The Sun in Mid-Career

the
Sun in
Mid-Career
Christopher Davis

Harper & Row, Publishers
New York, Evanston, San Francisco, London

Lines from A. E. Housman's *A Shropshire Lad* are reprinted (on pages 317 and 321) by permission of Cambridge University Press.

Portions of this work originally appeared in *Works in Progress*.

FIRST EDITION

Designed by Gwendolyn O. England

Library of Congress Cataloging in Publication Data

Davis, Christopher, 1928–
    The Sun in mid-career.
    I. Title.
PZ4.D2596Su [PS3554.A933]   813'.5'4   73–14309
ISBN 0–06–010989–0

75 76 77 78 79 10 9 8 7 6 5 4 3 2 1

Part of this novel was written while the author was a Fellow of the John Simon Guggenheim Memorial Foundation, for which assistance he offers grateful acknowledgment.

PROLOGUE | **1970**

●

The drawing in the letter from his daughter had a title under it: "Love Monster." The letter began, "Your Papaness" and went on. It was mostly about love. Anthony Gamble appreciated that, since love was something he was supposed to know about. Also, he saw the first purple lilacs of the year, the clusters of blooms ripening from the bottom, the top of each full flame hidden still and dark, like a balloon not fully blown up. He thought too of maleness. It was the day after the day that National Guardsmen shot and killed students at a university in Ohio not far from the one at which he was temporarily employed. "FIVE DIE TEN HURT AT KSU . . . REACTION TO TRAGEDY," it said in the student paper, the number corrected later to four.

Next to lilac, the fruit trees blossoming seemed paid for. Looking around, Gamble, who was forty-one, decided that this was minute one past the zenith of the sun, this very day, and that the sun had nowhere to go but down, not at first thinking that he meant himself. (Applause was heard. Someone was making the speech about truth. Voices echoed in academic halls. These were supposed to be seminars upon the question of the new war in Cambodia and the killings in Ohio, but they were speeches. Burn down the town, they said. Impeach Nixon.) He decided that the sun was in mid-career, that we were in the first moments of our afternoon, moving at last toward the evening, and high time.

Gamble rummaged among objects on the outside tables ("ANTIQUES NEW USED AND ABUSED" said the sign on the barn), and a boy with a boy's tough face said, "There's more inside." The man went inside and began to go earnestly through junk on the trestle tables, in the corners, inside the glassed cases, looking for something—anything—to buy: a walking stick, the sugar shaker his wife wanted. Pale faces clicked on for him from time to time in his constant conscientious effort to admit the reality of others.

He got near-charley horses in each thigh at softball. The shortstop had a long beard; the right fielder had a beard and shoulder-length hair. The present batter had a soft beard and a face of surpassing beauty. Gamble was shifted here and there in the field. Running for second base on a long drive into center, he slipped in the red silk dust and his foot twisted under him: two near-charley horses and a twisted foot. He played right on. Later, fielding in left, he ran for a fly ball clearly in center and collided with the center fielder, a tall broad man with dark hair, knocking the ball out of the academic's glove. The shortstop hurled his glove to the hard ground that had new grass coming up through it. Dark-eyed, breathless, sweating Ph.D. candidates. Around the small town's high school field were the back yards, garages, and old stables of Small Town, U.S.A. Looking, waiting now in right field, he arranged his face for the moment, thinking in sentences about the Saturday mornings of childhood.

Gamble's car was his father's trade-in Oldsmobile. He had left the Plymouth wagon for his wife. The separation was a rare one in the man's family. He had come to the university to lecture for the eight-week spring term for a good fee. It was too far and too expensive to commute, and so he had rented a small apartment and, temporarily a bachelor, telephoned and wrote home regularly. He went through the walletful of credit cards at the Shell station, and when he looked up everyone had gone. The two older attendants had, he was sure, only just disappeared through the door of the diner across the street. "Is anyone going to help me here?" The third attendant, a boy, had jumped into a customer's car and disappeared with it, tires squealing. He was entirely alone. The man arranged his perilous but still handsome face.

●

He got up in the morning, listened to the weekday radio preacher, worked out with the ten-pound dumbbells, made coffee, eggs, and toast, drank juice. He prayed at the shrine of his children's letters and gifts on a low table, to their photos. Nothing. He peeked around a paper curtain at the day. Both the room and he now smelled of Ben-Gay.

●

In summer pink and violet hydrangeas, which they called snowballs, grew coolingly on woody stems above cropped lawns. The children sat in canvas chairs at friends' houses, seashore heat on their bare shoulders, bare feet deep in the grass. They lived year round at the shore for a time, commuting across a causeway to school; and though, in memory, it was always summer, there had been cold days. The surf rolled nearby, ceaseless. It was all the sound of ocean, then, at the beginning of his effort to admit the reality of others. He would lie sprawled, overweight, on the hot sand of the beach before their house, brown as pudding, sullen-browed, gentle as a puppy, his broad rump presented to the sun, pressed to the globe, reeling with feeling, gold and green behind his closed lids, sweating coolly, just seeing his own thick black girl's lashes beaded with sweat or gigantically blooming with grains of sand, his cheek against his branding-

5

hot arm, scissoring legs in that silky quilt of sand as the patches marked by his fat satin body cooled it, grinding his boyhood into it, dreaming of views and valleys, clefts and deep water, dreaming of food, root beer. . . .

A friend was going to be a magician (that boy's father was a druggist), but it was really his older brother's friend. A girl in his class had a bad heart and would die, she said, before she could grow up, and he heard later that she had in fact died before finishing high school. Another boy had a bad heart too, or a bad something else, and was allowed a sidewalk car with a low-powered motor in it. Still another boy in an epileptic seizure slid from his chair to the floor in the school auditorium, while the air around the children grew thick. The normal things.

He replied to one of his children's letters.

"Darling," he began. Near the end, heavily, he wrote of "Mr. Nixon's new war," using that nursery style, expecting that his wife, whom he admired, would see. Simultaneously, he guessed that Cambodia existed, the dead had died and would remain so, even that Nixon was real.

He went to an auction of antiques in the evening, drove out through the flat, fresh-plowed countryside, parked the Olds among Ford and Chevy pickups, wanting to buy something. He saw a deep shadow box frame of carved hardwood, cranberry glass, an old photograph the color of dried blood of a man, a grandfather seventy years ago, bearing in his arms his grandchild who would be now himself a grandfather perhaps, perhaps dead. He would buy it, buy anything.

●

He had written a book about capital punishment and in the course of his research had interviewed one of the guards who took the Rosenbergs to their deaths.

"She was all right. It was him give us a little trouble," the

6

guard said in a low, practiced tone, accustomed to journalists. "She worked it out he should go first because he was you know . . ."

"What?"

"You know."

What?

"Shitless"—shyly. "But really there wasn't anything to it. It was no worse than any other I worked on. Sing Sing: I used to have a regular little apartment in the main block above the death house right overlooking the river. I done that for years, then I got moved with promotion in the System and come up to this prison. But no, I didn't mind. Is that what you're asking?" (Ready for this.) "People ask that. If they don't, they think it. No, I didn't mind. Over twenty years I done it." Sexually, he eyed the man who was asking, grammar wavering, his lean old cheeks pale as death. The history was the man; you did not abandon that: his history was himself. A clear longing: he played games with English usage, let it fail, sizing up his man from phrase to phrase, listening to his own nuance. He had loved the death he witnessed, he meant deliberately to convey (I'll shock you now), and death got it up stiff for him as nothing else. Put him in a locked room with a fresh corpse and a few instruments and he wouldn't guarantee a thing. "Did I mind? You mean the Rosenbergs or generally assisting at capital executions? General. Well, hell. Someone had to do it. I didn't like it, but I didn't think about it. It was my job to do." He gave the other a windowless look, deep-lidded, necrophagous. "You get these people in here asking. They don't understand. You understand." Yes. What did they know about death? They two knew, didn't they? "I didn't think no more about doing that than you would think about sitting down to eat a meal." There it was.

Then the tour.

License plates, tobacco being shredded in big slatted cribs; the black men doing most of the—kiss me—work, sweating blood, it seemed, in order to sleep at night. No communication allowed, though one of Gamble's books was in the prison library. Weight lifters with their sleeves cut off at the shoulders against regulations, fat bakers, freight cars of coal being unloaded; punishment cells aloft: all were thinking affectionately of death, eying the visitor across the silence. Their love came from brief, camera-shutter snaps of death. The man, unengaged, was witness, consciously included: put it in writing for us, writer: our sexual exchange across the gulf, love for the well-known killing guard, sharp grins back and forth.

●

In his dream another writer announced that his next book would get into the business of God, clear up the whole thing at last. Dynamite! But total ruin inside this unfurnished man. Wasn't that to be his own next book? Now all was finished and wasted—the whole work life—because another man was to be the first to do it. He was too slow, ought to have written the book years ago. There were no good ideas left anywhere. It was hopeless. Unless you had a reputation—that was to say a reputation—you had no chance; they took your ideas from you and left you with nothing for your next book, nothing but that old idea ground into hamburger: the first guilt, impossibility of forgiveness. And the tragedy of inventing what cannot be. It was depressing. "My *best* idea"—wandering up and down the hot dream streets.

"We wish to commend the entire student body for a sober, reflective, democratic expression of the intense feelings created by the events of the past few days. A creative and constructive use of the memorial period has been evident all over campus. . . ."

"Nixon will have words of conciliation for the young people."

"Listen, you other ones too—you jocks, you Greeks—they want to kill you too. It isn't just us!"—into the public address, the boy's green voice bouncing off the buildings around the

8

mall. "STRIKE" say the banners, "FUCK." He himself says it prissily: fu-uck—glances into a mirror after using the john (pissing, shitting, pipe the young boys' and girls' voices: "killing"—frankly), sees the man with thinning hair, gravel-pit acne scars, gentle eyes (he observes that people who are put off look up at the eyes: is that a way in?), thinks of the boy in the sand, makes him rise (he imagines he is compassionate, but he is cruel). The boy wore faded satinet violet-blue bathing trunks with a ship's wheel buckle on the belt. Fat pushed out the trunks under the belt, showed a fold where the arm joined the shoulder, made his thighs brush each other, drew lines across his waist, swelled his earlobes, filled his cheeks, thickened his eyelids. . . . It is untrue; it was not so bad. The man notices the boy's near-empty crotch, unarmed boy-girl, lets the poor ghost go at last to run with surprising grace and speed to the water's cutting edge, curl into a green wave, swim out, roll over and spout like a whale, while out upon the shaking sea rim gnats and cockroaches crawl.

. . . combed his hair in the mirror's gaze, combed his tangled brows, which grew fast now, gave himself a tired movie actor's look: masked mouth, empty man. The window shade was up, and he might have been observed observing himself. Kiss me.

•

"They came in with fourteen-inch bayonets fixed on M-1s. What do they want? You see that, you're going to move. No need to shoot kids. You don't shoot kids when you have that bayonet. They're supposed to know crowd control, but they are dumb farm boys, right? They get to see a crowd-control movie, hear a lecture. *I* was in the National Guard."

There was a broad field of winter wheat six or eight inches high beyond the yard of the house. A red tom swaggered near the lush crop, then came and wove itself like red thread

9

among the men's male legs and the women's silk ones. There was a barn a mile one way, a silo as far another, a line of pea-green trees on the south horizon, fresh-harrowed fields like brown lakes. People here are grains on a table. From the northern horizon black smoke crawled into the sky, dropped, and crawled along the rooftops. Was the university burning? Everyone at the gathering was a teacher or a teacher's wife or husband in the Department of English. They sat in a circle of chairs on the lawn, each with a cup of hard punch in his hand. It was informal, and a man with a tie would have been noticed. The sky was tremendous. Though it was evening, the spring light was going to last for hours.

Two teachers climbed into a red Volkswagen to investigate the smoke. Gamble in his chair, drunk, followed a filament of jet vapor up from Chicago; it seemed to take forever to feather and spread, and then the setting sun lit it so that it was like cream; he looked straight up into the flaring white funnel of the sky where a pair of swallows played. When the two men returned, they declared that it was refuse being burned near the airport, that smudging black smoke.

The owner of the town's movie house would put on his marquee, "WE ARE PROUD OF OUR STUDENTS AND CITIZENS TOO," because there had been no violence, in spite of the fact that some of the same students were picketing the same movie house because it had fired its newly unionized projectionist. A laundromat would also put a surprised congratulatory sign in its window.

Gamble and the visiting poet, who had changed for the occasion from her usual farmer's overalls, went over their host's books inside.

"Well, class was God-awful, Tony. Three guys showed and looked embarrassed for me. I give them"—a gesture of maternity, her hands on her bosom— "everything. You can *talk politics* through poems: plain talk. 'These events are very weighty,' I said. 'There is much poetry in them.' They want to talk about the New Mobe without poetry. I want to talk about the New Mobe with poetry. I have come here to give them . . . Look: Lorca; that says something. But they form their New University to give it to me, *which is all right,* except I give it to them in poetry. They're schmucks, Tony, between you and I. I don't read books. I don't know anything about *theory.* I give them—well, I shouldn't say it, I suppose. Anything they write is all right with me, as long as they *do* it. I lie down for them, boys and girls alike. I say here it is, come and get it, which of course puts them off, because the most liberated are really very, very uptight."

Gamble said something, and she looked at him, attention attracted. She said, "Of course, you're not even here. At least I'm here. Where the hell are you? . . . Lorca and Hart Crane. Good."

Some other English teachers had come in to look at the books with them. "I'm very deep into Crane now," one of them said.

"My uncle knew Hart Crane," declared Gamble.

"Yes?" Then the poet said, "Well, I don't suppose I'm really here either."

And one of the teachers joked, addressing another, "I wonder whatever became of Minerva," using the poet's name.

They walked to the campus together, and she paused now and then under a green tree to give a black, New York City cough. They passed Century Printing and Offset, which had refused to print the edition of the campus paper with one of her poems in it. "Bastards." The sun was hot but cutting treacherously under it came a cold breeze from Detroit. Spudnuts. Roy Rogers Roast Beef. Taco Kid. House of Donuts. Lum's. City Hall. J. C. Penney's. She leaned against a brick building to get her breath. She said, "I told 'em I have fantasies—daydreams: why mince words—about all-male nudist camps, and of course they laughed till they damn near died. If I don't like their work, I don't say anything. I'm supposed to say I hate their work. I can't hate anything an honest man has written down. It's all done with love, isn't it? A little blondie sits alone and loving and puts down a few words from her heart, gives it to me. . . ."

11

•

His uncle was a composer. His wife had recently died, and he came to the Gambles' seashore house in the summer of 1936 or 1937 to finish his opera. There too, for a few summers, the boy's brother kept rabbits in a cage at the rear of the house, one named Comrade and he could not think of the other's: Dmitri, Joe. They would push their restless noses against the chicken wire while ocean-bright sun slanted in on the wilting lettuce and carrot tops and searched the depths of their witless eyes. The boy would look self-consciously at the speckled pellets they made in their bowels and so readily excreted.

Everyone needful was at hand. Love, which was to be something he would be supposed to know about, throbbed in the plump hollow under his collarbone: his pity for living things. He *saw* his brother feel it too, but he could not *feel* his brother feeling it, which was to become troublesome. The older boy's clever long fingers upon the rabbits was love, upon their hard bodies under the rich fur. His brother's long-headed intensity was love, his wheat-dark hair, small closed mouth, ears close to the head masking mastoidectomy scars. His grandmother was there and his father, who, despite a dark intellect, made mother-in-law jokes.

The opera would make the uncle's name. He was a small, well-knit man of relentless, hot magnetism. He had a beautiful smile and was alternately gentle as a saint and ferocious. He had also the powerful blunt hands of the real musician, a broad Russian jaw, a large mustache. The boy and his brother adored him, and he was the second father.

•

They rallied on Mother's Day after the heavy union meal. Student speakers particularly addressed parents: "Join us!"

12

and it almost seemed that something would break that very moment. The grass was trampled with the weight of truth; students back from the Washington rally spoke; butts, shreds of filter tips were everywhere. The blacks—he had learned to call them that by 1970—were said to have planned a banner:

"WELCOME MOTHUHS."

They stood, the mothers, unloved everywhere, more or less of an age with the empty man watching them, well groomed, slim enough, hard-haired, and quietly jeweled for their daughters and sons, as if, since nothing else would help, that might help. A speaker talked of Greeks and freaks coming together, accusingly of uninvolved boys going back to the frat houses to pick their noses and suck on Oreo cookies.

"Gross," declared a mother firmly.

The few fathers present pretended to listen but in fact only felt their authority, never secure, further threatened. A wind came from the south and sweetly blew through them. The public address voices leaped around the quad like a handball: nonviolence; join us; adjourned.

During his own Mother's Day call, Gamble learned that his grandmother was dying.

"Well," he said on the phone to his mother after a time, "did they say how long? . . ." He was calculating it. Who would take his classes? Plane schedules. They talked some politics and about the Ohio killings, and his mother was quelled as she almost never was: killing children in America now.

•

Kiss me.

His evening class, as distinguished from the daytime creative writing class, had been supposed to be different from the usual thing visiting writers gave them. Hadn't Anthony Gam-

13

ble all but said so in his letter to the department head, which had been posted?

Lean graduate students looked him over at the first meeting, slouching in their seats, still friendly: farm boys and girls, Chicago boys, forgiving local girls. Every other one was a blazing fire momentarily banked. The boys were warriors. They slouched, cigarettes aloft or jammed into the corners of their lips, as if exhausted by their days. Certainly this should have been the right place to come at the end of their long day.

"The writer's function of showing things as they truly are is a sociopolitical function (people-moving) directed against lies (Dickens and others) that lead, e.g., to Cambodia: crusades growing out of notions of good and evil, right and wrong, virtue and vice, heaven and hell, progress and primitivism, Abbott and Costello. . . . If some crusades are better than others, the crusade at best is the implement of an incomplete truth. The writer's job, on the other hand, is the complete truth."

Irony. The novel was dead? Overly sophisticated, overeducated (academic) writers tended to be jocular faced with creative sterility and serious social problems, which, surely, was the beginning of the end of art: he named the Roman Empire in its dissolution and several fashionable writers; he hated them all. At which the warriors looked suddenly alert, then restless: fuck this and that. They began to grin. Creeper clawed at the night windows of the classroom; the air went yellowish. He saw them feel it, but he could not feel them feeling it. They began to shout. One—he would be a Master of Fine Arts—offered facts. Later, ribbons of Miller issued from his mouth and entered the ears of the rest, tapes of Joyce and Beckett. He was angry in a slouching, soldier's way; he had to tell them now that he would die tomorrow but was alive tonight, and all that the man addressing them had said was shit. Art was not nature. The padre-teacher had not said so, and he in his turn threatened hell: brilliant students made poor artists; in a pinch, he could have been referring to income.

"Far fuckin' out."

A long-haired citizen-soldier, small, smelly, goat-eyed, tattered, and hungry (he was actually hungry), nodded. His was a fatal wound, and he nodded grimly sideways: yes. He agreed. He nodded, clenching his jaws and sliding the tilted goat's eyes sideways and upward at the possibilities, looking them all over at once. He nodded his shrub of a head. "Far fuckin' out." But the other man grinned in a raspberry beard: no; and from one more came a web of *Catch-22*, and from the girls—the lag was seen—*The Catcher in the Rye, Lord of the Flies.*

The men, half-listening, checked their arms. The time was now.

"The writer as revolutionist. His idea can move people to action, not necessarily by telling the truth. What is the writer's responsibility toward truth when he has also, he feels, an urgent responsibility to effect political action? If the truth —for example, to have claimed in 1944 that Hitler was a human being and that that, in fact, was the whole trouble— disarms our forces in the field against Wrong, should one: *(a)* Set the truth aside, make peacetime truthtime, and devote oneself to action? *(b)* Lie, and write that the whole evil of contemporary conservative politics can be contained in an individual? *(c)* Disguise the truth? *(d)* Tell it at all risks? Camus spoke of dividing the artist-rebel's life: political activity alternating, in our ceaseless war, with times of withdrawal for"—kiss me— "work. Or . . ."

Gamble quoted his uncle, Alexis Weisshorn.

". . . the only sound loyalty is to the concept of work, and to a principle which makes honest work at least true, good, and beautiful." No alternating periods. Work and politics were one. His uncle had said that in an interview published in *The Worker* in 1938, Gamble declared.

The guns were showing.

Had anyone there heard of the composer Alexis Weisshorn?

The soon-to-be Master of Fine Arts, tongue and lips alive in the raspberry beard, freckled and scarred, eyes like green grapes, possessing this moment, condemned, seemed to have improvised the future in two minutes of easygoing agitation. Who had the balls to join him? Even one of the girls said she had. Gamble would have gone along, but he had been chosen as the enemy. All the others slid under their desks.

Work was the flesh of man!

They groaned with boredom.

Wasn't this the sort of thing they wanted to talk out in class?—not teacher to teacher but student to student. It was not. He made his second mistake, for which they could destroy him. "What do you want to talk about then?"

●

Gamble stood on a street corner outside the Roy Rogers and watched as boys and girls in a line waiting to board an orange bus touched each other. The man carried his laundry wrapped in crackling green paper and his Roy Rogers roast beef sandwich in a greaseproof bag. The children backed into one another, sniffed each other with flared nostrils, gave and received light blows, trod on their neighbors' feet, turned and grinned into the eyes of the one behind. They stood in a cloud of themselves, inseparable from each other. One boy pinched another, who was so accustomed to being a boy that he did not turn, went on with his dream. For the empty man, even the smell of the cooked meat in his hand was an offense.

He saw his history in flat shutters: doors turning on a corridor, people hard-edged, just disappearing into the side ways, the light cold. Or he lay under a hedge far off from a house at night. He saw, delightfully comfortable, the yellow lights of the dining room, undeclared, his, not his, and was content to observe, knowing others were well.

He had arranged for his classes to be taken by another teacher and made his round-trip plane reservation.

He lay under the hedge of yew, looked across frozen snow at the lighted windows. That was all right then, as long as they were all taken care of and having a good time.

●

They looked in on her, then retreated to wait, while Harvest House men and women, clinging to the corridor handrail or clutching aluminum walkers in their crippled violet-veined hands, inched toward them, apparently astonished by them. The place contained a permanent smell of disinfectant, rubber matting, and feces. A few inmates sat on bridge chairs in their doorways like village gossips and talked back and forth. The director, who was an old friend, and the day-duty nurse, whom Fran Gamble had got to know, stood by.

"The doctor stopped earlier. He said she's comfortable."

"Bless her heart," the nurse said.

Inmates glanced into Rose Weisshorn's room, then at the Gambles. An old woman in a pink wrapper paused before them; Anthony thought she was going to talk about his grandmother, but she said, "I got to get a message to my daughter. They cut me off from the outside."

"Write a letter," said Gamble's mother, interested.

"They don't permit it. I can't tell if the daughter's alive or dead. If you could get word they put me here, she will get word to the son in Los Angeles."

"Go back to your room, honey," the day-duty nurse said, "or down to therapy."

They tried again, and this time the nurse bent over Rose Weisshorn and said distinctly, "Rose, look who's here." The old woman in the bed opened her eyes. Beyond her through the sealed windows could be seen a strip of brown lawn and a grove of nut trees dusty in the May drought; the sky hung heavy as stone.

"Here are Tony and Elizabeth."

Rose's twisted slippers stood toe to toe on her bed step. Her hands, nearly fleshless, stirred across the turned-back sheet. "I wish it would stop." She took Gamble's wife for her daughter and addressed her, her eyes seeking cloudily among them but always coming back to the younger woman.

"She hears music," Francesca Gamble explained to the nurse.

"I'm glad to know. I knew she heard something, all right." She patted the old hands. Gamble's wife, Elizabeth, eased the covers at the old woman's feet. His mother sat down, put her bag on the floor beside her, and crossed her legs.

Rose said, "Alex."

"Cheyne-Stokes respiration," Tony wrote a few days later. "His grandmother goes into it. Actual pauses in breathing, approx. 20 sec. per pause. Called 'rowels'? Oxygen tubes in nostrils . . . tank . . . attached jar bubbling as ox. goes through it. Dextrose fed into arm. Teeth out. Jaw sinks and drops to one side. Breath like fire." He stood between the door and a frame-and-linen screen, crowding his notes onto the back of a bank envelope, glancing miserably at his subject. The heavy room door skidded from its stop, but the rubber hands tied to it muffled the blow. Blue daylight, hard as a mirror, sped by the dying woman's windows. Gamble's mother did not appear to mind the notes concerning her mother; constantly acquiring medical information, she often passed it on.

Rose lay on her side facing the door, knees drawn up, one hand on her hip, the other with a pad of gauze in the palm because she cut herself with her nails. "Odor of sour cologne," he wrote.

"She could come back to her regular respiration, or go on like this for days, then all of a sudden just sneak off. They sneak away. We keep an eye on them, but as often as not we miss it. Then we glance in and they're gone," declared the nurse. She was a portly woman, matte black, with brown flowers in the whites of her eyes. "She's just filling right up." Gamble put it in his notes.

They waited in a common room that had conversation corners furnished with sling chairs and tables made of steel and glass. Most of the paintings were by the director, and when he appeared he found them looking at his work. He had brought along an old man in a flannel robe and stood with his arm across his shoulders. "How do you find her, Fran dear?"

She said she felt that her mother was suffering needlessly. Why the oxygen? Was it really necessary?

"The doctor will be around. Ask him."

And when the paintings were praised: "Thanks, but I know a good picture." He steered the conversation. Did these younger Gambles know that his father had been a Lombard Street regular and been acquainted with Fran's grandmother in his youth—the whole family? "They called her Babushka, right? Banking socialists: the American dream. The Russian Revolution was fought in South Philadelphia. At least that's how it sounded at our house. My dad was red hot right up until the Soviet-German nonaggression pact, then fell away. And Alexis. We all admired Alex so much. A great artist . . ."

How long had his father been dead?

"He hasn't been. He's right here"—indicating the old man, who was now silently weeping. "Senile dementia. He recalls little now." He asked the old man, "Why are you crying, Pop? Meet Fran Gamble, her son, and this lovely . . . ?" Her daughter-in-law. "I find," he went on, "that the men tend to cry and the women to laugh in old age. There's one"—a woman all but lost in a wing-back chair, smiling and nodding, beckoning to them with a finger. She looked cheerful. "Presbyophrenia." To Anthony Gamble: "No, I'm no artist. I know pictures. Rem Levy, the dealer, started me. I had a gallery on Eighteenth Street for twenty-five years."

They waited for the doctor, and Francesca combed her

Lombard Street memories. She remembered a fire nearby and shutters used as stretchers to bring out the family. They were living then in Babushka's house; her father had slept in one room, her mother with the children in another; to this day she had nightmares about the smoldering smell of wet char. Or had it happened while in another house? Charles Gold, the mad poet of Lombard Street—one of Rose's stories; the Oak Lane house for Fran's recuperation from rheumatic fever; a large dog there named Colonel, which had belonged to a neighbor, and Alex in a sailor suit reclining upon the dog in a brown photograph; everything brown and tan: the boy's brown silk bangs falling away from his eyes like a curtain.

Rose used to look with misgiving at Alex's button nose when he was in the tub: too small. She would pull on it to lengthen it, which she lived to regret. Though it was not told now, this was a story often told. Tony wondered, why in the tub? There was the story of a maid in another house a year or two later, a compulsive exhibitionist, of Alex and Fran hiding in a cupboard and then being locked into it by the woman. Stories about living in California, the influenza epidemic of 1918 . . .

Brown or iron-black photographs, boxes and steamer trunks filled with music manuscripts and with the letters, journals, and books of Alex's dead wife, Eve, in the attic in Tony Gamble's house, which had been his parents' and his when he was a boy.

•

When the doctor came through the common room, the old people reached to touch his coat. "Brody, a minute. Meet mine family." His passage bent them as if they had been grass. "Brody, you butcher," they called genially as he swept by; even those who were very ill and silent watched the white-coated figure pass. He took Fran's hand in his, Elizabeth's, Tony's. "Gambles all." ("Couldn't it be, simply, that he's stupid?" Elizabeth would ask.) While Fran, buoyed by the hour of talk, remembering her intent but forgetting the pain that prompted it, smiling in fact, asked her question, Brody held both her hand and elbow, then, attentive, shifted his grip to her shoulder. Tony observed it. He would write, "Blond, broad-jawed, possibly ill himself; hard-hearted smile; pink German-Irish lids so fatigued they close for whole seconds at a time; speaks with lids all the way down but cracks them to listen; you slip your words in there, into the profession; ears correspondingly small—an old felon; yet he is the kind of man to whom people give gifts."

"Mother is still in the running," he declared at length.

"Yes, but does she—should she need to be? She shouldn't be, I feel now; I mean in your race."

The metaphor enraged Elizabeth for her mother-in-law. "What race? What running?" He turned the deep-lidded gaze to her, and they saw that he saw she was pregnant.

"I mean to say that Mrs. Weisshorn is responding to the things we do for her."

Fran was certain that she was in pain.

She felt little or no discomfort: occasional difficulty in breathing.

Would she regain awareness?

She was often conscious and aware.

"You can't win a round," said Elizabeth.

Fran said plainly, "I want you to suspend anything like intensive care except to relieve pain. I don't use the word discomfort."

He replied at once, "I understand *well* your feelings in this matter, and I respect them."

"But."

A nurse came by and said in a casual tone, "They have a water hammer in nineteen."

"Aortic valve malfunctioning," Brody explained. Fran, of course, was interested, and Tony turned away to write it down as a man might use a toothpick. The doctor said, "As long as mother is responding to our aids, I'll order them." He did not smile, but he did not frown.

Wasn't she dying?

"Suppose it was your mother?" asked Elizabeth. And to his reply she said clearly, "You're wrong."

Later, because of what she had felt herself required to ask for her mother and because she had done no good, Fran cried briefly and bitterly, pinching the bridge of her nose. On her lapel she wore a white and blue dove of peace badge.

●

He sat with the goat-eyed citizen-soldier in a student bar, wooing the boy for an ally in the difficult evening class. The other screened the glass of beer before him with his long hair, his mustache forbidding smiles. His Oriental glance slid admonishingly here and there. Something was always wrong —"Ah, *shit!*"—but also always right. He dealt up-from-under looks to the empty man. . . .

"Judas kissed him for money, didn't he?" The man was not for whores, and yet . . . He knew that Jesus was a man only and so resented the fact—his inability to believe what was false but what he wanted to believe—that he gave that kiss. The graduate student imagined the kiss aloud. He had been raised a Baptist on a farm, and Christ and kisses fascinated him. These particular blossoms—the man, his student, the university town, this talk—grew and died all night. There was a smell of frying meat, melting cheese, onions, and beer. Silken waitresses spun among the tables.

" 'Dazzling and tremendous how quick the sun-rise would kill me, if I could not now and always,' " cried Whitman's out-of-doors friend, " 'send sun-rise out of me!' " But neither could. Whitman might take them both (he took everybody!) and crush them into his 1880s emanation of sun-warm worsted cloth, male flesh, and tobacco (the out-of-doors) with a

22

roar of love. The young man looked at the older one without any kind of embarrassment, as if Gamble were stone—at the hair, the eyes (he looked into the eyes searchingly, head forward, making something out at the end of a dark passage). At length he said, "The other night I was at this apartment where they had a new baby, and after she fed the baby at her breast she let me suck too. It was far out, really great. Really" —the humorless slanted look intent. Then all of them had slept in one bed, husband, wife, bearded graduate student, and the infant.

How was that?

It was a change from sleeping on the floor.

He told Gamble about an older brother on the farm who would come out of the house to tend his vegetables wearing a silk dressing gown of their mother's and women's high-heeled slippers; a tall slim man, he would pick his way with wobbling steps across the furrows, cultivator in hand, chop the earth and pull up weeds like a friar. The neighbors didn't think much about it any longer. He would hobble across the road to the shed, pick out a potato rake or a hoe. The student would sometimes see him through a window caught by the horizon before he bent to his work, the hoe like a crook, his chin resting on it, dreaming. Pickup trucks went by, and their drivers flipped a hand casually. The brother had wanted to go into community theater in Detroit, but that was out of the question. "Not because of the loose ball, but he'll attack you."

It was interesting, said the empty man.

"It's all Sherwood Anderson country out there anyhow," the other declared. "No one notices. By the way, what was that shit in your English 570 the other night?"

FORM: Genesis: prototypical creation: to organize, to explain, to reduce the threat of annihilation: GOD: ORDER: BE-GINNING-LIFE-END: IMMORTALITY. The first human act, intellectually speaking, is to resolve death by imposing form on chaos. We are *(a)* self-knowing (autists) & immortal, *(b)* other-knowing, so that we learn of death; *(c)* persuaded of our

23

mortality, we try *(d)* to solve it by imposing form on our information.

•

He sat before a microfilm projector in the university's library and turned its crank, looking at 1901. Students sat before identical machines, seemingly lifeless, arms hanging at their sides. In 1901 cigarettes called Meccas cost five cents a pack, Old Penn Whiskey seventy-five cents a quart. Marconi had signaled the letter *S* from England to America.

Gingerly, Gamble conjured his great-grandmother. She stood by her desk on the second floor in the old corner building at Fifth and Lombard (the new bank would not be started until 1910), a heavy woman, smiling with her lips turned down, folded gold-rimmed pince-nez on a black cord around her neck. "Well, it's over, is it?"—to her son and his bride. "Man and wife." If she believed in such things, she could give a blessing. There on film was Babushka's costume in a sketch, page seven of the *Times*, May 13, 1901: balloon sleeves, high neck, long skirt with a loop of false buttons down its length; thirteen dollars for shirtwaist and skirt; the shoes eight dollars.

A student caught him as he came blinking out of the library. "Did you read it?"

Later, they sat in his office while the public address speakers scratched and popped in the quad below. Short stories and fragments of novels were spread over the desk, and he stirred them with a pencil as if they were being toasted, picked them up and glanced at their titles and through paragraphs, while the girl sat silent, bowed over her clenched fists. The president of the university was standing on a balustraded terrace across the quad trying to address the gathered students. "Come on!" they shouted. He smiled at the sky, waiting. Shirtless, the student chairman of the new Free

University knelt before him and slid the shaft of the microphone up and down, tightening, then loosening the tab that held it, his breath amplified in the acoustical quadrangle. "Fuck," he boomed.

"For though I am not splenitive and rash, yet have I something in me dangerous," declared the president, smiling into the elms.

In one short story an operating theater had just been bombed to daylight. A breeze fluttered equipment; restraints and unrooted wires swung free; a slow snake of blood ran down a stainless-steel leg, outdoor shadows were now printed on the blood-sprinkled walls: nodding palms, passersby. ". . . smell of roasting meat," Gamble read and averted his eyes. In another story a small girl hurled herself like a bird from window to window inside a deserted house, while the neighbors watched from the lawn: why had her family left her?

He remembered the present student's name, found her story, opened it ("She stood in her grandmother's kitchen and watched the soft old fingers, a knife in them, nipping the ends from string beans."), then closed it. "It's good."

The girl shook her head.

She sat bowed over her own knotted hands, shrugging, shaking her small blond head. There were holes in the knees of her jeans. "Yes, only," she kept saying.

When the story was good there was not much to say, and consequently the interviews were brief; it was the bad ones you worked over.

"Yes, only you say it's good and don't say you like it."

He had told them that was possible, even reasonable, which they hated. "I like it," he lied. They went on in this way. He lied emphatically. He *liked* her story very much. He supposed it was beautiful. She seemed herself beautiful inside and out, though unhappy now. He observed that her scalp was clean. She unlaced her fingers and began poking them into the holes in her jeans.

"Why did you try to avoid me outside the library?"

He said he had not.

"*Yet* have I something in me dangerous," boomed the president, laughing. Teachers and students were hanging out of school building windows to see, and finally Gamble and his student looked down. "He's only going to give some easy lip service to the whole thing," she said sadly. Frisbees flew across the heads of the crowd. A boy was climbing a tree to retrieve a fouled kite. "He'll kill himself." At length the president said that he would join the school and such of the community as desired to take part in the planned candlelight march through town. "Recognition and mourning."

"Protest!" interrupted a dark voice.

"It looks like rain," the girl said.

Why wouldn't she believe that her story was good?

She shook her head. "No one believes you."

After a time, the teacher thrust his hand through the window and a globe of water fell into it, warm as blood; black islands appeared on the dusty slate stones of the walks. "Raining." They recognized the visiting poet in the midst of the disintegrating crowd, hips broad in her farmer's overalls, gray hair across her back. She was looking at her cigarette with astonishment because the rain had put it out. They watched her pinch the hard black end between her fingers, then stare at her hand. She carried a leather purse in one hip pocket, a red handkerchief in the other trailing like a dangerous-load flag; a two-dollar watch was strung on a lanyard around her neck. The speakers had gone; the public address equipment was being packed up to be wheeled to another rally; a few campus guards (that they wore sidearms was an issue) remained standing by, elderly, detached from the weather, even from each other; and a student organizer wearing a black armband shouted instructions to those left concerning the march, where it was to form.

The girl said, referring to the poet, "Nobody goes to her conferences."

Later, Gamble snapped a rubber band around the stories, packed them with Camus and Ezra Pound into his peeling attaché case, and marched down a rain-dark corridor toward a window. The floor was tacky with fresh wax, and he saw himself rise in it like a fish; there was a smell of spring rain in the air. The point was that if one were in Cambodia oneself, it might not seem so bad. But he must not persuade himself that imagined death was really worse than death. In class (everyone had come) he said, *"Art* is messages sent in code from one prisoner in solitary to another. *Philosophy* intends to dispense with the code. If you can talk, don't write." Of course, not everyone was a prisoner or a jailer, but he assumed that the people in this room . . .

Afterward, the head of the creative writing subdepartment asked, "How did it go?"

All right.

"How was the first night class last week?"

That had been, to a degree, fucked up, but he was working on it. When the other asked how Gamble's grandmother was and learned that she had died, he shook his head gently. Though he was the younger of the two, he had a gray beard. They had drinks in the bar of the Holiday Inn, and Gamble talked ceaselessly about his family. His uncle Alex, the composer, had been killed in a Mexican town where he had gone to work. He had been beaten and robbed in the dockside area of the town near dawn. It had happened more than a year before but only now (he was taken by surprise) did this occur to him: "I feel guilty about it."

The eyes of the two men roved among the salesmen and businessmen at the other tables. One always died for another, the gray-bearded man said.

•

At night he watched a talk show on a TV set with one channel, which he had borrowed from a student. On the table next to his children's letters and a collection of three sea shells taped to a piece of paper, the gift of Gamble's youngest (he had never been away for such long periods, and they missed him), was a glass of gin, from which he sipped, and on the floor a litter of newspapers and student manuscripts. He leaned into the cities of the stories now and then but would not actually touch one. Except for the notes he took, he had not done any work himself in over a year.

The consul sent home from the place in which he was killed Alexis Weisshorn's belongings, like thorns to handle. Gamble had found a desk calendar used as a diary: "A good day's work, thank God" across a page in red grease pencil almost at the end. The light out, TV off, a display began at once. His uncle, black-ringed eyes palely mad with concentration upon lists and memos, ferociously frowning and scattering ashes over his Brooks Brothers vest, chewing his mustache, suitcases, sacks of manuscript dropped inside the door of the East Tenth Street apartment, got to work on the phone; first things: the maid, Mrs. Black; the *Times* started, the laundry, and dry cleaner; mama; Moishe; Lenny; Mary at William Morris; Aaron; Asher; Fran . . . He would have to be half the day on the phone, plugging into things again. He lit cigarettes as he spoke, smoke everywhere, flapped it away, regularly glanced at the Baldwin thick with dust, at the bags and boxes of work—the opera-in-progress. "Who else? As you hear. I'm back! Did I not! . . . No, darling, why cry? . . . Of course . . ." until he began to come apart, burning in the sun from the long windows, serenely, "correctly" he would have said, consumed, and shortly went without protest back into death.

ONE | **1912**

1913

1914–1918

1918

1924

1912

•

Alex went to stay at the Weisshorn house on Lombard Street for a long weekend during the Christmas holidays. He slept in the same room with his father on a cot and went everywhere with Saul. His father had been ill. Before Alex the family spoke of bronchitis, but the boy understood that there had been some sort of fight somewhere and that his father had been knocked down. When at night Saul removed the ascot he wore inside his soft collar and revealed dusty dark-purple smudges along his jaw, Alex stared.

"Don't worry, old man," Saul said, observing him. "All's well."

His grandmother, who paid for them, asked the boy, "How are the lessons? I hope you progress."

They had gone on the first morning to the conservatory, where she ate her breakfast. A window at her back looked down on a sunny courtyard. In a rank by her plate were medicine bottles, orange, amethyst, and blue, and a glass with a silver spoon in it. "I hope you're not missing a lesson."

"No, Babushka."

Saul said, "The teacher's also on vacation."

"My daughter Annette's a teacher," she informed Alex, as if he would not know that. She was a plump small woman who dressed always in dark brown or black. Her eyes were black, and she gazed directly at people, pausing as if to think before she spoke. Saul, slim and straight, bald though he was not much more than thirty, sat on the arm of a chair and smoked a cigarette for his breakfast. He took out his watch and glanced at its face through the smoke. Father and son were going to the zoo and later to the bank, but Mrs. Weiss-horn was not to be hurried.

"I hope your mother don't lose her head and rush you all off to California as she threatened."

"I don't think she will," Alex said, anxious to please.

Speaking as if the reconciliation would undoubtedly come about, she addressed Saul. "It occurred to me it might be wise to give up the place you rented for her and rent or buy near the park. It's convenient and still practically country. You might get a car like Jack's to go back and forth."

His face brightened. "The Packard two-seater."

They talked about the car and about bank business. In the afternoon father and son stopped at the bank to look at Saul's office, and Alex sat in the padded swivel chair and played with the porcelain wet-roller and typewriter. Sasha Volin, Saul's brother-in-law, was there. "Your father, being a radical socialist, is opposed to banking, which is why he's so seldom here, I imagine."

"I only come to scout the enemy."

"Not much he's scouting."

Later, Saul said in a serious tone to Alex, "It's true enough that banks and thieves are the same. If you rob a bank—which I don't recommend, incidentally—you merely shift wealth from one place to another, and the ordinary people still do without."

They visited Mrs. Weisshorn again, now in her office, and she stood up for them as a man would. "Are you enjoying yourself?" She made Alex sit behind her desk. He could look through the fan-shaped window down Lombard Street, which was filled with carriages and drays, to the Weisshorn house. Beyond were visible the tangled spars of freight vessels in the river. "If you weren't going to be a musician, would you work in a bank?"

He shook his head.

"I suppose your father has been talking to you. He has his own ideas about profits and values."

The boy listened to everything, knowing he would be expected to report to his mother.

He was free to run around the house. His aunt Susan, a doctor, had her offices on the ground floor opposite the seldom-used formal dining room. Her patients were women. If she heard Alex, she would come out of the waiting room—he could see a bright fire in the grate behind her and the ladies peering around the door—and raise her pince-nez. She was tall, dark-faced, and wore her hair in braided rosettes over her ears. There were two other sisters—Annette, the schoolteacher, who at twenty-seven was so absent-minded that she had had to think for a moment who Alex was; and Pauline, married to Volin. Dr. Susan was reading *The Psychopathology of Everyday Life*, and she brought the book "to table," which was how she referred to meals, and translated aloud in the clipped accent she had picked up during her years in Edinburgh. Both of the other sisters lived in nearby houses.

Volin used French phrases like a St. Petersburg Russian, kept Christmas in his house, as well as Jewish holidays, but raised his boys without religious training. "The world is a toy shop as far as I'm concerned. I take the most attractive things. Whatever catches my eye." He hung a wreath of holly in his office.

"As long as customers don't see," Alex's grandmother said.

Though he would be away for a few days only, the boy wrote his sister letters. A little snow fell. "It's like Dickens here"—thinking of the etchings that illustrated the books. "You should see Papa count money!"

There were bricks of them in different denominations, each bound in a strip of paper. There were also loose bills, which he sorted, rapidly counted, and bound into smaller bricks. The work was done after banking hours when the doors were locked. Alex was fascinated by the swiftness of his father's fingers. His thumb leaped to his tongue to be licked. He counted coins, flicking them like grain between his fingers, then rolled them in heavy green paper, tucked in the ends, and marked them with his gold pen. As he worked, he told the boy something about the bank's history in an instructive tone. Saul's father, who had died the year Alex was born, in 1905, began in the seventies sending steamship tickets to emigrants as a favor. "To help with travel expenses, he and your Babushka lent money too. And passports. We used the passports over and over. A family would arrive, return it, and we sent it with tickets and money to the next family. Before he married Pauline, your uncle Sasha acted as courier with the material and helped shepherd people. We brought over half the Jews in the city, it seems to me—the Russians anyhow. The Auerbachs bring over the Germans." He put the money away and locked the drawer with a key that was on the same chain as his watch. In motion or still, his hands, Alex thought, were beautiful. He swiveled in his chair, removed the cover from a typewriter, and began to write. "Delinquent account," he explained. "A finance company, of all things. Wolves and foxes. Ideally, we'll put each other out of business. You wonder why I'm employed in such a thing? *I* wonder." He ripped the paper out. "The bank evolved. I evolved. Period." He grinned at the boy. "Your father, in his weakness, takes the path of least resistance. You won't do that."

Saul sat, having lit a fresh Helmar cigarette, neat, dry, contained, his work completed. Alex admired the gestures and cleanness, the spare body, the snowy shirt, even the bald head with its fringe of dark hair.

They went to a Bach Christmas program, and Saul gazed around from his mother's loge seats, now and then nodding to someone. He shook his program as if he were shaking a match and then read the information it contained with apparent skepticism. Alex observed him look over the prettiest women and clear his throat at an old couple nearby who had fallen asleep, heads lolling. "They ought to be shot," he whispered.

"They look as if they have been."

The father turned red trying to stifle his laughter.

He introduced Alex to a beautiful woman during the inter-

34

val. "A very dear friend of mine," in a different-sounding voice. But the woman addressed the boy in the serious tone she used with Saul.

"I've heard a great deal about you from this doting parent of yours. Indeed, there are times when you are his sole subject of conversation. Saul, such eyes! . . . I would sincerely love to hear you play."

"I'll probably play with Stokowski in March," Alex replied.

She knew that. She nodded. Of course he would. She had red hair and wore a green gown. Alex stared at her shoulders.

"Saul," she said, looking deeply at him, "how *are* you?"

When his father said that it was not necessary to mention the lady to his mother, Alex replied with brilliant, total cooperation, "I even forgot her name."

There was always a group at the Lombard Street house after Saturday concerts. Mrs. Weisshorn sat behind a silver samovar and thrust cups at people, scarcely glancing up. An actor-poet, a recent immigrant brought over by the Weisshorns, recited in Russian and English, and afterward, while discussing the program for a Literary Society meeting to be held at the Labor Lyceum, Saul imitated him. *"Blow,* vinds, and creck your cheeks! . . ." which made Alex laugh.

"Maybe we should get him for the program," said Volin. Mrs. Weisshorn had kept her place at the head of the long table. "He shouldn't have attempted in English," she said, though the accent her son imitated was no different from hers. Alex's uncle, Jack Loeb, said, "He's well known in Russia. I understand the Czarist secret police want him. Two months ago he was walking the streets of Moscow in fur boots."

A Polish maid came with a tray and offered cake and sandwiches. Another girl was clearing from the earlier gathering. Their feet were bare indoors; out of doors they wore Saul's cast-off shoes. Saul mixed himself a whiskey and soda. The snow had begun again and Alex, sleepy, watched it sweep past the black windows and heard it hiss in the flue. A friend named Blum, a doctor brought over from Kiev by the bank's agency at the turn of the century, said, "Could we move ahead with this?" He was barely forty but gave an impression of age. "I want to beat the snow."

"A few flakes," Saul declared, "maybe an inch by morning."

"Get Emma herself to come down," said Sasha Volin. "She'd give her Haymarket anniversary talk. Also, they're celebrating Kropotkin's seventieth birthday in New York. Maybe we could tie into that."

Blum shook his head.

Saul stood behind his mother's chair, a hand on her shoulder. "Get Yanofsky," he said.

Blum once more shook his head. He smiled at the people around the lace-covered table, shuttering his eyes, which were like a tortoise's. If he was looking at one person when he closed them, Alex observed, he would be looking elsewhere, as if politely, when he opened them again. If Jack Loeb, who was also a doctor, made jokes, Blum smiled with his eyes closed, acknowledging the humor. "*I* don't especially like Yanofsky. I suggest to offer his Tolstoy lecture Mr. McCullough. You don't get overtly political at a literary society on a Sunday afternoon. Or sound out Gutman on scenes from Galsworthy's *Justice.*"

"Jack London then!" cried Loeb.

"We must," Blum said singsong, smiling, "we must begi-in"—singing to make fun of himself and his pronouncements—"to part ways with Miss Goldman at every le-vel"— like a cantor.

"*Mais, que voulez-vous?*" demanded Volin.

"Everyone's sick to death of Little Father lectures," Saul said.

"*Where* there's a political bias and *where* literature is the main interest, I say—*I* say"—opening his soft hands and smiling around—"which does not mean pretty Pauline says or commanding Babushka says—*I* say if we are being political, let's stay out of the anarchist camp. This is not ten years ago, Sasha Borisovich." Later, amiably: "Look, our Mozart

36

sleeps," though Alex heard him. "He'll come over to play with my Ruth—he and Francesca."

When they were in their beds in Saul's room high up in the back of the house, Saul smoked, and the boy gazed at himself in the violet mirror on the clothespress. When he squinted, the edges of the glass flashed rainbows. As if it were someone else, he heard himself ask, "How did you get hurt, Papa?"

Saul said nothing for a moment. He smoked, sitting up against his pillows, his glasses and flat gold watch and chain on the table beside him. There was an electric button above his head to call servants. The gas jets and pipes had been wired. There was what seemed to Alex a mountain of books on the floor by the bed. "All right," his father said finally, then was silent. But with the light out, he began. "I was, as I often am, talking politics in an all-night place with your Uncle Jack and some other friends, whom you've met but whose names you may not remember, Alex. There were some fellows at a nearby table. I sent beers to them, and one of them sent one to me—not to the table, just to me, no doubt because I was the one holding forth. Since I was drinking coffee, I thanked him and didn't touch it. Then later I walked with Jack and Johnny Finn—that one I've told you about who used to be a city detective and now works full time for the Socialist Labor Party—to their streetcar stop. It was just about morning, and after they were gone I was alone on the street."

Alex saw in the mirror the tip of his father's cigarette.

"I can't describe that morning. It was beautiful. The light ran along the car tracks; and then Johnny and Jack's trolley coming along packed with workers—the night workers knocked out, going home, the day workers fresh as daisies, the trolley bell going! The sun came up between a couple of warehouses, and I felt it on me—one of those October mornings! I felt just like a cat in the sun on that street corner. Did you ever sit in the sun and feel that way?"

Alex loved it when his father spoke to him like this.

"There's something about me like a cat, I guess. I like to

look on. It's lazy, irresponsible—but to stand in the sun, alone, like a cat very early in the morning! Do you know what I mean?"

"Oh, yes."

"Only I wasn't alone."

As Alex knew he could do so well, he was building the drama of the story.

"Here was the fellow standing beside me—the one from the restaurant. I hadn't seen him. Out of the dark he had come. Now, I had taken a liking to this fellow—a real working stiff he seemed to me. I knew he was listening to me carry on, and I thought from his manner he approved of what I said. He looked all right. And then the beers. It may be he resented my not drinking the one he sent over. Then, as I looked at him, I thought: No, it's not the same fellow. They look alike, but he's not the same, and at that moment—I had just said, 'Well, you seem to have missed your streetcar, friend'—he struck me. I had seen he was drunk. . . ."

"Why?" asked Alex in horror. Why had he struck his father?

"I'm not sure. There's a sort of worker who defends those who exploit him—take advantage—because he's been trained to think no farther than a frontal defense of whatever his present employment is. And there are others—criminals, really—who become the hired thugs of the money fellows. Mr. Marx called them *Lumpenproletariat.*"

"Is that what he was?"—understanding nothing.

"Well, but there's that other factor. I couldn't be sure it was the same fellow. Or maybe I didn't want it to be. But what motive? I wasn't robbed."

"Oh, Papa!"

"I shouldn't be telling you all this, I guess. But it wasn't bad. I was all right." And when Alex asked what happened: "Why, I was knocked down. My glasses were broken. I had bought the Sunday edition, and that was scattered all over the street. Some people appeared out of nowhere. I came home and rested. Annette read to me from *Bleak House*, with which

38

she's torturing the schoolchildren of the city. Susan read Freud to explain what had happened. I represented who knew what: society, the cruel father because I made no secret of my job in a bank. That I spoke in liberal terms took from him his last weapon. And so on." He yawned, crushed his cigarette. "The point was that I didn't like to think it was the same fellow to whom I'd taken a shine. As a matter of record, I finally decided that very probably it wasn't. . . . Anyway, that's the story."

Alex must have been asleep briefly. He heard his father saying in the darkness, "Jack Loeb said simply the man was a bum. It didn't seem to make any difference to him if it was the same fellow or not. But I suppose I felt guilty. What license did I have to talk? That fellow's fist that struck me at least was grimed by work as honest as the system allows. You get to thinking, blaming yourself. Hadn't I deserved the blow in a sense? As far as Jack or anyone else was concerned, it was an accident. I might as well have been struck by that streetcar. I do remember I thought of you fellows—you and Frankie. . . ."

An hour later Alex woke crying from a bad dream.

Saul turned the light on. He stood by the door tying the sash of his robe. "I'll get Susan."

"No."

He had instructions from his mother not to be trouble in the household. Calmer, he declared, "I dreamed about fire. It was interesting."

Still another Helmar. Saul gazed at his son. "Well, I guess you need a father in that family, don't you—you and Frank?"

Alex had thought he was going to say he should not have told him the story (it was clear to the boy that it had upset him), but he did not. Instead the father said, "You know, you make a decision like this and the years speed up. Suddenly, committed, a fellow foresees everything right up to the end. That's the problem."

In the morning they had baths, hot, then cold, and used rough towels. Saul matched things on the bed, arranging suit, shirt, cravat and collar, studs, as if he were dressing a dummy, then altered items, studying the effect. The room was filled with winter sunshine and caps of snow stood on the chimney pots beyond the window. Alex, still exploring after two days, found a series of marks on his father's washstand. Saul laughed. "A lot I'll attempt to explain but not that. Childish nonsense." The little lines were in the groups of five that Alex's teachers made, four upright, one slash across. There were nineteen lines.

The boy, courteous and unwilling to learn what he was not supposed to know, did not insist. He too dressed with care. It seemed important that the cuffs of his shirt be as clean as Saul's; he had scrubbed hard with his washcloth. He watched admiringly while Saul put wax on his mustache, which already had wiry strands of gray in it. Saul polished his gold-rimmed glasses, placed them exactly on the bridge of the broad nose, the ribbon in his top pocket. He put his silver into one vest pocket, gold pen into another, a handkerchief in his sleeve for use, patted every pocket a final time. Alex was dressed too. He patted his pockets to make sure everything was right.

An old man was sitting outside the conservatory door. "It occurred to me—I was going by—I could see her for a second."

"You were paid," Saul said.

The man was dressed in a long overcoat and overshoes. He carried a hay-colored derby held up like a basin as if to catch something. His clothing exhaled the cold of the morning. Grinning, Saul gave him a dollar, and the man pinched Alex's cheek and smoothed his bangs. "Bless the boy," he said with a phlegm-coated Yiddish accent. "A genius. Saulie, with your permission, I'll rest five minutes, then go."

The banker said to his mother, "I gave Zeide a dollar. Don't anyone else."

"Are you enjoying yourself?" she asked the boy. "I'm told you're leaving this morning. Why not stay? We didn't get him to play a piece for us, Saul."

"I'll play after breakfast, if you like."

Her furrier was in the room displaying samples, and she introduced Alex without looking up. She shook an amber-colored bead of medicine into a glass, which she then filled with water. Everything was vivid on this winter morning: the letter opener beside her plate, the envelopes with their bright stamps and black script, the plum-red border on her shawl; a china pot stood in shadow, yet light showed through it and stood radiant around it. A diamond flamed on his grandmother's hand.

The furrier, who was a lively man, went on taking skins out of his satchel and spreading them everywhere in the sunlight for effect. When Saul sat on a chair arm with a cup of coffee, the man flung a fur across his knees. "Mind the cigarette, sonny!" The pelts were brilliant. Delighted, Alex watched him fluff the fur, blow into it, straighten it out again with the hard heel of his artist's hand, ringed small finger sticking out.

"Saul, tell her this ain't goatskin. *She's a rich woman.*" He winked at Alex. Then to Saul: "You and I are skin merchants, right?"—which made the banker grin and throw a glance at his mother. "Right, Saulie?" The two, transformed into boys, rumbled with laughter. The man bent to his sample bag, shoulders shaking. Alex, not knowing why, began to laugh too, and Saul turned away. He tugged off his glasses to polish them, then ground the silk handkerchief into his eyes.

"What? What?" cried his mother.

Alex giggled and the men roared.

"My God, she's sharp, ain't she?"

The furrier shook his head.

"Don't tell me. I couldn't stand it," she barked, but not angrily.

Then and later while he was playing for her, Alex observed a look he had not seen before in his grandmother's flat eyes. They seemed to burn. Though she did not smile, it was certain she was happy. He thought that the burning must be what it felt like to drink whiskey; the effect, which he saw he had helped to achieve, made the boy happy too.

His father took him home on the train, and the happiness persisted. At one station, passengers descending, others waiting to climb up, a conductor with a liquid silver whistle at his lips, the world upside down in each bead of its chain, he understood that he could move these scenes; and when the train went forward once more it was Alex who had arranged it. At parting, Saul caught the boy's face between his hands and kissed him, while Alex hugged his father's arm in both of his and would not let go.

"That was what he said, was it?" his mother declared when the boy reported.

She was angry because Saul had discussed the reconciliation as if the decision were all his. "I believe there are some details to be ironed out before that's settled."

She sat erect, gazing into the untended garden of her house, drumming her plump fingers. But later, almost as if she had shaken herself into it, she cheered up.

Alone with her brother, Fran said ironically, "For our sakes." She was on the long voyage of recovery from rheumatic fever, which was why she had not been allowed to go to Lombard Street. "At least there was money."

Alex had come home with a check drawn on Babushka's own account pinned inside one of his pockets.

"It wasn't like that. She's not bad."

Alex described his visit in detail. At night, talking across the gulf between their beds, feeling like Saul soberly talking in the darkness, he told her about their father being knocked down.

"But it wasn't the same man," he said several times.

Why was that important?

"It's the most important thing!"

Each morning for the next week Rose defined and redefined love for her children; and during this period the moon, a round powder-white stone, hung in the middle of the blue sky. Mild and persistent, it came to stand for the word in the boy's mind. He was surprised to learn later that poets had used it so for centuries.

1913

•

He played Debussy—all six pieces from the *Coin des Enfants*
and three preludes from the first book. For his encore, Liszt's
Second Hungarian Rhapsody. Dressed in the belted brown
velvet suit his grandmother had had made for him, he stood,
a hand on the piano, bowing into the pink lights of the
Academy of Music. The lights were up on the audience and
after a moment he was able to pick out members of his family
where they sat applauding.

The Maestro observed him, brows bent. He gave his satin
trouser seams a final tap, then stepped from the podium and
hugged the boy, his cheek right next to Alex's. The orchestra
applauded.

"Good," Stokowski said in the green room. "This is talent
worth the work to develop." He did not praise too highly. He
smiled at Rose in a gentlemanly way that was intense and
remote; no particular smiles for Alex. No musical smiles, as
Saul would put it later, which was impressive. It was as if the
Maestro had said that Alex, at the age of eight, was an artist.
Saul and Rose stood with their son. All of the first desks came
and paid compliments. Weisshorn relatives and friends
crowded the room. Saul's cronies made a shy group in a
corner. Sophia Carson—she was the red-headed woman Alex
had met the previous fall—said, "Here you are at last in this
venerable house." And to Rose: "Mrs. Weisshorn, truly this
young one is worthy of the Muses' love." Pale, her dark red
hair notable, the woman stood for a moment by the door to
the street, then discreetly disappeared.

Something about backstage excited or quelled visitors.

43

"It's as hot as a kitchen!" Babushka cried irritably. She was a subscriber to the orchestra's funds, and Stokowski and Rich paid attention to her; but she spent her time fanning at cigar smoke with her program and at last asked Sasha Volin to find her a cab.

"She's pleased, all right," said Saul, grinning, his hand on her shoulder. "One genius embraces another, who happens to be her grandson, on the stage of the Academy before all her friends and half her enemies—the foreseeable and correct consequence of disbursements. . . ." He prowled, elated, around the stage, gazed out at the empty palace, up at the hanging sandbags and catwalks; he knew one of the austere stagehands and introduced Fran. "His sister . . ." The orchestra members kidded each other, packing their instruments into green plush nests. Stokowski, having said a word here and there, disappeared, and Alex, in much the same style, moved from group to group, attentive rather than talkative. He accepted congratulations soberly, as if someone else were being described. " 'Minstrels' was much too fast. I did it all too fast, but that especially." An elderly woman ("Very well dressed and decent-looking," Saul said) asked Alex to sign her program, which he did, turning red but not forgetting to thank her for her compliments. The street door stood open, and musicians were beginning to drift out onto the icy sidewalk; they would turn up their collars, light cigarettes, glance at the cold sky. "Workmen, craftsmen!" Saul said with enthusiasm. (Stokowski had spoken of work with reference to Alex's talent.) "They'll get a drink, a sandwich, or a light meal, then back for the evening's labors!" The possibility of Alex returning too had been discussed and decided against; but they kept speaking of it as if he still might.

"Enough's enough."

"He's too young," Rose said firmly.

They stood close, serious and elated, directing their enthusiasm toward details, keeping their pride private, yet each conscious of it in the other. "A taste at this point, so that he gets both this particular orchestra in order to learn from it,

44

as well as some sense of the dimension an audience adds."

"Exactly. It's enough."

Now and then Alex would turn to them with a smile that included both without distinction; he saw, triumphant, their accord. He was conscious of the secrecy of their pride in him.

A rime of crunching snow was on everything in front of the Academy. Sun blazed blue-white on it, blinding after the darkness of the theater. People paused on the curb, looking right and left, and drew deep breaths. Their shoes cracked the frozen crust. Automobile and carriage wheels spun, and horses snorted steam. Fran's mittens were blood red, Saul's cheeks pink as carnations, the whiskers of his mustache brilliant and sleek as ermine. Suddenly a lady sat down on the slippery sidewalk. Saul glanced at Alex and Fran and, while Rose frowned, began to laugh. Alex prayed that the lady would not notice. She was indignant but possibly not at them. Both she and the gentleman helping her were stout, and a stranger had to come and hoist on her other arm. (Saul offered but was too late, fortunately for his back, he declared.) Even Rose smiled at last.

Across the street in Walter's, Saul cried, "You missed it, Sash! The way her heels kept skidding out from under her, she looked as if she were doing that Russian dance."

"I saw it! I turned back!"

Saul described it all once more. They screamed with laughter.

"Stop! Please!"

As he tired, Alex's eyes brightened and the flush became constant. He sat next to Fran, an arm around her waist. She was pale and did not stop smiling. Saul and Rose were side by side at the other end of the table. At first no one was hungry. Then, after the concertmeister had gone, having settled them and taken a courteous cup of coffee, as if he had been a constraint they decided they were famished, even Fran; and she and Alex ate ice cream and cake. The intensity of the boy's mood increased. He sang passages he had played to show how he had done them badly; then he would be

45

silent, inaudibly polite, as if to say that this was what a little boy should be like. He did not stop observing. His mother would say that it was as if he were looking for a way to show his joy but could not find it.

"Never such a gale—a hurricane of applause in that place!" Volin was shouting. "For this child!" He pushed his fingers passionately through his hair, his eyes filling. Saul said, "The idiot next to me kept shouting, *'Bis!'* which is for opera only!"

"It means twice. Again!"

"He should have been shot," said Alex.

There were twenty in the party. They made a terrific noise. People at other tables looked at them with smiles. "Our gusto, our life astonishes them!"

They teased Alex about the lady and the autograph.

"I paid her to do it!"

"Well, you won't have to pay anyone. There'll be plenty of autographs."

Later, Alex climbed onto his chair to be Stokowski conducting Alexis Weisshorn: the sideways glance across his own shoulder, up-from-under eagle glare; the head thrown back as if to shake out long hair. He raised his arms, at first lifting the hands as if they were weights, dragging them limply up, then clutching powerfully with them. He rolled his eyes in despair at his orchestra, then widened and crossed them to smile sweetly at the soloist.

His uncle Jack could only punch Saul's shoulder. He could not get his breath. Morris Blum had brought his wife and their daughter, Ruth, who was Fran's age, a plump cheerful girl. She howled and almost fell off her chair. Dr. Blum chuckled and nodded, and Jenny, his wife, cried, "It's funny!" Alex's first piano teacher was there, and, as Saul pointed out later, he looked both delighted and scandalized by the irreverence.

At home it was impossible to get either of the children to think of sleep. The excitement had been brought to a pitch that was painful, and sister and brother were both near weeping. Alex tried to keep up the courtly backstage style, and that irritated Fran. They fought, which was unusual. As she had been doing for the past several months off and on, Fran meant to sleep alone, and Alex was injured. "Why won't she sleep with me? I hate that! Please make her, Mama!"

Rose snapped at them.

Saul had stayed out with his friends to continue the celebration, and Alex wished he had not. He had begun to wonder what the *Inquirer* and *Record* would write about his performance, or if they would say anything at all. He kept crying, "I'm worried!" as an argument. Fran was adamant about her privacy.

He shouted, deliberately infantile, "You're spoiling the Stokowski!"

When Rose recalled the lady who sat on the ice and their father's description of her, Alex shouted with laughter, then began to cry. Rose put him into a hot tub at one in the morning and made him drink tea with a spoonful of whiskey in it. He would have to discover means of dealing with excitement if he was to manage before the public, she said. It was a matter of self-preservation. As he saw, joy itself could cause trouble. Since his successes would surely be great, he was going to have to learn, in one of his father's phrases, to take it easy.

She read aloud to him, not showing the illustrations, which though harmless enough might have excited him, until he fell asleep.

•

The reconciliation would not work out. There was an incident with a maid, which involved the children, and each parent blamed the other, though they had begun to fight before that. Rose had been threatening to take Fran and Alex to live with a sister in California, and finally, to everyone's surprise, she would do so. Saul, at Susan's suggestion, made notes on the maid incident, and when the children were grown they discussed it. And still later, Alex mentioned it to a doctor in Paris, claiming that he had not been much distressed, though, as he said, perhaps he ought to have been.

He had skipped grades and Francesca had lost two years, so that they were in the same class in September. She was listless at first, and the teacher, warned, did not press her. Alex went at his customary lively pace. He helped his sister with fractions and parts of speech. The teacher got into the habit of glancing at Alex when Fran was not attending, brows raised.

"She'll get into the swing of it," Saul said.

"The room's hot, and she can't get used to the other children."

There was no contention on the point. Saul visited the classroom, charmed the teacher, and had a look around. "God knows it's warm," he said. "She's agreed to put Frankie on the opposite side of the room from the stove. I'd say the other children were in awe of her."

"It's a smell they have like sour milk I can't bear," Fran said, as if she were not herself a child.

It was agreed between teacher and parents that Fran would bring approved novels to class and read them at specified times. The girl told her brother that they would not be at the school for long anyway. "It won't last"—the reconciliation. "They're too polite with each other."

She read Scott and Thackeray sleepily all day. She and Alex walked home, he with an arm around her waist. The top of his head did not come to her shoulder, yet he looked serious, and the children and teacher took him seriously. At home she got into bed for the prescribed rest and read some more. When school was over for the day it no longer existed for them. They made no friends. All their attention was for themselves and their parents.

At first they were shy with Saul, conscious of a mature male presence in the same house with them. They talked too much or said nothing. Alex dogged his father's footsteps. He would snatch the man's neat scrubbed hand and cling to it. Fran, in conversation with him, blushed, tried to look indifferent, both shy and ironic. After a few months they began to grow accustomed to one another, and by the end of the fall term Fran was taking an interest in her schoolwork.

"It's going to hold up," Alex said.

"Maybe."

In Cobbs Creek Park in the spring Saul and Jack Loeb would jab at the freshly flowering shrubs with their walking sticks. "Lovely!" They sat on benches and made comments on passers-by that invariably led to polemical arguments, while Alex gazed devouringly at the same people, wondering about their lives. Occasionally, he was taken to a local pool hall, where he watched Saul with his friends, earnestly joking, a cigarette between his lips, the round slant-eyed face dipping in and out of the focused light. The men grinned and joked yet never took their eyes from the table. With respect, the Negro ball boy watched his father play: a shot that brought grunts of approval. Alex observed his father's hands, the others' faces, thinking that what he saw was beautiful. But he thought too that he did not much like it.

Coming from a Saturday matinee that had been considered too exciting for Fran, Saul and Alex met Sophia Carson.

"I thought it was divine," she said to Alex, "but I'll bet it was too lightweight for you. Don't matinees give you a headache—coming out into the sun?"

She invited them to her apartment, which she called a flat, put Alex on the sofa in her green parlor, and made tea. Would he be preparing another concert soon?—treating him as an adult. She interrupted herself to lay a womanly hand on his knee and gaze at him. "You are something of a wonder, you know. Saul, he is an astonishing young man, aside from the child prodigy thing. I am talking about something much more basic." Addressing Saul, she did not take her eyes from Alex. She said, *"He is interested in others."* He liked her. He saw that she had learned some of his father's style. "He goes out to others. He is of the world every bit as much as he is of art, do you see?"

"Yes, of course. He's wide awake."

"He sees me. His mind is triumphantly present. Saul, have you had a look at these eyes recently?"

She brought out a Swedish cake and questioned him closely concerning its quality. She gave him long looks, put her strong hand on his knee and squeezed it. Or she would abruptly lean back, glance around her room, then back at him. "Getting perspective." She was a year or two older than Saul, her flesh matte and cool with a crumple under the chin, faint hollows filled with blue under the cheekbones. "Do you see what color this place is, what hue predominates?"

"Green."

"Saul! And why green? He sees, of course! He sees all, managing just about to consume me with those marvelous eyes." She shook back her feathery sleeves to reveal plump cool-looking arms, reached to tuck aside Alex's bangs. "Looking at that noble brow in the meanwhile. Oh, God, Saul!"

He saw at last that she was foolish.

"What did she mean," he asked his father in the trolley, "that the green room went with her red hair?"

"Yes, I believe that was it."

He did not dislike it. He was impressed because the woman, though foolish, had made something out of nothing and kept the occasion lively.

His parents fought late at night.

"I expected it went without saying that that particular occurrence was out: her apartment. It should not have come to pass."

Well, it had come to pass, as she put it.

"I will not bear 'as you put it.' I will not bear performances with words at this point!"

Fran and Alex sat at the top of the stairs. "We can't sleep anyway." It did not seem like eavesdropping. Fran sat with her dark head against the wall, eyes closed. Alex clasped his hands between his knees. The maid, Minnie, had a room at the top of the house, and they had seen a light under her door. "She must be listening to every word." Fran decided that she would not go to breakfast because of the way Minnie would look.

●

The maid's full name was Minnie Turks. She had bouts of housekeeping energy that alternated with long gloomy periods when she declared she was bored. She had been hired by Saul's mother, who also paid her salary as her gift to the new household. Alex and Fran decided they liked her. She was young, very black and handsome, and when she was in the mood cheerfully high-spirited. There was a boyfriend named Howard, to whom she spoke on the telephone. She would put Fran or Alex on too. "Ask him what he's doin'," she would demand. "Tell him to ride out here on the trolley."

At some point during the talks Howard managed to insert the year's vaudeville tag: "On the other hand she wore a kid glove"—a joke that never failed to convulse the children, and Minnie as well. "On the other hand"—as if he were going to propose an opposite opinion—"she wore a kid glove." He worked as a cook in a restaurant and had a sunny Southern voice.

In the summer, on afternoons when Saul and Rose were both out and he was off duty, Howard would visit, and Minnie entertained him and the children in her room.

They sat under the gambrel ceiling, Minnie talking in a stilted way, Howard mostly silent. He was a husky short man, not as young as the children had expected, very clean-looking. He smoked a pipe and looked around contentedly.

Alex was a musical genius: "You ought to hear him, Howard!"

"We'll do that," he would reply comfortably. "Hear him on the piano."

Of course. Alex was courteous. Fran said, "He played with Stokowski."

This, when he first heard it, struck Howard apparently, and the children watched while he laughed, showing his powerful teeth. "On the other hand," Minnie said, giving him his cue like a vaudeville comedian. He finished the line and fell back onto the bed laughing. At length, still smiling, he was silent. Minnie was silent. She would look from time to time at the man where he lay on the bed. The children were quiet. There were odd-smelling bottles and jars on Minnie's dresser. A fringed bedspread served as a room divider. The drain of her sink hissed. The man would sigh and, with the stem of his pipe, draw signs in the air above his head.

Minnie one day told the children to wait downstairs until she called them. When she did and they entered her room, she looked at them oddly, and Howard kept his back turned. The room was stuffy.

"Go on!" she demanded; they thought she was speaking to them but really it was to Howard.

Startlingly, he pushed Minnie onto her back on the bed where she had been sitting. She had pulled her skirt up until it was at the tops of her gray cotton stockings. Her garters bit into the black flesh of her thighs. They saw a few glossy curling hairs. Howard, his back to them, fumbled at his trousers and then, improbably, lowered himself between the girl's spread legs. Fran said to her brother that they ought to go downstairs, but Minnie was watching from where she lay.

"I'll say when you can go."

After a time, the man began to pump his backside up and down, then in a circular motion; his pipe fell out of his hip pocket where he had put it. His face was hidden, buried in Minnie's neck. He grunted and groaned. Minnie calmly watched them.

Minnie liked to observe the children as they dressed or "went to the bathroom." She would say she wanted to be sure of them. Of what? The boy and girl had learned from their parents, from Saul in particular, that physical modesty was artificial and therefore wrong. The father did not hesitate to show himself naked before his children. Rose willingly undressed before them. They themselves undressed before each other, only just turning their backs, or before the Volin boys and other cousins in the same room at the seashore. . . . Rose encouraged questions, but they did not ask them, feeling no need to and not knowing how to put them. Alex had no notion as to the source of babies; Fran knew little in spite of a sophisticated manner. An aunt had a big stomach and was going to have a baby. It was Minnie Turks who had surprised them by connecting these facts. The baby was inside the woman's stomach, which made it big.

Fran whispered, "Don't look," but it was difficult not to. She said shakily, "It doesn't matter." It was mysterious and really frightening, but it was all right: probably perfectly all right, Alex thought, yet it might be better not to watch.

At last, after a shout, Howard was still, and Alex could not help a little laugh. The man said something to Minnie, face averted, and she said to the children, "You can get out now."

That was how babies started, Fran said. Of course. Not with kissing. It was that motion. She was not sure that Minnie herself understood and, since the girl and Howard were not married, felt it was her duty to warn her.

"Never mind," Minnie said, apparently having considered it. "I can look after myself."

Fran asked her brother privately, "Did you hate it?"

He could not say he did. Thinking of it years later in Paris, he would remember with surprise that after all Howard and Minnie had removed no clothing; he would remember their modesty.

"We won't go to her room any more unless it's just with her," Fran said, believing that he was worried.

"I'm all right."

But they hid when Howard came to the house after that. There was no question of going to their mother, because the girl had sworn to tell Rose that Fran had been asking about the aunt and had looked at Rose's stomach and said she thought her mother was probably going to have a baby too. It would show the dark bent of her thought as well as hurt their mother's feelings, which was not to be thought of.

On a Thursday afternoon, she and Alex hid in a cupboard. They insisted to each other that it was a game, like playing Hansel and Gretel. Minnie was the witch and would devour them. Fran felt dizzy, and Alex was crying. "She'll hear you," Fran whispered. It was terrible, yet also terribly exciting and a little funny, as if they had been thrust into the middle of one of the German fairy tales Uncle Sasha liked to read to them. Because Alex was crying, Fran began. At the same time it was almost hysterically funny. They sat among the pots and lids with their arms around each other like Hansel and Gretel in the woods. Of course, they made a noise. The cupboard door was thrust suddenly shut from the outside and latched, and they could not open it.

"Don't do that to me, you hear, Fran?" shouted Minnie in a rage when she came to free them later. "I was *lookin'* for you two. Why did you hide?" Howard had gone. The girl was furious, as if she had been ill treated. Fran sobbed and was unable to stop.

Dr. Susan came to see their parents that evening, arrived before Saul and Rose, and heard about it.

•

Both Uncle Jack and Dr. Susan checked them thoroughly, even giving them blood tests.

How involved had they been? What, exactly, had they done?

Their Aunt Susan wanted to know what they felt about

what they had witnessed in Minnie's room. What did they imagine it had been about? She gave Fran long probing looks through her pince-nez. She would begin the interviews in a bland, remote voice but soon became, Fran saw, auntlike and suspicious.

"It's not unreasonable for you to have been rather deeply interested, you know. It would be odd if you weren't. Of course, you watched everything. Why wouldn't you?" It was hard to explain that Minnie's looking at them had forced them to look back. They had known Minnie wanted them to look, and so they looked.

"It is feasible that to a degree, unconsciously, encouragement was lent"—to Rose in Fran's presence. She knew, in any case, that Fran was always in search of adventures. "I don't necessarily speak of this as a conscious process." And later: "The girl is too knowledgeable by half for her age. It works to her disadvantage in the last analysis." Fran saw the contradiction. Susan said that they would sit down one day soon and get things straightened out, no dark corners; but they never did.

Jack, who pretended not to be interested in the children's minds, put practical questions. Had either of them been asked to touch either of the participants during these sessions? Had Minnie kissed either child on this or indeed on any occasion? Had the children sat or stretched themselves out on Minnie's bed, used her third-floor toilet? Their plump, golf-playing uncle was serious-seeming, wagging the stethoscope that he kept taking out of his pocket and putting back without using. Yet Alex knew he was amused. He heard him say to Saul, "That was a nice dolly your mama hired. Don't you like dark meat yourself?"

Saul dismissed Minnie.

She was the victim, he declared, of a corrupt society's need for a corruptible class to serve it. What was more reasonable than that she, ignorant and kept so by the state's wish, should desire to corrupt children in her turn? It was not as if she saw herself as evil. . . .

The girl cried out, "I work my fingers to the bone!"

She was unhinged because, as Dr. Susan said, no one had demanded remorse. "Perhaps religion is called for. You succeed in frightening her out of her wits."

"Such as they are."

The girl stood in the hallway, her suitcase by the door. "I come up here on my own, work my fingers to the bone!" she cried as Saul lectured. "You done this! But I'm the one gets thrown out!" She blamed Saul, hating his coldness. "You done it!"

In October Rose bought tickets to California with money supplied by Babushka.

Mrs. Weisshorn commanded Alex in farewell, "You'll study hard." Their grandmother was in bed with a cold, and the interview took place in her room, which had an attic odor of old papers and moth repellent. Rose was not present. Fran stood at a window and looked down at Lombard Street, romantically at the fall-tinted buttonwoods and damp sidewalks.

"They have a line on a good teacher out there through Rudolph Samuels," Saul declared gloomily.

"I'm adding sixteen dollars a week whatever happens"— Mrs. Weisshorn to Fran. "You can count on it."

"Thank you, Babushka."

"When she decides to come back, write Saul, and he'll send the fare from me. Anything further is entirely his business out of his salary." She lay in bed amid a litter of knitting, accounting ledgers, and correspondence. "Don't kiss me. You'll catch the cold."

Downstairs, Dr. Susan took them aside. "Your mother's running away both from her place and her work. However it may appear to her now, she's doing a weak thing. You know, of course, the extent to which this has hurt your good grandmother."

"I *beg* you, Susan," Saul said irritably. "We don't require that at this point."

56

"You'll find no music teachers of quality. They make moving pictures there."

"Rudolph Samuels is taking care of it."

She spoke to Alex. "Keep an eye on Francesca." Fran was headed toward boy-craziness. "Drop a line now and then on her activities. Don't be afraid to give an analysis of what's going on. I will not fail to reply with a letter of advice. I tell this to you because I feel your mother is incapable of being objective about Francesca."

"I'm not objective about Fran either," said Alex.

"You must learn to understand the ignorance, the very real mental poverty of that pair—the servant and her friend—and to forgive. . . ."

"We do," Alex said. "We're sorry for them."

He said to Fran at home, "She's the one with the dirty mind, not Minnie." And to their mother: "Babushka said in effect it was all right for Papa to send us money without asking her."

Saul, when he came to see them off, looked shy. He had shaved his mustache the night before, and his wife and children, none of whom had ever seen him without it, stared. He looked vulnerable and naked as an egg. He was ten years younger. This violent act, as much as the parting, upset the children. How big his nose had become! And, in an odd reversal, the greenish slanted eyes had grown ancient and serpentlike. Also, they sensed that he had done it to show how miserable he felt and that he disliked himself, which was worrying. He looked like an ugly boy. Saul smiled and wept, blew his new nose into a handkerchief, back turned, shook his head in wonder at his own behavior, and winked at his children: "Okay, okay."

There were telegrams waiting in Chicago and Saint Louis: "ARE YOU WELL. REPLY COLLECT"; letters at Aunt Katie's bungalow in Venice, California.

"I must know at once if you are really all right and well set up there. The important thing is your health, and I empha-

57

size this. You will have wired me of your safe arrival, now I must know *in detail* about the children's state of health. *Is Alex all right—mentally. Did Fran suffer* ANY *ill effects from the strenuous trip???*"

Between the lines they could read his blame of Rose for submitting the children to what he called the adventure over his, Babushka's, and Susan's objections. But the tone was passionate. "Kiss them for me. A hundred thousand father's kisses. Kiss them good night and good morning. Their poor papa loves them more than he can say."

"And so on," Rose said of this and later letters, "but the draft on the Bank of America he was supposed to send in the meantime doesn't arrive until three weeks after it's due and then turns out to be for half the promised amount."

1914–1918

•

It was not unlike Atlantic City, except that the sun set in the ocean instead of the bay. Aunt Kate, younger than their mother, was cheerful as long as the children performed tasks assigned to them. When she was strict it was with regret, so that it was difficult for Fran, who had most of the household assignments, to be resentful. Uncle Herman, as their mother said in a rare excursion into Yiddish, was a nebbish—a soft, gentle, dreaming man, all but invisible.

The bungalow—never called a house—stood on a half acre it shared with a twin structure a block from the beach and fifty minutes north of Los Angeles by the high-speed trolley. The town was new, the commercial dream of a manufacturer of cigarettes who had patterned it upon the Italian city. There was a pier with attractions: freak shows, lectures, art exhibitions, and dancing in a ballroom suspended over the surf. The children's playground became the beach. It curved emptily northward beneath the Santa Ana Mountains. Not far south of them were oil derricks. They visited a Spanish mission with Uncle Herman and Aunt Kate, went to Santa Catalina Island, took a ride in the glass-bottomed boat, and visited Lucky Baldwin's Santa Anita ranch. Los Angeles, with its adjacent suburban towns, was booming. Their school was new and open with sliding walls in the Japanese style and flower-covered walks between the buildings. Wherever they went were the cool canals in place of streets, which made them feel that their new life was exotic and descriptions of which filled their letters. From their bedroom window at night they could both hear and smell the Pacific. In Aunt

Kate's front yard were bougainvillaea and hibiscus, names they quickly learned, and something called a pineapple palm. They took exploring walks as far as Ocean Park or went on the trolley to Santa Monica, feeling independent in the flowery air. They went to Los Angeles with Rose. In the spring they climbed the seaward mountain slopes to get blooming yucca. They found an abalone fishing village, and the dark powerful-seeming Japanese, so willing and cheerful, delighted them.

And Rose's job, though not easy, was a success. She was first a clerk and then, having shown flair, the buyer for Katie's shop, which sold apparel for women. It sounded like fun to Fran and Alex, but Rose's feet, which were accepted to be too small for her weight, suffered from unaccustomed hours of standing. Fran would remove her mother's shoes at night, thinking of herself in a religious-literary way, bring a basin of warm water and Epsom salts. . . .

"Poor Mama," they said admiringly.

They were aware of doing well on their own, and the consciousness was a tonic.

Rose earned a small salary and the major part of their keep. Fran made up the rest with household chores. Aunt Katie's daughter, whose name was Joy, was lazy and friendly. Alex had his music (a piano had been rented), which, with school, was recognized as his job. He and Joy helped with dishes or, if they did not, saw that Fran was entertained.

Alex was Charles Farrow. Fran, a beautiful widow in a Santa Barbara beach house, was Ramona Patterson. They also called themselves Whitethorn and Whitemont. The games had solved the trip west; now, when Fran felt she was being exploited by her aunt, they played her resentment out in fictional parallels, with Joy's enthusiastic help. She said, "Mother's impossible."

Minnie and Howard were also all but fictional by now, and they told Joy about it without difficulty.

"My gosh!" the girl cried. She was a pink-skinned blonde and flushed easily. "What did they *do?*"

They told her clearly, giving the story its harsh outlines, reliving it plainly yet in safety, as if it were a chapter in a novel. They were compassionate, as artists can be, finally assigning the blame to society; and Alex, unsmiling, did the comic relief. "On the other hand she wore a kid glove!"

"But it really happened?"

Oh, yes.

It made their cousin's cheeks flame. "My gosh!" It had actually happened, but it was difficult for any of them to believe it.

•

"My dear Princess," Saul wrote in one of his earlier letters, "and dearest Alex: I want you to help your mother as much as you can in this difficult time. She is not accustomed to daily work. Use the money we send each week in a grown-up cautious way—this is advice, after all, from a banker—putting aside something, for the proverbial rainy day.

"Frank, I understand and sympathize with your complaint. It is not unjust. But you are a guest in your aunt's house and must 'bear a hand' cheerfully when asked. Rose writes that you get into Los Angeles for pleasure—the movies, a restaurant—at least once a week and that does not sound too much like 'slavery' to your papa. But, Frank, stand up for your rights too and in a calm way ask Joy to do her share of the housekeeping and shopping tasks. Yours is a working community in miniature, and each of you is contributing to the weal according to your gifts and capabilities, for which services you ought to receive ample compensation in some form. The fact that Alex wants to pitch in on housework worries me, since we know his energy is already dedicated. Each of us ought to do what he does best. . . . Life goes on as usual here. The bank keeps us busy. I have my nights out with the famed 'cronies' (how many discussions on that subject!) and at the same time continue in my efforts to save the workers of the world. Only tonight I talked several of the bosses to death in the lobby of the Bellevue, but they were inebriated so it was hardly a fair fight." Seriously he wrote, "It seems to me that the concept of *work,* that is of honest labor toward a useful end, may be not only the greatest good but the only good we may know on earth. . . ."

"It's because we're supposed to show Rose and Aunt Kate," Alex said, remarking on the tone of these letters. It irritated Fran that Saul thought she did housework best; and Alex, his face taking on an expression of suffering joy, indicating stacked greasy dishes or the rugs and bedding they had to turn out onto the lawn every Saturday morning: "Not only the greatest good . . ."

"Frankie, there are things you are old enough now to understand provided they are explained straightforwardly," Saul wrote in reply to a dramatic letter of his daughter's. "You inquire why this must be, our separation, and I will attempt to answer. It sometimes happens, unfortunately, between a man and a woman that their love for one another dies and cannot be revived by any means, in which case 'the clean break' may be the wisest course. No, I do not think we can ever again be the real household you so touchingly talk of, but neither do I think that three thousand miles of distance (what a gulf it is!) represents the correct, the reasonable alternative. . . ."

"Love dies!" Rose said when she read the letter. "What a thing to write to children!"

"He shouldn't have said that to us!" Fran said to her brother. She hoped she would never be old enough to hear such a thing.

"Anyhow, he wants us home."

They saw that their mother was pleased with herself, that she felt she had Saul where she wanted him. In fact, on the whole, they were happy. The warm, Oriental climate suited them—"Los Angeles magic," they called it in their letters. Rose, for the first time in her adult life, was independent of her mother-in-law. Alex's music teacher was excellent, the school first class. The boy's talent was recognized and he was allowed to move ahead quickly in mathematics and languages, with or without grades, by the reform-minded teachers and principal. At the same time, he was urged to take part in athletic activities, at which he also excelled. The scented warm rain and sunshine seemed to act on the children, Rose said, as it did on the plants. They took hikes, played at producing movies on the beach, and surf-bathed eight months of the year. Fran's period of illness became fiction: the sad remembered child was Esther Whitethorn, a chronic invalid, irritable and languid; Alex was a life-exhausted, eternally joking doctor. They became tanned and grew taller suddenly.

"Your mother relies so much on flowers to describe how you two are doing," Saul wrote, "that I can only suppose it has something to do with her name."

They quarreled long distance, with the difference that it was Rose who used the irony.

"If the weekly allowance is a burden"—Saul had written of dull sessions, irregularities in commodities due to the Mexican war—"simply suspend it until she feels she can afford to resume. We are all right for money and even in a position to help out if you and Mrs. W. are feeling the pinch. . . ."

". . . thinking of your own good and certain you must have regretted the note after it was mailed, I did not show it to my mother. I repeat, as regards the war take no risks. Come straight back if you feel qualms."

"I will let you know," she wrote in the new ironic tone, "the moment General Villa is on the outskirts of Venice, but I assure you we are safe for the nonce."

Fran wrote, hoping to affect him, "Mama even has boyfriends!"

She also called them suitors: acquaintances of Herman and Katie who came to the bungalow on spring Sundays, borrowed a room to dress, and spent the day going back and forth from the house to the beach. One of these, a courtly

63

man with silvered hair and a mustache who reminded them a little of their father, was, he said, an artist, a writer, and an actor, and also involved in producing films. Alex admired him and worked hard to impress him, both with his music and with gymnastics (he once walked straight into the water on his hands). The man spent more time with them than with Rose. On a Saturday he took them to Los Angeles to see the moving picture *Civilisation*, in which he had a brief role. He kept talking about the great expense of the picture. He had himself, he said, once owned a mansion on Santa Monica Boulevard and a five-thousand-dollar Locomobile. "Oil was discovered on the land about a year after I sold out—naturally." He spoke in an anxious serious way about finding movie roles for all of them. Joy and Fran would be child actors. Alex would perform in a filmed recital. He would act as their agent.

"The next thing we know he's vanished into thin air," said Alex, narrating the events of their lives as they took place. Rose had sent him on his way.

"I've had enough of weak men to last two lifetimes."

"He was a bit exaggeratory," said Alex.

Through the eyes of the suitors they saw their mother's charms. The family sat out on the dark lawn in canvas chairs and watched the sunset: "A ball of fire dropping into molten lead," Fran said. Rose told the children about a man who, in her opinion, had understood something of the nature of love —a tragic figure.

The Golds had lived in a flat a few doors down on Lombard Street while Rose was still in residence there. She was secretary to a lawyer. He was a poet and held no job. Only later did they realize that he was a sick man and had been from youth. He was small, intense, and handsome and at that time wore his hair very long, falling over a Vandyke collar. He carried his poems with him, new ones every day. They were written in copybooks with his name printed on the cover as a child would do. Rose understood that he came to see her. In fact, he hardly bothered to pretend otherwise. She knew

64

he pitied her position in a household where the mother-in-law ruled and the son chased anything in skirts. He would walk with Rose while she wheeled Fran in her carriage and read aloud from the notebook, gesturing unself-consciously. The poet was a laborer, as worthy as any man of his hire. He was going to have copies of the poems printed—leaflets on bright paper—and go from house to house as Whitman had done across the river in Camden to earn his bread.

Fran thought she remembered the man dimly, but it was not possible.

The man was in love with Rose. It was as clear as day. Rose did not know how to take him. She was not "that way" about him.

"I wish you had loved him!" Fran said.

Their talks had been the best of Rose's life. Some poems had been dedicated to her. She was the subject, discreetly disguised, of others. Saul, needless to say, detested the man. Now and then the poet gave a reading at the Weisshorn at-homes, but he often did something alarming. He would fling his papers down and rush from the room because people spoke as he read. Once he appeared with his head cropped close, so that he looked like a Siberian convict. If anyone commented on the poems, unless it was to praise them, he became angry and gave Rose a scornful exclusive look over the heads of the others: this was what poetry meant in the camp of the Philistines. In the front hall of the house one day —it was a morning in May, beautiful weather—he tried to embrace her. He had liquor on his breath.

Alex tried to see his mother in the dusk. She *was* beautiful! Fran chewed on the inside of her cheek with concentration. An odor of geraniums, heavy and sickly, which the boy would remember, filled the air. Though the light had gone, its reflection remained, and a romantic sea mist had drowned the lawn and the legs of their chairs. A light went on in the bungalow, and they could see their mother's hovering face, a scrap of rounded cheek, the eyes, as Fran would say, looking into the past. Fran thought of silver evenings, the poet

Masefield, of the sadness of dead events.

Gold left, returned with a knife, "brandishing it," Rose said. He threatened her. A maid was screaming, hands over her ears, as if she could not bear the noise she was making; passers-by paused in Lombard Street in the sun. How vivid she was able to make it!

"He wanted to kill you!"

"He loved her!" Alex cried.

That was love, be it said, for good or ill.

He flung the knife onto the marble step, jumped down, and ran off, having harmed no one. She could see in her mind's eye, she said, the white marble step and sun flashing from the bread knife, the sheeplike people, their stares.

"He had to go into an institution," she said plainly when they asked. He had been there for more than ten years and would probably spend his life there. The children said they pitied him, but Rose said, "Think of the wife!"

The phrase about their father chasing anything in skirts—it had been supposed to come from the poet—stayed with them. Their mother had never used such an expression. "It's because we're old enough," Fran said with her wryness. Rose talked now about Saul's lady friends and referred to Mrs. Carson by name. For the first time, Alex thought that all this must mean his father treated women as Howard had treated Minnie. Rose said that all her husband wanted to do was kiss the girls and make them cry like the boy in the rhyme. She said it to Katie and Herman, but the children were there.

"A bit of a talker even in that. The fact is Saul was never up to very much."

Alex pushed this away from him, leaving it to Fran. They would sit on a bench on the esplanade to watch the sunset, Rose with her shoes off, Aunt Kate and Uncle Herman strolling arm in arm and gazing westward. "Your father was not up to a great deal, in fact," Rose said. "He's not the lover he likes to appear to be." Or they would sit by the hour under clattering palms in front of the bungalow. It was as if the perfume of flowers or the setting sun made her drunk and

66

indiscreet. When she spoke of Mrs. Carson it was in a tone of commiseration.

"She only means Saul's weak," Fran said to Alex.

They knew that. That was his character. But Alex, supposing she meant something more complicated, put it to one side, leaving it to his mother and sister. Why should he be told that his father was not up to much? He was too young. He would sit in his canvas chair on the lawn not listening, or rise abruptly and go in to play through one of the music books his grandmother sent every week, hearing under the music the patter of water from a neighbor's garden hose in Aunt Kate's eucalyptus.

"Mind you, I don't speak of charm. He had all of that in the world." So had Alex, he was told; and soberingly: "I'm not all that impressed by charm, though Alex's at least is entirely sincere."

"I can see why Saul couldn't live with her in a way," Fran said to him later in their room, "but he was extremely unfair to her."

They told their cousin about the poet Gold. Both he and Mrs. Sophia Carson, the latter created by Alex because he had had tea with her in her apartment, became principals in the bedtime serial. They used the green color scheme and gave Mrs. Carson a New York *pied-à-terre* with emerald couches and lamps, shuttered windows, and a bed hung with green curtains. A marble Psyche (pronounced "pish," Fran would remember years later) turned over her shoulder and gazed smiling down at her nude body. Mrs. Carson took Saul's hat. Something to drink? . . . The maid screamed at the sight of the knife. Pedestrians stared in horror. The knife fell to the step, glittered in the sunshine, and the madman fled into his dark future.

Joy, who was a year younger than Alex and with whom they shared a long bedroom under the eaves, recited her lines placidly. Alex and Fran amazed her, but she decided it was because they were from the East and because Alex was a genius.

●

His piano teacher lived on Figueroa Street in Los Angeles in a rambling Spanish Victorian mansion set in three acres of gardens. Her name was Edna Loux. She had been Siloti's prize student, then briefly a concert performer. Alex was her only pupil.

Fran accompanied her brother on the trolley from Venice and waited in a plant-filled porch reading while Miss Loux (she pronounced it "Lux") and Alex worked. Once shown into the big music room, Alex made, according to schedule, for a sideboard where cocoa and cookies were waiting. (Fran was served the same things separately by a maid.) Then he would go to the piano, set out his work, and begin. Until the work absorbed him, he made a picture of which he was conscious: back very straight, the almost adult profile already starting to lengthen and droop, shoulders broad, waist narrow. Miss Loux would make an entrance. He said (he had got the phrase from Rose in another context) that electricity existed between them, and it was true that he knew the moment she came to stand in the conservatory door. He would complete the exercise, glance up, rise with courteous haste. They played such small scenes, understanding each other; but then when they got down to it, both labored unstintingly.

She placed herself so that Alex could see her face. She would nod or slightly shake her head, a hand on the baroque piano case, the other on her trim youthful hip. (Fran declared that she was pretty.)

"Don't play to me. Be serious."

She did not approve of Alex's early performance with the Philadelphia Orchestra. There would be a point at which, having worked hard, he would need to get rid of some of what he knew; a time for an audience, which had paid to do so, to find out something about Alex and something more about a composer. This was to speak of the future and of professional life. There had already been local amateur

68

efforts, in which Alex had taken part.

She was a tall slim woman of forty when Alex first knew her. She wore no jewelry and had hard short-nailed hands. (Alex's own hands at this age were already powerful and broad.) She ate little, no meat, swam every morning rain or shine the year around from the beach in front of her house, and touched no alcohol but wine, of which she took a glass at each meal, including breakfast. At the same time, as she said, she knew how to relax. She lived in her big house with half a dozen servants and a chauffeur. The gardeners, who were Japanese, did not live in. The rest had come from Virginia with her years before (she was an FFV, as the children informed their father with enthusiasm—a member of an organization called First Families of Virginia: an American aristocrat), and some of them and all of their parents had been Loux family slaves.

"But she's wonderful with them," wrote Fran. "They're like a family. They call her Edna and because she's absentminded they have to keep telling her what to do. . . ."

There was a friend, a Miss Framingham, who had been a harpist with the San Francisco Symphony and was now composing. She visited for long periods and would sit in a deep chair at one end of the room, listening to Alex's work, or stamp around scattering cigarette ash on the Chinese carpets, fists in her pockets, frowning. "Nat bad, nat bad"—in a flat Chicago voice. She was intense and serious and eyed Fran with a kind of suspicion. "The sky's the limit," she told her concerning Alex, as if in warning. She would wander onto the cool porch, which was like a liner's closed deck, and stare at Fran, who was reading Tennyson for school or Scott for herself. "She intends Alex to be a poet of the pianoforte," she once said to her, a phrase that soon became part of their collection of funny tags. Invited to hear a finished piece, Fran would see the women exchange smiles over the boy's head that were, she decided, sentimental.

"They're gone on you."

For Rose, it was clear to the children, Alex's teacher had

courteous respect, as due the prodigy's mother, but little use besides. There was talk for a time—it set going a flustered exchange of letters coast to coast—of Miss Loux having Alex to live with her for a year in order to benefit from what she described as a total environment of music. The children talked it over in earnest. Perhaps she would adopt him. Saul wrote angrily, forbidding any such thoughts, and it boiled down to a month in the summer; but in the meantime the children had a good look at the life of the rich as it was lived when coupled with the excluding life of the working artist.

"It's a matter, finally, of dedication," Alex said.

The work provided incorruptibility. You might be served on crystal by a butler in a green vest, but if you had done your day's work there was no harm in it. It was all in the work. Work—dedication—accounted for the weariness in the midst of plenty: the hard, self-denying life. It accounted for Miss Framingham's suspicion of Fran (the sister understood) and the polite, bored lack of use for Rose; it accounted for the smiles, brief, almost bitter, as Alex played.

Alex (and Fran) observed this and in great part understood it: the artist worked harder than others, harder even than the bouncing brown cigarette-smoking gardeners beyond the conservatory windows, who seemed never to cease work. At the same time, because of the solemnity, particularly of Miss Framingham, the artistic life was also funny. They teased Rose, saying Alex ought to be adopted by Miss Loux; they joked about the boy becoming a poet of the pianoforte; but Alex wrote long letters to Saul concerning the value of dedicated, self-denying labor in art. And it was as if, so difficult was the life (even if a little absurd), in relief after the hard day, incorruptibly, anything went: "We get crazy on weekends," he wrote, "and Uncle Herman stares at us. But it's the reaction to Miss Edna's factory and Mama lets us blow off steam." And when his father mentioned all the riches: "The money doesn't matter to her. She works too hard."

Late in the fall Miss Loux and Miss Framingham began to prepare their production of *Messiah*, which was to be per-

70

formed in her garden amphitheater. Alex would play the solo harpsichord. Miss Loux would conduct. There were to be two choirs recruited from local high school glee clubs, principal singers from the Los Angeles Opera Company, the directors of which were old friends of both women. Admission would be charged and the money donated to charity.

"I do not think it's necessarily good to fall into the habit of living at Miss Loux's house," Saul wrote. "She may be a kind of genius even in her manner of living, but you mustn't get to thinking that all of life is the life of art, whether in action or reaction. Maybe the point is to be single-minded without growing narrow-minded. . . . I wonder a little about the professional aspect of your *Messiah.* That comes pretty close to regular public performance. Does she think you're ready?"

"This from the man who couldn't wait for you to perform with Stokowski," Fran said impatiently.

It was she who wrote the letters home asking for money or gifts of clothing, sometimes on her own, more often at Rose's dictation. Alex might not be ready to perform publicly, but the three of them could turn out to be part of that charity the money was being donated to. Fran appealed to her father on the basis of her mother's frailty, the difficulty of the work in the women's apparel shop.

"I sympathize with your mother's difficulties, children," he wrote, replying to a phrase of Fran's. ("Her feet can no longer support her weight for such long hours in the shop.") ". . . You may discern the obvious solution to the problem, but I will not underline it."

This and other letters were to turn up in a trunk years later, the irony in them revealed for the first time. Alex would say that they reminded him of sunlight and geraniums, sickeningly, but that he could recall little else of what he had felt. Fran would say she remembered everything.

". . . The European war with the possibility of U.S. intervention has created a monetary instability, the effects of which are felt even by us at M. L. Weisshorn, and that means

71

that there is little cash available. Neither your grandmother nor I feels it feasible to increase the current weekly remittance at this point. We will discuss it again in another month. Frankly, I would rather have you here for the money than three thousand miles off. Rose says she cannot simply 'up and come home. That's too easy.' We believe it is what she should do, easy or not. Ask yourself, Alex, why study with Alexander Siloti's pupil when, if you return to the East, you can study with the master?"

Alex massaged Rose's shoulders. Fran bathed and massaged her feet, distorted by bunions and corns. There was a podiatrist, as Kate called him, in Los Angeles who had worked miracles for her, but Rose would not spend the money.

"Oh, my pussy cats, that does feel good," she moaned under her children's hands. Alex worked on the plump shoulders and neck, feeling the resisting tension beneath the flesh. He was sprightly and talkative, but Fran would grow severe. Perhaps there was something in what Saul said. Why, for example, did Rose wear shoes that were unsuitable for work? Fran was hard on vanity. But the fact remained that there were days when, for one reason or another, Rose could not get out of bed to go to the shop.

The sister and brother were free from Saturday midafternoon, when their chores were finished, until Sunday evening, when homework had to be done. They would go to the beach with a movie camera made of cigar boxes—Alex in knickers, cap backward on his head, being a director. All the children in the neighborhood were movie-struck. Uncle Herman had arranged to have them taken through the Keystone lot, and they soon knew as much as their cousin Joy about the stars. Mary Pickford was earning a thousand dollars a week and Chaplin much more. Stars appeared at civic auditoriums, even Venice Pier, to raise money for the Allied war effort, later to sell Liberty Bonds. Their actual in-person size and voices, their rich clothes, the big cars made them simultaneously familiar and more remote. Camera crews and extras were doing location scenes everywhere, and—this was one of the great events of their stay—Chaplin rented a house not far from their own bungalow and lived there with his leading lady while a movie was being filmed nearby. They were not married.

"That's their business," Rose said to the children in the sturdy manner that came to her now and then. "It is not our place to judge. They may have a better marriage without that piece of paper than your father and I had with it."

It was nothing less than astonishing to walk past the cottage on a summer evening and see the great man in his shirtsleeves, a garden hose in one hand, cigarette in the other, the famous exploding crop of hair (no mustache, of course; they knew it was painted on), the bony face and dark eyes. "He looks so young! He looks like a boy of my age!" Alex cried. And there he was playing a hose on a yellowish lawn like anyone else's!

When the relationship and the household broke up (they read about it in the paper), Rose said bitterly, "Even that freedom was insufficient for him."

As she worked less, often no more than two days in a week, their mother resumed a girlish vagueness. She canvassed her children ceaselessly. Perhaps they should return home after all. Persistent and practical, Saul's letters attempted to persuade her. She fell into the kittenish style Alex and Fran remembered from the periods of worst uncertainty. Hers was "fragrant" self-indulgence; she loved them for "seventy-mental" reasons. Once more, all her stories of the past concerned her father and her brothers and how they had protected her from life. "They should not have done it. If they had been less protective, I'd be able to deal with things now. . . ." For the children's sake, perhaps, they should return to where opportunities were greater.

Fran and Alex thought they wanted to go back east, but they did not want to do it out of weakness. It would be then as if they had wasted the whole reason for the trip. It would be a defeat.

73

They rehearsed *Messiah* at Miss Loux's Figueroa Street mansion. They made expeditions into the foothills of the mountains on Sundays with friends. Once Alex practically carried back down a rugged slope to the trolley line a class-mate named Alice Roberts, who had twisted an ankle. She kissed him in front of everyone, which made him a hero in two ways, and Fran said, "Bravo!" grinning with pleasure. Later, at home alone (Joy, her parents, and their mother were in Los Angeles), they made hot chocolate and sand-wiches and sat on without lights, serious about the adventure. Alex had "managed" things, solved a crisis. It was not much, he said. He had discovered that he could deal with situations, if not in one way then in another. There was, of course, a class bully, and Alex managed him. Adroitly self-mocking, he cut him down to size. He would interfere where he had no busi-ness (and every business), look the boy over at his work as one might an expert in his line. Hadn't the other noticed, Alex would suggest, that the boy he was hurting was smaller, younger? His intelligence raced to manage the nuances of the situation. No one was to be allowed to behave dishonora-bly, even the one who wished to do so. He would have ob-served the sensual smile on the bully's face, understanding it and even sympathizing—the pleasure of hurting—as with an illness. Yet cruelty had to be stopped. Fran was the same. They were diplomats of the classroom and schoolyard.

They would remember these as powerful and successful days but ones that held, in the odor of geraniums for Alex and the memory of work for Fran, both nausea and mild longing; this, they would suppose, might have been homesickness. There were dance contests on the pier. Alex and his cousin entered them and won prizes. Rose's suitors continued to appear on weekends bringing their bathing suits and gifts of candy. At one time she had two offers simultaneously. But Saul never stopped urging them. What should they do? What did Fran think? Diplomats dedicated to easing pain, they could see what their mother wanted to be told. Finally in November, with *Messiah* six weeks off, it was decided that

74

they would return in the following spring but that they would not tell Miss Loux until after the performance.

●

Alex used to watch Miss Loux's men at their labor, taking advantage of the hour between the end of his lesson and luncheon. Alone or with Fran, he wandered in the designed landscape that kept turning back on itself. Los Angeles did not seem to exist beyond the garden walls. There were walks and hedged alleys marked by marble statues, waterfalls and fountains, a summerhouse. At the south end of the property were citrus groves and greenhouses, a vegetable garden. Everything that came under the boy's eyes interested him, and he soon understood a good deal of what was going on. He questioned the gardeners, liking their serious replies. They were all serious, didactic men, some no taller than he (Alex would not grow tall), and he felt a tension between them and himself.

He explored the house and sat with the servants in their quarters on the other side of a felt-covered swing door and here experienced the same pleasant tension, which he dimly designated a "correct" sensation.

"I was born into slavery," the old butler said to him in an orating tone. "I was a *slave* child. When I opened my eyes in the morning, it was to look upon the world as a slave boy. Think of it! I lived up in the house with my family and played with her daddy as a boy, then took care of her like I was her own daddy after he died." But he had been a slave in bondage! He estimated his age at seventy-seven but said he might be ten years more than that for all he knew. "Nobody cared to keep track." ("The fool," Miss Loux would say. "He was born the year before my father—1840—and is well aware of it. What's more, he never paid the least attention to me.") He sat at the kitchen table, arthritic hands folded over each other, it seemed to Alex avoiding the boy's eyes. There was a particular smell, as if his flesh, though clean, was too strong for water. (But when Miss Framingham said black people had a smell, Alex denied it purposefully.) The cook, his wife, worked silently and apart. Fran sat apart also, in a deep window, feet tucked under her, dreaming. The tiled floor of the kitchen sloped to a center drain, and into this the ex-slave spat now and then. He had allowed the small fingernail on his left hand to grow and used it as a toothpick. When his boiled shirt gaped and Alex saw corkscrews of white hair on the black chest, there was the pleasant tension once more: disgust and, in the unguarded humanness, delight. The man would catch Alex between his knees and imprison him, smiling yet looking to one side of the boy's searching eyes.

"Bet you can't get away!"

The butler was strong. Alex tried to pry apart the powerful knees. He knew the man was performing, and if he did not know what the performance was about, he knew that he did not mind it.

"Then shall the eyes of the blind be opened. . . ."

Miss Loux rehearsed the alto in the music room.

". . . I used to go down into the fields and observe things like a gentleman. The men and women in their bright clothes singing. It made a picture. That was all it was to me. That's what it was like for me. Nonetheless I was in slavery."

"Didn't you ever like being a slave?" Alex asked, deliberately naïve.

The other was an old performer, the boy saw. He waited for the reply.

"No man who was a man could have liked it."

Alex recognized the avoidance of truth, not minding, thinking of honor as something to be maintained by almost any means. He guessed that this man had liked it.

Fran caught cold and could not be part of the chorus, but she had threatened to become hysterical if she was kept home, so she sat between her mother and aunt wrapped in blankets, looking up at the North Star, which Uncle Herman had pointed out. Miss Loux and Miss Framingham, who played her harp with the orchestra, wore chinchilla capes. Alex was in evening dress.

The performance began at sunset to take advantage of the lingering warmth. Miss Loux waited for the swallows to finish their song and dance (a humorous shrug for the amphitheater; Jane Framingham's chuckle). She did a cut version. Her mixed high school and adult choirs were well disciplined but, as Rose would say, unexpressive. Alex's fingers were stiff with cold, but he endured and felt that to succeed against the weather, which made it impossible for the harpsichord to remain in tune, was of an importance equal to succeeding with the music.

A program note directed the audience not to applaud before the end due to "the devotional sense of the music." The tenor, a tall plump man, sat with his fingers calmly laced until his turn came to sing, then leaped up athletically and, though Miss Loux had asked him not to, struck a soldierly pose with one foot forward, hands supplicating. The alto when she was not singing had a sweet bruised smile, which she turned helplessly from the conductor to the audience. She became angry at "He was despised," and when the bass sang, "Why do the nations so furiously rage together," shook her head in wonder. With the Resurrection, the reassuring smile returned. Fran, who was feverish, noted the comedy to tell Alex, but she also wept.

Miss Loux stretched out her hands to all the performers and would not herself turn to the applause. Alex had to spring from his place and require her to turn. Conscious that the applause was also largely for him, he kept his gaze on her instructively: she had done it all, the audience ought to know. He kissed her cheek, on which, Fran thought, herself crying with emotion at the drama of the moment and the music's overpowerful effect, there were tears like stars. It was a triumph. Alex felt its electricity, the applause speaking directly to his body. He remembered his mother had said that such feelings could cause trouble (how had she known that? he wondered now, admiring his mother—everyone—enormously), but there was no trouble in this. And, both wry and emphatic, Fran would say later that night that God existed, that God was in the music. "Never mind what I say tomorrow," she declared wryly, knowing herself. "This is what I mean."

The children spent New Year's Eve with Miss Loux and Jane Framingham. Alex announced that they—he and Fran and Rose—would return to Philadelphia in the spring. It was decided. The women were wearing their chinchilla capes. Miss Loux gazed at Alex, smiling. Then she and the other woman went to stroll in the garden. The brother and sister heard Miss Framingham's voice, increasingly faint as they walked. "King of Kings, and Lord of Lords," singing deeply.

"Is she taking it all right?"

"I think so," said Alex. "Why not?" He made himself see it coldly. "It's a matter of my work. She'll have to get over it."

He sat in a big chair and read Browning.

"I think they're both tight from cocktails."

"She'd better save room for champagne."

Fran said she was going to drink a glass or two. "I want to feel it." Fran had a theory: you should try everything once when you were young in order to sort things out. They looked over the bottles the butler brought up, and Alex asked intelligent questions concerning them. At last one of Miss Loux's dogs bounded in, followed by the women, and Miss Loux swirled her cape off and onto the waiting servant's arm in a single gesture, and had a look at the bottles. She put out a hand to them. Was there nothing else? "What about our Nompere?" Her Virginia accent increased when she addressed her servants.

"What the heck difference does it make, Edna?" asked Jane Framingham. "We'll drink a glass and that will be that." She stayed behind while Miss Loux, Fran, and Alex descended to the basement bins, which were next to the game room, in order to inspect the other wine. The teacher said that some of the bottles she looked at were spoiled, though the children could not tell how she knew. Alex said, "It's a shame."

"Many things are a shame, Alex, and very likely a waste." She leaned against the shelves of bottles, ignoring the dust. Her face was damp and pale.

"*Not* a waste," he said firmly. He knew she was referring to his leaving and did not pretend to misunderstand.

"Oh, Alex," Fran would say when they were alone. "Wow!"

A few guests came in at eleven. Edna and Miss Framingham went to the piano, and Miss Loux played while the other sang in her rough voice several songs of her own composition —lines by Swinburne and Tennyson that she had set. Alex, who had not heard her work before, decided it was serious in a way he did not approve—like Southern California, uncertain and without a character of its own, so that solemnity became important in itself.

When the wine was opened, Fran drank a glass at once but noticed nothing much. Alex, a small boy again, sipped his with an expression that made Miss Loux smile sadly.

One of the guests was a tall golden-haired man in evening dress who paid court to Alex. He said he could see that the boy's feet were planted on the ground. "A prodigy with a difference. No one could say in all honesty that you were a beautiful boy onstage," he declared, "but in a sense isn't that all to the good?" He had been present at *Messiah* but had had to leave early. He asked casually if the boy would perform with the Los Angeles Symphony, of which he was a trustee and board member, in March. Alex was afraid not; he was not ready. "Not *ready?* Help, Miss Edna!"

"Not ready," she said.

"That one has a certain *je ne sais quoi*," Alex said to Fran, grinning, using a catch phrase, "and welcome to it."

At midnight he announced the "Auld Lang Syne Variations," on which he had been working and which had a scherzo that made these musically aware people laugh, though the man who had spoken to him earlier sang the words seriously, staring hard at Alex.

Fran and Alex kissed each other unsentimentally.

"Happy New Year, kiddo," she said. "I wish the best for us in Philly and in the new life, but don't tell the old dear I said it."

The chauffeur was waiting to drive them home. Fran had a date next day to see the parade, and Alex and Rose and the rest of the family were going too, though discreetly apart. Alex went upstairs to find their coats. Miss Loux and Jane Framingham were standing in the hallway outside the bathroom door embracing. They swayed, locked together. Even now there was a cigarette in Miss Framingham's hand. Miss Loux opened her eyes and saw Alex. Keeping her eyes on him, she turned her head and kissed Miss Framingham, which, Alex thought he heard, made the younger woman grunt.

●

New Year's Day was, for Southern California, wintry. There were flashing moments of sun and the Santa Ana wind came off the hills. In the morning Alex and his uncle walked near the surf, bent against the wind, though Alex kept looking out at the bar of blue water at the sea's edge. Uncle Herman waved a piece of tarry stick and sang bits from *Carmen*, which was the best opera ever written, he said. "*Tor-ee*a*dor*"—jabbing the stick into the yellow sand in time.

"And what New Year's resolution have you made, Alex?"

Alex wanted to find out if an ordinary person (Herman was ordinary; he and Fran said to each other that that was why they liked him) was bothered by such things. He asked him.

"Why, everybody kisses everyone else on New Year's Eve."

80

For Alex, intent on information, it was difficult to describe the difference to Uncle Herman. As always, the man was vague; he appeared to be listening for someone to call him. He knitted his plump brows.

"They were kissing the way a man and woman kiss in the movies," Alex explained, simplifying. "They were like lovers."

"Lovers?"

Alex resolved for the new year that he would not confide in Uncle Herman any more.

"What did *you* resolve, Uncle Herman?"

Oh, he would smoke less; that was always his first resolve and, he was afraid, always the first to be broken.

"He wants to live to be Uncle Herman forever, if possible," Alex declared to Fran on the trolley going into Los Angeles.

"Don't you want to live a long time?" Fran asked.

Under certain conditions. "I'd have to be in full possession of all faculties." He would have to be able to work. Fran wanted to live briefly and with great intensity and to burn up brilliantly like a meteor in the earth's abrasive atmosphere. "I mean it!"

Sitting together away from the rest of the family, they were thoughtful.

"I want to be able to work, keep developing in my work until the end. The real artists keep growing—not this prodigy stuff." Alex talked now about composing instead of giving concerts but did not say so to anyone but Fran. He declared on the high-speed trolley, "What I always thought I'd like was to come out at the other end of life not caring so darned much." He meant about love. He would be like a monk in a monastery, freed to work without the interference of the passions. "On the other hand—maybe this is what you mean —it's not worth making all that much fuss about." And when Fran asked what wasn't: "Life. I don't mean other people's lives. It's only that people are too careful of their own—Uncle Herman—and you should use your life."

"Saul."

"Well, he's right, though he doesn't really do it himself."

Fran watched her twelve-year-old brother. His soft drooping profile was turned away to the mesquite- and palmetto-covered hills. Something was wrong, though perhaps not very wrong. Alex glittered, it seemed, as one did in that first pleasant stage of a fever with which she was so familiar.

They met Fran's date in front of Bullock's, held a conference, and decided where to rendezvous later for tea. Rose complained of the crowds, but Alex did not mind. He liked closeness and touching—that other language—even the breath of strangers. Nothing was wrong with it, particularly today. But Aunt Kate developed a headache, and of course his mother's feet troubled her. They ended seeing a Fairbanks movie.

Alex spotted Fran and her date from a distance in what Uncle Herman called the Plaza, a palm-filled square with a fountain in the center of it. She was wearing her serge Peter Thompson with a big scarlet bow on it. Her wide-brimmed beaver, a Christmas gift from Saul, lay on the bench beside her. She had her feet, in satin slippers (no more boots), thrust before her and casually crossed. Her hair was to be cut soon. The boy, a football player in his senior year, a catch, sat stiffly. Alex saw that they were silent and had been for some time. The boy had taken possession of the corsage he had brought for Fran, twirled it into the air and caught it. Alex was touched by the showing off. He observed his sister's beauty, the boy looking everywhere but at her, the corsage of rosebuds and ferns in his big hands.

"Hi, kiddo, have fun?" Fran asked.

Aunt Kate was laughing about something. She had a choking laugh, rarely heard, that was like sobbing, and Alex, who was funny, tried not to provoke it. The football player had to go home, and the rest walked in the square for a time, made their way at length by streetcar to Santa Monica, and, since it was too late for tea, had supper at the Arcadia. A young waiter, Italian, they thought, or perhaps Mexican, smitten, tried to conceal a note under Francesca's plate, which her mother confiscated. (The contents, revealed years later: "You are an attractive young woman, should be on the films," with an address in San Diego that was his own apparently.) It was the night of New Year's Day, and already Uncle Herman turned an unlit cigar longingly in his plump fingers.

When in early spring the time arrived, Miss Loux and Rudolph Samuels, who had come down from San Francisco on Symphony business, took the Weisshorns to the Los Angeles station in the Loux Daimler. Uncle Herman was at work, but Aunt Kate and Joy came along.

"I am going to say something that may or may not sound odd, darling," declared Miss Loux. "Take it for what you judge its worth to be and use it or not." Plainly speaking, she said, Alex was too public. "Strange of me to say, since you intend to perform in public, but I wish you were secret, dear, and private, and perhaps less eager to please in general. Do I make myself clear? None of this is very different from what I have often said." Alex thought but did not say that he thought he was too little public, that a secret life was wrong.

"Let people do the work of finding out where you are, and they will beat that path to your door, I'm certain."

Fran was crying because the football player, having helped the chauffeur with the luggage, had stood at the curb in front of the Breeze Avenue house as they pulled away, his lips forming "I love you" to the retreating car.

Rose left everything to Alex, who found porters, took their Pullman tickets to have the berths confirmed, and saw that the bags were put aboard the right car. Samuels kept nodding and shrugging. He and Miss Loux disagreed concerning Alex's return to the East Coast. Alex, feeling under the circumstances rebellious and a little frightened, made himself cold, "amusing," as Miss Loux dryly observed. At the same time, his high spirits were genuine. Joy sat by herself, pretending not to be interested in the farewells, eyes red, and Kate sobbed (or laughed, as Alex would say later). During the first few hours on the train, they would be outrageous to guard themselves against the wrench of parting and because to leave was marvelous. They were going home.

"Joy, whose hand was never at her lips bidding adieu," was Alex's best, Rose would declare.

He had shaken by the hand first Samuels and then the chauffeur. Then he embraced Edna Loux, who was shorter than he now, as he remembered having seen her embrace Miss Framingham, and turning his lips to her ear, whispered, "Good-by, my dear."

●

A multimillionaire, one of the officers of the G. M. Pullman Company, had his private car in the train. Alex, who was curious, managed to speak to him in his straightforward way simply by walking into the car. Later, the man, whose name was Douglas, invited Fran, Rose, and Alex to have tea with him. There were the man's friends and business acquaintances, as well as what turned out to be a male secretary-valet, all sitting at ease in the rich velvet-hung, gilt-trimmed parlor. They quickly snatched up their coats and pulled them on when they saw Rose and Fran and then stood making polite conversation. They had gone the Southern Pacific route to El Paso and were now coming into Wichita on the Chicago, Rock Island and Pacific.

"We will be—ah—three minutes ahead of schedule, I believe."

There was a good deal of railroad talk and consulting of timetables and gold watches. The men asked Rose's permission when they wanted to relight their cigars. Alex had read about it in the progressive Venice, California, school, so he mentioned the Pullman strike almost at once. It was more than twenty years in the past, but Douglas became angry. Debs had been no better than a murderer and Altgeld a coward.

84

"I think the coward was the President, sending troops in," Alex said.

The millionaire stared at the boy.

"I believe that Governor Altgeld had courage and so did Mr. Debs, doing what they did against police and the whole U.S. Army."

Rose said, "I'm sure Mr. Douglas knows all about it, Alex, and you might learn something from him."

Fran's eyes smoldered, and Alex had gone suddenly pale, as if he would faint.

"Indeed I can tell you something about it, young fellow, since I was present and in on it from its inception to its denouement. Is that what they teach you in an American school concerning that tragedy—that Altgeld was a brave man and George Pullman the villain?" The other men grinned, looking down at the thick Turkey carpeting. "Great day in the morning," said Douglas, sighing and gazing out at Kansas.

Alex said stoutly, "I don't say he was. I say he should have listened to the strikers' just demands in the first place."

Douglas began in a patient tone to describe the Pullman model community, the medical facilities and schools. "But when we got into a little financial backwater and asked for their cooperation . . ."

It was paternalism. Fran had the word from one of her father's letters. Douglas's eyes opened in a comic way. ("He was still mad, though," Alex said later.) "You too, little lady? Great day. Well, I thought your mama gave you good advice just now, but maybe we can learn something too."

The men sat down, relaxing. Rose smiled gratefully. She was already composing the letter she would write to Kate and mail in Chicago concerning this new triumph of her children: arguing serious matters with the top men in the Pullman Company in a private railroad car.

1918

•

Mrs. Weisshorn had moved to Parkside Avenue, which was almost country and ten degrees cooler than Lombard Street in summer; and Saul and Dr. Susan, though she had kept her suite of offices on the ground floor of the South Philadelphia house, had gone with her. The major epidemic of Spanish influenza began in September. Fran and Alex had their cases in the earlier, less ominous summer epidemic, and it was felt that they were through with it. Rose's bout came. She lay in a darkened room while her daughter nursed her and ran the furnished house that Saul and Babushka had rented for them. To visit their father and grandmother, the children now took a trolley through Fairmount Park, "the scenic route," got off at Fortieth, and walked.

After the first terrible excitement, their father struck them as being just the same. He seemed rather small, but Alex knew that was because he, Alex, had grown. Though she was moved by their meeting, Fran said, "It never pays to expect too much."

He had hugged his daughter until she felt she was on the edge of unconsciousness, and Alex said, impressed by his father's passion, "You might have been in fact."

"Oh, my angel," Saul groaned. "My princess-angel." He thrust her away to see her. "Beautiful! Beautiful!"

He kissed Alex. He took the boy's cheeks in the palms of his hands and looked at him in his famished way. It was what his father had always been, Alex realized: angry with passion, demanding, as if he required that something happen at once as a result of the power of love.

86

This was what went on when Saul loved mankind, the boy would comment, stirred. "Even when he's angry, it's for love."

They gave themselves up to renewed love. At the same time, watchful, they saw that they had expected too much as a matter of course.

When Saul caught influenza Alex was allowed to visit because of his immunity.

Babushka said, "The war is ending and God sends this."

Saul had a small apartment on the first floor of his mother's new house—a narrow bed with a rough cover, a brass-fitted bachelor's chest, and English fox-hunting prints, for which he and Jack Loeb had shopped on Pine Street. He lay for several days while Susan watched for pulmonary complications, then he began to improve with a rapidity characteristic of the disease.

Dr. Susan said to her mother, "Since you're an agnostic, you're in no position to blame God. You can't blame the Huns since they've been hit harder than we." Babushka would stand in the doorway of her son's room, looking into it with suspicion. The epidemic had forced her out of retirement. She went to the bank every afternoon.

"I blame."

On their return from California, she had given each of the grandchildren a kiss and a five-dollar bill. When they visited during Saul's illness, they went upstairs to greet Mrs. Weisshorn first, then returned and sat for an hour with Saul while Rose, who had accompanied them in case she might be of use but unwilling to enter the house otherwise, waited across the street on a park bench. In addition to these there were Alex's and Fran's social visits and Fran's solitary ones, considered to be upon business, when she would see Babushka alone in her private parlor.

"Why isn't it enough?" the old woman would ask directly. "It was carefully calculated." The dialogues were generally the same. Even if you could find what you needed in the shops, the prices rose each week. "You don't budget yourselves, Frankie. *She* never will if she lives to be a hundred. Rose is spoiled." Her brothers had spoiled her. "It's up to you to make a budget and stick to it."

On her return, Fran would cry, "She's impossible! There's no dealing with her!"

By the fall of 1918 the allowance, officially from M. L. Weisshorn & Son, had been raised to twenty-five dollars a week. Saul gave a little from time to time out of an account in another bank. For Alex's lessons and music books, for Fran's singing and ballet, which she took up briefly, there was no limit. There would be money for any cultural purpose but never enough for coal. Shrewdly ("I must inherit the knack from her"), Fran persuaded her grandmother that school clothing was a cultural item.

"Pledge the man's credit, for heaven's sake!" cried one of Rose's sisters. Rose could not work, the sister pointed out: her feet. She ought to charge whatever was needed. "Let the Queen Bee take care of it and not with her condescending air of giving charity." But Jack Loeb said she could not. "He is only obliged to support his children and educate them and to sustain life in you, Rose. That's the law."

Rose did not listen. Whatever she got she used. When it ran out, through no fault of her own, before the next remittance, she sent Fran on the park trolley to ask for more.

With the epidemic, however, as if responding to an atmosphere of emergency, Mrs. Weisshorn became almost generous, writing a check and thrusting it at Francesca: "Before I change my mind!" It was as if there was less time and money itself was less important. On the other hand, she was apt to forget regular payments, which she was supposed to send herself from the bank, though her son said it ought to be treated as if it were any other piece of business and delegated to a clerk.

Saul lay comfortably in bed after the worst of his illness was past, glasses in place, frowning at the papers, his son reading in an easy chair in the corner. "Come in, Mama!" he would call. "It's no longer catching."

"I'll stay here," said Mrs. Weisshorn warily.

She stood in the door, watching her son as if to persuade herself of something, then went back upstairs, sometimes not having spoken another word.

"She worries," Susan said.

The death rate rose in early October, with a thousand new cases reported each day. The average number in the city during a twenty-four-hour period was, on a few October days, close to the number of cases recorded. The disease was not epidemic but, as Susan had taught them to say, pandemic. There seemed to be no place in which it could be escaped. It hung over the globe like a cloud of poison. "It makes the war look like a Sunday picnic." The children's aunt was overworked. She had her own patients as usual with their usual complaints. In addition, the Department of Health had assigned her to one of its emergency depots at a South Philadelphia police station. "Give me war any day," she declared. . . .

On a sunny Sunday in October, Rose, Alex, and Fran rode the park trolley; Rose settled herself on a bench with *Of Human Bondage* and a sunshade. Alex found a dollar.

"Look!" he cried, bowled over. "Frankie!"

It was astonishing.

It lay almost under a bench—a slightly crumpled, nearly new one-dollar bill. They took it to Rose. "It's so lucky!" Then when they set off again toward the Weisshorn house, they found another not a hundred yards from the first; and then, a few feet away, a third. They were wild with excitement. Fran, sixteen, normally very dignified, clapped her hands. Alex gaped. They looked around in panic to see if there would be more. They could not risk the possibility of missing one—leaving it for someone else to find. It was the luck they loved more than the money. To be lucky, Alex declared, was the best thing. Anyone could work hard (didn't Alex?), but to be lucky . . . They hugged each other, while Rose smiled.

"Look!" they shouted later at Saul.

He grinned.

"What should we buy, Papa?"

"Found money ought to be spent on something useless."

Dr. Susan appeared. They were not to excite their father in this way. She stared at the bills, disbelieving. "Put that back in Babushka's purse."

The woman banker left her bag—a large jet-beaded sack with ivory handles—on a table near the front door.

"She'll be down in a few minutes. If you put it back at once, I won't tell her you took it."

The banker, lying in bed, shouted at his sister, "What are you talking about?"

"You don't believe they found three dollar bills, one after the other, on the sidewalk on Parkside Avenue? You're a fool." She spoke bitterly, eyes darkened by exhaustion and anger.

"How *dare* you!" Fran wept, beside herself. "How do you dare talk to us . . . call us liars . . . call *Alex* a liar!" It was unbearable that her aunt would say her brother was lying: an impossibility. She might say what she pleased about Fran, to her or behind her back, but Alex!

The boy choked, trying to control himself. He was outraged by the injustice and by the fact that he wept; he ought not to cry.

"Oh, for God's sake," Saul said. "Why the hell do you do it? Make a fuss over some piece of nonsense! Here the kids were happy . . ."

No, no, no, no, no. Put it back, Susan had to say. Simply replace the money and nothing more would be said.

"Oh, God!" Saul indicated the chest, on top of which lay his wallet and change. "*I'll* give three dollars to put into Babushka's purse!"

The injustice was terrible. There seemed to be no bottom to it. The war, the influenza were of no account. As a result, that day and a good many to follow became a torture of explaining for them. It was as if night had been called noon.

"She's an exhausted woman," their mother said of Susan. "Try to put it out of your minds."

Rose, of course, read all the literature and, not believing in their immunity, constantly advised her children. Crowds were to be avoided. They were to carry at least three clean handkerchiefs; every cough was to be covered. "Your nose, not your mouth is made to breathe through."

Clean Mouth, Clean Skin, Clean Clothes. "The three Cs. The bowels must move regularly."

Everyone was reciting rules to everyone else. Saul's friends Jack Loeb, Gyp Gamble, and Morris Blum—all medical men —put themselves at the disposal of the Department of Health, which meant they were, like soldiers, under the command of the Surgeon General. They would find themselves being ordered anywhere at a moment's notice, from the river to Kensington, even north to Downingtown—wherever the sickness fell most heavily during a given week.

"Open your windows and let the air in, for God's sake!" Dr. Susan's image of a cloud of poison, which she did not mean literally, was the prevalent belief. "Get out of closed rooms and into the fresh air. Picnic for health!" "Wash your hands before each meal" was a headline in the *Inquirer.* "Your fate is in your own hands." Everyone was to drink as much water as possible to keep flushed out. Even Susan, a strict enemy of popular medicine, referred her patients to the newspapers for information.

"At this stage, they diagnose and treat themselves."

Few doctors still had their own patients. Medical school seniors were considered practitioners; the rest, freshmen to juniors, had been pressed into service as nurses and medical aides. (The President had been authorized to commission M.D.s.) At one point in early November, Jack Loeb headed a group of five doctors on a tour of Pennsylvania and Jersey towns in which local M.D.s were themselves sick or dead. There was an appeal to women, trained or untrained, to put aside personal tasks in this crisis. "Help us to check the death toll that is taking women, men, and babies by the hundreds every day." People were urged to turn their houses into emergency hospitals or to offer nurses working in local homes a place to bathe and rest.

Babushka had trouble making up her mind but at Susan's urging finally moved Saul to quarters upstairs and notified Emergency Aid that the ground-floor apartment was available. As it happened, it was not used.

●

"I am here talking about ordinary human decency!" Saul cried. "Even in this terrible human crisis, lines are drawn." He waved the newspaper at Gyp Gamble and Jack Loeb. Negroes were being sent to hospitals for Negroes, whites to hospitals for whites.

"What the hell, Saulie?" Gamble said in his slow voice. "In my experience they're happier among their own people whether they're living or dying. He doesn't want to die in the same room with you either."

"Oh, Jesus!" Saul shouted. "Think what you're saying. What *kind?* Kind? Humankind is the kind . . . Jew!"

Gamble stared.

They sat in Kelly's at nine at night, Alex with them (his piano lessons were in the evening, and his father saw him back and forth).

"What was that you said?"

Gamble, sallow with tiredness, eyes dark-ringed, let his cigarette drop from his mouth, twisted a finger in his ear pretending not to trust his hearing, while Loeb grinned.

"No, I am serious. You talk about the heroism of the people. I observe the masks dropping, the old depravities, long hidden, revealed. I remind you for what it's worth that in this country the majority of your leading fellow citizens wouldn't want to die or do anything else in the same room with you because you're a Jew!"

Gyp Gamble's eyes slid quickly around the restaurant. He was a tall, heavy man with the thick black hair and leathery skin of one of Buffalo Bill's Indians. He was the oldest of eight brothers, the youngest of whom would one day marry Fran.

"What are you looking for?" cried Saul, finding a higher level of rage.

"I am a little tired, Saul!"

Loeb began, "There are in fact good reasons for such hospitals—"

"Good in the context, good to our everlasting shame . . . a so-called democratic society."

"Saulie."

"Under Marxism—"

"Oh, God," cried Gamble.

"Oh, who?"

"Reb Saul . . ."

Gamble had stories—"fresh news"—of Kiev pogroms against Jews by Bolshevik soldiers. "Sir? No!" Saul cried. "That's anti-Soviet propaganda invented *here!*"

Alex's eyes, blazing, danced from his father to the others. He kept rolling and unrolling his leather music case.

"And if so—*if*—why pogrom, that word? Why not part of the general cleansing—a military action against those who, by the unwillingness to be committed, are in fact counter-revolutionaries? This revolution is deadly serious, my friend, not something, now, in a book. You get in its way at your peril!"

"Don't get unlucky?"

"Exactly! You do not. *You do not get unlucky.* Not now!"

"Under Lenin they have the epidemic."

"And worse without proper nutrition. But they are one people."

"That simply isn't true, Saul."

"It is *true!*" Saul shouted, striking the table so that the sugar shaker and little horseradish bowl jumped. *"It is true."*

"Lucian," Gamble said to Loeb, doing one of the old Rube Goldberg tags, "sweep out padded cell number six thousand

and thirty-two." They grinned, weary, but Saul did not smile, nor did his son.

Later, Loeb said mildly, "But what kind of constituent assembly, for heaven's sake, Saul? When the Bolshies don't like it, they send in troops, and then the dictatorship of the proletariat is looking down the wrong end of the gun just as before. You'll have civil war for twenty years at this rate. And just setting aside your imperialist wolves and jackals, they're *bastards*—excuse me, Alex—for pulling out of the war and leaving it all to us."

"Et cetera!" Saul said.

Alex, also scornful of such simplifications, only heard the beginning of Loeb's speeches. How explain the obvious? Uncle Jack should know without being told.

There were now a hundred thousand cases of the disease in the city. First schools, then theaters and saloons had been closed. There was liberty as well as danger in the air, which the boy found exciting. He would be on a city street at an unheard-of hour—the middle of a Tuesday morning—with his mother and sister. Rose would ask intimate questions of a shopkeeper, a stranger, who answered fully and seriously. The man's family appeared to be getting through it; they had had a death, not close, thank God. Streetcar conductors were courteous and sober, and the courtesy was returned. "People are brave, really!" Alex said. He was moved by the quiet acting out of courage. While it went on, it seemed to him the only important thing in the world.

"People are good," he said to Fran.

"It takes something like this to bring it out."

"Unfortunately."

But he was not sure it was unfortunate.

"HUGE HUN RETREAT," the papers cried. "BRITISH NEAR LILLE." The war went well as the epidemic did. Death could bring out the good in people.

Hope, not death, was in the air. As an example, the Russians were a free people. As another, it was observed, when they had been stricken in great numbers by influenza, that

94

the war could not go well without the anthracite miners. Saul pointed out that this potency, recognized in themselves as a weapon, must secure them the wages and working conditions they were now denied, secure them freedom, in short. Good came out of bad, out of violence, Alex's father said; not always, but when it came, that was apt to be the way. The notion excited and distracted the boy.

He found himself unable to study.

Saul pronounced: "Unless more useful work is found for you, do the work you know."

But Alex stopped studying for eight weeks during this period. Deeply excited and distracted, he told himself that his life of music might be over.

●

One of Babushka's servants, a girl named Helena, was infected. Fran heard that she had dropped a pot of tea on the best Oriental upstairs and when her mistress reprimanded her appeared to faint. That is, she sat heavily in one of the upholstered chairs, something she would not have done if she were well, covered her face with her hands, and would not speak. Two other servants had had cases, and it was time this girl got through hers. When Mrs. Weisshorn pulled her hands away from her face she did not appear to be conscious.

"Saul!" his mother called, going to the head of the stairs.

They got the servant into her bed on the third floor. "I've caught it!" she cried over and over. She said she was going to die. Babushka, who had at least half of a medical degree, as her daughter put it, said irritably, "Don't be foolish. You have a mild case if I ever saw one. You're fortunate to build an immunity so cheap."

Dr. Susan had a look at her, then stood with her mother and Saul in the hallway. "She's not too bad. Keep away from her, Mama, and let the other girls do the running."

Susan had been asked to lead a force of medical students and nurses who were being sent to Chester, where the disease had broken out with new virulence. Morris Blum came down from his work at the hospital, sat by Helena's bed, took her temperature and pulse, and listened to her chest. "A little rough."

"My back hurts," the girl said to him in Polish. She had had fever, but now her temperature was normal. At the same time, she complained of a headache and pain in the lower back.

"It could be something else." Blum was cautious, on the lookout for masquerading diseases. He kept nodding in his ancient way. She was feverish and at night made anti-Semitic remarks in Polish or called for her mother. Alex and Fran, who had got to know the girl, came up the stairs one afternoon without permission. They heard her cough, which was loud and frightening, on the way up. "We're all right," said Fran, who was interested in medicine and spoke of studying it. "We're through with it." They gazed in from the doorway, and the girl, her forehead damp, strands of pale hair stuck to it, looked at them, then away. "I'm frightened," she said, which took Alex aback, because he had been thinking at that moment and in those words the same thing about himself.

The children heard no reports. A week later they were told that the girl had been taken to a hospital and died there.

•

Annette still lived with her family on Lombard Street and felt it her duty to bring news of the old neighborhood from time to time, as if Parkside Avenue were exile.

"This item particularly concerns Saul."

She sat with her brother, Jack Loeb, Volin, and Alex in Mrs. Weisshorn's parlor, taking her time.

"What!" Saul cried.

The English teacher held her pince-nez, one lens up, lorgnette style. "I wonder how you'll react."

"Everything's a spelling bee with Annette," said Volin of his sister-in-law.

She gave her news in her own time. Solomon Zeide had died of the Spanish influenza.

"Well?" Saul said. He sat pulling absent-mindedly at his mustache.

"That's that then," said Saul.

Later Alex would remember the week he had spent in the Lombard Street house over Christmas and the pensioner his father had addressed as Zeide and to whom he had given money.

Saul, Volin, and Loeb saw Alex home on the park trolley.

"Death," Volin pronounced, "though ubiquitary at all times, in days such as these shows herself without shame." He gazed through the streetcar window into the dark trees. "Do you know that of all the world's continents the only one to escape thus far is Australia?"

Saul sat chewing the ends of his mustache while his son watched him, trying to guess what he thought. At last the banker said, "The only real barrier to mankind's progress is man, it seems, myself first and foremost."

"Foremost. Bravo!" Loeb said ironically. "Marvelous." The plump doctor did the work of three but was lively, ready for what he called "philosophy," which meant drinks and arguments. "Now you are trying to persuade yourself that you're a bad fellow."

"I'm relieved he's dead. He was a pain in the ass, Jack."

"You're permitted to be pleased."

He had a flask in his pocket and when they got off the streetcar offered it.

"Not now."

Jack grinned. "See how your father's sort of mankind punishes itself when it feels guilty? Saul thinks he can cure influenza by refusing to enjoy himself. And he called that maid of theirs who died superstitious because she believed in devils."

●

Morris Blum telephoned to say that Susan had come down with the disease while working in Chester and that he had arranged to have her brought back to University, which was his hospital. "We found her a bed. She's all right."

She had been working around the clock in the hastily organized health stations. Blum said to Saul on the telephone, "She was doing a bang-up job," in his Russian-Jewish accent: "beng-up."

Having gotten the impression, Saul reported to the family that Susan's was a less dangerous variety and that in any event, since she had had a mild case the previous summer, there was the acquired immunity. But Blum, when he came to Parkside Avenue, said, "We are dealing with special problems—discharge in the lungs evoked by a living virus, which has broken down tissue resistance."

When it was over, Saul would tell Alex the story. Visits were limited, and Saul was the family delegate. He saw his sister. "I blacked out for a second. It's one of my tricks. I faint standing up." Then he had turned, looking for the nurse, to say that the wrong bed had been indicated. This was not Susan. She lay, semiconscious, pillow soaked with sweat; her breathing sounded like the clatter in a machine shop. She did not recognize Saul. Of course from that moment, really from the first moment, as he would tell Alex, he knew she was going to die, and it became a matter of finding out how to prepare his mother.

"I happened to glance under the screen there and saw that a visitor had fallen to the floor. I thought: People are being struck down as if by machine-gun fire. No! Someone was praying, if you please—a *man*, kneeling, with his hands folded on his hat! It was all I could do not to run out of the place, that's how panicky . . ."

Poor little girl, Saul said he had thought.

"I tried to remember when we were kids, what she was like, but I couldn't."

He could produce no sort of emotion in himself, he said, and Alex realized that what he understood about his father Saul did not understand about himself. As if trying to start an engine, Saul tried to feel pity for his sister and was surprised when he could not. He and Alex went over it in Saul's ground-floor rooms. "I felt little pity for her. I looked at Susan on her deathbed and felt little. Now I feel nothing. A year from now I'll feel nothing. A bit of a cold fish, your father."

Himself terrified, filled with a pity that was in part for Saul's impotence to feel, Alex decided that his father's awareness could be better than pity. To accuse oneself was the bravest act of the mind.

"I'll tell you what it is," Saul told Alex, who had known it. "I don't really like people."

He kept the boy up until nearly dawn, each talking, each listening. This had been Saul's conclusion. He stood at a window. He added, "Generally, that is. To put it another way, certain people I love. The rest, nothing."

Alex declared, "At least you try to understand what you're like."

"Oh, I'm a great talker."

"In a good way. *I'm* a great talker."

"In a good way."

•

Fran and Alex came to the house in the early afternoon with their mother and, rather fearfully (what would she do?), climbed the stairs.

"She's still at the hospital," Mrs. Weisshorn said to them at once. "They don't bring them home under the circumstances." She sat so stiffly in a chair that her back did not touch it. Though she kept a handkerchief ready, she did not use it.

"It was as though she thought she ought to have one in her hand," Fran would observe.

Their grandmother looked them over. "You had yours. I only hope the immunity holds up. Frankie, when you have children, this is what may happen." She added in the belligerent tone that was typical of her, "So you cut your hair." She held a hand of each child; they were conscious of the opium smell of some medicine; and gazing at Babushka, Alex thought: It's like Fran's eyes.

"Does she mean I'm not to have children at all?" Fran would ask.

"I'm deeply sorry," Rose said to her mother-in-law. Babushka nodded. She kept looking around the room. "Saul!"

He was on the phone. The entire city, it seemed, was telephoning. When he came in, she said, "Ask your son"— "Esk"—"if he'll play something in her honor." Though Alex was present, Mrs. Weisshorn put the request to his father.

"John Finn telephoned to say that an old friend passed away in the night," Saul said. "He hadn't known about Susan."

"He was upset?" Babushka asked.

"Very much so."

"Where will he be?"

"Ashenbach's, Saturday morning."

"You should put in an appearance."

The brother and sister went downstairs, Alex to the piano. He played Mozart, knowing his grandmother liked it, though he remembered that Susan had not particularly liked any music. Fran turned pages while Dr. Blum's daughter, Ruth, plump, cheerfully smiling in spite of the occasion, sat on the final third of the bench. Only family and a few friends had been asked to this gathering to honor Susan because of the danger in crowds, about which the papers still carried warnings every day. The cremation, handled by the nonsectarian Brall Brothers, would be private, without ceremony.

They went upstairs again. Saul stood behind his mother's chair; he nodded approvingly at Alex. The others were silent.

"Your playing affected them," Fran would say to her brother.

In the evening, everyone gone (the children were to spend the night), Babushka asleep, they sat up late in Saul's rooms.

"We are so 'umble," said Fran, being Uriah Heep.

"Oh, we are 'umble," Alex said, nodding.

"So very 'umble."

Saul appeared with a sandwich in one hand and a cup of coffee in the other. He said, "Veddy 'umble are the Weisshorns."

"*Oh*, veddy!"

"Forgive the intrusion."

"I thought it was a ham sandwich."

"I am an 'umble fellow," Saul said. "I am an 'umble 'ebrew."

" 'E is . . . 'e is an . . ." Fran could not finish. Alex sputtered. "What! Say it! Oh, God . . ."

"No, no, only . . ."

It was so *funny*.

" 'E is . . . what he *said*. 'E is an 'umble 'ebrew!"

Saul, as if not sure at first that his line had capped everything, looked from one to the other of his children. Then, though he was too good a poker face to smile, his eyes blazed. He drew his lips down, smoothed his mustache, and tossed the killing line at them to set them off whenever their laughter seemed about to subside.

The next afternoon Fran and Alex walked in the park, going all the way across to the bluffs overlooking the river.

"It seems to me we won't know what we feel for a long time," Fran said. "It's like being in a war, I suppose. You're so busy with what must be done you don't realize . . ."

Alex, however, was ready with his feelings. "At first I felt

101

like Saul: nothing much. But I'm not like that. I should have felt something."

"You worried—"

"I worried about it, felt guilty."

"What's funny is Aunt Susan's the one who always talked about feelings of guilt—from Freud."

"But you know what I mean."

The incident in which she had accused them of taking money from her mother's bag weighed.

They talked plainly. "Didn't you wish it at the time? I did!"

"Of *course*. That's the whole point. We wished it, and now we think we did it!"

"No," Fran said, though that did not mean she disagreed. They would shout the pieces of each other's arguments at one another, agreeing. If a subject moved them to pity and consequently anger, they shouted accusingly, as if the other, instead of agreeing and pitying too, were the opposition. They were aware of doing it. "We get it from Saul." Generally, it was themselves they were accusing.

They worried because they had not liked their aunt and felt horror rather than sorrow when she died. Alex would say, "It's the waste that's the worst of it—now when doctors are so badly needed." And immediately: "Which is a terrible thing to say."

"*No*, it's not!"

It was low down.

"You're like me," Fran would begin. . . . Their thoughts, as they walked, fell into rank, began to make sense. Alex, typically interested in the way thinking happened ("worked," he would say), noted something odd. The faster they walked away from their house toward the river, the better and faster their thoughts marched. Was there a connection between motion and the thought process? When they stood over the river their thoughts stopped too; they could only gaze stupidly, emptily into the water (water was a factor; yes). And when they started back, perhaps because it was in the direction of the house, their chores, their mother, the same

102

thoughts fell darkly once more and pessimistic.

Alex would pause to put off getting home, hands deep in the pockets of his Norfolk jacket. "In *fact*, if you're only thinking of relative worth and so on, one of us or Mama would have been a lot easier to spare." And Fran, agreeing, shrugged darkly: "No."

Together they resolved things and rarely parted without a sense of having done so. But these nights Alex slept badly. More than once he heard the milk horse—the hollow thudding and jingling, carriage springs creaking as the man climbed up or down. He held his breath until their own two bottles chimed on the steps. He felt he was missing a point. It was a sickening, dead-weight sensation. He tried to make in his mind's eye a picture of the milkman—red-shaven, sleepy, drawing in the cold dawn air, the smell of raw milk and horse in a cloud around him. What was the point he missed? He could imagine the actuality of other people, but he missed something and of course could not know what it was. He thought sickeningly: Someone else knows more than I do.

He would turn onto his stomach and grind at the bed—an agony of comfort, the only safeguard against immensity—but then, strict, he refused the comfort. He heard his mother and sister stir on the other side of the wall.

"The thing is," he would say to himself, "I ought to get back to work."

The schools had reopened to get in a few weeks before the Christmas holidays, and he and Fran walked there together.

Talk always returned to Aunt Susan.

"What does it change?"—death.

Everything and nothing, Fran declared. "Susan would still be the same person if she were alive. We'd still be saying we didn't like her. We'd be saying"—all right—"what a bitch she is." Death didn't alter it.

On the other hand, it changed everything.

"Everything is *fixed* by it," said Alex, stopping on the sidewalk, afraid that the fluttering thought would leave. This had nothing to do with the usefulness of death. "Death says this *was* the person. It means you can go back into the person instead of always going forward with him. The end"—this was it— "makes *sense* of the beginning." It might be what death was for. (Was that the point?) Alex himself shook his head, and Fran said she did not understand at all. He stared with narrowed eyes at the streets. Stories, of course, were in the mind of the storyteller. There was still the dead-weight sensation of not knowing.

"You're just being an artist."

Maybe: it might be the point. *"That* could be God." His notions might thrill Fran when she understood them, but they left the boy depressed. He was in a bad state, Rose declared of him. He had not yet resumed his lessons, but she was reluctant to urge him now.

"Also, reality keeps getting in the way," said Fran. Mrs. Weisshorn, who seemed calm in her grief, had begun once more to forget their checks, and at last Rose dispatched both Fran and Alex to remind her.

"Here's your answer," Alex would say.

When they got there, they heard their grandmother crying. Having gone straight up to the closed door of the parlor on the second floor and paused before knocking, they heard a sobbing that was recognizable, though they had never known their grandmother to cry ("She cries in Russian!" said Alex), and their father saying distinctly, as if to a child, "I am going to ring Blum. Do you hear? He'll give you something, and you'll take it."

He found his children, and it was he who wrote the check.

"So there it is," said Alex, as if finally, of death.

●

One of Fran's friends, in the same class at school, took a place in their lives because she lived nearby. Her name was

104

Harriet Fishman, and like Fran she was older than the rest of the class—a placid girl who reminded them (sentimentally now) of their California cousin Joy, and who continued to wear her hair long and in braids, though she was sixteen.

"She's *nice,*" said Fran of her in the tone of someone worn by life who seeks simplicity.

They were often in each other's houses. Fran found it easy to confide in her, and the girl, simply, told Fran every thought that came into her head. She bought cigarettes called Deities and taught Fran and Alex to smoke. Her father made plum brandy, which he kept in the basement of the row house, and Harriet showed the Weisshorn children how to drink the top from each bottle and restore the level with water.

Alex would sit on an old glider in the basement room and hold his brandy to the light. It was red with amber currents eddying in it. At first it was like milk, then it burned. They used the same glass, handing it around, and Harriet, at her turn, drank deeply. It did not seem to affect her. She would drink, pass the glass, and affectionately watch her friends.

She admired Fran for her wit and the tart opinions she had of teachers and other adults, as well as for her dark good looks, but she was in love with Alex.

"She told me," Fran said.

"She's two years older."

"All right. She didn't arrange it." Fran said wisely, "I think Harriet will fall in love easily. Not to minimize this."

"I like her."

"She's *nice.*"

Really, Fran meant. The fact that she spent her pocket money on cigarettes and drank liquor made her seem peculiarly innocent. She was on the surface: plain, open. She was, simply, herself. "She's simple-minded, but I mean it in a good way. For example, Saul's simple-minded. Or not complex, I should say. It's how people look at things—people who don't keep questioning themselves. You're not simple; artists never are, it seems to me." She added, "I'm like Saul and a little like Harriet. It works on different levels, of course."

Now and then, deliberately, Fran left the girl alone with Alex. "Mama wants some things at the store. I'll drop in on my way back." She would ruffle Alex's hair, give Harriet a breezy pat. *"A bientôt, mes enfants."*

"Oh, if I could play an instrument the way you do, Alex," Harriet would begin. Or: "You are so brilliant, you and Franny. You're in another world than ordinary people." Her own family had not been touched by the influenza plague, and the death in the Weisshorn family impressed her. Everything that concerned the Weisshorns appeared to her to be outlined and bright: important. They were hidden, surprising, yet offered themselves frankly. They were polite. "I can't get over that"—a boy of Alex's age, his unembarrassed courtesy, his grown-up interest in others' opinions and comfort; the fact that Fran did not gush but addressed herself, a serious pretty teacher, to real problems. But she worried about the politeness too. "It's as if you're missing the fun."

"We have plenty of fun," Alex would say comfortably.

"Oh, yes?"

He could tell she wanted him to kiss her.

She hooked open the furnace door with a poker, holding a cigarette high in the air, lit a broomstraw, then used it to light the cigarette. When he took his turn he found that the end of the cigarette was wet.

"Oh, my dear."

She slipped onto his lap to kiss him. He could hear the floorboards creak as Mrs. Fishman walked in the kitchen above. There would be a pause, then the steps again as the mother went from cabinet to range and back. Alex wished Harriet would move her hips on his lap, but she sat heavily still, an arm across his shoulders. He was aware of the clean smell of her cotton dress, saw that its white piping was scorched. He observed the grain of the silk in her tie and the freckles on her throat. There at the heel of his hand her hip flared softly out, unstayed. Her soft lips covered his; her breath whistled slightly in her nose and tickled him. He remembered his grandmother sobbing behind closed doors, having hidden her mourning from everyone but Saul; he thought (deliberately? he would wonder) of Babushka's harsh grief.

Harriet said, "I like you so much, Alex."

He wondered if she would say she loved him.

"She kept pulling away and looking at me like this," he told Fran later, frowning curiously, being Harriet studying the effect on him of what she was doing. "It might have been a laboratory experiment." He had held his breath when she kissed him and thought: I'm being polite. He thought: I am an 'umble 'ebrew, and told Fran guiltily that that was what he had been thinking. Fran said she would kill him if he told her he had laughed.

"I thought of Babushka crying in her room the time we heard her."

"*Why?*" Finally she asked her brother, "Did you like it?"

"Yes and no," he replied. "I had the cigarette in my hand and wondered what to do with it. That rusty glider kept making a racket, and I was afraid it might collapse."

"Oh, God!" It exasperated Fran. "You're such a back number at fourteen."

"Not quite fourteen."

"*There's* an example of it right there," she cried, grinning at him.

But inevitably: "Think of poor Harriet"—the gift, as it were, to him. And this sobered Alex, so that when later he stood above the river in the park, eyes pulled sideways with the weight of thought, he said, "Yes, think of her." Then, bringing himself to himself, he squinted into the brown river. It was a warm day for December. A few sculls were out. Fran stood a little way from her brother. She had to get back. A young man was coming to spend the afternoon. Alex stood with his fists thrust into the pockets of his jacket. He chewed the inside of his lip, squinting fiercely into his future. He said, "I wonder if I *use* Aunt Susan's death." Fran said she did not understand, and Alex added at length in a distant voice, as

107

if to explain, "I am thinking about composing."

In any event, he would soon return to his lessons. He stood, small, trim-waisted, aloof, drawing crosses in the turf with the toe of his shoe.

1924

•

There was a rumor at the White Star pier that the Prince of Wales was embarking, and Fran's husband, Bob Gamble, in the party mood of taking trouble over such matters, pulling on his pipe, strolled over to the customs shed to see what he could find out. The ship rose like a cliff, disappearing from view above the roof of the pier. When it was all right to do so—the baggage seen to—the others boarded, and Bob found part of the group later on an upper deck.

"I'm afraid not," he said in a tone of concern.

"Oh, no!"

"Someone's putting a Rolls-Royce aboard. I saw it."

"If it's his, it would have a crest of some sort."

"Well, the royal thing of England, no less."

Saul and Ruth Blum had descended to the cabin, and Alex was seeing about their table in the dining room. Then Ruth came up again and said, "Come on. Saul had a bottle of champagne all this time, the stinker." She put it to Bob as a lawyer: "Is Prohibition in effect on board?"

"As a matter of fact . . ."

Rose, of course, would not go down. It was clear that she did not want to be where Saul was, but she said politely, "It's just exactly a ship at berth that causes me queasiness." She was now Mrs. Carson. She had remarried a few years before, delayed the honeymoon repeatedly because of her husband's health, and then gone abroad for a month. Fran's honeymoon and her mother's had been a year apart.

Alex came on deck to stay with Rose until the boat would leave, and Fran remained too, the three staring down into the oily strip of water or watching people throw paper streamers, mostly silent.

"Well, here you go," Fran said a bit moodily. "I'll make another prediction: this will be the first of many such trips." It was in the cards. Alex was going to study in Paris. Saul was to cross with him, settle him, and return.

At last Rose wept.

A plump matron at forty-four, now with money available, she wore smart clothes and hats, pearl ropes and fur pieces. "After the years of borderline poverty," she said dramatically. Harry Carson insisted that she and the children spend money—use it. (He waited for her now in the St. Regis lobby.)

"I order you to come over in the spring, Mama!" Alex would make her take him to Maxim's. They would go down to Cannes on the night train. "I won't leave unless you promise." His tone was earnest, important. He looked at her searchingly, as it were at a person rather than a mother, with great attention: she might say she would come and then not do it. "Frank, see to it she comes. I'm dead serious about this. You need the break and by then I'll badly need to see you and make my real progress report, not the kind you give in letters."

"Mama, the idea is to send Alex off in a relatively cheerful frame of mind."

"I'll stop."

Rose excused herself, tucking up the veil of her hat in a preparatory way as she went.

It made Fran impatient. "This is all deliberate on her part. She wants you to remember her heartbroken. Guilt is supposed to assure a speedy return."

"She's unhappy," said Bob Gamble, who had run an errand and returned. "It's natural enough to show it." He was tall, dark-skinned, and heavy-shouldered, though on a smaller scale than his brother Gyp. His manner was thoughtful.

"I'm asking her to sit on her natural feelings a bit!"

Now they, as a trio, gazed into the dark canal between the ship and wharf.

110

"It's interesting the way she's simply handed it over to Harry Carson, you know? It was like getting into a cab for her, marrying Harry. You give your destination, then sit back and forget it," Fran said.

"That's perfect!"

"Very good," said Bob.

"A perfect sketch of the way she simply handed over the reins . . . I will want to see her, though," Alex declared earnestly.

But Rose said to her son later, "The purpose of your stay is to study and work, and you need a free mind for that. You are not to concern yourself about me. I'm well taken care of. When I want to know what you're up to, I'll write and ask specifically. Don't anticipate and feel you have to report on every little thing. . . ."

"Well, I'm always misjudging," Fran declared with a kind of fierce humility when Alex reported. "She does come through where you're concerned."

There was a stir at the foot of the first-class gangway before the all-ashore, and they looked to see a handsome elegantly dressed man in the midst of an entourage. A passenger declared that it was the Prince.

"It's Fairbanks."

It was Douglas Fairbanks, the actor.

Ruth Blum, who was plump and freckled and wore her hair very short, put her hands to her cheeks and then dropped them. She cried in a tone that showed she was capable both of self-mockery and of being moved, "Oh, my God!"

Saul stood with an arm around her. The radiant man passed not three feet from them. The crowd of disembarking visitors pressed around, thrown uncertainly off their stride by his presence, forgetting their farewells. *Where was Mary Pickford?* He cast his astonishing smile in every direction. Alex and Fran gave each other their sardonic look, which meant that their luck was good. It was not the fact of Fairbanks (they had seen him on the beach at Venice as children),

111

but that his appearance now put this departure in the center of things where it belonged.

Fran nodded: right; and Alex caught it.

"Okay," he said.

Saul was tight. He bent Ruth Blum into a movie embrace, while she shrugged and rolled her eyes.

Alex cried, "Good Lord, why don't you two get married!"

Saul and Alex stood together, grinning down at the others on the pier as the ship, bells and whistles going, edged away. "If a problem comes up at the bank, Sasha," Saul shouted through cupped hands, "stay home so it can resolve itself!"

●

"But why join?" Alex demanded. "What sense does it make to put your name down? Can't you function as efficiently without doing that?"

Art and Communism were the themes on the voyage. They sat in deck chairs, wrapped snugly, taking whatever came on the stewards' trays, looking not at each other but at the Atlantic.

"You mean, is it necessary? No, not really. Not practically. Isn't it a case of willing submission, of, if you like, commitment?"

"Yes, I like 'commitment,'" said Alex. "I rate that very highly indeed."

They talked at length, conversations agreeable and unrushed. Alex was serious about wanting to know where *he* fit into the scheme. How could he not want to know that first of all?

"Very well . . ."

"If you state that art in the new society is supererogatory . . ."

"In the forming of the new society perhaps . . ."

112

Art came, according to Schönberg, not of ability but of necessity.

They went on about it pleasantly, though each would shout at the other.

"We are not here speaking of personal necessity"—the September sun flashing on the father's glasses as he sat up in his deck chair, flinging aside the blanket. "We are talking, I hope, of use. Before it becomes art, which is to say beautiful, it is first useful and therefore good; these are contingent conditions. When you separate these conditions, you are still a romantic. If it's no *use*," the father shouted energetically, aware as Alex was of the listening passengers on either side of them, "it's no good. If it's not good, it's not beautiful—Mr. Plato—and if it's not beautiful—"

"It's not art!" a bar acquaintance shouted from his chair nearby, so that both Alex and Saul roared.

The voyage was a good time for both of them, the correct sort of interval. They felt the tingling limbo of it, which was a compound of anxiety concerning an attractive unknown and the sinking inability either to turn back from or to hasten or slow progress toward it.

"To be voyagers on their way out . . ."

The young man and the older one loved to talk, but Alex was a better listener. They would run from point to point. ("We agree at the top of our voices.") They were always leaving something: "I'll get back to that, Alexis. Remind me." In the deck chairs they were wound to the snapping point with rage, an impatient desire to make or complete a point warring with courtesy, rigid in the Scotch wool rugs where others lay supine as prescribed. They went on at meals, over drinks in the bar, concerning themselves with revolution and art, death and sacrifice, and simultaneously they were ironically aware of the comic effect of being revolutionists—artistic, social—in first class.

"Romantic is precisely what I am not," cried the young composer. "The romantic's manufactured object is himself expressed." He was the classicist. "I work from models to express the race, if you please . . ."

". . . you say, 'Commander, I am at your orders,' in effect!"

". . . speaking specifically of music—its expression, its suppression, its exploitation. Now, I don't mind a correct sort of exploitation. I don't mind self-expression shaped, provided the artist does the shaping *of his will,* to a good end. I very much mind the notion of suppression of the aimed, call it personality force!"

"At your orders, Commandant. That's all. Period. Forget the rest of it, Alex."

"Papa . . ."

And Saul would shout, "That's all! All ye know and all ye need to know!"

"Oh, fine."

"We decided to throw you two overboard," an acquaintance would say, coming up to their corner table in the bar and laying a hand on the shoulder of each. "Nobody can stand you."

Alex found a chance to talk to Douglas Fairbanks, though it was hard to catch him by himself. He referred self-deprecatingly to the beach at Venice and to Fran's and his playing "movies."

"Well, there have been odder ways of getting started in the industry."

He was courteous (Alex was studious of such things), amusing, and remote. "Just remote enough," he would report admiringly, "to make sure that all we'll do in future is exchange nods on the promenade deck."

They talked about Chaplin, and Alex made a picture for the other of the comic actor watering his drought-yellowed lawn and his own amazement at the actuality of the man.

"Yes, he is a dear friend of mine," Fairbanks said, just as if that fact were not always being reported by columnists.

"His voice was rather high, but it went with him," he wrote to Fran, "and he referred to the 'movie industry,' which

114

went with him too in a way: industrialists are also swash-bucklers. . . ."

Alex worked out on the rings and bars in the gymnasium and entertained on two separate nights in the Neptune Room (he had begun by playing Debussy for friends his own age and wound up with most of first class for an audience). He won at deck games and the daily mileage pools. On his side, Saul initiated a serious flirtation.

Her name was Flora Harvey. She was a widow, an Australian who was going to Paris, then England to visit relatives, and meant to take six months returning home around the world.

"I advise you to plunge in," said Alex, worldly at nineteen.

"Do you know what you're saying?"

"I know."

Saul began by arranging to have her deck chair moved next to theirs and wasted no time in laying his hand over hers, playing with her glove buttons. She said she admired Alex's talent and talked about it at length, but in an absent-minded way. "I firmly believe that artistic talent is a Jewish trait," she said at last.

"Wonderful!" said Saul with a kind of angry joy to Alex when they were alone. "What is there about that sort of stupidity that I find I can't ignore?"

"Well, she's a challenge," said Alex.

Saul disputed with her in what he thought was a Socratic way. Did she believe that men had a duty to others or to themselves alone? *Were* there intrinsic differences among men?

"This reminded her of the fact that she had what she called a nigger at the table with her on a ship in the Pacific. Shall I tell her I'm a Communist?"

"You might save that."

"For the ultimate moment."

There was a day of stormy weather, during which the banker pressed his courtship on the near-empty decks while

115

Alex, keeping out of the way in a lounge, had glimpses of them, his father in a light topcoat bracing against the ship's movement, Mrs. Harvey, plump, her reddish hair bound in a scarf, clinging to his arm. A stormy silver-yellow sky rose and fell beyond them. He took mental notes for a letter to Fran. "The depression you noted shows distinct signs of dissipation. . . ."

"I'm working myself into a rage concerning her," Saul reported. "It's as if I need to for some reason. She's a blue-ribbon bitch."

"She's not so bad," Alex said. "Why should her political views matter?"

The man and woman teased each other in a challenging way; it was clear to the young man that they were attracted. Mrs. Harvey loved tea dancing. When Saul would not perform, she swirled Alex around the tilting dance floor, or if Alex would not, then one of the ship's gigolos, scarves flying, tight curls bobbing in the late afternoon light ("Sophia Carson had red hair. Do I run to that?"), her implacable nose like a dart (Alex's description), running the young men ragged.

"Not up to a grea'deal, are you, darling?" she would say, breathing heavily. "Yes, a gin rickey. Alex is marvelous, however, which more than makes up. All the gigolos are Semites too."

"You inspect them?"

"I ask them. Unlike you, they don't get angry, I suppose because they are not ashamed. You are Communistic because then you become that instead of something else you don't like. You might as well become a Catholic." She would stare at him in a musing way. "A Jewish banker is what you are, my boy; and you are a young, talented Jewish composer." She talked about the Rothschilds. She had had an experience in one of the banks. "What sort of interest would *you* charge me?"

"For you, dolling," he said, "twenty percent only. A boggin." But she could pay with her gorgeous body.

"Well, we'll see, won't we?"

Late in the evening after a great number of drinks, she would stare hard at Saul, eyes fuzzy, running her tongue around and around her lips, while Saul, who had matched her drink for drink, sat coolly sober. "So it's all perfectly straight-forward, is it? Whistle and I'll come to you, my lad. I'll tell you what the trouble is, though, and that is that you are extraordinarily attractive, God knows why."

"A perversion."

"During the rough weather the other day, Alex, your da' made a proletarian proposition. What do you expect I'll say in the long run?"

On the next to last day before port Mrs. Harvey, who was never seasick, failed to appear for the midday meal.

"Why don't you go see if she's all right?" Alex suggested; and, as if he had been reminded of an annoying obligation, Saul flung down his napkin and left the dining room. He found Alex an hour later.

"You missed lunch."

"I'll pick up a sandwich in the bar."

He said to Alex cheerfully, "I wonder how much you know?"

"About you and Mrs. Harvey or about life?"

Saul told him everything that had happened, leaving, or so he said, nothing out.

•

On the last night, the ship tied up in port and discharging its cargo, they talked about Alex's immediate future.

"I am not here discussing your talent or your ability to put it to hard work."

They had packed. Saul had taken his shower, then Alex. Saul put his last highball on the dresser, where it trembled with the dynamos of the ship; he lit a last cigarette. "You have a duty to protect as well as make total use of talent."

117

Alex granted it.

In a few words: Saul wanted Alex to be more reserved in his personal life. He paced their stateroom at one in the morning, both unconscious and, as Alex thought, conscious of his naked body. Alex dried himself with a towel. "Why 'more'? Am I unreserved?"

"You tell me you are."

A father was not supposed to use confidences in this way. "I'll tell Fran, I suppose, about you and Flora Harvey, but I won't use it."

"The point is, as you say, I'm a father."

"After all." Alex said, "I believe in taking risks."

"You are saying to your *father*, 'I have to risk myself!' Your 'self' means your life."

Alex was in search of precisely that. Why shouldn't he be? Saul would remember it as one of their best talks. Now, at home, they shared an apartment on Pine Street filled with geometric furniture, all in black and white (black carpet, white Steinway baby grand), and such discussions had become as routine and necessary as Alex's work or Saul's.

"Getting to what 'father' means . . ."

"A smoke screen. We are here two friends in conclave."

"A father . . ."

Naked, they shouted at each other.

"Be careful! *I* forbid needless risks with your so-called self. *I* forbid."

"Saul . . ."

"Demand, then! I demand essential care of your *self.*"

A father demonstrated self-preservation and a son followed suit. "You don't demand and require!"

Disembarkation procedure began at six. They would not try to sleep. When they were dressed they were calm. "Is that clear?" Saul asked, as if his son had not spoken. "Use this"—tapping his brow, which gleamed yellow, wholly bald now, under the caged ceiling light. "The world in which I have known you sometimes to seek diversion . . ."

". . . is tricky."

118

"He's of several minds about the game played with Mrs. Harvey, I suppose," he would write to his sister from Paris, "but whether it's his own excesses or the Place Pigalle kind, he's in a puritanical mood, for which I pay. Also, we're too 'up' for each other and need to be alone, me to get to work, Saul to misbehave without me watching. . . ."

Just before disembarkation Alex missed his wallet, which contained his passport and letter of credit, and he and Saul had half a dozen cabin stewards combing the corridors. ". . . totally irresponsible," Saul cried. "Where is your *mind?* I don't see how a supposedly normal human being . . ."

When the wallet turned up in a piece of hand luggage, Saul cried, "Idiot! Where was your *mind?*" They encountered Flora Harvey in the ship's salon, which had been set aside for passport inspection.

". . . always losing something, this idiot of mine."

"I had a husband like that. A possessive man who kept losing things."

She was cheerful, richly made up, the tips of her fur boa bobbing on the deck. They exchanged the names of their Paris hotels.

"See her?" Saul said to Alex. "I detest her." They stood briefly at the ship's rail, in no hurry to descend. There was a creaking of ropes and crane cables as the dock workers, still in the light of acetylene flares, finished unloading the hold. Silent, they watched what they supposed was Fairbanks's Rolls-Royce lowered to the pier. They breathed the port odor of cindery dampness and earth; whiffs of powerful tobacco rose to them.

"We're here."

"The first French we heard was like good rough bread," Alex would write. "It made the voyage appear what it had been right along: a scene, an artificial piece within which essentially artificial things were said and done—a holiday. Now that's over. I had spent hours at the ship's rail looking at the sea, which I love of course, but without the land one is turned too deeply—artificially—inward. You can't get at

119

what it contains, unless, I suppose, you are a fisherman, so it becomes an aphrodisiac for feeling. I tried this on Saul, who liked it. The smell of earth at war with the sea smell restored us to our duty, and we went at last, father and son, into an acid-smelling bar at the end of the customs shed, bought Gauloise cigarettes and a couple of brandies at eight in the morning, and looked at each other through the amber drinks. . . ."

Alex had said, "I hope Babushka comes around"—referring to his grandmother's disapproval of his quitting college and going to Paris to study.

"I'll handle her."

And then, Alex supposed as a result of the brandy and the hour, Saul said almost dreamily, "If sometimes, inadvertently, I make you feel like a little boy, remember she can do that to me."

"Not your usual style of confidence."

"No."

"But you resist her."

"I resist."

Then Saul said, "A marvelous, marvelous voyage," with belligerent happiness, as if he too were setting his foot on a new path.

TWO | **1925**

1926

1927

1928

1929

1925

●

He daydreamed like a schoolboy about Eve Schiff. He saw himself with her in a bright room overlooking the sea. They were engaged in conversation. When she smiled her eyes would nearly close above the high prominent pale cheeks. Randall Schiff, her husband, did not figure in the daydreams, except to be noted dutifully at the outset of them as a figure upon whom a door was closing. He thought: I am now thinking about this particular woman.

Hay was being cut. The sun would open a valley landscape —low shoulders rising gradually at first, then the peaks of high shattered stone above, and the summer sky, glassily hot, which in his intense imagining his eye pierced. The train's motion rolled the scene back: gone; but his dream was a constant dimension, himself running outward in place and time. The countryside made him think of Goethe; it made him nod assent. There was someone in a carriage in a mountain pass very near this geographical place, a mysterious box on his lap. Time did not count, nor the fact that the people in and standing around the carriage, just opening its door, taking boxes down from the roof, were fictional.

" 'Tell them I *am*, Jehovah said,' " said Alex. "What am I quoting?"

"Not Isaiah?" Asher Moak did not know.

"Isn't there a story in *Wilhelm Meisters Wanderjahre* with an uncle and nephew traveling through a pass in these mountains? A mysterious box of some sort?"

It rang a bell.

Passengers coming in and out of the second-class compartment said *"Gruss Gott"* softly to them, avoiding their eyes. "Americans look right at people, into their eyes," Asher said. "It puts people like this off. It's not polite the way we look immediately for something special."

". . . collect toll. Strangers must give something up at once in America or stand condemned."

A woman and a child, each carrying a small varnished suitcase, curtsied to them!

"Oh, my God," Moak said. "Did you see?"

The young men had bought high-crowned felt hats in Zurich. They wore them with the brims curled smartly, pushed down on their brows. One would catch sight of the other—they looked a little alike—and nod as if at a mirror. "You need our long Semitic noses to carry these hats off."

"Oh, God," said Asher. "You don't mean to make that picture."

"Oh, God!"

They sat in casual attitudes, Alex wearing pale flannels, legs thrust out, arms folded, Moak curled sideways into a corner. They glanced affectionately from what had become a stronghold of a job accomplished and their hats at the German-Swiss.

Moak *very much liked* (this tone, though mild, most people found unopposable) what he characterized as Hindemith's health and plainness.

Alex had liked nothing at the music festival but the Schönberg. Both had assignments to write review articles for musical quarterlies, and both had taken notes. Moak would not discuss the Schönberg: "A desert of technicalities."

They nodded in amiable disagreement when they spoke at all about the festival, but they were more often silent concerning it. They also disagreed about politics and about the potential adverse effect upon his work if an artist absented himself from his own country for long periods.

Alex had brought along a just-completed ballet, and Moak had gone through it in their Zurich hotel. Was that a desert of technicalities?

124

"The point there is that you have written and orchestrated thirty-five minutes more of sustained music than you have hitherto done. No, not a desert, but requiring technique of a high order to apprehend, then transcend, Strawinsky"— the great name uttered in Russian.

"I wish I had less respect for you."

They had made a place-name duet: "Schinzachdorf und Gelterkinden, Baselstadt am Rhine," and sang it in a church tone that convulsed their compartment neighbors, particularly children. Another, *È Vietato Sputare,* sung operatically, was no use except in Italian trains. When their talk threatened to become less amiable, Asher would sing. Moak, like Alex, had been a musical prodigy and youthful performer. Unlike Alex, though only a few years older, he had acquired the beginning of a reputation as a composer and musical essayist. He had also a sage air of knowing, an objectivity and certainty about art and the life of art that made people listen to him. Unopposably, Moak said concerning Alex's ballet, "I rather like the opening and the closing."

"That's six minutes!"

He tried his friend in a tentative way. Was Eve the sort of person who salted people away, so to speak? Did she have conquests?

"For God's sake, Alex!"

The younger man's head had begun to ache, and he examined symptoms, biting with concentration on the ends of his new mustache. They yawned incessantly. Alex, for a moment, was on the high-speed trolley between Venice and Los Angeles, analyzing life for his sister. He said, "I was an insufferable small boy. Were you?"

"No, but I'm prepared to believe you were." Moak was reading Lenin's *The State and Revolution,* which Saul had bought for Alex as a parting gift after settling him in Paris the previous fall. "Seas of blood," Asher would murmur. "It sounds rational in French."

Earlier, they had seen a highland sunset of clear glass green and carrot red that made Alex ache in the hollow of

125

his shoulder, the "heart" poets talked about, and he had decided that he felt the motion of the earth as it rolled eastward in opposition to the movement of the little train upon it, Alex and the good Asher, his friend, inside, the sun left behind. He remembered being in a train with his father, Saul's brow burning in a quicksilver winter sunset, willing the train to move.

Later, using the photograph of Milan Cathedral on the compartment wall, Alex tested his eyes, while Asher, pale and freckled, suddenly clearly ugly, appeared to sleep. The train had grown cold. Grit was in his clothes, in his shoes. The journey was permanent—the speedy, cocky going forward, the irrational halts in black countryside, the sound of boots crunching in the railbed gravel under his window: a lantern would gleam. These reasonless stops and starts more than the famous steady rocking of the train in motion generated sexual tension, so that he felt gratefully put in his place, like anyone else, he supposed, upon a journey. Everything had its sexual appeal—Eve Schiff in thought; that dozing old woman beside him; the boy snoring in the corridor corner, yes; even, for God's sake, the photograph of the cathedral. This was democratic of him. The tension, like stone—inelastic—hurt. He refused to touch himself, to masturbate. He wanted people: he hungered for them. For God's sake, he wanted even this old woman beside him whose dinner salad he could smell on her breath. Asher, of course. He told himself that he was serious about life.

"What are you winking at?"

He was testing his eyes. "Don't be funny."

"If they pass, they can help the nose carry off your hat."

"Listen," Alex said, grinning, "I'm in a serious mood."

He had had a serious suit tailored in Zurich. It rested in a box on the rack over his head. Asher had nagged like a mother, warning: "It's overcoating, for God's sake! You'll never be able to wear it"—a woody, German-looking three-piece suit of dark tweed with a leather-buckled belt, big leather buttons, and treasure caches in the lining. "Great

126

Scott! Alex, think of the central heating at home!"

The suit was part of his future. He would wear it at lecture-concerts he had planned for his living the following winter in Philadelphia and New York. He could see himself in it, serious (and not at all), the white smile (Eve's description) unavailable until later, and, because he was decidedly American, foreign in his own country: hands broad, nervous, square-knuckled in the buttoned cuffs; the gymnast's body banked in the overlarge jacket, as it were in armor.

"I can be someone else and simultaneously more myself."

"Which is the cold, dismissing side of you no one knows," Asher said.

He would seem at least to deal with the business of life and get through it, which was to be the Saul in him as he planned it.

Paris had been, he wrote home in various versions, the unmaking and then the making of him. Saul sent a stream of warning replies and when he became frightened wrote that Babushka was ill. ". . . talks in terms of seeing you. Of course, you are not to consider cutting short your studies."

"He says it, I mean it," Fran wrote.

He was taking no unnecessary risks, he said in a letter to his father, which was more or less the truth. The idea, one's first duty, was to be independent. He had learned enough about composition from Mme Boulanger, from Asher, and from his own efforts to begin to see how and where he would now have to buckle down to it. Time would have to be stretched, money made in order to cast off from Saul and, really, his grandmother. Edna Loux came through Paris on her way to Rome and told Alex that his flaws and virtues seemed to have been underscored by his stay: his earnestness and his courtliness. He wanted to know which was which.

"The point is that you learn too quickly, darling. If you've learned French manners, that's all to the good—even the hand-holding, which any woman likes"—the intense, frowning, energetic attention, the concern, always with a cigarette in his lips, for the person he was with superseding every-

127

thing. "And if you are earnest, that's good as well. I suppose I am not warning you against the good manners but the speed of apprehension. . . ." Her perfume had reminded him powerfully of Los Angeles. "How I dislike Paris!" she cried. There was a steady, misty rain. One of her porters, carrying too much, slipped and injured himself. "Yes, that's my luck these days." In the taxi going across the city to the Gare de Lyon, his former teacher said, "Don't be too cold."

"To you?" as if it was not possible.

She shook her head. "That savoir-faire with the porter, and the café, and the cabs! I'm damned unlucky. Don't get out of the cab. Why didn't you ask about Jane Framingham?" She wore a Persian lamb coat and a feathery hat, beneath the veil of which lines had bitten deeply; there was face powder caked in them. "Yes, take a look."

He went back to find the injured porter and talk to him, in order to let him know that what had happened mattered and to give him more money.

Rose paid her visit alone because her husband was not well. Sasha Volin appeared one day, portly and gray-haired, wearing the white waistcoat that he had made a trademark, and introduced Alex to half a dozen Russian émigré families and to the weekly "day" of one of them, which made Alex remember Babushka's on Lombard Street and which he twice attended after Volin left. Asher Moak had introduced him to the English and American artists in Paris, as well as to their Bohemian life. "You sound as if you are doing very well," Fran wrote, "and now is not the time to stint yourself on anything—art, fun, or what have you."

"I have met rather a marvelous girl," he wrote proudly.

It was at a party given by an American sculptor to celebrate the sale of a piece. The artist chewed tobacco and spat juice onto the white marble torso, then massaged the color into the stone, while a group watched him. "He's been doing that for days. It's becoming the most interesting toast color," Alex said to the girl. He had noticed her because of her looks rather than anything she said, which made him feel pleased with himself. She was very thin, with the blurred, starred, white look of an actress in a movie; her high cheeks had hollows under them; her teeth were not good, but she seemed to feel no shyness in showing them. Her hands were large and competent-looking, the nails bitten short (Alex bit his nails to the quick and looked to see if others did). Her hair was straight, a kind of gray brown, cut short. Her eyes were, he thought, black, though they would turn out to be brown in daylight. She was smoking but had no drink in her hand. Alex held a match for one of her cigarettes, and when it was lit she tapped his hand as if to turn it off.

He asked, "Are you German?"

She said her name was Saint-Simon; did that sound German?

"I heard you speaking German. Someone said your name is Schiff."

"And I say it's not"—as if he must choose. "Look," she said, "I am in rather a black mood. There's a wonderful old intellectual French actress in the other room who's going to do *Hamlet* in burlesque English à la Bernhardt. You shouldn't miss it. I won't go because I've heard her."

"Of course," he said, rising at once.

She sought him out later. "Perhaps the trouble was that I hadn't had a drink."

"Now you've had one?"

"For some reason I seem to mind that you'll remember me as stupid after this night. Or, what's worse, arrogant, which I am and which I battle in myself. I can hear the arrogance even in my apology. You happen to have caught me on a bad night. I sometimes use Evelyn Saint-Simon when I'm unsure of the ground—defensively. I first used it when I was put in a new boarding school. It was during the war and German names were mud. The point is that I got rid of you earlier because I heard myself becoming difficult, and that wasn't the impression I wanted to make. Now I wish you'd interrupt me."

"Try asking me a question."

"Why is it important about how you'll remember me?"

"Well, you're in love with me."

"Head over socks. Gee whiz. How quick!" Then she said, "Listen to us making smart dialogue. Of course, I take mental notes. I'll use it. The thing is you're making me feel better."

He said, "I think your looks, your cheekbones in particular, are extravagant."

"Oh, there's the descriptive word! At the risk of making you feel dismissed again: I advise you not to use such words."

"They're smart." The title of the marble torso, which had been sold to the Metropolitan Museum in New York, was *Volupté*. "Isn't that smart?"

"So-and-so"—the artist—"has a clear regard for what he's doing, what his career has given him, in this case an ironic regard. He knows a word has nothing to do with a piece of stone, but he knows the money customers feel it has or ought to for commercial reasons, and he is trying to sell them and understands that they have their selling job to do as well. I suppose at your age you think that cynical."

A certain kind of cynicism became practicality. It depended on the ends you went for. "In this case they are presumably good ones," Alex said coldly. "This man's living: his comfort. And of course, I see what you mean, that the stone stands anyway. But its title is a parallel creation and will stand too. Does he really want his ironic regard for museum dealers to be part of his statement in a hundred years?"

"All right. How touchy you are and how damned bright! You want to take a piece out of me because I turned aside your compliment." She said, "You know a woman mustn't respond directly. When I get home tonight I'll put down what you said, word for word, in my journal. I'll also try to describe your courtesy and the dazzling white smile in the brown face, and things of that kind. What kind? Well, that you listen, for one thing. When you were speaking I didn't listen at all, just waited my turn polishing up what I'd have to say, the point being that nothing you could say was going to alter my set speech. Then you came through, and of course

130

I had to listen too. My father's like that—like you—both attentive and incisive. It's simply courtesy allied to brains, which I love. I have such respect for that."

Did she mean he had good manners?—thinking of what Edna Loux had said.

"No, you idiot. I can't explain it any better, not if you're going to be thick. Of course, clearly, you're well brought up. No, it's as if you and my father had cornered the world market in courteous attention; and of course it's because you listen that you're able to reply well. No, look." Her manner had changed entirely from its first coolness. She put a hand on his shoulder, and he felt tension in her through the comradely gesture. "Concerning that Saint-Simon wretchedness: I won't lie to you again."

"Don't promise such a thing, for God's sake!"

"I swear it. I need to." And then, "No, look: will you ask Asher Moak about me? He knows me and can give you my credentials."

Soon she said she wanted to go home and asked Alex if he would like to go with her. "I came with three men, so it hardly matters."

On the way she quoted herself as having said to the sculptor during the course of the evening, " 'Do you know what I do when I look at that piece of yours? I draw myself up and try to be beautiful. I try to emulate it.' That was Eve in a nutshell, baby, under glass. The intention seemed to be to praise, but the real idea was to draw looks to herself, so of course that's how it got phrased. Self-love revealed. You see it for what it was, I know—a whore's trick. Nor did I much care if I suffered in the comparison, since the only point ever," she said wryly in the rocking Metro train (they both stood hanging from bars, though there were plenty of seats), "is to get the customer's eye."

He saw that she had been influenced by him, by his coldness toward the sculptor's calculated title, and soon, of course (Alex's "of course"), she saw it too. "I wonder, though, if this puritanical humor is really better than a black mood."

"It sees me through a lot."

"Yes, but I'm not you. I do the self-denying where it seems to affect production and nowhere else."

"Your writing."

"Yes, of course. That's what I mean. You'll misunderstand this: I'm obsessed by money and my work. You're not, so you can only give lip service to money grubbers. Do I mean lip service? When you're poor *you can't work*. That's how poverty grinds. I support myself by reading the latest German novels and seeing Paris plays and sending précis reports to M-G-M, which is the film company my husband works for. I get five dollars for each report. But if I send in five at once, I get a five-dollar bonus. If I send in none, I get nothing. You've heard of working for peanuts, haven't you? That's exactly what I have to eat for breakfast and lunch most days."

Alex was horrified.

"No, look." She grinned. "I've succeeded in impressing you, all right. Peanuts are nutritious as well as cheap, and I get one good meal a day at Stryx. The point is," she said, looking at him, "you care, don't you? I've impressed you. It takes three alarm clocks to get me up in the morning. I set them fifteen minutes apart. I work on précis from five to eight, then peanuts, then the novel, which I always mention in capitals, for four hours."

"And you've been so poor—hungry—that you can't work at all?"

"No peanuts, no work. You ought to see your expression! Of course, I'm stretching it. My parents are flops, so even when they have it I can't take it from them. I have plenty of friends, though, and only starve by choice. But the point is it's all tied in with my attitudes toward work—whether I borrow, how I starve. Though work is the core, there's a point at which I prefer not to work."

Alex said that he was also obsessed by his work.

"Yes, but not by money. You're the son of a banker, after all." Then she said, "But you listen to me! I think you are a very complete, sane person."

He wrote Fran, "The surprising thing is that we haven't run into each other before in this relatively small world. Of course, some of her friends are rather famous. Asher in a way is the least of them, which puts us both in our place, though he, I think, has read pieces of a long, ambitious American chronicle she's been working on for years. She's about your age or a year older, very intense and in-going, intelligent almost beyond what she needs for her work (I have a theory there), and has the kind of looks, carved without waste, burnt (exhausted in the sense of being well used?), that I admire, when I'm not admiring your Nazimova kind of looks, exceedingly. She is married, but she and her husband, who is a cousin of some kind and a businessman, are separated yet somehow still involved. . . ."

When Fran wrote in response, he replied, "No, I don't see her much because we're both in bouts of working." He said (Fran decided it was in a sad tone), "In any event, she has a great number of acquaintances almost exactly like me—in my position—to turn to in the idle moment. She'll be back in New York soon, possibly back with her husband. I've given her your and Bob's address, which I use as my own, and she may actually write."

He and Asher and Eve and a few others, before her departure for New York and the composers' for Zurich, made a farewell tour of the Louvre.

"Art is power," Asher said, "and power is not seized without hazard. Therefore the practice of any art is a high, perhaps the highest, of high-risk jobs, not excluding girder-walking."

"Art is work," declared Eve. "Simply and solely. Of course, any success in any work makes one feel powerful, and there's your real hazard."

They were crowding through one of the wings of the museum, an enthusiastic, gesticulating group. It was a spring morning in which the light, as the painter among them remarked, was as hot beneath its early coolness as if the city were under a burning glass. They argued about everything, disputing each piece, while the guards watched them uneasily.

"This stiff risked nothing," cried the painter, glaring at a well-known polished bronze shape. "He has not left his studio in twenty years."

Agreeing, Eve and Alex argued heatedly. "I'm quoting you, for God's sake," she cried.

Moak said, "Alex agrees with me whether he thinks he does or not."

"I agree with Eve!"

"Alex, you agreed with me," one of the others said.

The painter shouted "Croce!" over and over, like a crow, Eve said. When, outside again, he found himself in a little oven of the harsh light, Alex paused and raised his face to it, eyes closed. He saw Eve do the same. "I'm going to become brown like you," she said.

"I've watched Alex stand for half an hour in the middle of the Luxembourg Gardens with his big chin stuck up in the air like that," Moak said. "I saw Picasso walk by once and look at him. He was astounded."

"I want to go south—to Sicily."

". . . lie naked in the sun," said Eve. "The sun must bake right through to the marrow. The sea . . ."

Alex said—it did not sound odd to him because he had decided that he was that morning, just before Eve's departure, talking in a dream—"In everything, I agree with Eve Schiff. So-and-so is wrong. Asher's wrong, of course," though he felt Asher was right. "None of you believes that you will be dead in a very short time, that's the trouble; but I foresee all our deaths." He held his face, expressionless, eyes closed, to the sun.

Asher Moak reminded him of this in Zurich, and Alex admitted that he might have said it.

"Eve gave you such a look!"

"I was in a peculiar mood."

In the train, nearing Paris, exhausted, Alex dozed and woke. His friend slept bolt upright. Alex's dreams had been

134

desperate. They exhausted him by being both specific and explicit and made him feel guilty by failing to fit with his earlier notions of sexual pantheism. He tried shifting images in his mind, substituting sex for sex, to see how he responded. He shut down one thought, opened another, then became angry. "No censoring," he said to himself. "That's out."

On a station platform, having had coffee, eaten sweet cakes, and lit their first cigarettes, Alex asked Asher's opinion of Eve Schiff and himself "as an idea."

The older of the two young artists stared. "Yes."

And then: "I see. Why not?" He did not pretend not to understand, seeing Alex in another light. "You have capacity. I can't comment on the morals of it in you or her, though morality's a factor, or could turn out to be. Foreseeing trouble: okay. Trouble is creative in this case." He said, "You might manage it," which also meant that Eve Schiff would never be easy. He made no mention of Randall. "The great mistake is to assume people's responses. I'd back you," he said.

A letter from her was waiting at his hotel. (It would turn out that Asher had got one and a couple of others of their acquaintances—all written on the same day and filled with the same facts and figures.) Her father, who sometimes produced unsuccessful plays, had acquired the rights and was to coproduce a new Viennese comedy. Eve's mother, who had first come to America early in the century as the soubrette in a famous operetta, would star, and Eve was to translate and adapt, in return for which, she wrote with zest, she would receive "sixty-six and two-thirds percent of one percent of my father's two percent. I have already gotten $100. It's doled by my father, which I *don't* like, but not his fault. Mutzi and he agree to call me Miss Saint-Simon in the theater, at rehearsals, and so on, unless someone says to Mutzi, 'Is this your daughter?' Randall has been nice about this project, which startles me." Asher's letter said that Randall had asked her to move in with him when she returned to New York from the MacDowell Colony, where she was working.

"She thinks she won't, though."

"Perhaps she should," said Alex intently, biting his fingers and concentrating on this.

"We think of spending part of the summer together at Sag Harbor, which, Randall says, as a place makes him potent about me as a person."

To Alex she wrote, "I rather miss you. I remember how you go out to people." To one of their mutual friends she had written, "The novel goes ill at the moment, and since I came here to work on it I feel guilty, but the adaptation—i.e., money, getting-back-to-Paris money—comes first." And to that man, a painter Alex and Asher saw every day at the Dôme, after the same financial information: "I miss you a good deal, your outgoingness, your attention. . . ."

"She 'rather' misses me," said Alex, grinning. He said, "I'll see her first, however. I'm going home. Outgoing home."

•

Through a Paris acquaintance, Alex, ten days before he left, made an appointment with a psychoanalyst then becoming known among the wealthy émigré families. Asher Moak, who had himself been in analysis, warned him: "I don't believe it's for you, and it could be dangerous. Things like this have to be handled over the long run where it wouldn't matter if you became friends with the man or not. I can only suppose you're going there to hear something specific. He's not going to tell you anything at all."

The man did, however. He was a plump, fair, good-looking German sitting in a white-walled office (like a dentist's, Alex put in the notes he would make) on the top floor of a building on Boulevard Raspail.

The doctor said, "There's a lift," in perfect English. "Why didn't you use it?"

Alex was panting from the climb, which he had made with

136

more than his usual athletic energy. "Eying me!" he would say later to Asher, laughing yet dismayed. "It never occurred to me there were buildings in Paris with elevators." As if joking, he had replied, "My sister's the one with claustrophobia."

They were at odds at once. Alex thought: Of course, it's going to turn out to be a mistake. Yet seated in the cane-and-chromium chair, he gave what he thought was appropriate information with soldierly forthrightness. He offered the story of the experience with the maid Minnie and her friend.

The man looked irritated.

"I think the thing I'm trying to say is that if a lot of things left a mark, it happened that that did not," Alex said naïvely. "I have no fear of closed places. I did not think the act I was required to witness was ugly or wrong, and we even sympathized with that need to be on display. I have no feelings but warm ones, I hope not patronizing ones, for Negroes—a particular American problem," and so on.

"What are your ambitions in connection with composing?" the doctor asked.

Alex declared promptly, "I'm moving in a circle, a tight one, which I believe is what's needed at this stage." He would not be specific about this; it seemed to him that it had no bearing. Helpfully thinking that what he himself thought of as the compulsive precision of it would interest the other, he mentioned points A, B, C, and D, the terminals and starting places for the phases of his career as planned. "I'll straighten out and into some sort of forward line by 1927 or '28," he said.

"Why did you come here? It turns out I'm really curious."

"Well, about my sexuality."

The doctor said angrily, "The only thing I can do today is set up a schedule"—he said "shedule"—"of appointments. Do you work in the mornings or evenings?"

"I'm going home in a week, I'm afraid. Didn't Mme Rabinowitz tell you?"

Instead of replying, the man asked, "Exactly what is

wrong, as you see it, in your life of music?"

"Well, nothing or everything. It's not why I came. I've been reading and listening to a good deal of Strawinsky, Scriabin, and Dukas, and I'm told it shows. The last time I played one of my compositions someone said, 'Scriabin and Dukas,' in a congratulatory way. Generally, one's life of music in Paris being what it is, no one responds at all. I play a piece and then, arrogantly and without being asked, play it again—all very intense and I suppose irritating. It manages to steam up the mirrors, that's all." Alex, watching the man, was feeling at sea. "Can that be of use? I did want to ask something."

"Let me say that this is not a shop where you come to buy an item and walk out."

What brought that on? Alex said, "I really don't know how to address myself to all this."

"Have you a number of mirrors in your flat?"

"It's a furnished hotel room. It came with the mirrors. There are about three."

"Well, you are narcissistic, of course, and by extension homosexual."

"Why 'of course'?"

He was first stunned, though he knew he would have had to get to this to discuss Eve Schiff, then angry.

"I am myself," the other said. "Homosexual, that is."

"So it's all right."

"Yes. That's what I would try to persuade you to see."

"And this after ten minutes."

"It's you who limit the time. You came to have a definition of yourself and presumably my advice. For that five minutes would have been enough. The advice, if you can take it, is that it's quite all right. Speaking in ready-made terms, it seems to me that you were born to be just as you are, which if you like puts you in the clear." He went on in the irritated tone, underscoring the deliberately laymanlike phrases. "The practice of the arts, you will soon discover for yourself,

138

is neither steady nor particularly fulfilling. You need something to fall back on."

Alex would say to Asher, "It turned out, I think, that he was trying to convert me to some kind of Trotskyist socialism. It was all written on my brow. He saw that I could not be a success as a composer, so he was suggesting a hobby."

"What the hell did you want to know?"

"If, with my experience, I was committed; and I suppose in effect he said I was."

"And I say you're not. Among other things, you would always mean morally or ethically committed, which a man like that could not understand. Why couldn't you stop with the advice you liked?"

He had gone straight to a café afterward and, hands shaking, coffee untouched on the table beside him, made notes to use with Asher and later with Francesca for what had come to be called in their letters the big conversation. He would be frank with Asher but, when it came to it, less so with Fran, saying at last in her presence, belligerent as he could be freely with no one else, that he would write her a letter about it next time he went abroad. He did not know how much Saul knew but knew what Saul guessed. He was to be (oddly, he would think in the soldierly way) fastidious, unwilling to say flatly either to Saul or to his sister, who were confidants, what had been said at last so flatly and openly to him. Remembering something his father had repeatedly told him, Alex also believed that to be committed was to be made older; but since he defined age as the chance to work with full knowledge, he had thought that commitments were to the good.

Eve Schiff stood in the way, he told himself dramatically. Why "of course"? The presumptuous bastard! Alex paced the wireless deck on his way home, telling the doctor all the things he had thought to tell him since. "Why all right?" Not merely all right by the man's tone but very good indeed, very superior. What about its being quite wrong? He raged to himself, balancing along the slanting decks during the rough passage. He spoke to no one in the first days, would not use the gymnasium, which always cleared his thinking. He smoked too much, was rude to the stewards and then eagerly, insultingly, solicitous of their regard. He stormed up and down the decks behind the lifeboats, dressed in sweaters and his Paris beret, chewing ferociously on the cuticles of his thumbs and addressing himself. Why not wrong? If you liked, of course, then it might be all right to be wrong, as no doubt Alex was. Let the morality of it be at least as clear as the self-gratifying admissions, then if you pleased go and do wrong with a vengeance. There was no "of course" about it, no "all right." The presumptuous—what? He did not even know: Freudian? Jungian? Very likely an anti-Semite. He went to his cabin and added the thought to his notes. It might be somewhere at the root of the whole business. "But then would he be a Trotskyist?" he asked. "One cannot begin to see the end of possible perverse combinations," he wrote bitterly.

During the last days of the trip, he struck up a caustic, loose-talking acquaintance with a young man, the son of a woolen mill tycoon from Maine, who was willingly vicious and in whose company Alex felt he could punish himself for disliking his life. Then, when the young man showed a serious liking for him, Alex avoided him and kept to the company of the tycoon and his wife, with whom he fought concerning politics in Saul's choleric style. By disembarkation none of the family was speaking to him.

Of the experience with the doctor Alex said to Fran, "I suppose I wanted him to give me his blessing, an okay on Eve." It was as far as he could go just then in explaining his reason for having seen the man in the first place. When she began to speak to ease his dark misery, he cut her short. "I don't want you to try to understand yet, because you would and I'm not ready."

Another time, however, he said, "Among other things, the fool told me that my attitude toward work was, simply, wrong. There is an order of monks in Provence—men who

140

spend their lives chipping their graves out of granite cliffs. That's their whole work. This man said that that was what my work would become to me if I'm not careful. Asher loved it. 'Of course,' he said, which started a big fight. My God . . ."

But it was not a grave the artist made, Fran cried. It was a—what? "A building—something of use."

"That's it. Something useful," Alex said.

It was the grave's opposite.

1926

Dr. Carson, Rose's husband, died of a heart seizure in his offices on the ground floor of the South Broad Street house. He had been prepared for it and with his habitual thoughtfulness tried to keep "the business," which was how he referred to many things and finally called dying, as easy as possible for Rose.

During the last six months he slept on a sofa in his office, half sitting to relieve the pressure, medicines within reach, written instructions and a telephone on the floor by his hand. He still saw patients for two hours in the morning—old customers, he called them, who had started with him and wanted to try to finish with him. He and Rose had married in 1920. "An outgrowth of the divorce. A single blossom from that thorny bush, though I see comic overtones as well," Rose said.

Sophia Carson was the doctor's first wife and Saul's mistress. When it was decided by old Mrs. Weisshorn that divorce was at last in order, it was the two plaintiffs, Rose Weisshorn and Harry Carson, who had not met before this (Bob Gamble introduced them from rolling chairs on the Atlantic City boardwalk), who married when the decrees were final, while Saul and Sophia stopped seeing each other almost at once. "Which is merely typical," Rose declared; and Carson said, "We were a very temporary quadrangle."

He was a gentle, undemanding, philosophical man who read poetry in his spare time and had a discoursing style of speech, which had its influence on Rose.

"Saul," he pronounced mildly, "wants what he can't have,

which I find human of him. The divorces were a dirty trick because then he was on the spot. We made him choose." He told everyone what he had said to Rose when he asked her to marry him. "I'm not well. I'm no dashing lover at this stage of the game. I can offer security and I can, I believe, give you uncomplicated companionship, none of which, you may feel, adds up to the best of all possible bargains for you. I can also give you a gentlemanly game of bridge but no longer, as I could have until a few years ago, my flashing net game at tennis." At forty Rose was, to him, a beauty who could have any man she wanted.

Rose, of course, conferred at length with her children. Her manner from this point until her marriage, when, as in Fran's phrase, she settled back for the ride, reminded them of her early Venice, California, style: independent, optimistic.

"At my age one thinks in terms other than romantic ones." For example? Fran, serious, required her mother to examine her motives. "Security, for an important example. For you two as well."

"He's thinking about a bit of romance, Mama," Fran declared in her practical tone at eighteen. "He's crazy about you."

Alex found that he had to calculate his response with care. His mother would expect that the notion of her marrying again might "throw him," and he had to appear to feel reluctant and yet, as he and Fran agreed in one of their midnight talks, not sufficiently so to make her turn from her course for his sake. "Bluntly, we have to be damned careful not to queer this deal."

"When you started about love, I was afraid we were going to get Charles Gold, the mad poet of Lombard Street, again."

"That was romance, if you like."

At the same time, they were shy and uneasy. Their mother's renewed independent manner, the fact that she was doing this for them too, raised doubts they could not express directly. "I feel involved," said Fran. "It's as if the three of us are marrying Harry."

In the end, what it meant was that for the first time in any of their memories there was enough money and more than enough, and Fran no longer went begging to Babushka. Both Rose and she acquired, during the engagement, decent wardrobes. Rose bought six or seven pairs of shoes at a time; Carson gave them both seal coats and alligator bags. With Alex along as arbiter, they made excursions to New York (the parlor car on the train) to shop at Saks, and I. Miller, and Bergdorf, went to the theater or to Carnegie Hall, and stayed at the St. Regis.

"Perhaps not quite," Alex would say at almost sixteen, intensely, shaking his head at a hat in Saks. Dr. Carson bought him hand-sewn shoes and soft flannels, an elegant music case, an engraving to go in his room in their new home. Alex found that he wore the clothes well and enjoyed, as Fran did, buying things he did not really need. "My God, let's be spoiled rotten for once," he said. But their mother's fiancé, delighting in them all, proud of Alex's talent and Fran's wit, spent so unstintingly that they themselves, the puritan in them embarrassed, tried to call a halt.

"Save some for later when we really begin to batten," Fran said.

He accompanied them, when he could, to the galleries and theater, and took them to the Plaza for tea dancing, where he would watch contentedly, a freckled man with pinkish hair white at the temples and a row of forbidden cigars in his waistcoat pocket, while Alex danced with Rose and Fran. Fran was "Nazimova" to describe her beauty, which Alex would pick up and use thereafter. "The hearts you'll break at school!" His own and Sophia's daughter lived in New York, where she went to drama school, and there was a Palm Court luncheon at which the daughter was stiff and rude to Rose, whom it was clear she disliked.

"Oh, I can manage that one all right," Rose said in their suite afterward with her manner of strength. "You simply have to stand up to her. She's a chip off the mother's block."

The doctor took Alex to the University Club.

144

"Your mother in her way is a very capable woman but requires that things be taken out of her hands. She requires," he said in his rhetorical tone, "shoring up. Having had the love and protection of doting brothers in childhood and adolescence, the disappointment of the business with your father, she requires reassurance. I know you are fond of Saul, Alex. I don't dislike him myself. The point is that, underneath, your mother is a terrified personality. You do not simply take a pet and, by some private definition of freedom, set it free. I tell you this, which perhaps you know without quite knowing it, because I want not only to provide for your mother materially in the event of my decease but also in the matter of her emotional well-being."

"He's rather impressive," said Alex to Fran.

"Well, he understands her. Of course, in a way he's getting ready to pass her back before he's taken her on."

"But if he provides materially as he plans . . ."

They grinned at each other sadly. "We're being damned calculating. That's wrong."

As the time for the marriage came close, Alex grew uneasy. He had been struck by Carson's words at the University Club lunch. He said, "He's right. And it may mean that she should not marry at all. Harry seems to forget that if he's so sick, that's going to put her through something she may not be up to and do more harm than good in the long run." And he said to his mother, self-conscious in a way that was unlike him, "If you want to pull out of it, Mama, you needn't be concerned on our account," which made tears spring to Rose's eyes. To Fran, more sophisticated, allowing himself to be agonized, he said, "Of course, I'm jealous: the whole psychological thing. But aside from that, *are* we just disposing of her? Never mind what she thinks: what do we think?"

"Mama's doing what she wants to do, as always, and in this case we are benefiting."

On the marriage night, their mother and stepfather in Atlantic City, the two youngsters stayed up late in the solidly furnished parlor of the doctor's house on South Broad Street.

145

Alex stood waiting while Fran sipped the champagne he had poured. She shrugged. "If it's the best you can do." His face took on a rebellious waiter's look. "I suggest that perhaps madame is unacquainted with the best," in a sort of French. Did the American lady know how much he took home to his wife and children each week? He would comprehend if she did not wish to know. He sampled the champagne himself, at once became a sneering falling-down drunk, and presently became tight in fact. They raised to each other the last glasses in the bottle. They were Charles Farrow and Ramona Patterson.

"To Dr. and Mrs. Carson."

"To Dr. and Mrs. Carson. May she not be a disappointment."

"Oh, God"—choking with laughter.

On her marriage to Robert Gamble, Dr. Carson gave Fran a large cash gift, though the young lawyer was already making a comfortable living. And when Alex went to Europe in 1924, in spite of the fact that Dr. Carson disapproved of his quitting Penn, he paid his passage. It was Saul with whom Alex was living by then and Saul who accompanied him, but Dr. Carson matched the Weisshorns' allowance, so that the young man, as he put it (and as Alex quoted him to Asher Moak), could live *la vie Bohème* in comfort "without the petty quotidian irritations that are part and parcel, as well I know, of a needy student's life."

When he died, Alex telephoned Eve and got Randall Schiff. "She's out. Should she call you? Is something wrong?"

He told the other.

"Oh, God, I am very sorry," Schiff said miserably. "I'll have her call."

Collect, Alex insisted.

"I liked him," Eve said later on the phone. "And I'll talk about that to you, but just now I need to know about you. Are you all right and shall I come in?"

Harry had been reading, Alex had been told, the *Crito*. It lay open, face down, on the floor by his office sofa. Eve kept

146

grunting sympathetically, as if the words had been blows. Carson had taken the appropriate medicine, managed to telephone a colleague across the street, who had been alerted to the contingency, then put the book down still open as if he would pick it up again.

"Oh, Alex!"

When Carson's pulse stopped, the other man phoned upstairs to Rose from her husband's office. It was four in the morning. "This is Dr. So-and-so, Mrs. Carson. You may remember that we met at the College of Pharmacy fund-raising in the spring. . . ."

Several years later, swimming in the warm shallow waters of the Sicilian Ionian, they would recall that particular moment as being, except for its circumstances, funny; and Eve, encouraged, would confess that all she could think about while talking to Alex was that this was a toll call and she had begun, compulsively, to count his words.

"No, but I was unhappy as hell for you." She saw that he was angry. "How readily, when it involves one of your family, you betray me. You're the one who used the word 'lugubrious'!"

"I loved that man!"

"I tell you that I was unhappy for you."

". . . that you hadn't been listening."

She had been listening enough to get the story straighter than Alex was getting it. Did he remember the *Crito*?

What Harry had been reading? "It was Tennyson—'Break, Break, Break.' 'But the tender grace of a day that is dead will never come back to me.' "

"You told me that you were told the *Crito*. You don't remember!" She said, "In any event, it was your voice on the phone that time—how you responded to that death—to death—that made me begin to be in love with you."

Eve Schiff had traveled to Philadelphia twice earlier in that year to hear Alex lecture. She sat tense and pale at the rear of Witherspoon Hall the first time, and the second stood, as if ready to run away, just outside the door of the Poor Richard Club banquet room. She and Randall were living together "tentatively" in his apartment, but she kept her own. "It's thirty dollars a month I can ill afford, but it's my studio and bolt hole. It's also a place I can be private with people when I need to be."

Fran, as it happened, was away both times Eve came. Rose met her, and Saul, as well as Dr. Carson, in whose guest room she spent the night. Saul had been charming and attentive. Rose had kissed her. "Half of Alex's letters dealt with you," she said.

Eve made Alex take her to see the sights, but then did not look at them, and spent the time talking instead. She kept using the word "like," underlining it. "I like your family. I worry about meeting your sister because I think I'll like her, and" —mysteriously— "I don't think I want that to happen so soon. . . . Your father doesn't like me."

Alex protested, but she turned on him at once. "Never mind. But I see where you get your attraction and your venom. He asked me nothing about myself, and I think he never will. I don't say that's not okay in his terms, but you can see how it makes me feel set aside. Your mother said your letters dealt with me, which is only her manner of speaking, but that's what your father will do: deal with me."

"Of course he likes you. . . ."

The word kept ringing, underscored.

"Your mother likes me and your father doesn't."

They were in the museum of a historical house, and she looked seriously into each glass-topped case. "Dr. Carson has quality, I think, and is the genuine article. Understand, *I like your father.* He has the kind of solar brilliance before which I'm always helpless. You have it, but then you have other things as well. It's only that I see so clearly—and here I go again—that he doesn't like me, probably seeing in me a potential threat." Then she said, "I won't come back to Philadelphia because you're ensconced and I don't fit in." She was pale, tense, her slanted brown eyes fixed on him. "Do I look as if I belong?"

"No."

She looked foreign. He said, "In fact, you're not really here."

She smiled for the first time since he had greeted her the day before. "Nor are you." And at the station later: "Why don't we pull a disappearing act, go find ourselves wherever we really are?"

He pressed money on her for the train fare, and with reluctance she accepted it as a loan, then began to send him back bits of it, usually a dollar at a time with a receipt enclosed for him to return for her records.

"Money is my great—what? Horror, I suppose. I am very much a Communist and entirely absorbed in money, which I've been told is paradoxical in the sense that it is only apparently self-contradictory. Anyhow, I will be destroyed by money at last."

The Viennese comedy she had adapted for her father and mother had never gone into rehearsal. "In the theater you need not have had a success to raise money; you need to have raised money successfully. And my poor father and money are enemies to each other." She said to Alex, "You may have the touch. You can't tell about people." She wanted to know what he made from the lectures and was disappointed that he got a fee. "Why not rent the hall, advertise, and put the profits in your pocket instead of letting a lecture bureau fob you off with what can't be more than twenty percent of the profits?" She would grow insistent at such moments. Opportunities should not be wasted. "We are in fact always owed money for work performed as artists. We set to work without any kind of agreement as to reimbursement, like fools! I am owed God knows what in hourly wages for the three years

149

I've put in on my Guy Johns novel."

"I'm not sure we're owed anything."

"Oh, you're still a romantic. I'll have to kick that out of you."

"She's the romantic," Saul said angrily when Alex told him about these conversations. "She's owed nothing unless her work serves a specific cause and not then unless it serves it well. She has the aristocratic viewpoint. Does she imagine we can't do without novels?"

She had said a novel started the Civil War.

"Which is nonsense," cried Saul. "The Civil War was fought so that capitalist industry would be free to invent the twentieth century! Talk about romantic."

"And we can do without music, of course."

"Of course! There are plenty of good songs around to sing! To feel you are owed something for nothing is to give yourself a license to misbehave." He said, "What does Eve think I want to discover about her that I don't know?"

"Who she really is, I suppose."

"Does she sleep with other men beside her husband?"

"I suppose she does."

"Then I don't want to know about her. You see my point?"

"Yes, of course. He's a puritan. It fits," she said, hearing this. "But I must say it's encouraging that he asked. The difference between you and him is that you do battle against your puritanical tendencies, and he thinks his are perfectly okay. We'll make him commissar of morals and infant prodigies. I know something about fathers."

Wasn't it encouraging, Alex asked, that he reported to her?

"Yes, you're growing older."

At his Philadelphia lectures Eve had been, as she said, both terrified and filled with admiration. "You are marvelous," she said, "but I fear for you. The sheer talent you display is heaven-storming, like an overrich meal. You know no dividing lines." He was creator, performer, teacher, student. . . . She would stop herself. It was as if she were frightened by what

150

she said. "No, look: leave it that I admire talent and prepare to be admired."

Alex gave three lectures in New York at Cooper Union and saw Eve afterward. She approved of the heavy suit from Zurich. It was not incorrect to try to express something by means of costume. She used the word as Alex did to describe the behavior toward others of those obliged to lead by their talent. Alex's lectures and clothes were correct, his compositions not necessarily so yet.

Randall Schiff was with her. He was a tall, bony, Scandinavian-looking man of thirty, with hair and lashes so pale they looked white, and round sky-blue eyes. "Excellent," he declared with pleasure. "You play superbly, and your talk was good solid exposition. Now I begin to see what it is I like about the new composers." He said, "You have great intensity. Alex, you should be teaching in a university."

"Did you see that he was white with stage fright? There's the secret!"

They went with a friend from Alex's Paris student days to a famous speakeasy on Charles Street and had steaks. Alex and the other, whose name was John Gregson, would not let Schiff pay. Schiff asked Alex, "But do you mean you really dislike Hindemith?"

"He holds the record for pages written and the number of notes to the page." They talked music but not exclusively. Alex, high on success, was entertaining, and Schiff leaned back in his chair and smiled with pleasure, while Eve, proprietary, as if she were presenting him, looked down at the table instead of at Alex. She was, with her husband, deferential, almost silent. She sat back with heavy lids, looking from one to the other as if she were memorizing the talk, or, when Alex held forth, used her manner of the modest entrepreneur. When it came to the menu, however, she and her husband grew intent upon it, leaving the others out, discussing each item. And when the dishes came, each was examined sharply. "Why don't you just leave that, Randall?" she said of a dish of vegetables. "That's not for you." Each looked over the other's food. When Eve had isolated that portion of her steak she would eat, Randall gave a nod. "Good. Don't attempt too much, Eve." They ate, chewing thoroughly, almost in silence, except to comment on the food itself, glances fixed on corners of the restaurant or occasionally, confirming something, briefly on each other. "You could eat that perhaps." Or simply: "Good?" Eve drank a small glass of straight whiskey, Randall nothing. At the end of the meal each took a tablet from the same bottle, which Randall had in his pocket.

When the discussion over the check began, Schiff, who had a speech difficulty, began to stammer. He left the table for a moment, and Alex asked Eve, "Is he upset? Should I let him pay? It was really my party and John's."

"Let him pay for the coats and the taxi. Tell him you'll divide things up that way. He's terribly worried about your poor lecture fees and at the same time, like me, is a cheeseparer and ashamed of it." They talked about her husband as if he were a mutual friend whose problems affected them both. Eve asked, "Now that you've met him at last, what do you think of him?" anxiously.

"I like him immensely. He's completely natural."

She canvassed John Gregson.

"Ditto." John was a young, good-looking, not serious composer who wrote criticism and what he himself described as "small, attitudinized" genre pieces—mostly settings of surrealist poems. Alex stayed at his and his mother's apartment when he was in New York. "A very genuine person," he declared seriously. And later to Alex, walking across town: "That's a complex relationship, wouldn't you say? They seem so guilty about each other."

Alex said he thought complex relationships were the best. "I'm not sure theirs is."

"Well, mother-son? Father-daughter?"

"Both probably, but that's not necessarily complex." He was thinking of himself and Eve. "The way people are with

152

each other is mysterious." He found he did not want to discuss Eve. He telephoned her from Philadelphia the day before Dr. Carson's funeral.

"You are not to come in."

"No, I don't think I'd be welcome. Do you want me to?"

"No, I only wanted to talk to you like this beforehand. It shores me up to hear you. My father and I are both known to pull faints on such occasions. My own style is to be serious and responsible, taking everything on my shoulders, then keel over."

"Heroically telling everyone not to bother about you. Generally raising hell, in other words. I'm surprised about your father, though. Listen, of course when you say long distance that I'm not to come in, that means you want me, doesn't it?"

The funeral brought both sides of the family together. Babushka sent a basket of gladioli with a note saying, "Deepest regrets" on an engraved card: "M. L. Weisshorn & Son. Banking in All Its Branches." Saul appeared at the service, though not at the cemetery. Fran and Alex thought how hostile and alien, like a fox among chickens, their father looked in his yarmulke in this portly Jewish company, as if in a moment he would throw off his disguise, snatch someone up in his jaws, and run out of the door: as if, in fact, as Alex said, he were not himself Jewish. Alex was not surprised to feel no particular emotion. The painted husk in a box at the front of the chapel was not Harry Carson. When Eve, conscientious, had telephoned again in the morning saying, "No, but look, I can make the ten o'clock train if you want me," he was firm. "Save it. You're my bank account. I'm going to be using you but not yet."

After the buffet at the Broad Street house, Alex and Saul, Fran and her husband, and Ruth Blum met at Saul's speakeasy in the courtyard behind the Bellevue Stratford Hotel. Both Alex and his father were tight. "I thought Mama handled herself admirably," Alex said.

"Acquitted herself," said his father. "The perfect hostess."

"Sophia Carson looked well," declared Ruth Blum, who

153

was her victorious rival, in a plain tone. "That particular kind of beauty seems to go on and on, really from plateau to plateau."

Saul told the party what his mother had said years before concerning Carson and what she considered to be his bad luck in losing his wife to her son. "It's all right to change, but you shouldn't change from Cohen."

"*Why?*"

"Some mysterious business."

"It means descent from Aaron and the priestly caste," said Bob Gamble in his scholarly tone.

"I suppose that was it. Anyway, it was bad luck to do so."

"Gamble was Gamaliel, wasn't it?" Fran asked her husband, knowing.

"That's what my father says. Gamaliel, the Elder, I think, was Saint Paul's teacher."

Names set them shouting at each other, except Bob, who was as always calm.

"What is Blum? What is Blum?" Ruth kept demanding.

"Flower, of course! *Blume,*" said Alex. "My friend Fisher Blumenblatt: flower petal." The word in German for newspaper . . .

"Ugh!" cried Saul.

"No, not 'ugh'!" said Alex, enraged at once by this old challenge. "German is the best and richest, the most complete language . . ."

" . . . rooting of pigs!" Language shaped people and vice versa, and they were here talking about the only *natural* imperialists on earth.

"*Not* the English, of course?"

Their voices rang in the dark barroom. Ruth defended Saul. "Not in that sense. The Germans are God's own imperialists!"

"You see, I think at a certain point you commence to quote Miss Schiff. It's a filthy language. Pig talk."

154

"Do you know one word of it? A word?"

Alex was planning to study in Berlin, and Eve had begun to teach him the language.

"I know Yiddish!"

And what about that?

"Even uglier! Hideous!" he shouted. "Go listen to a couple of old Jews on South Street: pigs grunting."

" . . . inappropriate metaphor," said Gamble, pulling on his pipe.

"You're exaggerating a bit, old boy, to make your point," said Ruth.

"Hideous! Can I be clearer than that?"

"Yes, now spell the word for me. Isn't that what you do next? Papa, you're impossible," his son said. "Eve is Mrs., not Miss, by the way."

"No, no, that's a miss if I ever saw one."

There was an angry misunderstanding: had Saul intended a pun, which Alex would resent, or was he, as he finally claimed, referring to Eve's liberated unconventionality?

"We might keep in mind," Fran said at length, "that we were remembering Harry Carson over a drink."

At their own house, where Alex was staying for the moment, Bob Gamble told the young composer about Carson's estate. He had drawn the doctor's most recent will and been named the estate's executor as well as its administrator. The day before he had inventoried the safe-deposit box. "There really isn't a great deal to distribute," he said. Carson had sold most of his securities, not necessarily the right ones. The house was mortgaged. There was a great deal owing the estate by the doctor's patients, whom he had never pressed, and little chance of collecting. The daughter in New York received three thousand in cash. There was a thousand-dollar bequest for Sophia; about ten for Rose, which under the circumstances was a good deal. There was a small bequest in trust for Bob's and Fran's son Patrick. Gamble, of course, would turn his fees back to Rose.

When Alex told her, Eve said, "It means you'll be doing Berlin on a shoestring, which is all to the good. Only the poor get to know that city."

1927

•

During the fall and winter there were periods when Alex saw Eve Schiff frequently and others when she was, as she put it, unapproachable.

"I'm trying to work. That's the first thing always: Guy Johns. If you interfere or put me off, you're my enemy, I don't care who you are." There was no special footing, no distinction between him and Eve's other friends in this, which when it did not make him jealous was a comfort. She would say on the phone, "I'll see you, but I'm in a state." Or irritably: "You talk a great game about your work, but you always seem free to come and see me."

"I've been working very hard indeed."

"As you should. Okay. Now have some regard for this, I assure you, extremely difficult swamp I'm in."

Randall Schiff was in England as part of his job with M-G-M and to see a specialist about his speech difficulty. Eve had given up her smaller apartment and was living in Randall's on West Twenty-fifth Street. "Unconditionally. He has agreed to think in terms of a divorce and has authorized my father to explore the wherefores with his lawyer. Probably he'll pull back at the last minute, as always."

"It didn't seem to me that his stammer was a great problem."

"It manifests under pressure. It's my belief that since he knew he was going to see the doctor, he allowed divorce talk in order to be stammering freely and show the specialist how bad it can get."

Alex laughed.

157

"I'm like that too. We're economical and practical. No, but it's bad for him, this business. It makes him impotent." She meant impotent in bed. She did not hesitate to speak of anyone's sex life, her own included. She showed Alex her husband's letters, which were intimate and clinical: the meals he ate described, irregularities of bowel movements, erotic manifestations. Her own letters, some of which she handed over before sending, were filled with affectionate anxiety, though they were less intimate, which pleased the young man.

During the periods she allowed Alex to see her, she would range the length of Manhattan from Harlem to Greenwich Village in an irritated fury of restlessness, visiting everyone she knew in a chain. She took Alex along in this dark mood and introduced him casually (her friends were writers and poets that year, except for Asher Moak) or ignored him. Once, she took him to a party and left it with another young man, disarming Alex later by saying that her behavior had been unforgivable. "I'm not disloyal. It's the last thing I am."

She blamed her work, Randall, the humor of that winter, which was wet and dark. "I feel so poor and ugly. I want to be back in Paris, yet how the hell am I going to scrape together enough for that! I damned well wish I had a banker for a father!" She knew New York well and saw to it, as a solemn obligation, that Alex learned it too. He must not think that her love for Paris altered her love for New York. "Or for Berlin, for that matter." She did not love simply one man; she loved several. Each of "her cities" was a book, a work: "All of America is contained in New York, all of what's uniquely American. The rest may be wonderful, but it's something else." And when Alex argued: "No. Not this particular winter, baby. I brook no arguments. *My* American book is this city."

She was in a fever about her work.

"I've damned well got to get going cutting a path to someplace, if, as I think, I'm not going to live long." When she saw Alex, it was between bouts with the novel, so that she was always in a rage of anxiety. When she was working well and her mood was good, she would not see him.

"I think you expect something," she declared once. And before he could reply: "It's a bit presumptuous, don't you think? I let you kiss me once or twice because I enjoy that. But lots of people kiss me, you'd better know, and I'm not committed to them. The fact is it would be much to your benefit if you were to keep clear of me during this time."

"I suppose you mean that if I were to force you onto a bed . . ."

"Oh, don't talk about that. I mean that you seem to expect something and that there may be nothing there for you."

He did not allow himself to feel that their relationship could cause him jealousy yet. He knew there was at least one man, a young unpublished writer named Fraser, with whom she went to bed. It seemed to him that she did so clinically, as a cure for her discontent. As if he were speaking of such a possibility generally, he suggested it.

"Oh, yes, not only possible but a good notion—someone who does not permit demands and himself demands nothing." Fraser's apartment was near hers, and they often ate lunch together at one place or the other. Late one afternoon, Alex met her at the Russian Tea Room and knew without doubt—her temporary ease, the sliding unfirm looks she gave equally to him and to the dark roomful of people, the way she ate, ravenous at first, then not at all—that she and Fraser had just made love. He knew it, feeling it, as if it had been he in bed with her, or for that matter with Fraser. He cut short what he thought of as the privilege of jealousy. They went over the large menu item by item, Alex deciding. He was both amusing about what they would eat and concerned, knowing Eve's dislikes. Sauces were withheld or served separately to be tried out; vegetables, forbidden contact with each other or the main dish, were served on plates of their own. They divided dishes both to save money and because the portions were too big. He conferred with her, frowned ferociously, fraternally at the impressed waiter, whose wrist he clutched in his powerful hand, until at length he felt her turning to him and away from Fraser. He managed this, he observed, without a pang of what he understood as jealousy.

She watched him then, amused, sleepy.

"You are the eighth wonder of the world," she declared. "Where did you come from?"—comfortably sleepy, yet now focusing on him.

He used a phrase of hers: "Out of the blue."

Years later, she would remember the afternoon vividly. "I knew you knew where I had been. No one could have secrets from you. The point is that even though you say you weren't, you were jealous."

"Not a bit."

"You were, in your terms, 'normally' jealous. You were in a rage, but it was bled white, all the heat pulled out of it by your terrifying self-discipline. That's what attracted my attention that afternoon: that you knew and that you were angry as hell but that you didn't think you were angry."

"It's simply not true."

"Oh, true. You see, a large part of my problem during that lousy winter was that you wouldn't make a proper pass at me; so I was aware."

He would see her to the apartment on Twenty-fifth Street, where she often dismissed him at the door, not hesitating to make him feel young (she was older than Fran) and without standing. They were supposed to have a German lesson every time they met, but by February the sessions had stopped. "I'm too selfish to be a teacher."

"Or you lack the endurance."

"Oh, good. I'm glad you're not afraid to take me on."

He was not.

"Good"—absently.

If she invited him in, she went at once to a sitting room window and looked out in order, as she said, to orient herself. "I'm a little claustrophobic. Yes, I'm well aware your sister is. If you don't mind, we won't talk about you and your sister now." She often wore men's trousers, to her mother's dismay even in New York, and would stride back and forth across the little room, thrusting her hands with their bitten nails through her hair or into her trousers pockets, smoking constantly. "I liked you better in Paris those few times. I liked myself better. I remember I was rather open with you about myself, full of self-dislike yet quite calm."

"You gratified yourself. The cure was in the diagnosis."

"I like that. I compared you at once to my father. How I love my father, and even my mother, at that distance! But my God: I *said* you were bright, didn't I? And you really are bright as hell. . . . Of course, isn't it true that you in fact do your work so many hours a day, six days a week? And without any fuss. Whereas I'm prepared to destroy myself *about* work. If one is to be injured, it should be by means of the work itself. This place stops me. I know Randall will have to sleep here when he comes home, and of course I'll sleep with him."

The apartment was the sitting room, a bath, kitchenette, and two tiny bedrooms, one of which was Eve's studio. All the rooms were the same, untidily crowded with newspapers, books, and journals, the walls covered with photographs, Impressionist reproductions, and postcard seascapes. Even the bedroom, which had been Randall's and once as bare as a religious cell, was now crowded and untidy, ashtrays and coffee cups everywhere. She showed Alex her grandparents in a photograph: weighty, contented-looking people in the garden of their house in a Berlin suburb. "They raise weeds exclusively. They're the best—to me!—darlings in the world." There was a recent picture of her father in a soft collar and pale Panama that tilted steeply across his forehead. "He goes suddenly theatrical for pictures, the angel. He's a frustrated actor, and I think if it hadn't been for Sylvie might have accomplished something in that line. He worked with Reinhardt in the Deutsches Theater." He was a slim gentle-looking man with a cropped gray mustache and spectacles. "Of course, a photo shows nothing"—in her soft tone, not quite looking at it. In a corner of the frame was tucked a snapshot of her mother, the actress-singer Sylvie Tudela, and she removed it to reveal her father's slim hand with a cigarette in a holder. "I may want you to meet them. Sylvie has something good now, a Sacha Guitry adaptation, so that she's at her best."

She revealed to Alex, in a moment of good humor, what she called the publishable details of her life: "My sunny side." She brought out the volumes of her journal, black leather-bound books, which she opened at random and read from. "School nonsense . . . Here's Paris on a rainy day, rooftops and all." She read the description aloud. "Not bad. Not so bad, baby"—pleased. "You're in here, but I'm not showing that yet. This is very important to me. It's the substance of me: absolutely real, my friend. It may be the only thing I will have done." The handwriting in the journals was regular, unhurried, in letters so small that Alex had to bend close when she put a page briefly before him. "Of course, some of it's grubbiness about my obsession." She meant money. She showed a few of the monthly accountings, which went right into the journal. Ten dollars for a review for *Dial*, sixteen for doing some typing for a playwright friend of her mother's. "*Sparkling Champagne* adaptation: $50." It was a good month, she said. Alex went through the listing of expenditures, chewing angrily on a thumb. What did she mean—a dollar ninety-five for breakfast? For a whole month? Lunch was entered at three dollars and twenty-nine cents, dinner at only a little more.

"I don't breakfast, except for coffee, and I'm treated to the other meals. You see I'm all right. There, look at medicine: eighty cents!"

She showed him more photographs. Randall in Paris on one of the bridges, and with Eve on a dune at Sag Harbor. "I'll show you those dunes one day. You love the sea as I do. The most marvelous day two summers ago, Randall and I swam without our suits—it was completely unlike him—then had moonlight behind that dune or one exactly like it. This girl"—indicating a photograph—"is the lover of So-and-so"—

a famous actress. "She has been married. She has what I think of as true duality. In this instance, she is the lover and giver. And she is very serious. I like her." She might want Alex to meet *her;* she might not, as if it somehow depended on him. There was Eve's narrow bed, carelessly made, a collection of stuffed animals arranged on it, photograph portraits of Lenin, Rilke, and George Bernard Shaw above it, the three alarm clocks about which she had told him beside it. There were more little seascape postcards, and she hesitated over each one: stormy, indistinct scenes. In the studio she stood silent, letting Alex look around. This room was neater, the desk bare except for its portable typewriter and jar of pencils. There was no manuscript visible. "I put it away, right out of sight. I become physically ill if I look at it after work."

Occasionally, if her work had gone well, and she was not anxious about money, and he happened to be available, she gave Alex tea and made conversation. Her telephone—Randall's—rang constantly. She would talk to Alex about the people with whom she had been speaking, analyzing character and motives. "Yes, but what is it that makes him tick?" She discussed her friends for hours, with passion. She loved music and, as Alex saw, understood it; and here she was humble, listening. About books she raged, laying down the law, and Alex listened. If Alex saw her home after a party, they weighed each of the guests. So-and-so was "cryptic, not entertaining." If it was someone new, he was solemnly considered, measured: she did not like him on the phone; there was little "proportion" to him, et cetera. Condemnation was in terms of work. "He will not get down to it, and he doesn't care! How can he not care? My conscience drives me to my grave!"

"And you want company."

But she could not joke about work. "It's the unforgivable one."

"What about Tom Fraser?"

"Well, what about him? It's what I dislike about him."

Politics interested her, but she would not read newspapers,

163

and the political journals that cluttered the apartment were Randall's subscriptions. "I can talk some about French and German trade unionism and now about Sacco and Vanzetti in this country, and that's it." But she had read all of Marx and Engels, and Alex, as he would report triumphantly to Saul, was learning his socialism from her.

But it was people—those they knew and were currently seeing—who were of greatest consequence to them both.

"What did you think of my friend Walter Ferguson?" Had he talked to that girl Eleanor Glenn, the poet? Could he see that she was pregnant? "Of course I know who. He gets girls into trouble on purpose. He should be sterilized." They gossiped, in fact, openly and with vigor, but also with seriousness. It happened that the people Eve knew were well known or becoming so, which gave the talk weight: they were significant, these people, as if in spite of themselves, and talk about them was central, serious. People were significant.

She discussed Randall, not hesitating to reveal intimacies of their relationship. She saw Tom Fraser and other men, and though she did not yet tell Alex that she went to bed with them, she did not trouble to hide the things she knew about them. The point was, Alex saw, she took them all seriously, intently seeking out and acknowledging the due value of the weight of each, and her intensity was no greater or less concerning them than it was concerning the composition Alex had written and performed in the New Composers Series with Asher Moak and Gregson and others, or her family, or his, or the union-conscious waiter who had served them their dinner.

Alex told himself that Eve should not sleep with other men; it was this, in all likelihood—the complicated, rationalized guilt—that had caused her dark humor and so threatened her work. He referred to it obliquely.

"And don't you have your nights in Philadelphia?"

"And in New York. But I'm in a cheerful frame of mind about them."

164

"No guilt."

"None I can't handle."

"I've pointed out how wrong you are to expect things of me," she said. "I'll be exactly what I will be, won't I?"

They went to Eve's apartment after the opening night of a play in which her mother had a small role. (Eve had, punctilious, sent her opening wire with its correct combination of punning and hope.) She paced angrily, smoking. "It's such rotten luck, the Guitry thing falling through. And this curdled nonsense we just saw is sure to flop, which will turn her right on my poor father, and then *his* failures will be thrown at him. Christ, I hate failure! How the hell can it be the path to greatness when you look at Sylvie? Anyhow, the trouble is that art has one path only, and the third-raters simply get trampled in the crowd. *God* damn! Yes, and second-raters like Evelyn Saint-Simon. I am so *sorry* for her!"—ambiguously.

Then, angrily, dry-lipped, she kissed Alex. They sat on her bed and embraced. She kissed him silently, his face between her hands, drew away and looked at him. "Out of the blue," she said. She had grown abruptly gentle. When he tried to take the lead, she submitted briefly, then resisted, and stood up.

"I'm going out again when you leave."

"Which means what: Fraser or someone else?"

"Someone else this time, I rather think."

"You rather think! Do I know him?"

"I don't know"—smiling. "I rather think not."

He stared at her. "Don't go out!"

She shook her head. She said to him, smiling in the broad Oriental way, "I'm being disloyal to Randall, you know, not you."

It was not true. Not now.

"Oh, the divorce is nothing, no more than the marriage anyhow. I tell you I am being disloyal to Randall."

"Which is what you want?"

"Well, yes, but don't be only ingenious." She said, "I am speaking of *loyalty* now."

It confused him. "Then don't be disloyal to Randall or anyone, I charge you! It damages particularly you. Isn't it the last thing you are?"

"The last thing." She grinned, head now back, eyes sleepy. She said at length, "It seems you are the most important thing ever. I think I like you too much." And again: "Not now. Do you understand? Not now."

Later, he remembered the heat of the word "important." He was staying at John Gregson's apartment in the East Sixties and that night sat up late alone with a drink. It had been a hint, but it was a clear one, and in the morning he sent carnations, which she had said she liked, "Not now" on the card.

Eve brought her father to one of Alex's lecture-recitals and afterward to the green room to introduce them (her father had been ill and unable to come to Mme Tudela's recent opening night). He was shorter than Alex had expected (Alex was short) and plumper, his skin smooth and pink. His posture was military, and he actually tapped his heels together and made a stiff bow as, still holding Eve's hand, he shook Alex's. He referred to his little girl. Then they met Mme Tudela at a theatrical restaurant on Broadway, she having come after the curtain of her play. She was plump, pretty, glittering. She had a Viennese accent and an expression of rueful charmed surprise. "I like your young man," she said of Alex, a gloved hand on his, emphatic; and Alex saw that she did.

Afterward, Eve was cast down. "Those things never go well. My fault." She asked, "Do you think she seems so? She's Jewish."

"I don't particularly know what it means to seem so, unless you mean looks. Then no. I like her very much."

"Of course. Father's a *von* but doesn't use it. Neither will Randall unless he wants to get something out of a snob."

Alex said plainly, "You mustn't be a snob," which she said cheered her to hear him say.

She declared later the same night, "Look, that was all, Alex, such as it was. I have now a special lover. I tell you this straight, Alex. Don't see me again." She had been, she said, naked in bed with the man not forty minutes before meeting her father at Alex's lecture, and she was going to return to him now, was in a fever to. She was crazy about him—an expression she never used.

Was this the one she rather thought he did not know?

No, it was someone else.

•

Alex went to the MacDowell Colony in the summer to rework his Paris ballet and begin on a cycle of songs, setting Whitman and Dickinson poems. Eve came at the end of his second week to begin a sustained stint on her novel, and they fell into a relationship that was different both from the strained erotic one of the winter before and from the comradely one of her visits to Philadelphia.

Eve said humbly of those months in New York, "I was doing nothing. I was useless."

This place was devoted to work and at the same time, since this was the summer when the executions of Sacco and Vanzetti were to take place, to politics: the drawing of political lines and taking sides. People they spoke to, whom they had known before, seemed altered, darkened by the imminent deaths, as if aged. They said, "Now is the turning point." Nothing could be the same, and everything and everyone would be irrevocably changed. Eve said proudly, "When you take artists and turn them inside out this way, you are going to find something good." There were exceptions, but they proved the rule. She was devoted to art as to the guild of a trade. She was clear-eyed, steady, now working steadily. "I'm in love with it again," which meant her work. "When it goes badly, the pain is nearly unbearable, but it's pain and you forget it when it stops. This other thing"—the darkness of the summer—"never stops, and you have to put it away from yourself to get through work." She was pale, tired-looking, and apparently content. The divorce looked as if it would work out. "I haven't been seeing people," she said meaningfully. "Man, woman, or child. My mother calls and says I'm stabbing her to the heart because I refuse to lunch and have our customary gossips. 'Destroying your father' is the other line. She says I think that because she's an actress I can't take her seriously, which is her own guilty conscience speaking. When I don't see my father it's to shield him from my rotten humors."

She said, "In short, I'm behaving myself."

Casually, on the porch of his cottage after the working day was over, Eve told Alex what she supposed was the cause of her dislike of her mother. "When I was small, at the very worst and most impressionable age, she was"—hesitating, though the word when she chose it was typical—"disloyal to my father. Sylvie was the toast of Vienna at the time or something, and that must have excused it in both their views, because he worshiped her art. I've had to watch out for this in myself: any behavior goes since everything subserves work." (This, he would tell her later, rang a bell in him.) "I knew about Sylvie because, since they were really children themselves, they confided in me, their child. I simply chose my side."

Alex, accustomed to the idea of protecting people, said, shocked, "How could they let you know it?"

"To see if I'd bark, the way you test yourself with dogs to find out if you're a good person. Sylvie was made to feel guilty, poor dear, and became as good as gold, but it was too late, and here I am, the bearer of my childhood. But isn't everybody?" When he reverted to it at another time, she said, "Don't tempt me. That was Schiff in a nutshell, com-

168

rade, thinking of herself while the State of Massachusetts prepares to do murder"—bitterly, which told Alex that the confession had been difficult in spite of the casual tone.

About her work she was in a fiery, chaste mood as well as, as Alex and many others there that summer were, creatively active. She spoke to no one but him except in the common rooms at the house and then insisted on talking only of the Sacco-Vanzetti case. If the subject was changed, she fell silent, turned inward to her work, or rose, and left. Mrs. Mac-Dowell, who gave her colonists at least one evening of her husband's work, did not play that summer. The resident Fascists, as Eve called them—a writer and an elderly composer, both Californians—could enrage her with a word, and she and Alex often found themselves shouting in duet. "We are not here speaking of humanity in the abstract, nor of justice as a concept, but of a community of frightened people— monopoly business, in this case—arranging the deaths of these men of certain age and aspect in order to set an example. And you discover that everything is very real and necessary indeed, and that you are observing a real function of our justice as a didactic tool available to the state, and then you discover to your dismay that when necessary the state, in order to teach, may also kill. The truth of guilt has nothing to do with the matter now. It is a necessary function of our sort of society occasionally to kill in this way. And you may be as sure of that necessity as of the reality, just as needful —the mucus-and-flesh-and-blood actuality—of its present victims."

It would have been Alex or Eve speaking interchangeably. They were precise and simple (these were ABCs), thriftily making auxiliary points within points, using words for attack, angry, sardonic; at last, themselves persuaded of the reality they described, despairing.

But work was in the front of their minds as well. At ten, whatever was being discussed, they would say good night to the others, part from each other with a nod, or if they felt sympathetic a kiss, and be in their separate quarters by ten-

169

thirty. After a particular angry session, they agreed to say nothing more of a political nature in the evenings, feeling the uselessness of it. "It's not the time for this kind of talk. This is not a classroom time."

After MacDowell, Eve was going to Cambridge to stay with a friend, a Harvard teacher named Henry Petit, and to join him in the work of the Emergency Committee. "I will do little or nothing, in fact, because I'm frightened by crowds and demonstrations," she said candidly, "but I'll be in Boston, which is what I need now. Is that selfish?"

He said, "If your own work is going forward, the honest thing may be to stay here or go back to New York."

She studied him, amused and angry. "I think it's correct for you to tell me about honesty. Really. Let me tell you that my work, though it's going, ain't necessarily going forward."

She came to see him (it was an infraction of the Colony's conventions) during the midday meal, which was served in the studios. She had a box filled with manuscript and called out from the path, "Okay, baby, be it on your own head."

Alex took the afternoon from his own work and read half of the chapters, making notes.

She said belligerently in the evening, "In the first place: am I any sort of writer at all?"

"Why ask me? I assume you're at least a writer. The point is I'm not and can't speak professionally, which you knew and which must be what you wanted." He was cold-seeming but also physical. He stood close, occasionally touching her. "Now, I find that you go on about your characters' motives too much for my taste, when I'd rather be hearing from them or, better, seeing it all acted out more. Guy Johns is wooden, plainly speaking. I won't attack this job in any other way, and I know that if you give me any credit, I'm making you suffer. The heart of the book is not there. There's a hole. You're conscious of it and do narrative through the blanks, talking to distract us from this—what amounts to the nonexistence of the Johns character."

170

She said, "Remove him and you have nothing left," with a laugh.

"As good as."

"Then I'm not a writer! Not!"

"Wait—"

"Not!" She laughed in a shouting way, as if in relief. "Good! Just so, casually, does a real humdinger of a crisis sneak up! It's happening, isn't it? You're saying it to me! Oh, baby, this is the moment, because I respect you more than Asher." Almost at once, she became quiet. "No, I'm ready and willing!"

He was silent, then, nervously tugging on the ends of his mustache, began to talk about her novel, while Eve listened, nodded or shook her head, and herself put in a few words to disagree or agree. At length she ran to her cottage for a notebook. "Let's get it straight."

They took a walk; then they returned to sit in his studio and talk until nearly dawn. Alex spoke from his notes and under her intense questioning. Eve smoked without stopping, shoved her fingers through her short hair, and took her own notes. When he was "wrung out," as she put it, she snapped the notebook shut, thrust it into her pocket, lit another cigarette as if angrily, shaking back her hair, and said, "Now. What about you? Let's have it."

"I'm not going to tell you anything."

"Something. Tit for tat."

He grinned. "You mean more about Saul and Fran?"

"If that's all you can drum up. No, look: let's hear about your loves."

His heart pounding, he asked, "Why?"

"Oh, why not? I'm one of them, aren't I?"

He said, "Yes, absolutely."

" 'Absolutely' threatens it at the outset." She gazed at him, not smiling. "And of course you'll want to know if I love you. When I'm in love, it's the sentimental head-over-heart stuff, as unconvincing in the real life of love as in my writing about it."

"I know you're potentially very good, which was why I could speak as I did. Don't pull tricks."

"Potentially! Hope for me! You also know what I'll go through when I'm finally alone in a room."

"Stay with me."

"And the worst is I'll be thinking of myself and not two against the State of Massachusetts." And she asked, smiling, "Do you want me in bed?"

"I don't."

"You are damned wise. You see that I'm trying to turn the tables and won't allow it. At once I grab for what power I can get because you have hurt me like hell—using love and my other woman's weapons, what you call tricks: of course, whore's tricks. Absolutely, I love you, which is why I'm hurt." She said, "I *need* my writing."

"You still have it. But in any event, I can't give it to you in a bargain."

She was pale, curled into the room's armchair, her cigarette aloft. He saw tears on her cheeks.

"Aren't you taking away my work?"

He had assumed he was giving it to her, in a sense anyhow.

"Oh, good. I wondered. What about what I said, or do you consider the context?" And when he said he did: "Well, that's where you are ignorant, stupid, and bad. I say I love you, and you allow yourself to think of it as one more trick."

"I told you I love you as well."

After a time, she said, "I had a syphilis scare this spring, did I mention it?"

"No."

"Have you ever had one?"

"Yes," he said. "Clap too."

"My, and so young." She took a breath. "All better now," she said with ambiguity.

At his door, saying good night, she declared, "You are right. I want to have moonlight but better not." He had asked

172

her to visit him and his family at the Gambles' seashore house, but she refused. "Why don't you come to Boston instead?"

He had to work.

He took her in his arms, but it was she who spoke. "You are exactly right to the millimeter," she said in a firm tone.

In the few days remaining, they spoke exclusively of music —of Alex's work, of Asher's, of the work of other composers who were trying new things. Eve's comments were to the point, utilitarian. She was impatient with the air of holiness she found surrounding musical matters, the mystery. "It can be discussed after all by laymen," she insisted, "if common terms can be found. It's the same problem with medicine. Then snobs pick up smatterings, turn around, and try to mystify and sanctify in their turn." She had written an essay upon what she called music-literature but would not yet let Alex see it. He said, "You've never judged me, but you've allowed me, unequipped, to judge you."

He played his new work for her, and she said after a silence, "Well, marvelous."

He lit a cigarette and busied himself being a host in his cottage. She took the sherry but did not drink. "Do you need anything more than that to work with?" he asked.

"You're not yourself yet, I'll add anyhow, whereas Asher Moak has been from the start nearly—himself and unique." She went on about Asher. "He has something like religious faith. It's under everything. Isn't that needed for a concert program?"

Alex agreed.

"And you see structure—never mind what kind it is—some sort of structure in him; whereas your tracks are so well covered you almost make another path. I mean something different from work's being overwrought. What's more, Asher can get a full physical effect without sex suggestions, which I like. His string quartet.

"The songs you've done," she said finally, "are good, though slight. They keep up muscle tone, which I approve."

173

She took his planned career as outlined: it was just the kind of scientifically outlined self-analysis she would put into her journal. "Bear in mind that you mustn't be rigid about phases. You must allow the world's needs a chance to alter your course, to jump you, for example, from B to D."

"Certainly," he said. Such central discussions between them were particularly unself-conscious.

During their last evenings at the main house, they spoke to each other and did crosswords. When general talk turned to politics, they looked up and heard out the reactionary artists ("Doesn't that have to be a contradiction in terms?"), and were silent.

"What I remember chiefly about the period, aside from the earth-shaking undercurrents, is that you gave me a chance to get back at you, which was you at your best," she would say.

They did not talk about love again. It was as if that was reserved. In their good nights and their final MacDowell farewell Eve was cool and Alex, as she was to inform him a few years later, "imprecise for once. Not one bit sure of what you wanted or even of what you were feeling."

•

Alex shut himself in a third-floor room of the shore house with an upright piano, its front panel removed, and worked with self-punishing concentration. Frantic in the evenings because he could not work again until the morning, he said he disliked what he was doing. "How the hell can I learn to leave in some of the bad stuff?"

"Talk about arrogance," said Saul.

"No, really . . ." Susceptible, he had picked up mannerisms from Eve. He quoted something she had said about too carefully covering the seams. He was grim, distracted, irritated by his father's observation. "Why doesn't he go into the city to the bank?" he asked Fran.

"It's his vacation."

Yet mostly the three were good friends. They sat on the beach in the afternoons and took walks at night by the summer surf, oddly silent for them. Alex watched the lights of shipping on the horizon. Quietly, they talked over the developments in Boston. If Bob Gamble was with them (he commuted to the city by train), they appealed to him on points of law. There was, notably, an absence of holding forth, of speechmaking. The summer had taken on a hard character: remorseless. It was like sun on metal, they said. Life was about to be removed from the two men: "Just pull them out of life, like pulling a couple of teeth. Horrible."

"The whole business of death"—Dr. Carson's phrase, which they used; but they drew no conclusions. The relative silence to which they were reduced, since it concerned death and since their talk was never, normally, about death, led to more silence. They felt the strangeness of it. Alex made angry decisions about his work. It was hash. He played it for them and by the force of his angry baffled state required them to agree that it was no good. If they knew in theory that death was the inevitable weapon of the other side, they could not believe that they were about to see it used; falsely, Alex played this fear into his work.

Eve wrote to him from Boston, and on the weekends, with the Blums now occupying their own rented cottage (Saul and Ruth were officially engaged), the young man read her descriptions to a silent group.

Saul stood seemingly aloof. Ruth sat cross-legged on a beach towel, Sunday papers around her, plump features solemn. There had been a reprieve to August twenty-second. She read various items and comments. In reference to the complex maneuvers, Bob Gamble said, "They're trying for what they call a writ of error to take it to the Supreme Court now."

"They arrested Dorothy Parker," Ruth said from her newspaper. Her mother, fully dressed on the beach, sat reading and smoking in a canvas chair. She was a compassionate, unironic woman, elderly before her time, who did not believe that the sentences could fail to be commuted. "You'll see." Where was Brandeis in all this? she asked. She read, lips stirring, smoking in angry bursts. Where the hell was Mr. Grover Cleveland?—meaning to say Calvin Coolidge. When they realized the mistake, they roared. It became a family classic: "Where the hell is Grover Cleveland?" She went ahead, reading the list of arrested demonstrators. "Don't we know a Bessie Kimmelman? Toledo, it says."

Saul and Rose ran into each other that summer. Rose was staying in the Gambles' Philadelphia house and came down on weekends, often in the car with the Blums. Her remarriage and widowhood had enabled her better to accept the character of her children's father, as she put it, and she even consulted him. "There's no point in the children going to Boston, is there?"—speaking of Alex and Fran, who periodically discussed it.

"Of course not!"

It irritated Saul: romantics loved on-the-scene drama, the lost-cause feeling. "Who suggested it? I won't have it."

Dorothy Parker had been roughly handled and was reported to have said of the policeman, "The big stiff!"

"For what it will accomplish, affairs up there are well in hand," Dr. Blum pronounced.

Saul said, "The Italians are seeing to their own."

Alex cried, "The world is up there seeing to its own!"

"All right," his father said, subdued, conciliating. "Okay, I grant I might add weight if I went and that I don't want to go." He lay in the hot sand, daily papers and left-wing journals around him. "I'm not drawn."

"Thayer sits on his porch in Worcester," Ruth read. "He smokes a cigarette, it's reported. He goes out on the links."

Saul descended to the edge of the surf, taking Fran and Bob's son, Patrick, with him tucked under one arm like a football. Alex watched the narrow brown back and bald head, the boy's small pink back. Pat's intent gaze was fixed on the double handful of sand crabs Saul had dug for him.

176

"It's hard to get past Papa's manner," said Alex.

"And Blum's remoteness."

"Well, I'm too frightened about it myself to think quite straight." Later, he decided but did not say to Fran: That's it, of course. Saul's frightened.

They went guiltily to a speakeasy Saul knew—Morris Blum, Bob, Ruth, Fran, and Alex, Saul in the lead. "So this is your low life," Blum kept saying. He had a volume of Lenin, which he had absent-mindedly brought along, and they made him turn the title side down. "We'll be lynched, Morris!"

"Let them try!"

They walked back on the beach in order to allow exercise to ease their guilt, though they had stayed only an hour.

"It's ridiculous," Fran said. "We're talking about one drink each."

A reef marker blinked red and green on the horizon. The sky was dense with stars, the Milky Way white hot, flaring in a brilliant powder across the southeastern sky. They sought constellations, Bob Gamble naming some of them. The party broke into beach-watchers and star-watchers, and the latter kept pausing, craning, and pointing. "Follow those two bottom stars on the Big Dipper straight up to the right. There! Very faint . . ."

Saul and Blum argued ceaselessly.

Strollers passed them or came looming out of the night going the opposite way; but near the Gambles' house the beach was deserted, and Fran suggested a swim.

"What, naked?"

"Oh, in our underwear. Why not?"

Alex argued for it: the danger of going into that blackness, from which the breath of the sea, immense and cold, rushed out at them. The brother and sister, who saw it as a risk, wanted to do it to absolve themselves. Saul saw it as a midnight dip, merely, and instead of discussing it began to unbutton his shirt. Bob Gamble was starting to walk back to the house. Ruth said, "Oh, my God." Saul went on arguing. "Why

177

is it that we all refrain from pointing out that those two are anarchists?" It drew salvos, even from Blum, who despised anarchists but knew the times and his audience. Ruth, in pink underwear, paddled near the shore, arguing, covering her breasts when anyone came near. Blum stood dressed on the hard sand. Saul, he said, was stubborn, reactionary, in fact. Saul shouted at his future father-in-law from the water. "You want martyrs now!" He was pointing toward the deep ocean. "The future's not up the coast. It's out there!"—the east: Russia.

Alex had plunged in, naked, and swum far out. Fran could not keep up. She said later—the two of them sat on the beach until nearly dawn—that she had been certain of his intention to challenge his doubts about himself in this terrible summer but that she had been unable to conquer her fear concerning his strength.

Saul had not met anyone halfway. "They go up, stay at the Ritz or some such place—Dorothy Parker, for God's sake!—and do their damnedest to get their names into the papers. That's what's going on there."

"You can be a socialist in the Ritz, Saul."

"You cannot!" Precisely that: you could not! "You can be *shit* at the Ritz. Period!"

"Exclamation point," said Ruth.

Blum declared maddeningly from the shore, "You're upset, Saul." And Ruth: "Where is Mr. Grover Cleveland in all this?"

But Alex, alone with Fran later, chilled, unwilling to go back to the house, wept talking about Sacco, who had at last broken his protest fast at the urging of Vanzetti and his wife. "When it was hopeless, then he decided for life! When it was hopeless, Bart said, 'Now you eat something.' Because not to eat was to give the bastards something and to act to no purpose. Oh, Jesus," Alex wept. And then: "This is why I'm no good. I fall apart." And still later, without self-consciousness: "Of course, one has to do something about it after all."

Eve came on a surprise visit, bringing the history teacher

178

Petit with her, a week after the executions. She said, "We're staying for a few hours. Then we go to New York. I must get back to work." She was pale, thinner than she had been, restrained with Alex, who treated her as if she were a soldier returned from the front.

"Of course, I should have gone. The work I've done isn't worth anything. Now I must live with the fact that I did nothing."

"No. Practically speaking, you needn't have. It was a circus of warring political factions. And if you'd gone simply to have done something, then we're back where we started." But she did not seem interested. "I'm going to beg, borrow, and steal and go and join Randall. Don't look me over that way," she said. "You know I pervert everything."

"I would have said you just go in a circle."

"Would you?" She was exhausted, clearly uninterested in Alex. He saw that she had come to tell him this. "I need Randall badly—his friendship."

It was a Sunday. The Gambles' house and the Blums' cottage nearby were filled with guests. Mother McLeod, already so called though she was little older than Saul, was there with her daughter Janet, who had been a girl friend of Saul's years before, and Nikolai, her son. She was a professional union agitator and organizer with a reputation in the labor movement that was to become legendary.

"My recruiter," said Saul in a courtly way. "Business ought to be booming."

"That's it." She was tall and stern, yellow-white hair knotted carelessly at the back of her head, her skirts brushing her shoes at a time when young women were wearing them above the knee. She and Henry Petit, Eve's friend, had known each other for years. The Harvard teacher was a small man with hair parted in the center and a severe aristocratic face. He wore a Palm Beach suit, a spotless Panama, and white shoes. Eve and Petit and Mother McLeod sat fully dressed in the shade under the boardwalk, making a kind of team, Alex felt, that shut others out, while Nikolai and Janet

179

changed into bathing suits. Eve said little. "To all appearances we lost an important one," Mother McLeod was saying, "but my conviction is, as your comment suggests, that by this act the movement has gained a hundred thousand adherents." Rather heavily, speaking without haste, she teased Saul with the freedom of intimacy. "I wouldn't make ideological hamburger out of this, Rothschild. From the viewpoint of most of the power in this country, the only important thing that happened in August was General Motors splitting two for one. I'll bet you noticed that yourself, didn't you? What a position to be in, to have to read the market pages like a thief in the night! Saul, I don't say people will fall all over each other now to unseat the reactionaries; but they've committed murder in public this time, right in the lens of the camera."

She and Saul consulted apart from the others. Alex said to Eve, "A prince and his priest. She catches his ambiguity about this."

Eve, shadowed and striped by the boardwalk above, would not respond.

"You have a faculty for making friends feel they had just met you and had better behave."

Looking away, she shook her head.

Petit was saying, "Fuller was never anything but the forlornest of hopes, ever. And Brandeis hadn't the least intention of delaying until October and the new court; and his view was not unreasonable, recognizing the constraints, the corrupting pressures upon our judiciary."

When her children came to the beach and Nikolai, pale and tall with red spots on his shoulders, had trotted down the beach and plunged into the surf, Mother McLeod said, "He's doing first-class work recruiting in Pittsburgh. I assume I'm among friends." They would be leaving within an hour. There was a constraint among them that Alex could not identify. He saw that Saul, who had become plain in his dress over the years, liked neither Petit's looks nor his manner.

"Say, what do you do all summer, Saul? Lie here under the

180

boardwalk and look up the ladies' skirts?" Mother McLeod asked.

Was it idleness, the world revolutionist itching with ennui on a Sunday? "Everyone's getting on everyone else's nerves," Alex said.

"We've just been handed one hell of a defeat. We're not terribly interested in your prince and his ambiguity," Eve declared. "I don't see eye to eye with Mother McLeod on this either, by the way."

Petit took Alex aside later. "Alexis Weisshorn," he said earnestly. "I have heard such things about your work. No, not just Eve—Asher Moak and others. Eve, of course. She's in a state, isn't she, but about other things too. She came to Cambridge. We were together on the night of the executions. She said nothing. What could she say? one felt. She wanted to look at the sea, and Frances, who is my wife, drove her to the beach. It was not to solace herself but I believe to remind herself of the irresistible source of things." And later, intimately, in the same rehearsed-seeming tone, which Alex assumed was an effect of lecturing: "There are two levels of enemy, Alex. There is the social enemy, now known to be control of money under competitive and exploitative conditions (and we are on our way home there), and there is the enemy of the spirit, for lack of a better term, which, contrary to dogma, also rules in our dear U.S.S.R., and which is, simply, darkness. Ignorance: the fatal failure of even the best of people to know themselves, frankly to admit themselves . . ." And so on. The air was gray with irritation; everyone's teeth were on edge. A wind blew up, whipping sand against their legs. Alex felt that if he understood Eve's friend, then he did not like what he said; yet he liked the man. Eve herself sat as if she were stone. Petit told Alex that he owned a villa in Taormina, where he spent vacations and sabbaticals. Eve had promised to visit him; now Alex must. Yes, he would like that. Saul stood aloof. Fran was with her son by the water's edge. Bob Gamble strolled in the surf, pipe between his teeth, the fresh wind whipping his bathing robe. Rose sat alone, smiling, her feet in tiny white rubber slippers thrust out before her. Alex felt as if his mind would split apart with irritation. Eve had been looking at him, but when he spoke to her, she turned her face away.

●

She walked between Asher and Alex, an arm linked in an arm of each. They had had a couple of drinks and were now on Fifth Avenue in the October dusk.

"Look at them!"

"We are identical to them," Alex said.

"Of course. I don't mean that. No, but look at their faces, won't you, with the sunset on them. They blossom! They are so beautiful! They're on fire! That man's eyes flashed fire!" The white dresses of the women blazed, the white collars of the men, their shirt fronts, the whites of their eyes, and their teeth when they spoke. It made her weak with a kind of joy, this moment. "All the eyeglasses are in flames!"

Asher laughed, but Alex took her seriously, himself feeling the joy of that slowed moment. Eve ran ahead, walked backward, and pretended to operate a movie camera. "Perfect, you two! Oh, Alex, you are the handsomest ever. No offense, Asher."

"None taken."

"You are both blooming in this light like apples! That building is painted bright red by the light. All the sunsets in Europe are pallid beside these! Why am I going?" She had that day had her final typhoid shot and would set sail on the *Europa* next afternoon. Both Alex and Asher were to see her off with others around, but this was, as arranged by Eve, their private farewell. She did not lower her voice. "Is it possible to love you both? I mean in this nagging sexual way," she cried, dancing backward into the pressing golden crowd, darting glances over her shoulder. "I'm *so* sorry"—to people she bumped. "Don't look German, Alex."

"It was only the objective disapprobation of the drama critic," he said, grinning.

"My God, I am shot!" She clutched her hands to her narrow breast and staggered against a wall, so that passers-by stared. Over dinner she told them about the doctor who had given her the injections. "An old family fixture who was always lecherous about my mother and then about me. Anyhow, he kept inquiring anxiously concerning the onset of menstruation from the time I was ten, and now suddenly he wanted me to undress for an injection in the arm. I said, 'Please just skip the cartoon situations. I'm not in the humor. . . .' "

"You weren't in the giving vein," Asher declared. "Rather, he wasn't."

"Wait a minute. That's potential. Marvelous!" She did not laugh but examined Asher's mot intently. "How could you work it?"

Alex said later in Asher's room in the Algonquin Hotel, "No, look"—serious, half deliberately sounding like Eve—"I wonder if the picture you make of yourself—on Fifth Avenue, for example—is any kind of likeness?"

"Now you're asking for a sock on the nose," she said warily.

"No, I'm serious. You're not really bold that way. I wonder if I like it."

"To be bold is my desire. If I can successfully pretend, I expect to be allowed to do so." Then she became angry. "Who gives a damn what you like, Alex?" And at once: "Stop me, Asher, when I start being like this."

"Stop me," Alex cried, "since I started it."

"No, thank you. I'm doing no stopping."

Eve was going on angrily, "Hell, Alex is integrity itself."

"Now, what does that mean?" asked Asher Moak.

"Why, simply that he's the same with everyone. He has fun, he makes love in exactly the same way with anyone. He's cut from one cloth."

"If that's integrity, then that's you," Alex declared.

Looking over some music, at last moving to make peace,

Asher said, "You two would be more polite behind each other's backs."

Alex, thinking to change course, told Eve about a girl he had known in Paris who had also linked an arm in his and another man's and skipped between them up the Boulevard Saint-Michel to the Luxembourg instead of up Fifth Avenue to the library. She listened with cold attention, staring. There had been a—what was it? A déjà vu there in front of the library's lions. ". . . so powerful it made me ache."

"For that girl?"

Naïvely, he still felt he was only telling a story. "She was an anti-Semite. Her dot evaporated during the depreciation of the franc, which hurt her father's feelings. He blamed the bankers, so of course she did. Bankers are Jewish, and when she learned that I was a Jew and that my father was a banker, she went to town."

"I don't understand. I remind you of her?" Eve was pale. "I remind you of a dim bitch of an anti-Semitic provincial French cutie who skipped?"

Alex saw that apparently she had. He said nothing. It was as if suddenly he were not with friends and had to be careful. Asher cried, "Whoa! Start again!" Still angry and now alarmed, Alex said, "It's way out of hand. Right. I'm categorically sorry, darling."

"But you don't *like* me!"

Next day he brought to the boat as many carnations as he could carry.

"I saw you rushing the gangplank, snarling at navvies and tourists, wild-eyed, looking like Chaplin," she said. "If you'd allow yourself to be entered, you'd win every race in sight. No, I think Chaplin's handsome. Are all these for me? I don't like carnations that much." She held his hand with both of hers, digging her nails into his palm in a rage. He saw her parents, her father not quite looking their way. There was Tom Fraser. There were no women in the party that he could see except Mme Tudela, which he pointed out at once: "Speaking of comedy."

"Yes, it's comic, I suppose. You're really fearless. What's more, I tell you I'll have myself a time with the First Officer, whom I've glimpsed already and who seems all he should be, which is funny too. And Randall again on the other side. I expect him to interest me now that we're almost divorced."

"Is everything manner and tone? This is all right." To apologize, he said, "Yesterday—my tone—was due to your notion of a special pre-farewell."

"You wanted to see me alone." She nodded.

She talked at length, urgently and secretly, to Asher Moak, their heads together, while her father and Alex spoke. "She worries about me," said the stiff-mannered, kindly ex-officer. "My health. Could you assure her that I'm well? And she sends us sums of money, which she can't afford. She does without needlessly. Do you correspond? Then I'd be grateful if you were to mention these things."

Before the all-off, Eve said to Alex, "I know you love me. Last words. I wish I had a little of either your integrity or your talent. Some love is lost: it was that bitch with the *Antisemitismus.* No, forget Fraser. Concentrate on me. Good-by."

On the train to Philadelphia he felt jangled. He had said, "This is all right," as if to make it so and now felt it had not been. New Jersey was ugly under its ceiling of clouds: the black landscape, the pinched dark people around him, the smoke grit underfoot. It was all as dark as death. Manner was nothing. He must touch people even if they turned on him.

●

Fran and Alex with their father and Ruth Blum spent the week beginning the day before New Year's Eve at the Traymore in Atlantic City. Bob was to join them, and Saul had arranged for the second evening at a place called Lubeck's, known for seafood, Scotch, and a clientele that included fa-

185

mous gangsters. Alex went with his father to choose the lobsters and champagne, and Saul and the owner, a former Philadelphian, conferred at length. Ceremoniously, they were passed through locked doors into a vault filled with bins of wine and cases of whiskey and gin.

"Paradise!" cried Saul.

"Now you got something on me, Saulie."

They stood in the midst of the illegal plenty and talked about liquor smuggling and mutual friends, while Alex, not unpleasantly excluded, fascinated by the casual, just off-center, "well-acted" style of the two men—their worldliness—both admired his father and enjoyed being his son.

After dinner, which lasted until nearly ten, they went onto the boardwalk, bundled to the eyes against the Atlantic wind. Bob Gamble stood tall, portly, and good-looking at the boardwalk rail taking health-giving draughts of the icy air through flared nostrils, as if he were on the deck of a liner. Ruth wore a new coat with a fox collar, which, in the fashion, was too short for her looks. She was pretty but had a joker's solemn manner and candid gaze: a shrugging way of putting things.

"Well, there's your moon, all right."

"Look how those clouds cling to it," Alex cried. They had argued through dinner about the imminent execution at Sing Sing of a couple who had murdered the woman's husband. It was an antidote to what the previous summer had been to be able freely to shout about this, unintimidated by the force they had set themselves to stand against.

"What *use* is it?"

"We are here talking about . . ."

And Bob's slow, final opinions, to which even Saul listened with respect.

Death had become something they could manage once more, Alex would say at length. "Liberating, isn't it? We'll let those two take all our sins out with them!" But in fact he felt freed, as did the others. They looked clear-eyed, not in the least tight, into the winter sky, which was stained sulfur and

186

pink in the tunnel of the moon. They stood at the rail, half frozen, staring up.

"Too damned dramatic!"

Alex quoted a favorite of Eve Schiff's: " 'I had an affair with the moon, in which there was neither sin nor shame,' which is not the case, we hope, with Saul and Ruth." Casually, as if it did not matter to him, he told Fran and the others Eve's word for love-making.

"Does she call it that? Well."

Saul said nothing.

"What can you say, is that it? I see how it could be embarrassing." He was not embarrassed, but Fran said later, "You shouldn't throw away good things like that."

"I can say anything to people I love."

"You can't."

He would not let Eve, himself, or the others be made less. "What's the Malacca for, Papa—to persuade us to your views?" They walked south, leaning into the wind, Fran between her brother and husband, Saul and Ruth moving ahead. Saul's barking laughter reached them and Ruth shouting in her candid voice, "What? Oh, my God, *what?*"

"She thought . . . no! What bone? Oh, my God!"

Saul waited for the others to catch up, a frail hatless figure canted against the wind. Ruth went ahead, weeping with laughter. Gamble grinned in spite of himself.

"There isn't?" Ruth kept turning to ask. "There has to be!"

". . . fantastic compliment to the sex."

Saul leaned weakly on the rail, a hand to his hip, laughing and coughing, and Ruth, good-natured, laughed at herself. "I assumed there was a bone in it!"

Conventional and contented, they went to the Traymore's New Year's Eve gala in the big ballroom. Bob Gamble stuck to waltzes, though he was a graceful dancer. Alex, Fran, and Ruth did the fox trot and tango as well. Cheerful, Saul sat them all out, erect and youthful. Two of the water tumblers

187

on the table had gin in them, and he sipped at one, not greedily, and smoked.

"Isn't that Harriet Fishman?" Fran suddenly cried.

"From Strawberry Mansion!"

She and Ruth ran and brought her over. Their old friend wore a fringed gown and carried a bag of gold mesh. Her blond hair was piled high on her head. Though she had not seen them in years, she said immediately to Alex, as to a final judge, "I wouldn't get it bobbed, see?" She stared at him in her old placid, wondering way, then greeted Saul. "Oh, I recall *you*, Mr. Weisshorn. How is your mother? I was always amazed: a woman banker." And when she heard that Fran had a two-year-old boy: "Oh, my gosh, how lovely! I think I must be barren. I'm on my second honeymoon, so it's nee Fishman twice. Wait a minute!"

They were laughing by now.

"Two honeymoons with one man or two different men?"

"Oh, two different. That's not either one of them over there. My husband had to go up to New York. I think this one's a gangster. So is my husband." She sat down, held Alex's hand, ignoring the man with whom she had been sitting, and gazed at him with swimming eyes. "You got so beautiful and important-looking."

He danced with her, and then Bob Gamble did. "As a lawyer: do you think they'll really execute Ruth Snyder and Judd Gray? She deserves it, the butch. I hate her type."

Bob said to Fran, "Your friend's had a few, I think."

There was a floor show, and the vocalist, rising out of a dark well into the spotlight, spangled dress blazing on her black skin, sang blues.

"She's good," Alex said.

It was, somehow, a vitally important moment.

"Oh, gosh," Harriet said weepily. Later she said to Alex and Fran, "You were always so intelligent! I never met before or since two such intelligent people. You wouldn't believe the passes I made at this boy—practically threw myself at his head. Or someplace. Remember the *orgies* in my

188

basement?" She took her room key from her bag. "Got it?"

"Got it," Alex said, nodding at the number.

"Okay. I leave it to you." And with no change in tone: "I heard about you giving concerts and meant to go."

When Saul learned her husband's name, he said, "He's an antique dealer, but I suppose you could call that being a gangster," which made Harriet laugh until she hiccuped.

"That's right!" she kept crying. "That's right!"

Near dawn Alex, Fran, and Saul sat in a boardwalk restaurant over scrambled eggs and coffee.

"I wish she hadn't kept saying 'orgies' "—using the hard g Harriet had used.

"I'd be willing to take part in an orgy with Harriet, I believe," said Saul, pronouncing it that way. "What went on when you took her to her room?" And when Alex did not reply at once: "I'll say this for her. At least she isn't one of those willfully destructive man-killer types. In fact, I know a few less polite terms for such."

"Papa," Fran began warningly.

"I mean only that I like Harriet."

Alex said nothing. He watched his father, who sat smoking, sitting at the restaurant counter in a youthful alert pose, overcoat flung open. He had tucked aside his plate, a match extinguished in the barely touched food. His coffee cup was almost full, and he had let it grow cold. Alex understood—he felt it—his father's strict communion with his cigarette and with his son, at whose glance he glanced himself aggressively from time to time, as if with right. Fran had seen Ruth, who was tight, to bed. Bob Gamble had greeted the New Year and gone to his and Fran's room. Now and then, looking away from his son through the restaurant window at the cold boardwalk and ocean, Saul would pass a hand across the top of his bald head or flip the ash from his cigarette in one of those geometric gestures that were, as Alex had once said of them, the sum of such gestures, a fine actor's.

Later, Alex and Fran sat in rumpled evening clothes in the Traymore lobby, feeling dissolute because children had come down from their rooms fresh for the new day, the new year, and they had not been to bed.

"I admire Saul," Alex declared. "I'm like him. And I see the self-love in the statement—as well because he loves me. He can use himself for effect, and so can I. I approve of doing so. The trouble is he's saying, having none: I have a right to you —of me. But here's what he says, and he's correct: if we're to serve, then it's no holds barred, given the predetermined end, the effect. Saul doesn't simply dislike Eve, though he does that. He feels she will run me over, so if he can he will throw himself in her path. He's astonishing. He has no god but the effect and has no doubts as to which effect is the correct one. I wish I could be so sure. I know damned well I'm going to have to be about something and soon, because I find I can't hang my work or my life on what goes on inside art. That idiot in Paris might have been making sense. I must somehow take it and use it the way Saul does himself; a people's opera: why not? But I'm not nearly ready, and I worry about my motives—running out in front as I do to be seen, wanting a kind of advertised life: the whole theatrical aspect of it. Admiring Saul, I can admire myself *without guilt*. Not nonsense, perhaps . . ."

He said, "You look every inch the desperate flapper curled into that chair with fur up to your chin. I hope Bob tells you you're beautiful." He asked courteously, "What about you?" And then he said, like Eve, "No, look: I mean it."

"I also need to be of use. Let's go back. You moved from Eve to art in a stride. They're exactly the same to you?"

"I'll try to make them so, maybe. Or is *that* nonsense?"

"That's nonsense. Did you think I was hoping you'd stay with her when you took Harriet up?"

He said, "I require people who will try to run me over, just as Saul says—put me right out of business; otherwise I'll never know what my work is worth. I can't ask you or Saul to do that for me. Maybe I can help in turn by running over them. Over her"—meaning Eve.

"And the physical part?"

"Oh, absolutely," he said to his sister, grinning. "The physical part."

She said, "I was thinking only of tonight with Harriet, not a lifetime."

After a moment, he declared, "Eve has a not-good skin and bad teeth—small, not healthy—and her nose is wrong."

"Delightful. What a gallant lover!"

Alex slept all that day and then went out on his own at night. When he returned to the room he shared with his father he found Saul awake.

"Are you all right?"

Alex was drunk. There were pinpoint spots of blood in a spray across the front of his shirt. When it was clear that he was not himself hurt, Saul asked, "Are you in trouble?"

The younger man declared that he was not. "Oh, somewhere, perhaps, in the whole genus trouble I'm in trouble." With himself, he might say.

"Why should I have to see you like this?" It was as if he resented being sober when Alex was not. "Some ruthless men run this town. It isn't a good place to play games. If it's anything requiring advice, let's go downstairs to Bob at once. Is it?" And then: *"Were* you in a fight?"

"There was fighting where I was."

"You're careless. My God!"

"Yet I see it's all right."

"What does that mean?"

"You don't mind: it's all right."

Neither spoke. Alex had folded his overcoat into as small a package as it would make and placed it on a chair. "I may be doing this from time to time this winter," he said in a different tone, formally. "I don't mean just slightly perilous things. I haven't got my bearings, and it will be evident from time to time. You will assuredly worry, but you are to worry as little as possible."

"Having been warned. On the other hand, I don't mind. It's all right."

"That was hasty. It referred to another level."

"You're to be warned that I will worry a great deal. Or do you expect to get off scot-free? Worrying is my necessity. What would Francesca think of all this?"

"Ask her." And, turning it off by being tight: "We're both warned then."

"Is it Eve, this crap?"

"To a degree, this crap. And a bit my work. I'm getting old for a virgin."

"That was all in your Paris letters. You're not. *Then* I'd be worried."

"I was speaking metaphorically of myself vis-à-vis this whole business: life. So long as it goes, you don't care in what manner the virginity's lost, do you?" And then: "We're too used to these intimate late-night talks. We can't shock each other." He went into the bathroom, leaving the door ajar, and stood urinating. He sang resoundingly, sounding drunker than he was, "Vee-*zah*-vee life!" He said over his shoulder with emphasis, "I must absolutely"—grunting and sighing—"absolutely be of use!"

"So of course you render yourself useless to prepare."

Alex said, "Papa, why don't you want me to love a woman?"

He could not tell if his father heard.

In the early morning, guiltily, Alex put on old university gym shorts and sweat shirt and his Paris beret, and ran up and down the hard-packed sand near the surf, his jaw, with a twenty-four-hour beard bristling, thrust forward. Saul was waiting perched on the edge of a stack of tarpaulin-wrapped beach chairs. At once he said, "If I said anything to upset you last night or the night before in reference specifically to Miss Schiff, I apologize."

"I apologize for two nights in a row on the town and for being tight in front of you."

1928

•

"I'm not doing much," he wrote to Eve. "There are moments, too mild to be called attacks, of nervous stomach, though Blum thinks they may be symptoms of chronic appendicitis. Of course I'd rather think I'm not responsible or that I could cure myself by 'calming down.'

"I've picked up a German shepherd pup from an old friend of Fran's who's become a vet, and I spend an hour before breakfast every morning in a city park trying to train him.

"My grandmother, the matriarch, is ill, and the family—Saul—is at a standstill. I visit her and discover that I'm fond of her. I mentioned you and she said, 'We dealt with banking Schiffs from Frankfurt. There's a Baltimore branch also.' It's her heart, and it is to be taken more seriously than my stomach.

"You will have heard by now from your parents of my evening with them in New York. I felt they could not afford the very good meal they gave me, which included wine and Camembert. I was shown snapshots of you and Randall, and then your mother said, 'The divorce was an ordeal for us all, but Eve insisted on going through with it. Now here they are the best of friends again!' They seem really at sea. Your father said, 'I only want them to be pleased with their young lives,' which was appealing. He wondered why we are so unhappy about what we do. When he was young, artists were delightful people who had fun when they weren't at work and even when they were. 'Eve makes such a funeral of it.' And so you do, and me too. He blames the war, which was the death of sweetness, and he says that melody in music died at the same moment. The death of all self-affection and illusion, he called it. The machine was born earlier but the war gave it its perfect expression, which is death in the long run. The ugliness and smoke and death make their kind of sense, but it's not one to be expressed by melody.

"I argued that machines can be the opposite of death, citing Russia's new machine society, that melody may be part of one more useful machine and useful itself still as such. He said, 'You sound like Eve!' Do I? . . . Then, as if it was not apropos, Sylvie spoke of some friends of hers, frankly, as her Park Avenue patrons and patronesses and said that she would arrange introductions for me. That I will need a patroness seems a matter of course to her, and your father said, 'In our society the artist learns how to accept.' I played the MacDowell songs for them, and Sylvie said I was a good performer among other things, not specifying the other things, though. She also said she thought I was good for you but not to let that become an obligation because she doubts if you are very good for me! . . ."

"There spoke the true and blue Sylvie," said Eve in a brief reply. "She wrote too and said that you had been 'frighteningly charming' at their dinner party, but apparently you didn't scare them enough. I have had to send $25 of my hard-earned M-G-M dough, very likely to pay for your Camembert. You see what you let yourself in for when you get involved with other families. I can't explain to them or to you about Randall and me. It's no longer love, God knows. I don't know what it is: habit, mutual compassion. I think he wants to settle me before he quits me entirely. Unfathomable generosity in him. He has a girl friend in America, and I know he loves her. Yet he won't go to her. How good it would be to have all this kind of thing settled and be devoted strictly to one's work! Isn't that motivation uppermost—getting the sexual stuff out of the way so that one is no longer in its toils? More about the dog, please. A dog seems exactly right. . . ."

". . . going through all my work from the initial 13 yr old Mozart imitations up to sketches for a Sacco-Vanzetti one-act

194

opera, getting rid of things. Nothing's good. It's nearly settled that I'll study with Schönberg, maybe go over in the spring, use the summer to drift, then Berlin. . . . I want to talk to Schönberg about drama, *Pierrot Lunaire*—speaking melody with strict rhythm. *Sprechgesang.* Striking the pitch, leaving it, dropping into street talk: the music is a silk hat, the talk strikes against it—workers walking out. Do you know the piece? You with your moon love would be knocked out: *Der Kranke Mond* is the flute. *Der Mondfleck.* Moon sickness . . . A.S. is miles in front of everyone. He has written me, congratulating me on my decision as an American to return to our 'original and proper source of supply, which is German music.' He says the war cut it off and that we've been writing Franco-Russian music since. Maybe not nonsense . . .

"I've redelivered a couple of my Cooper Union lectures and detest them, feeling now like an actor, not a composer. Isn't my job, *my only job,* to compose?

"I prowl Greenwich Village with Johnny Gregson after the lectures and complain that I write too well, which amuses him. He cries, 'Oh, too marvelous to be true, Alexis!' I say, 'Yes, too effing delicious, luscious; Cellini where it should be Giotto,' if that's what I mean. John's mother waits, insists on knowing what we've been up to, and nods approval no matter what. 'We've been out effing and raping, Mother.' She's a tall plain Boston type, very angry at conventions. The husband-father is never brought up. She says, 'It's all right with me. Anything goes.' John's trying to raise money among her friends to do a New York harbor documentary film, and he brought a sailor home one night, as if that was the way to begin. 'Look at the planes in his face, Alexis! Think how he'll photograph.' The man couldn't stop talking, afraid to put a foot wrong. When he came to a pause he filled it with worried sounds to show more was coming. 'You are living life such as we will never know it,' Mrs. G. kept saying, which appeared to offend him the time he happened to hear it, since clearly this Park Avenue stuff was the life. Johnny slept with him, and in the morning Mrs. G. and I heard them shouting at each other from behind the bedroom door. 'I'd hoped they were getting along,' she said with dismay. . . ."

". . . rather put off by your coolness, which amounts to moral judging, though you clothe it in humor. What about *your* sex life, or are you voyeuristic? The fact is, isn't it, you disapprove of poor Johnny. . . .

"The dog? The nervous stomach? Your grandmother? Give me news. Are you coming abroad? I want to talk to you, and so does Randall. There are several particular things to discuss. . . . Yes, your job is composing: yes, yes. And mine to write novels. But don't be aloof and cool, please! If that's necessary to your work, then you are improperly motivated and work and man both may go down the drain.

"I picture you with the dog. (Why will you not tell me his name?) You are stern, demanding. If he misbehaves, you are wounded and look away with your jaw stuck out while he cries for forgiveness. You are politely surprised that you could be refused your reasonable request. He ought to have wanted to do what would be so good for him without being told. But when he obeys, how you love him! . . ."

She wrote again the same day, replying to another letter of his, which had crossed hers: "You say absolutely casually that you are going into a hospital for what Dr. Morris Blum calls 'preventive appendectomy.' Randall went to his doctor to ask about this. It's nonsense of the most frightful sort, he finds. Are there no surgeons here in case of an attack? Or in Berlin? Only the best in the world! This is utterly wasteful, though you seem so proud of it! As if you were a soldier—no, an explorer getting ready for the Pole. Do you know what it is? It is Weisshorn egoism. Unforgivable. Why, after all, do you never say *anything* in your copiously worded, funny (yes) letters? I wonder! I want to talk to you, because I can see that writing is you at your weakest.

"By now, of course, it's done and you have a foot-long scar. Of course, none of this is the point, is it? You have something to tell me and you are not telling it. You *appear* to go to the heart of things. I say: don't do Sacco and Vanzetti now—not

196

directly. You will miss them if you try. You must find something that stands for them. But you must please speak to me. No, it turns out. You are indirect with me and direct with *that real death.* It can't be done!

"All right: my own work goes not badly. Johns is now Porter, and this change symbolizes all. You put me through this, you know. It is at the root of all my hate and love for you. I believe (and of course this will put the hex on it) that Guy Porter has, by accretion and by sweating him through my pores, begun to acquire a resemblance to reality. Something more: he comes close to looking and sounding like you. What do you think that is worth?

"I'm enclosing a poem with Randall's notes in the margin.

"Now you say the dog, still nameless, has gone back to its kennel. A black mark against you.

"Will it interest you to hear that I am at the moment chaste?"

". . . It might be of interest (though I don't see why, really) if I thought you still were by the time this gets to you. If we are going to talk, then I'll save my answers to your charges. My solid news: operation a success, grandmother better. How can Johns-Porter become me? You must be leaving ruts and gouges in the rest of the people. Are you accounting for that? Of course, I don't know. The upshot: *our need to talk.* (But why Randall's? Or is that unsensible?) I'm doing *Kritik der praktischen Vernunft* with a dictionary. I begin to believe that inevitably the means to good ends in everything must be unpleasant ones or at least 'noble concessions.' Why not control one's nature toward a good purpose? I'm just approaching this, which is, of course, moral dynamite, covering as it does everything from accepting patrons (Sylvie) to being, rather making oneself be, in love: a sort of dishonesty, in fact. (Don't judge this too quickly.) Why be controlled by our freed natures when we refuse to be controlled by a society and its particular requirements if we disapprove of it? . . . I am deeply sorry that this appendectomy business scared you. I ought not to have told you. Fran says that when I was drugged and drunk just before surgery, I spoke of you. When I see you I will speak *to* you, and I will do so directly. If you are wrong about why I can't do S and V, you are right that I can't do it.

"The handwriting: I'm dictating to Fran. She is pregnant once more, by the way, and beautiful. . . .

"Your friend Henry Petit came to my last lecture (last for all time) looking like a jockey-size Woodrow Wilson and said in effect: know yourself, do not judge yourself. Interesting and sympathetic man, unhappy because his wife is ill. He says you and I are fated."

This was crossed by a letter of hers to Alex. Randall had been in London and returned:

". . . adored each other. The sense I'd had of closed living, of the horror smell of flesh and soiled things (not real, yet real to me!) was dissipated by him and by generous spring rain that was like laundered linen. But now hours later I'm heavy again, stifled by Randall and Paris in sunshine. We are seeing each other like lovers, not living together. He has decided I'm in love with you, and not in our old comradely way, and that the only 'healthy' thing is to deal with the fact. I'm not sure Randall knows what is healthy, yet I believe in love and perhaps only in that. Now I'm not working well, but I expected that too. Things are dark, not desperately so: no feeling of things being out of my hands. I have pretty much stopped thinking about you.

"Twenty-four-hour hiatus," she wrote and described dining and touring Paris at night with a group that included a number of well-known writers and painters and excluded Randall. She named each of the celebrated people and put in titles of books, then wrote, "No good. I carry myself—the spirit lugging the body—and am afraid I was rather a blue note in the company with its jingle wit and riddle games (why do 'important' people raise such a stink about the minor pleasures?). If I'm not working, how can I relax? I managed to get to bed with an English boy in an unexpected resolution to a sort of limping, sad friendship, which amused and cheered me, then cast me down, of course, even lower. I wish I were dead but must wait. Of course, I would not say so if I were really desperate. I told Madox Ford that I will die at thirty-three, and he was shocked and upset, believing me completely. It was a little surprising not to be disbelieved. You predicted it years ago, but then who could believe the child *you* were? (Of course, you are the only good one, I begin to see at last.)

"I had a nightmare that your operation had killed you and woke weeping and inconsolable. Then I knew that nothing could kill you. Did I say that *I* have, I think now, an incipient breast tumor? Also, since you did not inquire: Randall's London miracle man has so far succeeded in intensifying and diversifying his stammer, poor man. Apparently I did not enclose that poem with his marvelous comments. I am Masefield at best. I preach a fine meaning-follows-sound line (Carlos Williams and modern music), being 'hep,' but out pours Christina Rossetti. . . . Sylvie writes (s)mothering me with injunctions; my father is 'being killed' by my absence this time and by lack of cash, though Randall now thinks he can get him a movie company job. But my filthy Guy Porter will kill me first! I suggest that you avoid Paris on your way to Berlin for your peace of soul. With that in mind, here is my grandparents' address there. Trust me in this: *you will like them.* By next spring maybe, if you will be in Salzburg, I'll come to you there for our talk.

"It's amusing to reread this and see that I said I had stopped thinking about you. But in fact I don't wish to see you. I had had no moonlight at all in weeks and weeks, then Randall setting me off and the boy following! Now, as if sex were wrong—my sex—I feel a sort of nervous breaking down, a grit-in-the-teeth irritation that will not go away. I am not like some women, but for love with weight and consequence, to avoid the triviality of most of it, I would pull a man off a bus, if he looked right, or by the hair out of a café. . . ."

"My news," Alex wrote, "is that my grandmother, whom

we called Babushka, has suddenly died. It was kept from me until I got out of the hospital, I don't know why. I say to my father, the one to be emotionally affected and the one whose involvement affects me, 'Are you okay?' And he says, 'Perfectly.' But he's not. It's odd. There was a depth there I did not expect. I was not permitted to attend the funeral because I was still recovering, even though I was at home in the apartment I share with Saul. Amazing how I accept my treatment as someone 'special.' I deplore it, accepting it! My father was very plain in his dealing with everything but of course fooled only himself. He pulled a faint as the velvet covering collapsed when the coffin on its elevator went downstairs. That is, he fooled himself concerning the depth of what he felt. At night he was calm-seeming once more; but I kept feeling, terrified, that he was like a man, like Nijinsky, who can hesitate in the act of falling. He came into my room at three in the morning and said, 'I'm scared.' Jesus! And, of course, just as if he hadn't said it, I asked, 'Are you okay?' and he said, 'Perfectly'! Then he assured me—with what a strange, unaccustomed gentleness—that in spite of this and in spite of the stock market tying up cash, my plans are not to be altered. But of course I am at least contemplating a postponement of the sailing date.

"I am entirely well now. Do not simply toss off 'I have, I think, an incipient breast tumor.' Give!"

"Too many things to say," she replied, "angry things, loving ones. Here are headings. You are to talk to me—*to me*, that is, though not yet. Your business of controlling one's nature: horror! Once more, it is bad of you to have given up on the dog, once having begun; *this surprises me very much.* Was that out of Kant too? Fran threatens me, I feel. Why? Your father too. Now will you be dishonest with me? Of course not, so why talk such *merde?* I am deeply sorry about your Babushka and about your father's grief. I see that you will not allow yourself to be protected too much. Do I dare suggest that you don't postpone your trip? Perhaps you should not unless it means bearing a crippling load of guilt.

As you say, you are a composer. Now get to work, baby.

"Tumor a false alarm. It is all but entirely absorbed.

"Now. Feel that terrible, loosening pleasure of beginning, of your future hunting you down! Be unresisting. Let it reach you! It is morning. Get off the hook!"

●

In a day, by attending, he learned to call it the Ku'damm —the broad, café-lined central Berlin boulevard—and walked up and down both sides of it in a state of excitement, each time venturing a little farther from his dock, which was his hotel. He found Potsdamer Platz, peered intently into German faces, as if learning them. He knew there was poverty—it was famous—and it interested him deeply, but he knew he had not yet seen it: a legless man, a one-armed veteran. . . . He was wary, gleeful. He learned with speed. It was Saturday. He had telephoned and found, to his pleasure, that he could not see Schönberg until Monday evening.

Menus threw him. Alex had read Kant but could not order a meal with certainty and had already had to choke down something he detested because the name in German had a sweet sound. He sat with a newspaper in his hands, not trying to read it, left a handful of reichsmarks beside his cup, and walked restlessly off, a waiter staring after him. He strolled up and down, looked in again with raised brows in case there was a question about the bill, and tipped an imaginary derby to someone who stared back.

Later, he took a tram to Friedrichstrasse, which Asher Moak had recommended, and gave it a narrow inspection to rehearse his evening. He pulled on his Paris beret, tilted down to the top of his nose, and smoked holding the cigarettes between his lips, face thrust up to keep the smoke from his eyes. He looked around the promising streets.

The hotel room was damp. There was the usual wardrobe.

It loomed toppling along one wall. There were a squat bow-legged dresser and a shaving basin on a stand painted to look like marble.

He took his time.

The look and smell of this homeless room appealed to him. It was old, oiled, waxed, timelessly refrigerated: above all old. The drapes and carpet had an odor of hay, the rough bed sheets a damp carbolic smell, the ballooning bolster an electric smell of silk. When he undressed, he kept the wardrobe door open to use the mirror on the inside of it. He was ceremonious. The appendectomy scar showed itself to him— long, puckered, red where the stitches had gone in, violet at the line of incision. Naked, taking his time, he studied the peremptory orders on the back of his door, went to the window, and tucked aside a cold drape. The next building was a private home, windows blinded. Beyond lay a scrap of street with an old-fashioned carriage and pair going by under a lit gas lamp, pale in the afternoon light, a tree—were they lindens with that mottled scabby bark? trees were a problem —and a baroque curbside pump for horses that had a scallop shell lower down for dogs. He thought: Here are all of Berlin's secrets up to 1914—chewing on the cuticle of his thumb. He had tried the bath down the hall near the head of the stairs and found it occupied.

When at length he sank into water, which he kept painfully hot, his experience, his present consciousness, pulled into lidless focus; Alex looked back at himself, into his history, as if through a reducing glass, and saw nothing either serious or alarming. The heat made his temples pound. When he rose he had to do so slowly. "I propose to establish progressive stages of certainty." Who was that? He had seen Eve for two hours between trains in Paris; thinking of her, briefly, bleakly, he knew the nausea exiles feel. Then he thought, as Eve would have had him do (he told himself): No, I am at the center, in the beginning.

In the long northern twilight, dust dropping from heavy dry leaves, he walked out into the city once more. It was unseasonably hot. Businessmen swung off trams, coats over their arms or, sleeves flying, over their shoulders, bowlers and straws pushed back, looking up into the old trees and hot sky. Women and men in shirtsleeves stood in front of their tenements. Windows had been thrown wide, doors stood open. Now all the terrace cafés were filled; Alex stopped at a table for two where a man sat on after another had risen. *"Bitte?"* But the waiter was slow and, swiftly just, sweating lightly because of the bath, Alex rose and walked off without having ordered. Plane trees; they had to be, their old leaves like leather. He found a garden terrace with trellised vines and graveled paths that suited him and drank a beer. He looked out as the street moved past. An angle of the café building threw a shadow across his table under its umbrella, so that his hand lay half in shade, half in sun, the hair on it flaming. The beer stood bright in its shaft of glass. Discharged, Berlin's business world moved swiftly in counter-columns. He stirred the lazy hand to touch its knuckles against the stein, hypnotized. With concentration, a child nearby ate pink ice cream. Briefcases, brown and black, lay on tables. A slender woman with a fat escort eyed him; Alex nodded as the man looked up, so that the man returned the nod. Good! Alex had cleaned himself with care and shaved twice. The hotel bathroom when he entered it had smelled acidly of violet cologne. The street odors were heat, horse dung, tar, and the exhaust of automobiles. The next table had ordered sausages. The beer was like earth, and the earth and trees smelled of bread. The woman was lovely, her square-necked gown where it was visible beneath her coat cut low, made of shimmering blood-red cloth; her thin throat had been powdered, yet freckles showed themselves to him at five yards; the lids of her bright brown eyes gleamed as if greased, and the eyebrows had been painted on, high and arching, her own plucked and powdered over. Her blond hair was as short as a soldier's. She looked at Alex, Alex at her. He said, "Pregnant moment," to himself. He loved her thinness. He thought theatrically, using words, "Marvelous eyes, like a hunting dog's." And: "Eve." The woman's escort shrugged to show his indifference.

Alex dined without menu difficulties in a street off Friedrichstrasse—cutlets and cold Rhenish wine—saw a play called *Sundig und Sufi*, a farce, of which he understood enough (he would see important drama later), and afterward sat at a table on the balcony of a beer hall, from which he could look down upon the crowd below and the stage with its backdrop of papier-mâché Alps and band members dressed in *Lederhosen*. It was very noisy and smoky. At the next table, which touched Alex's, was a man who had brought along his small son. The boy remained for some time bent earnestly over a piece of paper, drawing, then showed the drawing to Alex. He had written *"Maus"* as its title.

"Good."

The boy and his father were fair and blue-eyed. The latter wore work clothes that had been darned and patched and seemed small for him, as if they had been bought originally for someone else. He nursed a beer. "My son"—in English, with a shrug, as if to say, "These artists!"

It was a good drawing, Alex thought. He focused upon it with the solemnity of a man who has had a lot to drink: nice mouse. The child, who could not have been more than six, showed no sign of sleepiness, and the father appeared to be sober. Berliners, there for the music. Yet oughtn't the child to be in bed?

A party of businessmen in silk hats occupied a table directly beneath him, and Alex could look into their platters of sausage and potato salad. They lifted steins, waving them to the thumping music: caricatures, bourgeoisie on the town. Guilelessly, one reached, as Alex observed, to stroke the behind of a woman serving him. The boy's father also saw this, cocked his head at Alex, gave the same rueful shrug, and drew his lips down. The cartoon man's hand had a flashing ring on it. Each of his companions sat confidently, legs apart to accommodate a paunch, waistcoat straining: Grosz cartoons. At the table next to them was an exquisitely pretty

204

very young girl in a short gown; next to her a bearded man in a Bohemian-looking velvet jacket; a blind newsman still in his high hat with the name of the newspaper he sold printed on it, mouth ajar as if to take in the music.

The blond man touched Alex's arm and indicated the table beneath with his thumb. *"Kapitalismus."* He waved the hand at the balcony, banged his own chest. *"Arbeiter! Proletarier!"*—fixing Alex with a blue gaze. The boy was embellishing his drawing, crouched over the table, holding the pencil stub tightly.

Later, Alex felt ill in a particular way, the sensation familiar and elusive: heat in his throat, an ache in his joints that was not displeasing. A degree or so of fever, perhaps as much as ninety-nine point four, he decided. He had smoked too much, but that framed the feeling, made sense of it; and drinking, he concluded, helped. He would remember that he had felt he was one of those who benefited in illness from liquor and tobacco, at the same time aware that he was thinking nonsense and that he would have to deal with whatever was wrong with him in sober daylight.

Now, at three in the morning, he made mistakes deliberately. He had left the beer hall. A tout persuaded him to a dance floor table in a nightclub. He decided, after a third trip to a w.c., that he had had enough beer and switched to whiskey.

A girl sat with him, her face blurring. "Fox trot," she kept saying. Observing the dancers, he thought: I *like* grotesques. He searched his pockets for his little appointment book in order to make notes, describe the types. "Most interesting." The bath had been too hot, then walking in the treacherous autumn cool-warm breezes, coat open, sweat drying on him. . . .

He could not look at the wheeling stars. The *Arbeiter* was beside him, saying, "Alex?" He did not remember having given his name, yet he must have.

Where was the artist?

He had taken the boy home.

Naturally. Alex's German seemed to come with ease now. He found words he did not know he knew and understood much of what the other said. It was astonishing to run into the man again. They walked on Unter den Linden (*these* were the trees), the man talking readily, Alex buoyed by a powerful hope, not daring to look at the sky.

They found a café in Joachimthaler Strasse, having walked all the way, and drank beers, nodding at each other. The man, Alex decided, looked very tired; he had patches under his eyes. Didn't he have to get up to go to work? He wished to hell he had. There was no work. The beers cost a mark, and Alex put money on the table.

"Are you at the Hotel Adlon?" The man had seen Americans there. The Esplanade then? He sat straight, thick hair in a bar across his brow. He appeared to be as tight now as Alex and blinked sleepily, talking less. His name was Wilhelm, he said, which he disliked because of the Kaiser. Yet it did not matter, did it? He said he had a song to teach Alex: *"Aus den Raumen der Fabriken, Aus der Schiffe tiefem Schoss..."* And later Alex sang for him, "The workers on the S.P. line to strike sent out a call. But Casey Jones, the engineer, he wouldn't strike at all. . . ."

Wilhelm grinned. "Fine!"

On the street he sang, "Gwine to lay down my burden down by the riverside . . ." softly, well, he thought. And, "Fine, fine!" Alex cried enthusiastically at the other's attempts at harmonizing. Had Wilhelm heard of Professor Arnold Schönberg?

The other slid into shadow as they walked. The night was cooler. Now and then the blond face loomed, large-boned, broad across the cheeks, then disappeared. Alex discussed *Sprechgesang*, which was the thing that had moved him to come to Berlin, to the master. Had Wilhelm not heard of *Die Glückliche Hand?* *"Wie schön du bist . . . O du Schöne . . ."*

"I sing *and* talk," Alex sang and spoke loudly, his light voice striking the pitch, sliding into speech. "Sitting here, drinking beer with Wilhelm, my friend . . ." though now they were walking. Where was he? Alex was suddenly alone, which was death. Presently, the workman reappeared. Alex decided he loved him.

In Alex's room the man said, "I will borrow a few marks." Now that he knew where his new friend lived, he would bring the money back in seven days when a certain sum was expected.

"Certainly."

Der Kranke Mond was a flute; *Der Dandy* a piccolo, a clarinet in A. Hard to sing. Alex tried. Well, then Wilhelm must know Brecht's *Im Dickicht der Städte.*

Wilhelm sat on Alex's bed. Was there whiskey? He sat straight-backed, exhausted-looking, now and then raising a dirty fist to bite its knuckles and stare over it at Alex. When he understood that there was no liquor in Alex's room, he said, "I need a drink."

"We've had enough."

The other had taken off his jacket and turned back the cuffs of his shirt. His arms were powerful. An old tattoo on the right one said, "Johann," stretched pale, as if he had been a small boy when it was made. Was that his name? "My other name." He was laconic, eyes sliding around the room with disdain. He liked the Adlon. "This is not much of a place."

"Bitte?" But Alex had understood. He asked, "Was that your son?"

Yes, why not?

Where was the boy's mother? Then Alex threw some marks onto the bed. He said, "Go on, better leave now. It's time for me to get some sleep. I must work in the morning. Pay me back when you can."

"No, no." What was the rush, for God's sake? Suddenly the American wanted to get rid of him.

Alex felt, as he had before, both ill and powerful, onto something better than hope. "You insult us both."

He could not force him to go.

Indeed he could, be assured . . . fully capable.

Alex stood, head belligerently low, looking up from under. The young man said, "You are foolish, I think."

"Go on."

"I don't mind that, Alex."

The young composer advanced a step and struck the other, shoving the heel of his hand against his shoulder.

"I'm not *particularly* drunk," Alex declared loudly. And, "I deserve to be struck," the other cried simultaneously, which Alex said at once was one more affront. He saw in any event that the man would stay, which was what he wanted, though he was irritated. The wardrobe door hung open. He glanced at himself in its glass and then, with drunken politeness and in order not to seem vain, kept his eyes on the other.

When he woke past noon it was raining. He checked, found his money intact, watch, other items: all right. His head was splitting. A blue headache. He had a cold. He was supposed to visit Eve's grandparents, the von Schiffs. He would not, and he could not take this throat to the maestro's house, for Christ's sake! And when it came down to it, why was he studying composition at all at the age of nearly twenty-four when he ought to be composing? None of it could have been any more mistaken. He began a letter to Eve, but instead scrawled a note to Asher in New York. " . . . nonsense about guilt. It is there, fixed and ideal, like truth. Isn't wrong wrong? If not, how in hell are we to define right? We can't say that something is wrong until it suits us to do it, then call it right!"

He took the letter to mail in an afternoon exactly unlike the day before: wet, cold, black, blowing. He kept his rage raw, strode along with his collar open, coat flapping, to see if he could not turn his minor illness into a major one. He bought a newspaper. He was old, unshaved, ill; he smoked on the infected throat. He found a filthy restaurant with insolent waiters, black thumbprints on the plates, sputum on the floor. He rattled the newspaper and raged dangerously at the sulky tough man who brought his food. He examined his Berlin evening: that, precisely that, was what Alex Weisshorn had done: Alex's performance. Excellent! he thought bitterly; nothing wrong with that, he hoped.

1929

•

Randall and Eve arrived in Salzburg in the spring. Alex had come from Berlin to work, and he planned to stay for the festival and review it for a musical quarterly. Clinically precise, Randall began at once to analyze their situation. He introduced it by saying, "I know what you can't know about Eve, of course."

They sat in the Café Lohr and, in Randall's words and under his direction, had it out.

"We are going to say everything."

"If you don't keep being prefatory," Eve declared.

Alex had dedicated to Eve his just completed one-act opera. He had performed it for them in his studio in a private house near the hotel at which all three were staying. Now they had come out to the café.

"Randall is going to give us his best German manner."

"I don't mean to speak of the lightning and thunder of creativity just yet, though we must get to that," her ex-husband said. "I will say that I know Eve is in love with you."

"Is this what you knew that he did not?"

"And what perhaps you did not. She watches your every gesture. She has at this moment a famished look I know well, and it's for you and your work. Mark that"—as if in warning, smiling.

"Of course you're tight," Eve said. "Does it still count? Or do I mean of course you're right? Anyhow, Alex knows it."

Randall, who had not stammered yet, said, "Eve is in love at last."

"Such an anticlimax. Please put your boat ticket away.

You'll lose it. Isn't it that you're finished with me at last?"

"That's it for me, not it for you."

"He's finished with me, so he brings me around to you. He's unwilling to leave me on the loose in Paris."

"Now I must ask, are you in love with her?"

"You can't marry me to Alex without his consent. I want to talk about the thunder and lightning if this is what you meant by saying everything."

Randall was going home soon. He carried his steamship ticket with him and had taken it from his pocket to show Alex. Probably he would remarry. Neither he nor Eve said who the girl was. "Are you?" he insisted.

Was Alex in love with Eve?

"Yes," said Alex.

Eve said, "And the opera is only magnificent!"

"Her famished look!" Randall cried, missing her humor. "If that isn't love!" He hesitated perceptibly each time he used the word. It was as if he had just turned his attention to this matter of Alex and Eve and everything was still new to him.

Alex repeated to Randall what he had said to Eve the previous fall in Paris. (Randall had been absent on business.)

"Having agreed to say everything," Eve declared once more with irony. "Were you aware?"

Randall said, "No!"

"I felt it wasn't my business to tell him," said Eve. And then: "What are you feeling?"

"Well, nothing really," Randall replied. He stared at Alex. "I didn't know, and I'm chagrined for Eve, I suppose. In fact, I don't know if I believe you." He said worriedly, "If you're lying, that's an insult to her."

"Having offered something of myself," explained Eve.

Alex saw that the other man's cheeks were red; he was blushing; Eve was too.

"I'm not lying."

Eve said, "Something else for Randall to cope with."

The stammer had returned. It made the man silent.

They remained for a week. Alex went back to scoring the

211

opera, which he had begun in Berlin with Schönberg. Eve and Randall conferred in their room and over meals. Alex joined them at night.

Randall said, as if objectively, "I recall gestures and words and even a bit how you walk, though not now, and perhaps that doesn't mean anything."

Then he would appear to forget the subject.

At the Café Lohr he discussed Alex's work, while Eve would look first at the young composer, then at her ex-husband, head back, smoking. The smoke curled up and she blinked it away. At length she interrupted. "Weren't we saying everything? Are you finished?"

Randall finally asked Alex, "Well, but you have range? What do I mean? Not to use clinical terms"—which, normally, Randall enjoyed using.

"Have I been to bed with women? Yes."

"There!"—triumphantly to Eve, not thinking it might have been she.

"I knew that," she said. "What does it mean?" She offered nothing, waiting.

"I don't want to talk about character. I don't know my character, and I'm not going to go looking yours over like a doctor or a man with a job to offer. We might as usefully talk about money. That's going to loom a good deal larger for you both than this business," Randall said.

"Which means that you trust him," said Eve.

"Well, he's putting it up to you squarely."

"If that's all, I can commit us both. I'll say this: Alex has the loveliest smile and eyes that ever came down the pike."

"Ambiguous tone," Alex said.

"*White* smile."

"Also, your metaphor leaves something for other novelists."

Schiff had had no part in the end of the exchange, which was as near as she had come in his presence to showing what Alex would call the fact of her anxiety.

Alone with him in his hotel room, all the manner absent,

she said, "What Randall can't get from you is what you think about it. Your 'by way of being,' which was how you put it to me at the Stryx in Paris, if you remember."

"I insist on it," he said. "I don't like it or approve of it, which must mean that I wish I weren't as I am. It's not simple, though, and don't hope it."

"But I suppose he would mean to ask if it's permanent necessarily, the homosexual aspect."

"Not necessarily. The will operates, and then I see that I'm changing all the time anyway."

"So you should have said, 'I've done this and that,' not making it sound final. But you sounded to Randall—and here we all are in Salzburg—as if maybe you wanted to escape, so he was upset for me."

"Of course I'm scared. I desire you."

That was all right, she said, smiling: "On both counts. It's only Randall I wanted to assure. I warn you I mean to love you completely. That means completely, baby."

"Fine."

She shouted, laughing, "A missed cue! And you may be saying fine in another tone before long. What I'll learn from you will be about work, and in return I have a thing or two to teach. The point is there'll be time. We'll get third and fourth chances. This isn't it at all. We're not in love yet, only proposing it. I permitted this playlet in the first place to pay Randall part of what I owe him, which you've understood."

"In fact, we don't have to say a word more."

She said seriously and emphatically, "I must get to work."

It was, then, an understanding.

Another day, again alone with him, she asked, "What about your sister? It's Francesca I envy. The only immortal relationship and the only honest-to-God romantic one—blood, the common experience. That knocks me out. I'm not worried about this emotional—sexual *au fond*—business, but you can't guess the envy I feel of your papa and sister and the rest —your absorption."

"I'll be absorbed in you."

"Naïve guy. No doubt."

She sat looking half asleep in the armchair in his room, smoking constantly; she was thinner than he had seen her. When he said, "I've got to get some weight on you," she replied, "If you're going to be tender, I'll probably cry." He saw tears in her eyes. That, he said, was earth-shaking.

"Yes. Right. I'm finished speaking for Randall, and you will always be right."

They were together through most of the next several nights. Eve said, "I perceive that you'll talk my head off if I'm not careful, and I begin also to see that in every way you will be the teacher, since I've never learned to think beyond the room I'm in or the person I'm with. But not yet. This is really just to look. Am I dreaming—that you could love me?"

Except in Randall's presence, neither offered to touch the other. During their talks she sat in the chair and Alex lay at full length on the bed, hands clutching at the ceiling as if he were reading something there, pulling it down to look it over and discuss it. She watched him with the intent open expression that Randall had described as famished. When Alex talked about his work, half shouting passages of song, and about how he meant to use it, she became so silent and concentrated, opening her eyes wider, as if by that means to hear better, that it was nearly impossible for her to regenerate her own talk afterward. Silent, they would watch the windows turn gray. He paraphrased her about the future hunting them down. "I have the feeling now. Is it what's called an intimation of immortality?"

"It helped people invent the notion of immortality."

He took Eve and Randall to restaurants where he was known, where the waiters had become his comrades, ordered meals and wines with seriousness, lit everyone's cigarettes, had Mozart Festival stories ready for them—being a host. They treated one another with affectionate courtesy, and, before Randall, Eve and Alex kissed. "Lovers' kisses," she said, kissing him deeply. These were, as she had often said, her communion. "Moonlight is something else again."

214

Randall appeared to be neither approving nor remote. The kisses were a talk from which he was now excluded.

"You don't know much!" she said to Alex, however.

Just as they always had, Randall and Eve discussed symptoms at length. Alex listened, biting his mustache and frowning, offering prescriptions and parallel difficulties in himself or in his family. The young composer had an infected finger (attending, he always chewed on his cuticle with nervous concentration), which was a matter of importance, Eve said, since it interfered with his playing. They unwrapped it as if it had been a relic, heads bent over it. Randall had just the thing among his medicines, and he wrote on a napkin in the same microscopic script Eve used a regimen of treatment.

Sightseeing in a church on their last afternoon, she said to Randall, "There will be no difference in how Alex and I talk about you in or out of your presence."

"Of course not," said Randall.

When they said good night in Alex's room, Eve would return to her room and Randall's and go to bed with him. ("We had moonlight on two occasions," she said some time later, "but it wasn't in the same class with our kisses.") On the final night Eve remained with Alex, and though they did not make love she slept with him; and the next afternoon Randall and Eve left together.

Nothing was quite decided. They understood that they had not talked about anything really, and they had a sense of rawness and disorientation, of peril. They were both, they declared later, frightened. She would return to Paris, see her ex-husband off, and get her work together. "Money is the major factor," she said musingly.

"If I say meet me somewhere, will you?" she asked.

He wrote Fran, Rose, and Saul separate letters saying that he thought he and Eve were going to live together. "It's being arranged, rather an attempt is being made at an arrangement." They were brief letters, almost identical. "Of course, it may fall through," he added anxiously in each case. "If it does not, I will be very happy."

Saul did not reply. Fran wrote, "I am pleased and know you will be good for each other. Your work life has required a secure base and this, I'm sure, is it. You and Eve will strike fire from each other, and if that sounds romantic it only reflects what I feel. I am deeply moved. What do you mean —an attempt at an arrangement? Money? At the moment it's all right, though Papa and Sasha at the bank are starting to tread water like the rest. (Sasha says, I think, that the dough they lend belongs—'en effet'—to First National! A system, your honor.) Anyhow, I'll let you know if there's a problem. . . . Mama, of course, twitters and is jealous. She wonders if you won't get arrested if you produce passports with different names at hotels. . . ."

There was a letter from Rose saying that she knew Alex and Eve would enjoy themselves and hoping, without being specific, that they would be careful. And there was a note, a surprise, from his aunt Annette. "It is no business of mine at all how you conduct your life, Alexis, and I heard of the proposed change in your mode of living quite by accident. I am reminded of the liaison between Frédéric Chopin and George Sand and of the intense morality, really, of Baronne Dudevant's attitudes, not to say Chopin's. For them their art was the moral arbiter. What was good for it was good for them and the world, and ordinary or conventional behavior had no bearing upon them. I believe that an exact equivalent exists in the two cases and that you and the young novelist Miss Schiff will find your shared lives of rewarding mutual benefit. . . ."

He wrote again to Fran:

"Why do I find your letter cool in its tone? (You have every right to show what you feel. I only want to be sure what that is.) Especially as I must stay over here, money is of the first importance, but I'm earning a little (that piece in *This Quarter* brought $40), and Eve earns regularly, and we'll eke it out. Things being as they are there, I'm writing Papa asking

216

him to halve the remittance as of this date.

"The work's finished—scored as well: fifty minutes, which is too much for a one-acter without chorus, yet it does not seem to sag. I played it for Randall and Eve and got good reviews. It's dedicated to her as the songs are to you, in case you didn't know. Now what? If I send the new piece, can you get it to Stokey? It must serve as a stepping stone, at least to the Prix de Rome. . . .

"What is happening to me, what makes this the great cross-roads, is the realization of a need to be a better person—in a sense you will understand. As with everything, at base, it has to do with my music more than with other factors. . . . There was an experience, a key one—nothing at all overt— with that butler of Edna's years and years ago: a secret recognition between us, ex-slave to new slave. Were these the beginnings or is one simply born to it? That with that black servant, whom I loved for a corruption I sensed in him and wanted both to emulate and correct; seeing those gardeners through Edna's windows as I played, women everywhere close to me, between me and them—a world of women (including Herman?)—that may have turned me: art and women, with (it was literally dark, as it happened, the kid-glove kids too maybe) maleness—not speaking of Papa— prowling beyond reach, saying in effect that I was in the wrong shop and had better get out on any terms if I wished to be useful and, well, good. Now, can I get out of the second world?—rather, join the two?

"I have a typical letter from Aunt Annette, sounding as all our family does as if she doesn't belong to it, giving her seal to Eve and me. But no word from Papa, not that it's needed! I'm packing it all up now. I look around and love the room I've worked in so well but warn myself against loving rooms. My final gesture will be to put back on the walls all the *vergolden* mirrors and sepia scenes of Rome, say good-by to my landlady, who weeps for music of and in itself and says of my Carolina lynch-law opera that the world is better for the sweetness I bring it, then I won't look back."

217

Randall Schiff wrote a note on French Line stationery.

"I have just left Eve. It's over. My heart is with you both, as well as my warmest hopes and wishes for the future. Your sincerely admiring friend . . ."

"But if that was the point at which you panicked, when did you come around?" Eve would ask.

"I didn't. It was an act of hostility meeting you. I hated you. You were killing me. I went like a soldier to meet you."

She would say, grinning, "And I settled your hash, didn't I?"

THREE |  **1930**

•

January 1. But really two hours into Jan. 2. Dinner at the Petits' and quite all right. She is really ill and only put in an appearance, looking regal and remote, in actual pain I'm sure. She appeals to Alex, who, as I observed, does not mind illness, and he caught me up on it, trying to get me to say he fed on it. He's had one or two (he claims five, but it's not true) bad days and is spoiling for a fight, which I don't give him. He was all smiles and belligerence at dinner, brilliantly angry at one of Henry's guests, a local official, and being dangerously frank about Fascism, though the man had charm and a cool head and would not be baited. Borthwick, the horrible English writer, was also there on my right, but since he knows that Alex is a Jew and that I am "with him," as he rudely said, he could only be silent, at least to me. He is a good writer some of the time. Villains are sometimes great artists, Alex points out, but I say I don't see how that can be. "Dostoevsky was a Jew baiter," he says, "and so was Degas."

Alex suffers in a way, when he is not working well, that makes me certain I will fail him. He goes silent and steely, becomes businesslike, alert, poisonously courteous, picks fights with waiters, and generally makes himself disagreeable. I try to reach him, knowing the importance of what he is going through, but it is not easy to do. I can only say "I love you," feeling muddy myself, yet putting him first on purpose. At the same time I tease. "You haven't been out of it for a week," I say. "It's two days." I can't help being accurate. He says now that Taormina—perhaps Sicily as a choice—was a mistake for us, meaning for him, because there is too much

221

expatriate social life. In fact, *I* have not worked in three weeks. Alex says, "How can you bear it?" because he could not. Tonight I said to him, "What you don't understand is that now, thanks to you—my love—I have a sense of survival that lasts for whole hours at a time."

On my left was the Petits' local doctor, a plump lecher who emphasized opinions with a hand on my knee, and once as if by accident well up my thigh—he all pink and silver with a high starched collar, me sallow in the reflection in his eyeglasses. I kept glancing at Alex, who was being amusing with the American countess whose concerts he will do in the spring, and he seemed to catch on and did a, to me, hilarious parody of an irritated husband, frowning and rolling his eyes at the doctor. But in fact the man's hand, clean as could be, the nails pink and gleaming, a few black hairs on the knuckles, rather set me off. Also I was drinking, which Alex was not, though he would say he had been. Borthwick was eying Alex and at one point asked, "How old is he?" I said who? And then, because I can't hold out against these bastards: "Twenty-five." He grunted enviously, drunk. Alex's looks and style—he can be funny even when he's angry—are compelling. He is one of those who draw the glances of a whole table, for whom people listen, though they talk to the one next to them. Even when he is quiet, attending, there is a ferocity in his silence that compels people's looks. Petit proposed toasts, including a vague rabbity one to "Democracy." For a moment I thought Borthwick or the official was going to propose Il Duce, but neither did. Henry's chair is under the portrait of him by Colin Brady that shows him seated in an armchair, wearing tails and topper, in the center of Red Square, which the Fascists pretend amuses them; the whole scene was quite good. At the end, very medieval, Henry sent a servant with a lantern to light our way downhill, which meant half an hour down for the poor man and an hour back, and a tip from Alex, which we cannot afford. And then despite extremely troublesome kalooah brought on by the drink and the pawing, no moonlight. Alex, as if he were tight, went to sleep at once.

●

January 9. Alex is going through the old journal, inspired by the fact that I have begun entries again. When Graziella has cleared the table after lunch, he moves into the sun and sits sweating and bare-chested, "going at it." I'm not supposed to watch, but I do from my window, and he becomes aware of me there. "I don't remember this happening!" he calls. The sea is spread out behind and below him. Lizards run across the wall, then down and over the terrace. Once I saw one go across his bare foot. He glanced at it, then at me with a happy grin.

I have begun to work a little. Just getting Guy Porter— over 1000 pages of him—from the suitcase under the bed, along with the bundles of notes, is a victory. Now I'm only reading. The verdict: it could be worse. I think that resuming this journal helps objectify. Alex, of course, is now working, though to have told him the machinery had been running for him all the time, out of gear, would have been tantamount to suicide. The thing is that what he's trying is classical, the manner monumental, non-naturalistic, generic. It speaks of Death, Love, not by example but directly, against which I've warned him before. Yet, by God, his talent seems to carry it, and each song has that iron quality of having existed always in precisely that form!

Concerning the journal and his objectivity, I say, denying his idea of himself, "But you are better than other people!"

". . . having to see myself through your eyes without liking what I see and at the same time having to be cheerfully remote," he interprets.

January 10. My Italian is stiff, limited to what I can say correctly, but Alex simply plunges in. Graziella's brother Carlo is in the hospital in Catania. In all likelihood it's a gallstone, a disaster for this family, which relies on each member's income to manage. Carlo is a waiter in one of the restaurants we go to in town. Probably there will be an operation. Graziella has been with us only a month but we—Alex especially, of course—already know the family and its difficulties and are considered by them to be friends. She is plump and untidy, though clean, and filled with anxiety concerning her relatives, even when none is called for. There are two other brothers, both waiters in cafés on the main square. The father is chronically ill, an angry man, a secret Communist (though one sees not all that secret) who runs a scissors-and-knife-grinding hole-in-the-wall in town on a lease-share basis. They are bitterly poor, all of them. The whole country, of course, is desperate. Those here, attending to the whims of expatriates and visitors, don't do as badly. Alex and I are going to take the bus to Catania tomorrow to see if we can be of help. Graziella wept with nerves, and I did too.

At work.

I hear his piano (getting that down the path from the road is now one of the local sagas)—the handful of notes played, tried out rather, varied, tried again, the line sung in his sweet high voice (yet it is powerful), like a window part opened on sound, and it makes me still. I am motionless, my work set out in sections around me, the notes in "German" arrangements, with indexes and so on. I'm oddly content.

I have tables arranged in an L under the window, as in New York, but with a difference! Here I see the vine of bougainvillaea, the wall of our neighbor's grand house, his fig, citrus with the yellow and orange pocked fruit in their black leaves, clumps of cactus (Petit says cactus in the Mediterranean came originally from the New World!), a patch of dark blue sea crossed by fishing boats, the white-layered horizon and blue-black sky, lizards!

This morning when Alex came to my door at his break, punctually at ten-fifteen, I said, forestalling him, "Not too bad. Something good is coming to the surface"—the point being not to throw him off, since he always has his own next session to handle. He wanted to know, as he has asked before, if my hearing him was part of the problem. I said, "There is no problem just now. I'm absolutely okay. If I thought your consciousness of me would make you timid, I'd set up somewhere else! Thank God, you don't try to keep the strength out of your voice."

●

January 19. Sunday. Some queasiness. Alex off to swim alone, then up to town to see the countess, possibly Petit. We dislike Sunday. If he runs into Henry's doctor, he may bring him down, casually, as if for a drink. My skin has begun to react to the sun, and I must keep out of it, I suppose. Damn my luck! Alex is the color of stained wood.

He came back rather late. I was in bed in the room, no light. My God: Sunday! We both take it off from work and of course should not. There is my stuff on the tables, yet this is now a bedroom. I am dark, unhopeful. Alex tried to be amusing for me, meaning that he *was* so, only I could not respond. I kept having to go out to the privy, which must have been off-putting. Yet when we went to bed—early, Alex pining for Monday morning and his work—we had what might have passed for a good moonlight, then, at his suggestion, slept against each other like spoons, which I adore. Now, in the morning, hearing him, I am filled with the idea of survival.

January 20. Having gone over into this day . . . Remarkably hot. A good swim, though I stay in the shade of the rocks afterward. We swim far, far out, Alex going slowly for me, sidestroking and talking all the way. Marvelous! We see Graziella watching from the balcony halfway up the cliff. "My God, look at us! Look where we are!" White, blanched-white cliffs with the lush road running zigzag down, making all green, as if it were a river. A dark blue sky, which hangs low. The sea tugging at our legs. It desires us, of course. Alex says he is always seeking the horizon and longing to reach it, but I long for the deeps. Sometimes when I say so, I get what he calls "the look"—drugged, he claims, as if I am hoping for it at once. Then he is angry. He knows when I say I love the sea, I mean it. What I seem to want is to drink it in, have it inside as well as out, which happens to be death: surely the most desirable death. The sexual symbolism noted too. I am evidently in a manic phase but not too scared of it.

Also, I'm eating. I ate breakfast. I will polish off whole platefuls of Graziella's pasta, cakes, steak, drink wine at every meal. I seem to want to smoke three cigarettes at once. It's not sexual, though of course it all is. One isn't sure which comes first. Alex says of it, oddly, that it's innocence. "Right, baby," I say. "I am innocent. And what is more"—making him laugh—"I really am." . . . When we rented the house we took down the mirrors, since we are readily distracted. Now I mean to put them back. Alex, being a genius, can see such excitement only in terms of work and assumes mine is suddenly going great guns. But how could it, he wonders, since yesterday's mood? Of course, I did nothing but listen to his beautiful work, my head helplessly turning to it in that lovely room made blue by bougainvillaea. I will be good for weeks on this! Yet, don't I know the penalties!

●

January 21. Actually put the mirrors back up, making Alex grin. I demanded, dragging him before the big one in the hall, as if before a judge: "I may look sad and you may look tense, but Jesus, we're young, without a line or care! Look how smooth!"

"Beautiful."

"Well, you are!"

●

January 25. At night we undressed before the mirror in the dining room, which is Alex's studio, while he kept glancing at the upright as if it were a policeman, then we walked naked to the one in the hall. I turned him and myself this way and that. We didn't speak. He took the initiative, and I deferred. If I could make him stop thinking that the next day's work will be affected by this night's pleasure! It's all sin-penalty. Of course, I'm the same, only I take time to do battle against it, whereas Alex minds nothing, is at peace, as long as his core—that is, his opera—goes. Apologetically, he indicated the appendicitis scar (distracting the gods from my red spots), and I, unstrung, knelt before him, which had not been my intention, since I have been bending efforts toward full moonlights. So that was that, except for something perfunctory for me later on in bed.

When we finally got ourselves down to Catania, it turned out that Carlo had discharged himself from the hospital, and Graziella had failed to inform us! "Then he must be well!"—angry and relieved. But Alex felt there was more to it. Graziella, when we told her, kept shaking her head. *"Maleducato,"* she said of her brother. It seems, according to her, that he actually is not well but on the other hand is very

227

lazy. She looked distressed. Alex says this is a habit of self-pity she's fallen into.

Still hot—unbelievably for January. We walk down to the beach. The fishermen look me over. They hide their women in dark clothes inside dark houses—women, donkeys, babies all together—and of course look at me—or did—as if I were the Babylonian woman in my trousers, with my cigarettes, or (gosh!) in a bathing costume. Alex gets tough admiring looks, as if he had had the courage to bring off something semi-criminal. But now they are more or less used to us and even give a nod or raise a friendly thumb. At first we wondered when they worked, thinking the high-sided craft with their lookout eyes on the prows never went out—Alex concerned about resources and adequate income—that perhaps there were no fish. Now we know these men have been out and back before we wake in the morning and taken their catches to the Duce-built auction wharf for weighing. Of course, prices are fixed, and they get next to nothing. They're brown and handsome, with Greek eyes and narrow powerful bodies —the legs and feet lovely. Old or young, it's the same. They get very old rather young, the way actors do, retaining beauty. They cook their breakfast—fish, of course—right in the boats over fuel-can fires and pass around wine and loaves of fresh bread the size of bicycle wheels. Cats arrive by the dozen and are tossed entrails and other treats. Alex has made the acquaintance of one family, and we are offered breakfast, a courteous ceremony of invitation and refusal.

The noon swim: the sky gets white with heat. Floating far out, I compose whole acts of plays. Perfect dialogue. Perfect, all-encompassing histories! Fishing craft sit on heat islands. There is no horizon. The colors of the men's shirts and ker-chiefs ashore, the flags on the wharfside trattoria are faded to near white. I think and immediately say, "I would love to see Asher!" I apostrophize the sun, but Alex addresses his toes. My play, finished, produced, is a success. "Don't look into the sun, for God's sake!" Alex cries. "You'll go blind!"

I describe the threat of the depth beneath me. I ask if he

228

thinks I love death, and he gets clever, quoting my own description of my mother as being "in full cry" after life, applying it to me. He wants to deny my ease with death, jealous of it. Trickily he says, "But if you do, how can it be wrong?"—as if what I really wanted was to be wrong!

"Can you see Graziella?"

We wave.

"Look at this place!"

I say, "My Lord, the Sun!"

I mean Alex but am too shy to say so.

At night, sweating to achieve moonlight (Alex calls it contending against the devil), I say, "Imagine the sun while I imagine the moon."

Back on the beach, I'm aware of the men looking at my breasts in the wet bathing suit.

●

January 27. Alex has played the difficult scene, now resolved, I think. And he played the ending. I had to grit my teeth, feeling trampled upon. I would not cry. Petit, who was there with a friend of his, looked as if he had been flung against the wall. I talked later to Alex about feeling greatness in it, and he said, making no denials, that I would not feel it throughout.

We had walked up into the hills above town before supper with Petit. A shepherd who plays a pipe and tambourine in one of the *caves* in town lives in an actual cave three miles outside and above with his wife, who is desperately ill. Petit will take us there one day. This time, however, we returned, and Alex played, and Petit was miraculously reduced to silence, so that his friend stared. There is a pattern of ill wives here. I suppose I will be one.

A good moonlight, except that his bobby kept slipping out. Reviews (précis) thus far (month past) for M-G-M: *L'Enfer d'Amour, La petite Infante de Castille,* the Erika/Klaus Mann book, *Koenigsmark, Si le Grain ne muert.* Income: $25. Alex gets his remittance, but now, with the bank's doors all but closed, it is made up by his father and Fran (really Bob Gamble): about $50 a month. I'll holiday from précis for one week, get into Guy P. . . .

Afterward, Alex demanded of me belligerently (the boy claiming his treat after chores?), "Do you love me?"

Irretrievably, irrevocably, helplessly.

"Yes."

•

January 28. After watching him read the journal of Paris–New York, '27–'28, for an hour, feeling I could get away with it, I said, "Where are you?" He gave dates.

"I'll bet you're having trouble being objective about that stuff."

"I'm never that."

"You are." Daring to tease him and make a point. "It seems to me high time you began to mind a little all the good rapes and fucks I've had."

Meaning, of course, that he takes it too well, cutting himself adrift from his own emotions. He saw the lesson, which sounds insufferable in me, only I know that if he's protected in order to work, he will accept that.

•

February 5. Still good, though the weather not what it was, the air thick without being cooler. I'm working each day, and Alex works with the energy of his genius. I find my mind on his work as much as mine. His libretto concerns the Achæan

230

League and Aratus but with contemporary parallels, deliberate anachronisms, and so on. Even his last piece had classical references throughout. "Why is that necessary always?" I ask. It gives him a peg to hang things on; yet he can't do it without being satirical about it—parodying the sugary neoclassicism of the past decade—which means that he wants to be free of it. It's not what I meant by indirect, acknowledging a fashionable (nearly finished) trend. Yet he does it marvelously well, as Asher has already said in an article. His ability to be funny in himself and in his work, something my solemnity seems to provoke, is his strength and weakness. I've projected and outlined a *Modern Music* piece touching on theater themes in music, comedy, tragedy, etc., and Alex approves . . . In fact, his libretto has become so generalized by now, meaning simply the exploitation of man by man, that with minor changes it could, and perhaps should, become a garment workers' strike in New York's Lower East Side. I said this, and it made him irritable because he saw the possibility, which in turn threatened. "Don't take out your high good humor on me." He persuaded me it could not work, however.

I should be writing but I'm doing this. A letter from *The Bookman* offers $40 per month to do its French and German "Notes" on a trial basis. What power the prospect of money brings!—unimpeded views of the horizon.

A reply to my letter to my father, in which I said that Alex threatened to become "literature" to me, that the sense of my mission seemed to be fading. "You feel guilty," he said, "because you sense me 'waiting for a book.' I am waiting for nothing from you except to hear of your happiness, which your letter seems to tell me you have at last. Now there is nothing to wait for." Alex failed to see this as ominous. He is distracted by a letter from Fran saying that her older boy, Patrick, is ill, apparently seriously, with an infection. Oddly, nothing—the weather, these somber reports—affects my joy, which continues to ascend. There is no trace now of a fear of failure—that I will fail Alex. If Patrick is very ill, knowing Alex's ties, Alex ought to go home. More anger, again because he is tempted by what I offer. I would go back to Paris, I suppose, and wait for him. At some point anyway, when this work is complete, he should be in the U.S. arranging performances. He ought to try for the Prix de Rome again, and that can best be done at home. All of it has us fighting in a manageable way. I think of the bitterness of his having to cope —go through things away from me—but it's a selfish feeling. He says he's not going anywhere. Why am I thinking of ways to deal with being apart when he has no intention of leaving? . . . Patrick has an ear infection, not an ordinary one.

●

February 10. Alex has written a killing piece for *M.M.*, which will make no one, not even Asher, happy. He talks about Asher's mystic and penitential ego in the new symphonic piece as being simply un-thought out; Hindemith's "fatal virtuoso gift"; Gershwin as being short of breath; Křenek deadly, trying to seem irrepressible. And so on. We argued but agree basically.

●

February 11. Alex in a black mood, work halted. He has lost his wallet with passport once more, which is one of the symptoms, and stormed up to the police insulting every Fascist in sight for failing to pull it out of thin air for him. They remembered him from last time. *"Calma, calma"*—which is meant to infuriate, of course. They made him fill in forms. There was no money in the wallet.

Then we had his birthday—placid except for dinner. We went to the San Domenico, my disastrous choice because I wanted to see the gardens. It was beyond our means except for a saved-for celebration, and Alex felt affronted even before we ordered. The least negligence enraged him. The staff, with the antennae of their race, caught on to him and were rude in earnest. Alex did not rest until he had frozen everyone into ironic acquiescence and low bows. And then, to punish us all, he left a gargantuan tip.

Our fight followed, flinging insults at each other as we walked Indian file down the path from the road to the house, Alex helping me over small stones, me quite good, I thought: catlike, contained yet available. Of course, I wasn't. We "went through" my father. I was accused of being wrapped up in him, which I admitted. A female Orestes. I said, "The trouble is you can't think of the appropriate lady Greek." Then his father, and the fur flew. Speaking of the tone of Saul's letters—I find them whining and nagging in an old-maid way about money, health, and behavior (meaning me) —I said that the man had in effect died with his mother, that he was an adjunct or parasite of her, and that Alex must take care not to maintain the same relationship with his father, which his father would of course welcome. Oh, boy! Altogether cleansing, though, and I tried to steer the energy to a moonlight. He resisted, as I now think he should have, feeling that that would be a form of babying in the circumstances. We were conscious of the fact, and it was ultimately our way to peace, that Francesca had not been brought into any of the arguments. I had sometime since agreed that he was not in love with her any more than I am with my father, nor she with him. (Knowing this on both sides—dealing with whatever truth might lie in the "pop" psychological stuff— is at the basis of us as a possibility in the first place. Now they are unassailable Articles.) I told him that at times like these I think of her as my only friend. Yet I do live in fear that Alex will fall in love with someone else.

February 14. Patrick is no better and no worse. There is talk of an operation but as a final resort. I sit and listen to Alex hammer at it, trying to smash down the barriers between him and music. I go and lean against the wall, close my eyes, and, instead of thinking of the little nephew, pray for Alex's work!

I'm typing out—remembering it—one of the passages—August '28—which I had suppressed for Alex's reading of last month. It was about him, naturally: after he had been in Paris, made his confession, then gone to Berlin. Randall was away, and Max Luddon carried me off, doing his well-known special raping stuff to the American gals—to Luna Park, all as it were delicious childlike fun—and to that three-asterisk place where the food is dreadful (or anyhow I don't eat when money is spent), and all the time I was thinking of Alex: his shining smile, which is his joy for his life; his work in life, the devotion to it; his conscious act, as an artist and a man, to go inward in order to go outward to others unselfishly. I had an hour or so, knew what Max would expect of me (quite properly) as the end of his expensive evening. And in fact I had already as much as promised it. So I went back to my room to dress for theater and had a *crise* of immense importance, one that led ultimately to the agreements with Alex in Austria later: me as a devil wrestling both Alex and Max—the image of it—a fight between Alex's qualities, *what he is*—his eternalness—and Max's raping kind of life-love, in which people are put to his uses rather than the other way around. And Alex won. "No, I won't!" I actually cried. Because of course, ordinarily I would have gone straight between the sheets with Max. I had stripped off my clothes—it seems ludicrous in recollection—and was literally running around my room fighting it! Of course, I was tight, and there was the physical pressure, but in fact I quelled it! Rather, Alex did. And when I saw Max the pressure had utterly gone. I did not go to bed with him, though I had said I would and he is so

234

sad a man (and just then very angry as well). But it would have been empty. . . . My Valentine to Alex.

In the evening, swimming, I said, "What I call your ruthlessness forces out self-pity, not self-sympathy. On the whole I find that I have pity for myself and little sympathy. Your being the way you are is one of the reasons I trust you. Where did you learn that?—to see yourself as part of the landscape."

If it was true, he supposed through trial and error, seeing what worked.

We swam to where the sun was past the shadow cast by the cliffs. "We are getting into each other," I said. "Turning to each other."

We went seaward with the shadow, then back, teeth chattering, bumpy with cold, across the black water, and toweled ourselves before the fishermen. This feels like winter.

"I think you deserve to be protected for your work."

It irritated him.

I'm starting to do something at night, and it does not go badly. Alex reads novels, goes to see Petit and his guests, sometimes doing the hot spots with them. The shepherd with the ill wife plays in three nightclubs, running from one to the other. Yet he is, Alex reports, a dignified man who respects his talent and does not complain of poverty. After it all he must climb up the mountain, sleep briefly, and be up at dawn boiling milk for cheese. The poverty of the island is heartbreaking. Of course, only Communism can cure it. But how is it to come about? Any soldier needs nourishing food on which to fight, but Fascism sees that none is available. Now that America is learning what hunger is like—the invention of hell must have come from the experience of hunger and seeing hungry children—it will bring about a change and soon. But again, food has to be found for the fighters, food even before the weapon of knowledge.

Alex comes home, I wrap up my little paragraph, and we talk in bed. The party had taken Graziella's brother Carlo in tow. He is idle, angry. There *is* an operation needed, but he can't afford it, can't find work. He wants to enroll in the waiters' school here and then go to Palermo or Naples for work in a hotel, but there is no chance. When Petit went off with his tambourine boy, Alex, Carlo, and the shepherd talked. There was also a young fisherman from our beach, the grandson of the one Alex and I call Saint Peter, who regularly does the night rounds, and he joined them. Alex is making notations of the shepherd's songs, some of which he thinks must go back to Homer, and wants to pay for them. Money . . . The shepherd said he admires *me*—a woman writing books. To him any matter of the intellect is more important than anything else!

"Of course, he won't take anything, will he?"

"No," Alex said.

I said, "Did the boy"—the young fisherman—"make you an offer?"

"He doesn't any more. Borthwick was there, and they seem to go more or less together."

It's the worst thing of all—the worst thing hunger brings about: the selling of bodies. I asked Alex if he was tempted. "No."

I have written Randall saying that there have been few moonlights of the true sort between Alex and me to date and as a result feel disloyal. Yet it's the kind of thing I have always told Randall. Ultimately I'll tell Alex I did so. I said in bed, "I need what you give me because it comes from you, not simply because I need it."

•

February 16. Sunday! I forgot to say that the wallet had not been lost at all but was behind a cabinet in Alex's workroom, where Graziella must have knocked it while cleaning. He had to go and explain to the police, which was difficult.

I find an edge coming on this phase. The weather has to do with it, the north wind starting its stuff. We walk to the beach

morning and evening but not to swim: silent before breakfast, talking plenty before supper, up and down the rocky
strip, eyes fixed on the sand or on the horizon. When he does
not respond to my talk of sea life and sea death, I say, "You
had better take me seriously!" The fishermen watch out of
the corners of their black olive eyes. One sits asleep, a net
upon his knees. His legs, crossed at the ankles, are slashed
with pale scars, desiccated, showing the long bones. He
wakes abruptly and uses Alex's arm, as a child would, to pull
himself upright. "You are something magnificent," I say to
Alex later.

●

February 18. I'm conscious of the entrance of illness, its announcement like notes of music. A presage. Me being me, it
is thrilling.

Alex has finished the journal, excepting recent stuff, and
has been going over Guy Porter. He makes notes, no comments.

Rudeness is one symptom. The postman, who had been
delighted by the relationship between the young artists and
always passed mail over the threshold in two parts—"Signor
Weisshorn! Signorina Schiff!" mangling the names—complained about the trip down the steep rocky path and the
quantity of mail. I let him have it with both barrels, and Alex,
seeing me upset, did too—poor man. He simply wants bigger
tips. He used to carry messages: "Signor Petit *dice* cocktails!"
—crying it out from the road. Now I suppose he won't. In any
event, letters come. We are to be descended upon in April
and May—Edna Loux and Jane Framingham, who has been
very ill. (For Alex, it's as if his mother were coming, which
is not beyond the realm of possibility either.) Asher may
appear with Johnny Gregson, who, Asher writes, is in a state,
and Abe Rappaport, Moak's new prodigy, and perhaps Fisher

Blumenblatt, who turned out to be a mutual friend of mine and Alex in our pasts. The Paris people are all either coming here or going to North Africa, where things are very cheap.

Patrick not well. I see it working on Alex. . . . He has resolved the impediment in his opera. Henry came down with Moyer, who is the Petit secretary–jack-of-trades, and two lady guests, Americans who landed in Palermo and are "working their way up" to London, from which they will be discharged back to America. Both are rich, and Henry is thinking of them, or one of them, as a patroness for Alex. Alex performed marvelously, doing the whole piece, improvising incomplete parts. I am reminded that he is immensely theatrical and dashing—a first-rate performer. For one thing, he plays well, which, with the power of the words—the silky horrors described—impales people, particularly those new to it. Like all good actors, he is suddenly enlarged in the room in which he performs, occupying the place of at least two ordinary men. This, with his transparent admiration of his own work, his belief in it, is fatally charming. Of course, he is the courtliest host imaginable.

We walked into the hills afterward, feeling triumphant. Inspired, I said to Alex, "You're my sun," as I have before. "The importance you give our doings! You say, 'We must now go to the top of this hill village and look down: the utility, it being us, of looking down. *We* must.' We lead, do what's needful, and, duty done, advise others, making them worthy." And then, lofty in spirit as well as in fact, on the threshold of our mornings as artists, *blooming* (me with an illness in the offing), we did actually look down through orchards of almond and olive, mimosa and pine, across the villages all the way to the sea. Of course, there was satire in my address, but Alex took it seriously and disapproved. Wasn't it enough to be whoring with potential patrons without this self-love?

Alex is an interesting man.

I see that when he does well, as in the day's performance, he must punish himself at once. He chews angrily on the inside of his cheek, gouges a finger with his nails as he talks until blood comes. When he says something good, he is angry with himself and punishes his beautiful hands.

He talked about his fear of becoming a personage, an actor in the scenes of his life, rather than the artist who creates the actors. He feels he must get outside of himself and see everything! Then what about me? I, who exist in the moment only and now only for him, have, I fear, been devoted to the idea of work. Have I transferred to the idea of Alex?

A muffling of sound, the sensation drugs induce.

I dreamed solutions to structural problems in Guy Porter and got up at midnight to make notes. The notions are no good, of course, and I'm writing this instead. . . . I think I was rude to Graziella today. Alex assures me I was not.

For précis of six novels: $30, plus a $10 bonus, which was a miracle. Not a bad month—really three weeks.

Definitely getting sick. I will tell Alex tomorrow.

●

February 25. Alex coming down with it too, so we are to be ill together, which is perhaps to the good.

●

February 26. He keeps going in to look at his manuscripts. Mine are locked up out of sight.

Petit's doctor comes with flowers. He makes me lie down and searches my meager body. With Alex, he's perfunctory. "I'll listen to you play your composition when you're better," he says as if to reward him.

Bronchitis. I say bronchial pneumonia. Much coughing, feeling fevered and ill.

239

●

February 27. The moon full. It blazes.

●

March 1. In like a lion. Still ill. Night after night of full moon. We try closing the shutters but they cast shadows and enter the fever dreams. The moon is like an ice sun, filling every corner. We lie facing away from each other, coughing and sleepless. When we must rise, we cast jet shadows in the snowy mooniness. We smoke a puff or two, cough our heads off and talk. Quite ill.

We assist each other to the privy, our way clear, sky blue as night skies in Christmas illuminations, stars pale, as if shocked by the moon's conquest. Clouds are red close in to the moon, bone white farther off. Only in the back of the sky can one find darkness. One feels that with light such as that no sun should be needed again. The sea is a final glory, giving meaning to the light. And the fishermen are all out, scattered from here to Greece, showing dim running lights, for no flares are needed to see.

●

March 3. Having fights, which means improvement. Angry, we try to sleep, legs tangled, unable not to touch. I say we're between drowning one another and saving one another, but Alex wants none of my talk. When we fight, it is with viciousness, accusingly, raging against each other.

•

March 4. Our mailman brings the letters in packets of ten or so every four or five days to save himself the climb. Randall is sending messages about needing me. Fran writes that the boy need not be operated upon yet. A check from M-G-M makes up for much.

Persistent kalooah and Alex no help. I'll make a play for anyone Asher Moak brings who's the least bit normal.

•

March 5. Moony nights. We are not only ill but really half mad. There is no one like Alex, who understands everything beforehand. He says he is moving toward something. I ask him to tell his most regular sexual fantasy, and he comes up at once with a textbook dream that's not what I meant but is of interest.

He is a child mendicant—a beggar in a shawl—and someone, his sister possibly, takes him in, babies him, and promises to keep him safe from harm. She seats him at a window so that he can look out, safe and snug, on the world he has escaped from. He has been given tea and a sandwich, and he eats and looks on. He doesn't see this as sexual in itself but recognizes it as being at the base of a maladjustment—an instilled wish to acquiesce in any attention being paid to himself. The tension of his life is his resistance to that temptation, he says. I had been talking about fantasies of bottoms and public shame, not an image prepared over the years, but, as he says himself, his madness is self-control. He admits anything, respectfully and sexlessly, as if he's talking about someone who's dead. I am supposed to speak in textbook terms about my urges: the little girl watches her father shave and plots ways to get rid of mother.

Not that this business of resistance in Alex isn't all-important. I rack my brains, feeling that the opportunity may slide. (He *has* said he is moving toward something.) If I praise him, he turns on me. But he demands praise as he does love. He demands love and throws it in my teeth: the child is not to be indulged. And he fears a loosening of the tension, upon which his work discipline is based, so that I'm warned not to try to cure him.

I make my way down my own narrow track. I tell him I'll go to bed with anyone. I tell him naughty stories. He listens politely.

I dreamed that I woke at noon and lay in the hot white room. (The ceiling was stained blue, as it is in fact by the bougainvillaea in the window.) My alarm clocks lay broken on the floor around the bed. Alex came in dressed in cream-colored flannels—vest, trousers, jacket—dark blue shirt, white tie. "Well, it seems we brought one off," I said.

"What?"

"A perfectly marvelous moonlight. I came three times."

"But I was out last night."

Oh, baby.

It was midnight when I woke from the dream. I told it to Alex, and he laughed in a way which meant he appreciated it as literature.

●

March 8, 9. Unsatisfactory moonlights. "Helping each other out." . . . The doctor was making one of his tours of inspection of my breasts and discovered the old lump. I said it was in the last stage of being absorbed. Such items seem to increase his sexual itch. He dotes on my boniness, my pallor. His plump fingers met around my upper arm and he was in ecstasy. If I were alone in the house, I'd let him get in bed with me.

Henry came with the news that the head of the Soviet trade delegation in Paris is to be a house guest next month.

242

He is terribly excited about it. He stands in the road because he is afraid of infection, shouts at our bedroom window, and we shout back hoarsely. He sent in a new pamphlet, which Alex and I read to each other. Most interesting picture of the American Negro, in fact Negroes everywhere, as being really one nation in themselves—that is, an oppressed nation. White and black proletarians are not identical but allies in the class struggle with the mutual aim of overturning the capitalist enemy. Alex objects. I say that it is functional revolutionary technique based on the sound theory of recognizing and encouraging nationalist roots. Alex insists on identity and starting at the top—internationally speaking—but that is simply not practical. . . . A good talk.

•

March 13. Something is building. This is the longest manic phase I've ever known, and it continues, oddly, in spite or very likely because of illness, to climb.

His nephew is to undergo an operation—a mastoidectomy: very dangerous. But probably it is finished with as of this date. Alex is frantic. Coughing his head off, he began to pack manuscripts. I said, "You must go," meaning it, yet knowing that from another point of view he should not, and already wondering how I will live without him. I think he must go or there will always be blame, for himself and for me. Probably I would wait in Paris, and we would meet in Rome in the fall, he having gotten the Prix. I said, "It may be that I need to be on my own again now in Paris, working as I did before. We may be better for each other after a separation."

A letter from Fran to me—generous and loving—about Patrick. It was Tony, the baby, who always suffered from ear infections, and so this came as a surprise. The burden, anyway: Alex is not to come. He would not be of use.

But I began strapping up my own manuscripts (how I love

packing work!) and planning how to get out of our lease. I said to the doctor, "Alexis is going to get a boat in Palermo. Is he well enough?"

"He's as strong as a horse"—perhaps thinking that then I would come and sit on his lap in silk underwear and pull his bobby for him. (In fairness, at the prospect of being on my own, I do think at once of ways of misbehaving.)

●

March 15. Cables. "Operation a success. Pat well." But from Alex's father: "Pat fair after surgery."

Alex cabled: "Require truth, nothing less." Which, he said later, will probably stand as his only immortal line. In the meantime, we postpone plans. Alex, in his anxiety, is like an injured dog. He eyes me but doesn't turn to me. He would bite if I touched him. He goes in to stand over the table on which his orchestra score, just begun, lies open, humming through clenched teeth. I stand in the door and watch him against the light. His eyes are washed pale. His lovely Jewish profile hangs over the pages. He looks ill, ravaged, and simultaneously in burning good health. His scores are works of art. If he makes an error—a spot of ink—out goes the whole section. He looks over the pages of beautiful notes as if it were graphic art, singing the notes as easily as breathing. Then I love him and determine to give up everything to him.

●

March 16. He asked for a cabled reply from Fran.

March 17. No word. We have moved to chairs on the terrace.

Alex had been steadily consuming the new Guy Porter. He chose this morning on the terrace for giving his reaction, which led to tonight and everything else.

"It's no good," he said.

He denies those words, but it amounted to that. He disliked it and, being Alex, a soldier of art, said so without ceremony, though he spoke with all the urgency anyone could have wished. He went on about it, going into chapters and paragraphs. I will not reproduce my notes here. He kept turning aside to cough into his fist, his nervousness intensifying the cough. Here is what it amounted to, all of it true, I think. I'm in love with a romantic image of myself as the moody bitch, and all the major characters, heavily equipped with my ideas, are mirrors to the image. He pointed out that both the minor people and the figures in my journal are objectively conceived and therefore realer. I am not to think that because I claim in the journal that John Cournos, or Morley Callaghan, or So-and-so said something, that they actually said it, nor that a book character did not say something simply because I made up his name. It's much more a case of keeping one's eye on the subject—the real tree—instead of one's idea of it (Cézanne's painting of a tree, or, equally fatal to art, the perfect Plato tree). When instruction walks in the door, art flies out the window. Style. He says that the journal's "non-style," which serves subject, tends to work. The novel's style, "oddly sexless, Germanic battle hero, unconquerable, and heavy, and marching before the subject," does not.

And much more. He was good both in himself and in what he said. I wanted to cry out, "How can you know all this at your age?" but it would have seemed defensive. He tore down, then produced ideas for cures—practical notions, usable suggestions, leaving me with something for the next day: turned me inside out, looked over everything, turned me

245

back again. There was an exhilaration in this, unlike the MacDowell session, which is indescribable. "If I'm romantic, then I'm slavish, self-abnegating, and frightened," I said, but he claimed that was massage, too quick on the uptake. "Well, then I must kill Christina Rossetti in myself anyhow."

"Yes."

"Even if it kills Eve."

"Of course. How can you expect to profit if there is no risk? You mustn't use this criticism of one novel for general purposes, though."

I had to keep trying the pain points at which the novelist could be killed and still manage not to take it personally!

We talked—he mostly—for three or more hours.

One of the examples he used of good stuff was the passage in the journal about Ian, the English boy—his virginity, looking for a hotel and finding one (the Palais Royal, I now recall), the electrifying discovery in myself that I was going to respond to his need, and then doing so. . . . All of this in recollection acted on me and on Alex. It was clear that it was acting upon us: both the story and the resurrecting character of Alex's killing criticism. I began to talk about Ian, his red elbows and knees (the ungainly beauty), the eyes of a blueness that colored his eyelids and upper cheeks, his failure, then success; above all, his need. It was how music acts on people, the effect of it on Alex and me.

And of course, having gotten at last into our appropriate roles (if that's it; I don't know), immediately after Graziella went home, we had our best moonlight ever.

●

March 18. Word at last. "Pat in no danger. Trust me in this." Which made all perfect.

246

●

March 20. It was no accident. The moonlights are good! I told Alex I want to send a cable to Randall. I'm half serious.

"I promise I won't get pregnant," I said, and we stared at each other. Wouldn't it be odd?

Blissful days.

●

March 22. We are no longer ill, yet we aren't well: for my money, perfection. I'm not going into motivations, except to marvel (snobbishly) that Alex and I are so readily available to currents. We simply responded to each other and are really in love. Whatever we were before, it was not just that.

He is working. I'm not yet. I lie here convalescent and hear him. It is spring. Graziella brings *olio in brodo,* which is her prescription, I smoke a cigarette, and that's lunch. Then I go with Alex to the terrace and, with this journal on my lap, look at flowers. They crowd around like the faces in Paris streets. The anemones are all colors—Oriental red ones in beds under the wall, dwarfish pale ones in shades of violet; each has a collar of leaves, from out of which its neck grows, getting longer every day. There is celandine—Henry comes and gives the flowers names since Alex and I are ignorant—which looks like a big buttercup and is used here, he claims, as a purgative. Veronica—a lot of conceited white and blue faces. They are all from Keats and Wordsworth, the names. I lie on a pair of chairs and gaze around, while Alex, slim with weight loss but hard, leans against the wall, against the sky, and looks me over, welcoming me from the dead. The big stuff: our hills, now yellow with mimosa and broom (almond gone); a spring sky, which means it is pale instead of that deep-dyed French blue; and the sea. The sea is perfect at this point, cross-ruffled by the nonstop winds (we are protected by the cliffside) and by the wakes of craft. It is transparent to a depth of some feet, then there is a hard dark layer, concentrated, cyanine. Farther out it is black.

Graziella smiles. Alex arrays himself with elegance, responding to our love. He breaks a sprig of rosemary from the bed at the terrace edge, rubs it in his brown hands, and brings me his cupped hands to sniff: piercing, minty.

●

March 23. I write Francesca, he my papa. "If it comes to it," I wind up, "and he must return in order to set up performances and try for the prizes while I remain, I will manage because now I know our relationship can handle separation. I'm *for* Alex. That is what has happened to me these months —learning to belong to him. Some part of this has been learning not to fear you: may I be as plain as that? . . . Fran, with your courage and your plain-spokenness and physical beauty, you are only magnificent. When Alex spoke of you years ago —glowingly, of course—I visualized you as the grande dame with bosom and glasses on a string. Then I thought, seeing snapshots: she's only a flapper, though a lovely one. Now that I've reached this port and all is a love fest for all, I am humbled by your steadfastness, which I say at the risk of embarrassing you and calling forth denials, and by your manifest unselfishness.

"I have got, I must tell you, a kind of mystical religion, people and place oriented: Alex, Randall, my father; the sea, certain rooms, certain paintings and pieces of music; actual things: objects, pantheistic, to pray to in my life and work. So I pray and have prayed, I tell you not for publication, for Alex, and young Patrick, and you. . . ."

I showed this to Alex, and he showed his, which answers for me one of my father's. My papa had been ill but mini-

248

mized it, of course, and Alex probed for facts, saying in effect that protecting me ought to be in his hands at the moment.

"We've said nothing about our illness."

"That's as it should be, of course," he said.

The sense of being at the dawn of things: how high we ride! It has gone past the question of survival, and I know I cannot fail him. Alex: this being, this talent . . . He watches me, lights a cigarette like a French tough, lets it hang between his lips, ducking away from the smoke, looks me over.

•

March 25. A plateau of genuine joy. Shakily, we go down to swim, lizards scattering before our feet, and proceed sedately in the warm water. Our house shimmers on the cliff in bands of violet. The sun beats around us, and we keep swinging into it, treading, the heat in colors against the insides of our lids. Alex sketches out a section of my nature for me, and I listen with attention. *"Am* I like that?" He reverts to my want of sympathy for myself, pointing out that nowhere in the journal is there a reference to my Paris poverty of seven years ago: the fact that I was hungry. He doesn't allow that I'm uncomplaining, only that I'm unjust.

"You mustn't leave things out."

Surprising insight.

We talk about homosexuality, not mincing words. Alex says it's wrong. It's fruitless in the obvious way, unproductive, therefore wrong: the developing Marxist in Alex. He is offhand about social difficulties, though I point out that the expatriate life helps that. One's acceptance of it in oneself, he says, is a little like "the business" of being Jewish, not meaning that it's wrong to be, he says conscientiously. "I'm cheerfully a Jew as long as there's anti-Semitism."

I'm half a Jew and not cheerfully.

Anyway, his point: it's wrong, and one does wrong, and that's that: human. The bad part lies in calling it right because you do it.

"Well, there can be no doubt that you still stand accused of integrity," which is meant and taken as a compliment.

The evening swim, and we are ancient, shadowed by the history of this sea. We kiss. I kiss him, winding my legs around his, half pulling him under. I put my hand inside his bathing trunks. Threatened with drowning, he has to keep from struggling and all the while smile.

"Isn't that carrying politeness too fucking far?"—using the word, as occasionally I must, now in this dark water—"smiling?"

I display a scarlet scratch.

"Did I do that?"

"With pleasure."

I feel myself go weak.

"What?" he asks.

"Nothing."

"What—kalooah?"—seriously.

"You make it sound like a symptom of illness," I say.

"It is." Which I love.

●

March 31. I'm taking no pills for the moment. On Alex's side there had been a little difficulty of impotence, tied to his work, we believe, but which led at last to good things.

Asher and the rest in a week.

●

April 2. I picked a fight, it doesn't seem to matter now what about.

●

April 5. Alex forgives me. I submit to him. Back at work.

●

April 20. Sunday. Asher has been here with Jack Gregson, Gregson's mother, Abe Rappaport, and the poet Fisher Blumenblatt. The last-named, who once edited a fairly ambitious literary quarterly, is a worse scalp-hunter than I am. He was in Vence last month when Lawrence died, sniffing. He is dark and frowning, yet not impressive. "I cannot understand people"—Mrs. Lawrence—"who will not answer mail." I can. Rappaport is Boulanger's most brilliant student to date, including Asher and Alex in the comparison. Koussevitzky will perform his First Symphony in the fall. He looks at people, even things—the sea, I notice—in a starved way, black eyes blazing, says little, eats meagerly, neither smokes nor drinks. He got to Alex and me at once. . . . Gregson looks unwell. Asher says it's drink. He smiles nervously, face filled with cheerful tics, as if even in his melancholy he cannot shake this old habit of happiness. Asher worries about him.

Asher himself was superb in his management of us all, individually, in the first days. He has the regal confidence of the leader born. I hungered to be alone with him, then when I was spilled everything. He said, "You and Alex are right for each other." He has promised to look at chapters.

Of course, I can't believe I'm right for Alex and kept insist-

251

ing about it: perhaps therefore Asher's encouraging statement. Yet Asher's not like that. Alex and I talk of the necessity of going our separate ways for a few months, and Asher says it would do our relationship no harm. I pray that it won't!

Mrs. Gregson is a sketch: dour and silent except to encourage her son to take another drink after he has finished one. "Should I?" he asks, and she replies, "Why not? We're celebrating," or something of the kind. He sits at the café table holding her hand and drinks gin while she drinks coffee. Then he goes to the balustrade at the sea end of the town square, and gazes out, hair flying.

"Not Italy! Greece!" he cries. "Mother, we must learn this place."

And she, calculatingly, looking over the expatriate types, "I'm learning it."

Rappaport, after studying me, declared that I was the most *striking-looking* person he had met. Only that!

"Don't painters fall all over themselves trying to get you to sit?" His own appearance—eyes especially—is so strange that Graziella told me she could not look at him. Of an early article of Alex's taking contemporaries to task, which Alex's articles seem to do, Abe said, "I think it's *merde*. All that stern duty"—but in an objective, inoffensive way.

Then of course Alex goes into Abe's work, and Abe into Alex's, and the fur flies.

Alex is happy with friends here, at his charming best, performing, fighting, listening in his consuming way. I sit aside, content, and observe. It is amazing and lucky to know people such as Asher and Alex!

We've taken tourist walks through town and up into the hills. Without his mother John is better. We swim on our stony beach. Alex is magnificently fit next to the others, a mahogany athlete. Rappaport is hollow-chested. Gregson carries excess weight around the waist. Asher is as smooth and small as a twelve-year-old boy, his shoulders dusty with freckles. I looked them over, pointing out Alex's physical beauty, which made Asher laugh.

Gregson paddled around, tight even while he was swimming. *"Is* it the Ionian?" he kept asking, as if he had fallen asleep and awakened in the wrong place.

When Petit accompanies us on our walks, wearing his knickerbockers and carrying an olive wood stick, he keeps us to the sheep paths, saying that the best Sicilians—bandits?—never use roads. We storm in and out of icy churches, my trousers and cigarette getting angry stares, eat cheese and bread under fig trees beside the road, while Blumenblatt cries, "Bread! Wine!" and shouts poems into the valley. Out from under the trees the day is as hot as burning paper. ... We went at last to visit the wife of the nightclub shepherd. The cave is really that, with a room built out from it on the steep hillside to house a donkey and poultry. She lay on a mattress beside a fire in the cave, smoke escaping through a crack in which we could see blue sky. Alex tried to stop her, but she got up to give us goat's milk cheese and wine in clay cups. The shepherd, Moorish-looking and with a curling cap of gray hair, treated her tenderly but did not help.

Depressed, down again through villages; children playing in gutters that are also the sewers; men without employment lining the streets to observe us; women and livestock together looking out of the bedroom windows. . . . The church landlords, long supported by the aristocracy, now by Fascism, have caused and encouraged this unabating misery. Tears stood in Asher's eyes. Blumenblatt fell silent. Then Alex, choosing his moment and with an air of triumph in the circumstances, told me by means of a general announcement that, by the way, M. L. Weisshorn & Son had closed its doors.

●

April 22. Three morning hours without work. Asher and the others are going to stay long enough for a party Henry's giving for his Soviet trade delegate, then go, probably to

Rome and Florence. Perhaps it's best, since I'm not working at all with the excitement. . . . Alex has had drinks twice with Abe, and now I have. Abe gazed at me with the fine eyes, paid compliments, and talked of seeing me in Paris at some unspecified date.

I point out to Alex that whereas he may feel liberated by the failure of his father's banking establishment, I now see instead of important work endless précis of pop German novels in my future. And of course it means Saul will be after Alex, pathetic in his hard-boiled picket-line style. (He has already written saying he might join us now that he is unemployed; a threat, translated: come home.)

●

April 23. An argument. Elements of real anger in it.

●

April 25. And another, concerning, humiliatingly, money.

Now it's Edna Loux, for our sins, with her companion! They checked into the San Domenico, had the drapes pulled to shut out the sun, and got into bed. Alex and I then had to come and be reverential in the dark. The Framingham woman, whom I had not met, seems stupid and is certainly gauche, though Alex appears to be fond of her. I gather she is quite ill. I don't mind Edna under ordinary circumstances. She speaks Italian and French like a streak.

I said later, "Well, there's your patroness, don't you think? Better get busy on it, baby."

Just liberated, he was in no mood to be talking of slavery. Signaling the start of the battle, I said, "The other one will

254

be dead soon, and then Edna will be ready. She's the obvious one."

Loux brought lavish gifts, understanding how to corrupt, as the rich always do. I got silk underwear and stockings, sizes supplied by Fran Gamble, Alex a silver-mounted case of shaving things and endless blades—again Fran's advice, Alex having complained of the lack of good blades. What I needed, in fact, and have plainly asked for of everyone, was a couple of American typewriter ribbons.

Alex accused me of being obsessed by money, which is true, but he said I spend my emotions as well, "investing or reserving them"—my lack of sympathy for bourgeois sufferers such as Edna and her friend (or for myself)—which is untrue and unfair. He pretends he wants to be given something for his work, but he doesn't, so he damns money and makes it a metaphor for everything despicable. He hated this because he thinks of himself as practical. "You and Francesca had to beg it from a greedy, rich grandmother or trick it out of her selfish boy. How can I trust you to understand what money is for?"

Our hands filled with Edna Loux's gifts, we went down the hill fighting.

●

April 26. I swear to submit, then cannot. It's not that he in any way demands it but that I feel it must be done. I love him crazily but spoil it by failing to serve him, that is, to be of worth to him and his art. Yet with it all—and I will one day learn to say to hell with my libido—*not* such bad moonlights. (The outward-tending effect of having exciting friends around, especially, perhaps, Abe Rappaport, has rather inflamed us both.) If only Alex were not so courteously comprehending! He allows the reasonableness of anything I do, even when he fights, temper lost, while I allow him nothing. It means I resist acknowledging him to be, as he is, superior to me.

A letter from my father has me frantic with guilty feelings, which Alex "understands"—a gentle note, nothing at all between the lines.

A night on the town with the whole crew. Not extraordinary.

•

April 27. Thinking of the last time I saw my father. It was at the boat two and a half years ago. My mother had brought her usual pound of chocolate from Schrafft's and an old fox boa of hers, which she must have told herself would suit my intended style of life. I sent it back with Papa. He sat with his hat on his knees while I did my stuff with Tom Fraser— all the current loves: Alex was there with carnations. He had brought a book, my poor father—something heavy from the Sanskrit inscribed to me in Latin; and he smiled and nodded, as if it was quite all right for me to kiss men and ask of them the advice I should have been asking of him. Later, he was formal, made me open my telegrams and read the flower cards, and reminded me to write thank yous, all of which could easily have been skipped; and we went over the ship in the usual way. I think I seemed impatient. I know I didn't do well. At last he went with a handshake, the poor old Prussian. He was having a hard time, and I couldn't help or wouldn't. I expected a last-minute contact, but it didn't come. Leaving the ship he was heartbreaking—careful not to stumble or look back.

Something unaccepting is taking over in this book. Is it because Alex said it's well written? I only want to say, with tears, that I miss my darling Papa and wish I were more generous.

256

●

April 29. Another night out. We cannot afford them, and then it makes getting up in the morning a triple-distilled hell. Asher tries to make it clear that he and his group are partying, out to get everything they can, and that he understands we are on a working routine and have to get up. But it's we who insist on coming along. I do, I admit.

We met Graziella's brother. Jobless, Carlo hangs around cafés and taverns with his glowering air of planning barricades and whispers with other young men. They are unable to afford so much as a glass of wine and are stiff about accepting treats. He is hard-looking, broad-shouldered, with a laborer's hands as powerful as tree roots. . . . At the other end of the scale is Saint Peter's grandson. By day he works as a fisherman, bare-legged and tattered; at night he gets himself up in patent leather and a striped suit and offers himself. He and Jack Gregson are negotiating something, while Jack's mother looks on benignly. Abe watches everyone. Blumenblatt wants a girl, but there are none to be had, apparently, except me.

I asked Carlo why he did not bring Graziella with him, why women had to be shut up like nuns. He would not condescend to reply except with polite phrases, disclaiming personal animus toward women. It was as if I were a donkey and had spoken, and he was surprised not by the meaning of my words but by the fact of my speech.

He took us to see his father. At near midnight the man was still in his tiny shop hunched over a grinding wheel. He glanced up, nodded, and that was the whole of his intercourse with us. He is almost as small as a dwarf, has a bitterly grooved face and tiny work-twisted hands: he is like the child to his own son. We watched him for a moment bathed in the spraying sparks, and Carlo regarded us with triumph, as if he had made a point, which I suppose he had.

We wound up at the shepherd's club. His wife, he said, is somewhat better, but no one believed him.

•

April 30. Daily visit, now routine, to drink tea with Edna and Jane F. The latter sits in her tapestry-hung bed, gray and flaccid, while we wave cigarette smoke away from her. "Alex was a genuine prodigy," she assured me. "The real McCoy." Smells of paregoric and stale air almost do for Alex, and he has had to dive for out of doors more than once.

The American countess's spring concert series—all experimental music—is set. Asher has helped Alex with the program but refuses to stay to perform.

Funnily, each of us in separate tête-à-têtes has told Asher all about our sexual life together.

•

May 2. No real work. Part of my depression is due to having to check sailings for Alex; also the imminence of Asher's departure.

A fairly serious pass from Fisher Blumenblatt. It was expected, but it made Alex cold and angry, which would have pleased me except it seemed exaggerated. Leading into the discussion, I said, "I would have preferred Abe."

Topics: sex, friendship, art, money—treated in, for us, their ascending order of importance. In the final stage, as always, we accused ourselves instead of each other. I believe, simply, that I am supposed to make him happy. I know I do not. Alex feels he is not satisfying me, conscious, I think, of the implied accusation.

I show him this day's entry, but he says in effect, "So what?"

No moonlight, though it was indicated.

●

May 5. Henry's party was yesterday. A kind of empty orgy. Once more Alex has managed to get rid of his wallet with all his important papers. And I've lost a key notebook, so that's that as far as further work is concerned. We pulled on damp bathing suits and, with cigarettes trembling in our hands, got ourselves down to the beach. Alex punishes himself, gnawing his poor lip to shreds.

We had been in the street at four in the morning with Asher and Carlo, and Carlo stopped to talk to a woman who was carrying a basket of loaves on her head. When he returned, he told us that the wife of the shepherd who sings had died the day before. We had gone to hear him and found the place closed. "If we had the courage and intelligence to organize!" Carlo kept saying, impressed because they had had to close the place.

"Perhaps they did it as a tribute," Asher said.

That was bullshit. The shepherd brought in the tourists, Carlo said. "My God, that poor woman," he said, at last not failing to remember her.

I'm sunk.

●

May 6. Three days more of my Asher.

At the party he had said, "Put the novel aside. I want you just now to do a straight autobiographical piece." Close to Alex's view . . . Alex's wallet, empty, was in the dust by the front door of the house. We are not talking about it. A tavern proprietor came down with my notebook, and idiotically Alex tipped him the equivalent of three dollars. He has always been a coward about tips. Of course, the waiter found the notebook, and the boss appears for the reward.

I keep asking, "What shall we do? That poor man's wife is dead."

"We'll see him."

Not today, however.

●

May 7. Silence.

●

May 8. Asher leaves tomorrow. Long talk. That is, Asher talked, I attended. The contents of Alex's wallet—papers, everything but money—was shoved under the door during the night, so we are grateful.

●

May 9. Asher and the rest took cabs down, got on the train for Messina, and that finished that as well. Alex handles me skillfully. A good letter from my father, but I hardly look at it. We don't discuss plans. I don't leave the house at all. Alex has been to see Henry, but I can't bear the idea. His party was my idea of horror, which is my fault, not his. By my choice, no moonlight. It turns out that I am not at all insatiable.

●

May 10. A letter from Fran. The boy is unwell once more. That puts the cap on it as far as Alex is concerned: I see decision take over in him.

●

May 11. He has seen Edna and her friend off. I would not. At Henry's party she told me, just as if I were not the person involved, that men like Alex were better on their own. When they repress the "difficulties" of their temperaments in order to make concessions in marriage, their creative work suffers. I told her I thought that was nonsense and hadn't noticed Alex repressing anything. But there is something in it.

I am rather shaky. Graziella keeps looking in on me, afraid I am sick again. She has made a horribly sweet tea from leaves in the garden.

The upshot of Asher's session with me at Henry's party: he is trying to say and won't quite that I am not a novelist.

The Soviet trade delegate, on his way home from Paris and prepared to linger among Henry's capitalist delights, kept talking about bread and steel—I thought in an ironic way, but they all—Alex, Asher, Abe, and others—sat at his feet. Then both Asher and Alex played recent compositions for him. Blumenblatt got into a fight with the anti-Semitic Englishman because the latter claimed that the rich Jews of London tried to sabotage the Allied war, so that while we smiled at one end of the terrace, there were screams at the other. I got tight—one of the smilers—pretending that Asher had meant something else but knowing I would eventually have to face what he did in fact mean. Everyone kept gazing at the sea, which was sunset pink, and at the puffs of lavender cloud that stretched out, shredded, and hung down. "Pink water!" people cried, discovering it again and again. And I, "being

261

happy," hung onto Alex or Asher or Abe, saying, *"So* tight!" though I was not out of control, and looking at the pinkness as well.

Over and over Henry indicated to new arrivals himself in tails in Red Square, his Monet, his Oriental horses, the miniature theater at the top of the house; the guests responded over and over, until Eve Schiff began to cry—I think it was in the factotum's bedroom. I said to Alex, "From now on she will require increasing amounts of attention. I advise you to cut your losses." They kept opening the door and asking about me, rather pleased at what was taken to be a liquor disaster—Henry, the trade delegate's wife, who had admired my trousers, even Edna Loux. The silky doctor came. He sat on the bed, smoothed my arm, and inquired after those parts of my body he could not see. Henry told me that the English novelist had been carried home drunk by two of his ruffians, thinking that it was Borthwick who had upset me. I said to Alex before everyone, "You mustn't feel guilty because your work is going well."

We made up an after-party party, Eve insisting she was all right. Calmly, I said, "I'm serious about tackling Edna for subsidization." Asher said, "Why not?" himself having someone. No one could see except Alex the state I was in.

"Would you believe," said Blumenblatt as we walked, "that Borthwick believes he's a socialist? Only he says the Soviet Union has missed its road."

We then came across Carlo, and he joined us. He and Alex made political speeches. Asher smiled and Abe looked bored. John Gregson caved in and was dropped off. Petit and Moyer had come along. Henry hung back like a pasha, while the secretary approached prospects in whatever café we happened to be in at the moment; and finally, at a signal, Henry went, saying, "I'm off to misbehave, I *think."* But it was only the same old tambourine boy.

Blumenblatt removed his shoe, put it on the table, and filled it with sugar. He improvised a ritual, making crosses in the air, which was tasteless and dangerous, since there is always a plainclothes policeman hanging around in these taverns, and they don't like comedy concerning the Church. The left shoe, for poetry, he said. It was dreary. I kept thinking that I was outside myself looking on and at the same time felt horribly trapped within myself, my throat aching with repressed hysteria. We went doggedly to the other night spots, even Asher silent at last. Alex did what has become his set piece about cherishing one's wrongs, insisting upon their wrongness, and employing the guilt sense to do better and persuade others to do so. At the same time he was funny, sounding like a cantor or like old Dr. Blum, his father's father-in-law. "I don't mince words, my friends. After all, it's wro-ong to be wrong: the whole notion indivisible"—or something. He clowned, teetering like Chaplin on a wall, doing a quick little ballet turn at the top of a street and teetering back, talking all the while. Apparently Abe had not been listening to all that puritanism, for we lost him between cafés—it turned out, I think, to Saint Peter's industrious grandson. Asher said we were like the ten little Indians. This sort of thing had never bothered me before, but now I was angry. I had been talking to Abe seriously, and then, as if none of that counted—and I suppose it did not under the circumstances—he simply disappeared. Asher and Blumenblatt argued with Alex ceaselessly, claiming that his view was subtly antisocial and antirevolutionary. Fisher Blumenblatt kept shouting that the people cannot be wrong, which, when it was translated, delighted Carlo. They had turned him out of the Catania hospital without doing the operation—gallstones—saying he was all right, but he thinks he was not all right and it was because of his political reputation, which had Alex raging. I simply went along, feeling feverish. *"Ha sempre ragione, il popolo!"* Carlo cried. . . . It was then that he spoke to the woman with the basket of fresh loaves on her head and came back and told us that the shepherd's wife had died.

Blumenblatt went off, then Asher. Carlo walked us to our door. We were silent. Alex and Carlo embraced, and then

Carlo embraced me. I was drunk.

In the morning: Alex's wallet and my notebook gone.

"You're angry because Abe went off with someone," I said to Alex on the beach.

"I thought that was you."

We wrangled about it. It turned out we were both jealous and rather bitter. I detested the beach, the sea, the indolent fishermen. The particular family, which Alex in his chronic desire to know and be known had befriended, grinned and waved; then the men turned aside to spit. I said to Alex, "Don't you see them?"

I thought it angered me, but it was really Asher's sentence on my work. She can't bear that quite.

Now a letter concerning the nephew, Patrick. He will die, of course, and no doubt I will blame myself for that as well as for everything else.

We walked up and down the beach that morning after the party. There, big as life and with a load of netting on his back, was the young man who had gone with Abe. I said, "This place is poisonous! Look at that!"

But Alex said it was good, "correct." You had your night; you got up and did your work.

It was a black morning. The sky was absolutely black, as if thick with poison. You speak of corruption. These people are dogs. Never mind the Church and the heel of the state. They've been dogs since Julius Caesar. Alex was badly hung over as well, but he hadn't my motive just then.

There had been twenty dollars' worth of lire in Alex's wallet. Neither of us mentioned it, because it was so staggering a loss.

I said, "They do or say anything to please and soothe, but all the time they're thinking of taking a bite out of you. They're all fuckers! Of course, Carlo stroked me, you know, when we said good night. Where indeed! He stroked my ass in that corner by the door! I hope it rains shit on all these people and that their fish turn belly up." I told Alex that we must not mention Carlo's name in connection with the missing wallet. "Not!" Of course, he took it. We had found it, empty, just by our door.

She will not survive, it goes without saying. There is no survival. Plainly: *I* will not.

Alex has gone back to his work, as he should, but she won't survive, which will be her method of failing him. There is certain to be a failure. I said to Alex on the morning after the party, *"Did* you give me a perfectly good moonlight?"— prepared to survive— "I can't remember." He had.

She is quite ill. Cramps coming on.

All these men speak of loving men. They sequester women, hoard art, money, sex. There is nothing left for a woman.

●

May 13. Alex had been walking on the hills above town. I was packing up my manuscripts and notes, putting on labels, using Randall's as my return New York address. I even got a couple of précis done. Alex began shouting from the top of the path at the road.

"She isn't dead!"

He came in dancing. "My God, she isn't dead! What the *hell* was all that from the baker woman the other night?" He was in a glory of joy. Resurrection. It had been a mistake. The tavern owner had closed up because his own wife was ill; and then the rumor, or so we reconstructed it. He had seen her, seen that she was not dead.

What he doesn't see is that she will die anyway and probably soon, so I detest Alex's air of triumph over death, which is intended to cheer me.

I'm now through with this journal. I showed the end bits to him. I could see that he was on the verge of pointing out that I had not made anything like such a dramatic speech on the morning after the party. He had not known that Carlo,

265

drunk, caressed me in the dark, nor that I think Carlo, embracing him, had picked his pocket. I created that dialogue for the journal's sake, and he has learned in this way, reading.

He said nothing. When he talked of it, it was as if I had spoken on the beach, and about Carlo he said, "Do you really think so?"

Tonight I said after a compliment of his, "You're the one, though. Sanctified. We agree in our century that we will not confuse the man and his cause, but you say the man and the cause have to be identical."

"What about Ian in Paris? That was sanctity in spades."

"Sanctity in sweat socks, you bet! Don't be naïve, angel."

But he must have been wondering now if I had made that up too.

I named the ones who loved him, a long list with every name I could think of—in this place, in New York, in Philadelphia, in Paris, in Berlin. "Everyone loves you," I said. "You're the one."

Alex had brought white carnations with his news of the resurrected woman. They are all over the house.

●

May 14. On my way up, out of the deep water.

FOUR | **1934–1936**

●

Eve's father died in 1934, and she stopped eating. It was a story of cause and effect, classically severe, that became famous in the family. "For all practical purposes," she did not eat.

In photographs she stands white under her sun hat, knees sharp against the wide-cuffed trousers, arms, like sticks in a starched boy's blouse, folded over her waist, which is astonishingly small. She smiles, knowing, into the camera: "As you see, here she is." Behind her in the picture the Mediterranean is bleached, a white dish; close to, in the black, gray, and white grains, a cigarette is sketched between her fingers.

She had conceived a distaste for her own body—a neurotic response not to be countenanced, she said. "How can we make me behave?"

On a street in Paris, trying to address a policeman, she burst into tears, and at night wrote Randall and Alex (she and Alex were married by then), describing the event. "I don't do well alone any more."

She wrote a posthumous letter to her father and sent it to Alex, listing the symptoms of "her loneliness" in script so small that a magnifying glass was needed to read it. "I wish we had had a better talk before you left. . . . Sorry you felt you could not let me know you were leaving." It was covered by a note: "Alex, enclosed an exercise in mental sanitation, the efficaciousness of which is yet to be found out." She herself arranged for treatment. There were two "irresponsible" weeks at Divonne-les-Bains near Geneva, for which Alex and Bob Gamble paid. She catalogued symptoms.

"I don't like having to sweat, I notice, and this rather than skin problems becomes the reason for avoiding my sun. Did I exhibit that as long ago as Taormina? I think it began later —can you confirm this?—in Mallorca, the compulsion to be dry and cool, the sea bird image. I dislike more or less intensely all of the bodily functions, which is why I eat as little as possible."

It was wrong of her, because she recognized that whatever the body had to do was right.

"Though I'm the first to laugh at outhouse jokes, admit the body's obligations, my own wastes are odious. It is a fact— that is, my feeling is. The things I have to do to remain alive are unattractive."

She saw that the fact that she understood her symptoms was a symptom, which was funny: "Alex, you'll make a song of it."

Saul said to Alex, "She intends to die."

"Not at all. She only means she doesn't much like being alive just now."

She was too deliberate to allow herself to see deeply into her purposes. She intended to stop misbehaving and get back to work, let Alex get on with his instead of serving her. All this fuss about her body was not worth it. At which Saul— they were having breakfast in New York prior to Alex's embarkation—made an angry noise with his tongue.

"Papa, no one's asking."

In another of the bleached photographs she stood with her feet precisely side by side, as if that were in her favor, and smiled broadly. She was about to turn, go into the house to write the insect letters. The road would be empty as soon as the doctor's wife worked the camera's shutter.

"Of all times for Eve to be alone," said Fran.

She was better with Alex. She had never meant to argue with good food; there was no money for that. She beamed at the meals he arranged to put before her in restaurants. Excellent food. Imagining that hungry people observed her, she was grateful, and at length ate a piece of broiled fish. She began to work again. A week before Christmas in Brussels, they went to a meeting, part of a Communist party convention in a public hall, were arrested, and deported to France, which Eve liked having happened once the manuscripts and her photographs of friends had been recovered from the hotel. In Paris she signed up and got a card, using the name Evelyn Saint-Simon, though Alex held off. "It has improved my health," she said in a letter to Francesca.

At home, Dr. Blum persuaded her to undergo surgery for the breast lump, which had reappeared.

Waiting, Alex noted in outline form ("More compulsively even than I should have been," Eve would comment) his reactions.

"1. If she should die—nothing beyond that—the word die like the edge of nothing. 2. But probably no chance of dying —except if the heart goes bad—and all the coffee and all the cigarettes—a sudden weak heart. 3. If the operation is futile —all this for nothing—and I forced her to it, with my 'nerves' and talk of something over my head—or did I? She isn't as forceable as that. 4. Long stretches of nothing on the top— no subject matter for the black senses, but it only waits for the moment when it can rush into meaning and words. 5. Endless day—yet parts of it over too soon—the moment when Blum came down—'It's all over'—where have I been the last hour? What was I doing? 6. The actual time of operation—the moment when I couldn't have answered a question. 7. What will they discover? a. a full-grown cancer b. totally unforseen condition c. necessity to take off breasts. 8. Constant recurrence of memory: Eve like a baby of two stalking back into the hospital room, sullen: 'I want to leave this hospital. They have no toilet paper.' (This one I can't think of without weeping.)"

Told he could see her, he broke it off. Later Eve said, "7c shows your ignorance."

She was all right, the growth benign.

She would write at the foot of Alex's outline, which she preserved, "How touching when the paragon misspells unforeseen."

In the fall they moved into an apartment in New York, and at the end of October Eve spent a week in Bellevue Hospital, malnutrition diagnosed.

"Misbehaving a bit apparently," she wrote to Fran.

She asked Fran to come and take care of Alex; and Fran, not understanding the summons but willing, came in by train for a night or two—she had a part-time job and there was difficulty in arranging the trip—to find that there was nothing for her to do, since Alex spent all his time at the hospital.

"What I really want is for you to persuade him to get back to his work."

"What am I to say to her?" Fran asked her brother.

He was bitterly irritable. "What do I care? Tell her I'm persuaded."

In fact, he had set two Langston Hughes poems, which he played for Fran, so that she could report that to Eve.

The couple visited the Gambles before Christmas. Patrick and Anthony, Fran's boys, stared at the beautiful woman who was like thin metal and who leaned against their familiar kitchen table, making it unfamiliar, using both frail hands to support her cup of coffee. They observed that she smiled at children and spoke to them as if they were adults. Alex did that too, but this was different. Eve's eyes burned. She would seem to need their replies, then would suddenly swing away, attention gone, then back again. Her skin, thin as paper, was spotted, but they did not mind it. Their Uncle Alex was funny, foxy and fast, running to help Eve or Fran, conferring solemnly with the maid Effie about how Eve's meals were to be prepared, while Eve protested that it did not matter (which was what worried them all), but his gaze did not burn in the same way. When she was not looking at them, they stared at her.

"December is one of my months," she declared, astonishing Patrick, who thought it was his because his birthday was in December. She asked when he said so, "Is it your favorite?" looking at his long head and wan face with interest because he had been near death.

Accompanied by the boys, she and Alex took long walks in the cold suburban streets with their dog, a German shepherd, but only when she was feeling well. Eve had bought the dog, named Very, the previous summer.

"Heel!" she cried in her rather deep voice. The dog was living with the Gambles, because Alex and Eve had decided that New York was no place for him after all, and the boys, thinking of him as theirs, tried not to be resentful.

"Very, stay!" she cried, and he obeyed.

She said, looking at the boys, at Pat particularly, "Male children," admiringly. They waited, but that was all there was to do with them—her admiration. Then she would turn away.

She looked around the suburban kitchen as if it were the moon. At midnight she and Fran mixed Ovaltine, which was prescribed for Eve, and had talks.

"We're seeing no one in New York."

Eve had talks with the maid Effie. "What is your life *getting* for you? What will it get for your children?"

She and Bob Gamble, who were good friends, had talks, and she said to Fran that she deferred to real men. When she passed the Gambles' mirrors, she did not look into them. Though she could not afford them, she liked fashionable clothes, as Fran did, and they talked about suits, coats, and shoes, but she rarely looked at herself.

In New York on New Year's Day she wrote, "To the works of 1936!" in a new journal.

As always, in order to work, she had set up two tables in an L and on them arranged manuscripts, notes, typewriter, and a marmalade jar filled with pencils. When she heard the piano and Alex's voice, she began to work; that was her electricity, she said.

Alex composed short pieces, sardonic in tone, for theater revues, for the Workers' Laboratory Theater, for Labor

273

Stage. He had joined the Composers' Collective. Early in the year he was given a job teaching musical composition and related subjects in the New School, and here he developed his ideas about popular opera and serious musical theater. He wrote articles in which he said that composers who divorced their music from other aspects of life sought to escape reality, and spoke of "the inescapable ties of music to the conditions under which it is composed." Eve wrote in *Modern Music,* "Music with a specific purpose"—and she had said that this was the sort she preferred— "cannot be given over to any one style or manner. It must be flexible to be useful. The proletarian composer must be able to control not only the emotional response of the listener but also the use to which it should lead." Brecht was a guest in their apartment. They had met Eisler abroad and had discussed these matters—educational art, technique subserving content, "a theater of the front line."

"Teaching-music must be a call to action," Eve wrote, but it must move both the working and the middle class. Alex provided an example of method: when a scene in an opera of his threatened to be sentimental, he slashed it across with dissonance: he instructed the worker, held up a mirror to the bourgeoisie, and persuaded the intellectual.

When she was well enough, Eve gave an hour or two a day to volunteer work at the League Against War and Fascism. Their friends were composers and writers, most of them left-wingers, though not all. In January and February Eve was eating regularly most of the meals put before her and she had gained and was holding a pound or two. They went to Harlem for jazz, to Café Society on Sheridan Square. They began to give parties. Occasionally Eve telephoned Fran to say that they had accepted an invitation but that she did not feel up to it: would Fran come and accompany Alex? And then when Fran came, Eve would feel better and decide to go after all. She said, "It's all neurotic, what I'm doing"—Alex having complained for Fran because Eve had ignored her at a party: "Ask Fran, if it's feasible at all, not to hate me just yet."

When it was suggested to her that she see a psychoanalyst, she said, "I should, of course." But it was very expensive, and she did not feel she could justify borrowing to go to one. "Nobody has money now for that kind of thing."

In March she stopped eating once more, again "for all practical purposes," and this time spent five days at Bellevue, then a week with Alex at the Blums' house in Philadelphia under Dr. Blum's eye. Sylvie Tudela came in with a play for which she was the casting director, but Eve, though she would see her mother every Saturday night in New York, would not see her here, feeling that she had been followed. "The whole idea is that there be some sort of sanctuary from mothers." She got out of bed, borrowed money from Ruth Blum's purse, leaving an IOU, went to New York at midnight, and telephoned Alex at dawn asking him to return there at once. "I can't bear that houseful of rich arguing Marxists anyhow, and they plainly detest me." (In fact, Saul and Alex had fought at breakfast that day, the father crying at last, "I command you not to go to her! She's dragging you under!")

Though Eve went to her desk every morning and took no medicine until noon because it dulled perceptions, she did not now work. Lunch for her was a glass of milk with sugar in it, and they had fights when she would not drink it. "I cannot swallow it!" she cried and became interested in what else the words meant about her behavior, so that Alex would find himself fighting farther and farther from the point. He moved between a hostile and arrogant manner and one of persuasive charm, both motivated by fear. When he panicked, he telephoned Fran, and, unless one of the children was ill, she came in.

He said, "I can't leave her for five minutes." He was now afraid she would die. It was as if his presence sustained her life as his music did her work. But when she felt better and began to eat, they agreed that he must go to the artists' resort called Yaddo in Saratoga for at least a month in order to get serious work done.

She wrote every day to him, said that she was eating and even doing a little work of her own—the poems again. He telephoned each evening. John Gregson was there, he told her, and one or two other old friends, and she spoke to them on the phone. Then he did not call for several days, and she (she would say that she had been "prophetically frightened") did not dare pick up a phone. Her mother wired for her: "Eve worried. What's wrong?"

John Gregson had committed suicide. Eve must not hear about it, Alex said on the phone to Sylvie. But she did within hours from someone who had heard from someone else, and when Alex returned, having cut short his stay, he found Sylvie in their living room, Eve in bed, the shades drawn. Eve said, "I understand you were the hero of the occasion. You took charge like a soldier." She was proud of him. "I'm all right. It scared hell out of me. My heart stopped beating, and I really hoped that was it for me too."

●

Alex arranged outings around a meal. This was an essential scene in the dramatic story on which the boys, Patrick and Anthony, were to be raised.

There would be a matinee, an art gallery, and a walk if the weather was good to the restaurant. Alex would have been there earlier in conference with the restaurant owner, an old friend "from happier days," as the man always said: a particular sequence of dishes, not too much of anything, wine "in the offing" but not shown, a table against a wall because Eve felt insecure unless her back was to a wall, dessert choice narrowed to two items in order to avoid discussion. When she was in her place, Eve would gaze nearsightedly around at the

276

waiters, all of whom were in the conspiracy to persuade her to eat and who tugged at their ears pretending not to observe, and at friends dimly seen. She herself seemed to defy illumination in such situations, in these old basement restaurants painted in leftover speakeasy brown. She turned constantly, as if trying to turn out of the frame of a picture and leave empty the space she occupied. She often excused herself and left the table. For the brief periods during which she was settled, she headed conversation toward her symptoms, as if to pay for the attention she was given: "All this psychosexual manure concerning my poor father," gladly admitting causes, buoyed by the unity a meal provided. (Leaving restaurants was as depressing as leaving the theater when the play had been good, which did not stop one going, she pointed out.) They had not talked about John Gregson's death. Eve had gone to see his mother, walking the twenty blocks uptown, acting, as she said, a scene, and then walking back to return to bed. But in restaurants, in the near dark, she spoke of John as she did of her father, with an appearance of sympathetic calm: "Death and food," she said.

"The waiter loves your way of making him laugh."

"I wish I knew why John felt he had to go away."

She talked about people she had known—in boarding school, at the University of Chicago, in Paris and Berlin, in the New York theater world. She enumerated lovers, classifying them according to the degree to which she respected their accomplishments. Alex came out first. She talked about the sea as if it were an enduring friend, reminding Alex of aspects of it they had observed together. Endlessly, she analyzed her character, using the third person: "Her object has been to be scrupulously fair, never judging, but this is tied in with her sense of guilt. . . . Great self-repression—oh, yes, you don't know, baby—and *little* self-control, overconscientious to a degree, stubborn, haughty, *not* vain despite what you may think, given to passionate friendships rather than love, avid for the feeling of life, impatient of loving except in narrow limits . . ." And again: "The point is, of course, that she had an object in herself. She loved herself best!—speaking in the past—but when she found something she valued more, she loved that more!" He watched her look dimly around and looked too: a silver dish cover glowing, an orange exit sign, a waiter's coat in the darkness. "That particular ability was not native. It was given her, miraculously, by life. . . .

"The most important thing was that she wanted to write, but instead became a sort of stenographer. And the hard and most important *fact* was that she had to make a living—she had to!—and didn't write. No, that's taking it down in shorthand, my friend. The book simply didn't get itself written. Gifted, oh, gifted . . ."

She would excuse herself, move slowly among the tables, pause to speak to a friend.

"It's the cramps," she would say, returning. "The most astounding pain but brief duration."

They talked politics, Alex, with her, having become increasingly caught up in daily left-wing tasks; in Eve's description as if both were on the central committee and everything they decided was to be acted upon at once. If, in whatever restaurant they had come to, they encountered a reactionary or Trotskyite acquaintance, both turned away, and Alex would go pale with anger and suppressed nervousness. Several times in restaurants he had been in near fistfights with other men over questions of politics, and once a headwaiter, a friend, had begged him and the other man and Eve to leave.

The courses were brought without fanfare, a platter set before Eve. She would look at the food without seeing it, push it aside with annoyance, as if something had got between her cigarette and the ashtray, and go on with whatever she had been saying about politics or her symptoms, then excuse herself once more, let the food grow cold until her return.

"No, I see that I must do something"—not in the third person, since action was proposed. Her doctor in New York

278

had a brother at Massachusetts General Hospital, a trained analyst as well as an internist, to whom he had spoken about Eve Schiff. Something would have to be paid as part of treatment, but there was no question of the terms being an obstacle. The point was that the man who treated her physical problems would be the same one to whom she talked about the psychological ones. It was tempting. "Anyway, they value me!" she said in triumph, but also ironically. Of course she would go, she said, since she was assured that it would be of use. "I consider myself under orders."

Another time in another restaurant: "Not possibly. Not now. Much too involved . . .

"I'll just try the ladies' again."

People stood over their table to talk about John Gregson or politics. Asher Moak held Eve's hand and said, "My God, how we waste people in this country!" He grinned sadly at Alex, who had just published a harshly critical judgment of one of Moak's concert works (" . . . a good chance for terse musical reportage wasted in up-to-the-minute travel-slumming music"). "Our new leader," Asher said.

And Eve later: "Joking very seriously, *I* think!"

Once, she was gone from their table for over thirty minutes, for the last ten of which Alex hung miserably around outside the door. Then he barged in.

"Is it that long? I don't feel too well, in fact. Look at you in the ladies'!"—laughing. "No nausea to deal with this time. Everything's so muddy, really, these days. Out: smells."

Returning to the table, she declared, "Such a lovely meal. How I'm bitching up!" She no longer spoke of survival or of failing him, but of herself in an objective style: ". . . The point is her mind was depleted by the years of taking shorthand or doing other men's work." She used her skeletal hand, a cigarette burning in it, as a flail, emphatic, eyes nearsightedly dark in one of the basement rooms. "She found her possible function as a woman in a love that was a love for life . . . taught herself that she could not write! . . . Years passed. She sat. She typed."

He drew her attention to the carefully planned meal.

"I hadn't forgotten. All my favorite things."

But she ate next to nothing: according to legend an oyster cracker with ketchup or horseradish sauce on it and then coffee. The meal would have cost ten dollars.

"Bitching up!" she cried in the taxi on the way home (there was no money for cabs), remorseful. "What I put you through!" She told him for the hundredth time, as she admitted, of her father seeing her off on the last trip, knowing he was dying and would not see her again. His final kiss, his eyes then. The Telegraph Building as the boat drew out at dusk, seeing still her father's dreaming gaze. "I collect only farewells."

Eve observed that certainly she appeared to be trying to join her dead father but that that was only appearance; she asked for high marks for self-restraint. At whatever points the collection of symptoms that was supposed to be her wish to die would yield, she claimed she fought valiantly, though Alex did not grant it.

"Say dutifully."

"Say that then."

They sat together another time in her doctor's waiting room. "It sounds romantic and brutal," she declared, "but I'm not really interested in dying, psychology notwithstanding—the apparent desire—and I have no respect for your interest in my dying. Besides, don't kid yourself. I don't intend to do it. If I were going to, why would I be making such a play for you and me? What I need," she said, "is bucking up."

She wrote to the Boston doctor a long letter done in several drafts, of which Alex kept a copy. It said in part: "35 years old, health usually good, nerves not good. No children or pregnancies. Breast cyst caused by unspecified glandular disturbance removed"—she put the date—" . . . lived in New York and Europe working at sedentary jobs (translating, typing, journalism, etc.) on an average of 10 hrs. a day from 1920 to 1934, except for three summers spent working on novel (part-time novelist otherwise). Aug. 1934 went to Mallorca and began new novel. Same month father died; same month cessation of menstruation. Sept., beginning of diabetic difficulties; no more real work from this date. Travel Divonne-les-Bains. Weight 92 upon leaving Europe in March. Tests in New York (your brother): no organic defects, simple secondary anaemia. Later tests, same results. These by Dr. Morris Blum, Philadelphia, included X-ray of abdomen, which was negative; basal metabolism minus eleven; blood 'surprisingly good.' What it boils down to is the fact that E.S. cannot swallow, which is to say: practical but no theoretical disinclination to eat. . . ."

She wrote her mother across town, explaining why she would go out with Alex but not to see her. "Very important for me to go out in evenings with Alex, partly because I at least get properly prepared toast, mostly because if I'm with him and can eat one teaspoon in his presence I make much more psychological progress. No energy for others after that . . ."

And to Alex, in a letter late in the winter, insisting that he be with her at mealtimes whether or not she ate, she wrote (he was in the same room): "My only idea (and hope) now is to take a spoon or two with you in the restaurant, then TAKE REST HOME AND EAT IT THERE. (*You* must find right places.)" She used the upper case on her typewriter for emphasis and as if to set this against her hand, which was all but invisible by now, and her voice, which was all but inaudible: "SPE-CIFIC: I got chill sitting in the last two joints (no need for doctor to know which when you tell him of this aspect, because they are good and he'll say no to them for other tries) WAITING for what I thought might be the right sauce—and what was. (Which I ATE when I got home, you recall.) When I got home, coughing, WITH CHILL, which you knew about, you didn't have training merely to go ahead without a word and make a hot-water bottle and a cup of hot water or tea. (YOU MUST TELL HIM THIS AS TYPICAL.) . . .

"The point is that to fall off in my eating before you is the

281

most serious defeat, for it gives everything to that energy and horror in my mentality that concerns my father and food—eating for him—by which I'm to gather that, simply, you are supposed to have been the cause of his 'going away' so that to eat for you is betrayal of the first love, et cetera. . . ."

She wrote microscopically one morning before dawn, "My love is all you" at the top of a page, as if it were the beginning of an essay, and gave it to him at breakfast. He ate (she required it of him) and she, tensely watching his spoon lift and drop in his hand, did not.

In the spring they borrowed the Boston apartment of a friend of Henry Petit, and Eve began treatments for malnutrition and kidney malfunction under the supervision of the analyst at his hospital. Once each morning, six days a week, she saw the analyst in his private office. Alex remained in New York on the doctor's advice, and also because he had his weekly lecture to give, but came by train on weekends to take Eve to a concert or play. She ate now regularly in small amounts. Though she weighed less than eighty pounds, she felt, she said, very well. She was engaged in writing a political article for *New Masses* and in composing a sequence of harsh, rhymeless sonnets, which she described as being unlike anything she had attempted and which she would read aloud to Alex or have him take into the park alone to read if she was unsure. His severity did not waver. Some were good, some not at all. He gave useful reasons for his judgments. She gazed at him in the borrowed rooms. He was pallid and too thin, fevered-looking. He had celebrated his thirty-first birthday earlier in the year. His eyes looked, she said, covered; she had tried "weed-grown."

"Nonsense," he said clearly.

She grinned: only that?

Except for teaching and preparing a share of several concert programs, he was not working. He could not.

"Are you bitter?" she asked on one occasion.

Politics aside, she attempted a practical description of his

282

musical achievement to date. He had managed an integration of experimentation: primitivist, classicist, popularist. Most significant of all, he had swum clear of the Schönberg insistence upon perfection, the ruthless insistence that led more often to paralysis of art than to daily work, and of the Edna Loux insistence upon genius, which had led, too often, to despair.

"You will work. I mean on a very large scale. You're ready now."

She had consigned her novel, wrapped in brown paper, to the future. (Early in 1970 it still lay in the attic of Anthony Gamble's house.) Alex was tired, drawn fine, probably coming down with a spring cold, but she gave this no attention. In effect she was through with him. Talking of loyalty, she observed that the only safe and sound one was to one's work. "Let's leave it at that." Then relenting: had he seen his dentist? A happy man, which was what Alex had been, did not tire easily; yet here he was, seemingly finished. But Eve said, "If I'm only nonsense, you're only tired. No, I asked you. *I* won't go to the dentist." She had been to dentists too often. She would write a poem about a dentist wringing his hands beside a grave, mourning his good work lost in the dead.

There had been no moonlight in months.

"My choice at last," she said. She hoped he did not feel he had to be chaste on that account. And then: *"Is* that unkind?"

He sat at the old-fashioned piano with its carved panels and ball-and-claw feet, one version went, improvising, as Eve, who lay on the sofa behind him, read over and over in a whisper a sonnet, this draft of which both had tentatively approved. When she stopped reading, he turned, knowing that she had died.

"You can't write it and make people believe it," Anthony Gamble would say thirty-five years later.

"Why not? It fits in with her general style and unpleasantness," his wife would reply.

●

"EVE DIED. SEND $200 CARE WESTERN UNION FOR CREMA-
TION. I AM ALL RIGHT"—to Fran in Philadelphia.

He wired Eve's mother. "DARLING SYLVIE. EVE DIED THIS
AFTERNOON. NO PAIN. RETURNING TO YOU 24 OR 36 HOURS.
BE BRAVE."

Saul, hearing from Ruth who had heard it from Fran that
Eve was dead, said, "Thank God. Alex hasn't done any worth-
while work in five years." Then he said that he did not mean
that and was sorry. When he saw Alex, he would tell him he
had said it and was sorry.

"I'm all right." Alex telephoned to Fran from Boston. He
would be out of touch for three days. He was not about to do
anything dramatic.

"You feel a sense of relief," her father said to Francesca, "as
I do. As Alex does. But he can be hurt by it."

("Papa's not bad this time," Fran would say.)

They did nothing, waiting out the three days, staying near
the telephone. Bob Gamble came home early from work
each day to share the waiting.

●

He took a cargo steamer from Boston with their luggage
and Eve's ashes in a box and sat on deck watching the lights
of the coast.

A deck hand said, "I see you somewhere."

Finally Alex decided it was the young sailor John Gregson
had brought home to his mother's apartment years before.
He turned away, then back. He felt guilty and, as always,
allowed guilt. The sensation was one of burning. His thighs
and back flamed and itched with guilt. He said, "I don't think
so. Anyway, I can't recall."

The man looked at the box knowingly. He kept an eye on

284

Alex during the voyage. If it was the same one—and now Alex was not sure—then that man, he remembered, had talked ceaselessly. This man was silent.

He ought to tell him that Gregson was dead; he said nothing.

On one occasion, plainly, the other said to him, "Don't do nothing funny, okay?"

When Alex opened the box to empty it into the sea, conscious. of the sailor watching, he observed that among the ashes were bits of bone—he recognized a fragment of pelvis and hip joint—and fainted. Then the man was right there with him.

He got a cab from the pier in New York, stopped the driver after several blocks, and got out. He said, "You bastard, you can go straight down Ninth to Twenty-third and across! What kind of money is a man supposed to have these days for you to try crawling across town on what is it?—Thirtieth or something?" He tried to hit the man, swinging wildly, but the other would not fight.

●

Patrick and Anthony came downstairs ready for breakfast and school, and there in the living room was a suitcase with Eve's initials on it, closed, and ashtrays filled with crumpled cigarettes, a number showing their mother's crimson lipstick. Alex was upstairs asleep in their house. The fact gave everything they would do that day importance. He would be there when they got home.

A day or so later, employing the disguise of being seven, Anthony Gamble asked, "Where is Eve?"

He watched his uncle closely.

He, Patrick, Fran, and Alex were in the car. The river lay on Tony's right. He had asked his question, having rehearsed it, where the river turned and a crosscurrent made the water, which had been dull soup, flash. Tony imagined that he put his hands into the river as they went and parted it to show its secret, junk-filled stomach. He knew that Eve was dead. He stared at his uncle as Alex, exhausted yet smiling, sensing that Anthony did not quite believe in his existence, turned to look over the seat to attend to the child in whose existence he imagined himself to believe wholly.

The river fled into a line of willows. Fran drove, grimly smiling, gloved hands on the wheel. Patrick, tall and pale, struggled out of his endless thought, surprised by this sign of life in his brother. Each one, in the midst of his thoughts, attended. How would Alex reply?

Later, trunks came and were put into the cellar, then over the years moved from house to house. After his grandmother's funeral in 1970, Anthony would at last open them and find Eve Schiff's journals, manuscripts, and letters.

1937–1941

•

The Loyalist soldier had a word with some children in a sunny city park, bending seriously down to them. At the edges of the movie screen the park became hotter and paler until it was like fire seen against the sun. Before the fountain, seated on a bench, was a soldier with a bandaged head. Women and old men sat on benches nearby.

"They go about their daily lives, trusting the men who guard their city."

Suddenly women came tumbling from tall tenements, laden with what looked like bedclothes; a sound, apparently of their wailing, blended with sirens. There was a glimpse, and no more, of men carrying a fluttering form that was what of course it could not be: a dead child, her legs flopping limply. She was gone.

Anthony turned to search through the darkness for his mother and his brother. His mother had bent toward the man in the row before hers and was in conference. Patrick, two rows behind, gazed calmly enough. A hair jumped and flickered, magnified in a corner of the screen; and from that direction, drawing Tony back, women again came running, dragging children by the hand. They were dressed in black, stumbling across streetcar tracks that were like the ones in Atlantic City. A white-haired woman stopped and looked into the sky and in a moment was alone. The camera glanced away. It constantly looked, then averted its gaze, though it had showed the child who must have been dead.

Later, there was a moment when everything went white, the voice groaned and was silent, and Anthony's mother continued to lean forward, white-browed in the projector's funnel of light, listening, then speaking a few words to the man who sat before her. He would make the collection speech. The audience watched the blank screen attentively until its pictures leaped up again. A poster of a crying child appeared, then a row of coffins in a white room. The film shifted and jumped. Tony watched the screen but also observed the effect of the fast, undetailed glances at death—the images spinning down the bar of dusty light—upon the audience. They sat in the ballroom of the Morton Hotel on Virginia Avenue in Atlantic City. In a wicker basket (made in China) on the empty chair beside the boy were lapel pins and armbands in the Loyalist colors. His brother had pinned one of the bands around the sleeve of his jacket. A man near Tony, seated on the hard front edge of his folding chair, breathed rhythmically, emotionally.

"After the day's work, citizens of Madrid train in empty lots."

They crawled across miniature ranges of hills, the city beyond them. A sudden picture, interposed, was of Adolf Hitler, saluting and as always tightly smiling. "Germany and Italy want Spanish steel for guns." A girl donated her blood; others stood in line to donate theirs. Ambulances were needed, doctors, medical supplies, blood. . . .

Anthony would help to stop Fascism.

He and his brother passed the collection baskets. Pat started his down one row. If it came back on the row below, he kept it going; otherwise Tony took it and started it again. Pat did the same with Tony's basket. The collection speaker, the man with whom their mother had been in conference, was himself a doctor who had come from the fighting fronts around Madrid. He spoke quietly of the death he had seen at first hand. (He had not averted his gaze politely as the camera had from the real horrors.) If this audience felt it could donate money, he was asking it to do so for the people of Spain, and for the Republican cause, and to help preserve world freedom and peace. Times, he knew, were still bad. . . .

The meetings were held every six weeks on Sunday nights. If Fran decided the boys might benefit from a particular one in the educational sense, she let them come and put them to work. Because the programs ended late and she had to help close up and perhaps drive the speaker to the station before their own drive over the causeway to the Gamble house farther up the coast, and because it was half an hour to school in the morning by bus, Fran would keep them home the next day. In that case, she telephoned on the Friday before and told the school principal of her intention.

This chapter of the Medical Bureau for Spain, of which Fran was a founder, had helped to raise ten thousand dollars in its first year for an ambulatory field hospital—a front-line emergency unit for the wounded—and was on its way to buying another.

•

They took their excuses to the nurse together on Tuesday morning.

"It's terrible, that war," the nurse said. "I read all about it in the *Press.*" She pushed Tony gently to the window, tugged the lobe down, and peered into the boy's ear. "Oh, dear."

"We weren't sick, Miss Anderson," Pat said patiently. "It's in the note."

She had been told by Fran that the family was trying the seashore year-round to find if the air would help Anthony's chronic ear-canal infections, so she always had a look anyhow. (Pat, as if his operation in early childhood had been enough, was now all right.)

She said, signing their slips: "Snippers, I understand they're using. That's against the Geneva agreement."

"The snipers are on the Loyalist side," Pat explained. "They fight the way we fought the British, Indian style, hiding all day in a tree, for example, and then firing. They get left behind the enemy lines. . . ." Commanding her attention, soberly, Tony's long-headed, fair-haired older brother described dumdum bullets to the school nurse in order to give her something to be upset about. "The Falangist cuts an X onto the nose of his bullet—into the soft lead," the boy said, "and it explodes inside the victim." Miss Anderson winced. What had he called them?

"Falangists." The Fascists. "Oh. Dumdum bullets."

"My," said Miss Anderson.

Her office was in the junior high building, and in these halls, where Anthony did not belong, Pat was remote from his brother, not unkindly denying him but already tuned to work. Yet he took a moment now to pause and shove a thumb at the pebbled-glass door they had closed behind them. "Snippers!" he whispered, convulsed.

Tony was required to describe his educational evening to the class, which he did not mind doing. These were now images remembered in the morning. He said men had carried a dead child from a bombed house. *Heart of Spain.* Reserved because he could not yet describe it was a man caught in midstride by death, in the act of running: his rifle thrown away as he skidded, falling sideways across the slant of a hill, his black beret flung violently off. This, in fact, was more terrible to Anthony than the child, but he knew the child was effective, and he could describe her. Aware she was impressed, he saw his teacher blink rapidly.

"The meetings are to raise money for ambulance units. My brother and I help after the collection speech." He went on about it, at ease before the class. The smartest girl, hands folded on her front-row desk, gazed at Anthony with blue eyes that widened, then blurred. He had taken the button from the collar of his windbreaker and put it on his shirt: "Save Republican Spain." He hardly listened to himself speak. Each desktop was a pond of light. The blackboard at the side of the room, though erased, still said, "Yorktown. Cornwallis. October 19, 1781." His remoteness began to conquer him. The gardens in front of the houses across the street from the schoolyard, gray-green in winter, were like so many dollar bills. The nurse had not liked what she saw when she tugged at the boy's lobe. His ears seemed to echo with his own words, pinging distantly. "Falangists . . ."

●

He looked away from the possibility of pain and did his homework without being asked, as if to buy it off. His father was considering another Ford instead of the Plymouth he had been considering for months (there was a private strike-breaking army in Dearborn, which was a heavy factor in the balance), and Tony cut the cars out of the glossy display book and drove them around the borders of the Persian carpet. From the top of the house (the garage-studio would not be built for some years) came Alex's voice, high, pugnacious, powerful: the same chords smashed at over and over. The boys' uncle had come to write additional material for the opera *Pilgrims, Revolt!*, which was to be produced late in the spring or in the fall as a Federal Theater Project. Pat sat in an armchair, a hand to his brow, a book on his lap. Fran had gone in the car to meet their father. The pain fluttered irritably near and pried at the boy, who kept trying to slide away. He had cut out a newspaper photograph of his favorite Penn football player (it was Pat's favorite, and Tony had learned from his older brother): Johnny Welsh, with a big number 8 on his chest, charging into the camera, one arm straight out, ball tucked into the cradle of the other—only 150 pounds— and won a game with him. Tony meant to play football. (Pat would be an assistant coach, perhaps, while he was at school.) The boy played on the carpet, plump, sleek, turning his back on pain, until his father came in and said, "What's wrong?"

Alex said when he came down, "Oh, Jesus! So soon again? Poor baby."

Anthony said he was very sorry, and before anyone had time to be touched by this he was himself touched, and began to cry both because of that and because of the now admitted pain. Bob Gamble was examining a leather fleece-lined pilot's cap the boy was supposed to wear with the flaps over his ears. Brenda, a pale Negro woman, stood in the kitchen door, a spoon in her wet hand. They sought the source of the pain, alarmed and armed. It was as if a bat had got into the house. "Look, he wears this cap with the flaps buckled over the top of the head," his father said. Patrick waited patiently for the evening paper. "What about an aspirin?" asked Alex, both at sea and practical. "Start him at least."

The doctor would come. If an abscess developed in the canal of the ear, it would have to be lanced, which was painful. On the other hand, it might not happen. Fran sat by his bed. "It worked itself out the last two times. This pain will ease up soon." Crying, she suggested, did not help much, so Anthony stopped at once. Alex came and read from a picture book to distract him, which made Tony uncomfortable, because it was not the kind of thing Alex did. It hurt terribly for a time. Then, just as Fran had said it would, it hurt less. She smoked a cigarette, waved at the smoke, then put it out in the toilet. They ate dinner without him, and he heard bits of the conversation, its tone quiet; he heard his name spoken. Probably, he thought, it was his own fault: his usual carelessness in the face of warnings. He had not worn his cap at all, let alone with its flaps down. He had played until he was in a sweat, then let the breeze cool him, not putting on his coat. He did not confess this foolishness of a few days before but was aware of it.

Tony was ill for a longer period than usual, and while he was convalescing Fran hired a tutor, and herself, during long walks on the beach, schooled him in the multiplication tables he had never mastered—a problem at the base of other school problems. He gazed out to sea. It was as if he were securely on top of something looking down. With Fran he felt poised, right (in his element, Alex would have said), and recited the times-six, times-nine over and over to the surf, while Fran prompted and the big German shepherd, Very, ranged the beach. Every afternoon Tony's tutor, a retired teacher, came and worked with him for an hour. He read the books he wanted to read, sketched, using his father's equipment (Bob Gamble was an accomplished weekend painter), and took walks alone, avoiding his friends.

One of the Medical Bureau meetings was held during this period, and Tony went to help as an independent: not an adult, not a schoolboy. There was Pat as he had always been, but Tony was not the same. He observed this occasion from a middle ground. Instead of sitting, he stood by a side wall, arms folded like an usher, and listened to the collection speaker.

Later, they drove the man to the station. He had been a professional labor organizer, they learned, and he talked of the Loyalists as workingmen holding the line for the rest of the world against imperialist Fascism. It turned out that he had been beaten by goons while organizing an Ohio plant. ("Goons!" Fran used the word, smoking and frowning angrily as the story unfolded.) It had happened several years before. He had been hospitalized for six weeks. "Oh, Christ, what a time, friends"—turning in his seat so that he could address Fran and the back of the car at once. Pat, in a new spring topcoat, stared. "They worked me over good. I was no use for the plants after that. I checked in at New York headquarters, then drifted a little, caught up with my reading; and then I got into this. The workers now see Spain as a political battleground where their own war's being fought." He was gaunt and tired-looking. "This is a Ford," he said, sighing, looking around it. "That bastard, but it's a good machine. I've had Fords get me out of a scrape or two. Everything adds up in due course. How's Alexis?"

Their uncle was in New York once more. The man nodded. He had a knowing, preoccupied air, as of one who makes time for everything necessary, the arts included. Tony watched as he stood on the sidewalk in front of the station, a worn black suitcase hugged between his knees, searching into a billfold for his ticket. He had been beaten by angry men with blackjacks and night sticks. The wallet had metal corners. He tugged out half an inch of a thin sheaf of one-dollar bills and, apparently unconscious now of the Gambles in their Ford waiting to pull out into traffic, counted his money.

Tony had been out of school so long that when he returned the other children were astonished. "Anthony!"—as if they had not expected to see him again: as if he were a guest in the classroom.

There was one more public meeting before the summer season and, then and in the summer, pay parties at the Gambles' house to raise money for blood and ambulances. Alex brought celebrities to speak or entertain. On one occasion a group of the actors in rehearsal for *Pilgrims, Revolt!* came down in two cars and did scenes from the opera, Alex accompanying them and playing the villains. That night the boys' mother made the collection speech. Pat's face flamed; he kept his eyes on the living room rug. Tony observed that his mother's hand with the yellow sheets in it shook and prayed for her not to be nervous. As soon as she began, Morris Blum called from the back of the room, "Inaudible here, Fran." Alex sat at the piano, head bowed, chewing a corner of his mustache.

"Well, we are holding them at Guadalajara," she said, voice trembling, "but the toll has been heartbreaking. Madrid is bombed daily. The Junkers and Hydro-Heinkels"—stum-

296

bling a little over the names—"can come in apparently very low over the countryside at the speed of a fast automobile, or bomb from a height. . . ."

She spoke of the need for sanctions against Germany and Italy and of the need to continue to urge Great Britain and the United States to supply Republican Spain with arms. Sasha Volin said, "Well, that would apply to the Soviet Union as well, I should think, Fran."

She said, "Oh, yes." Saul, who, cuffs turned back and a towel tucked into his belt, was keeping bar, said mildly, "Mr. Volin, the partisan view is all yours just now. We are urging everyone." And someone shouted, "Guns have no loyalties!"

". . . really want to express this all in a better fashion. I am, basically, just a housewife reading these reports in a pleasant room over breakfast. I want to express myself violently but feel I'm not entitled to take that position. What is needed from me and from all of us here tonight is something less self-indulgent than anger. . . ."

On summer weekends the house was crowded. Mother McLeod came and sat in the Gambles' living room on a hot Sunday, family and guests standing around in bathing suits. She wore a long dark gown of heavy cotton and old-fashioned high shoes, her ankles swollen above them. In a napkin on her wide lap was the sandwich she had been given; she juggled a Tom Collins and a cigarette. At the same time she sought papers and pamphlets in her bag.

"I'm an old-time Back Bay type myself," she said. They had been speaking of Henry Petit, who had been seen at a Trotskyite meeting in Chicago. "People like Henry are offended because Mr. Stalin has bad manners and isn't interested in art or the life of the spirit, which is what Henry calls pederasty. He's been trying to get in touch with me, but I'm hiding out." She called to her son. "Fetch that case of papers out of the car, Nick. I can never find anything."

She was to address a summer fund-raising in the Gambles' house.

"This gal's hour is coming too," she said earnestly to

297

Brenda, who brought her something, looking up into the startled face. "I'm going to tell you the same thing I told Bill Patterson ten years ago in Boston. 'Bill,' I said, 'all minorities are black.'"

Her son Nikolai had been in Spain on the new northern fronts and would be returning in another month. He was a thickly made man with an uncertain style of speech. The boys knew from Fran that his mother had been born into a wealthy family, broken away from it early, chosen the fathers of her two children as the owner of livestock chooses sires, and left each after each pregnancy. They took Nikolai to the chicken-wire cages at the back of the house to see Pat's rabbits and then stood by, embarrassed by their own emotion, to observe the soldier's interest.

"I was raised on a farm until I was ten and always had a rabbit. These look like good ones." He said he thought that one day he would like to go back on a farm and work it. It was hot in the sun. The man looked at the rabbits, then out across the low dunes to where the sea glared. Tony thought that the chosen father must have been a farmer who loved animals. The boys were acutely conscious of the fact that not a month before, Nikolai had been where men were killing each other. Tony tried to think of a way to ask what it had been like to kill people or see them die but could not. Patrick actually said, "How are things at the front?"

"All right. We'll make it."

They went swimming again in the afternoon. Mother McLeod sat on a newspaper under the narrow boardwalk to watch.

Bob Gamble, it turned out to the boys' surprise, did not like her. "He says she takes advantage," Pat reported, not understanding. The whole left-wing movement was its own worst enemy, Bob said, and deserved its failures. They observed her where she sat in the shade smoking and proofreading an article she had brought with her, glancing up now and then to smile at the bathers approvingly.

"Don't knock yourselves out, comrades," she called. Pat

298

looked around the beach. Though one of his rabbits was named Comrade, the word spoken in public had a violent sound.

Tony went with Ruth and Saul, who were spending the summer with the Blums in a nearby house, when they took Mother McLeod and her children to the station.

"These people don't even qualify as refugees, Saulie," she declared as they drove through Atlantic City's Negro district. "They are prisoners among us"—gazing at the warehouses and store churches, the peeling old wooden tenements. The street corners were thick with the unemployed, many, as Mother McLeod pointed out, fresh from the South. They turned reddish amiable eyes on Dr. Blum's expensive car. They seemed to Tony to be waiting for the future very modestly. He pitied them. (I am not colored at least, he thought with guilt.) One day, of course, he would help end their waiting. Saul drove and kept flicking his cigarette with his thumb and shooting his cuffs in anger at the injustice set forth here as if on a stage, agreeing with his old friend. The car rocked in the tracks behind a streetcar; sparks showered from the switches. It was a moment Tony would forget and, years later, recall. Their car, he would believe he had felt, had gone through this neighborhood like a flame, their good will effecting change for good, the car itself with its special occupants (if the Negroes only knew!) a medicine. When they stopped for a light, Tony, looking up from his snug and dreaming back seat, saw a young Negro woman lean over the rail of a second-floor porch. She turned her head lazily up, then down the street.

". . . come up from the South searching for jobs that don't exist waiting tables, chambermaids, end on the streets . . ." Neither Nikolai, a soldier, nor Janet, a grown woman active in politics, ever interrupted their mother. The girl on the porch, looking through him, then focusing upon him, said lazily to Tony, "Hey, darlin'," and the light changed to green.

A few years before Alex's death, when the nephew was older than Alex was now, Tony would be at the wheel of a car on this same street, his uncle beside him—they were on their way to pick up Rose at her apartment—and he would stop at the same light. Remembering, he would try to describe the revelation of that moment: the threat of the black girl's actuality. But Tony was never to be able to tell Alex even the simplest anecdote clearly. Alex would say with irritation, "Of course," seeming not to understand or understanding well.

•

It was odd to have the seashore house as their year-round home, to come back from school, get into bathing trunks, and go to the beach. Summers seemed both longer and nonexistent. There were to be three such before the return to the city, and Tony would remember them and one or two afterward with a pleasure that was at once nonspecific and specifically sexual.

The house was filled with naked people. Bedroom doors stood open on rooms packed with naked men; a door flew open upon half a dozen women changing their clothes. (He was to guess too late that some liked his looking.) If he went to find his parents, there they were just getting out of wet suits. Ruth and Saul would stand back to back in a corner of the bathroom half naked. Tony, plump, avoided nakedness yet was tempted by it, and he gazed with prophetic eyes at visitors lying on sofas, Noxzema smeared across their red shoulders and thighs. There was a smell of wet wool and baby powder in the house, and he would always associate the smell with flesh and summer.

He spent his mornings on the beach. If it grew hot, he rolled into the boardwalk's shade and lay there, striped by the light. In the afternoon, having eaten too much lunch, he would go in search of a friend, though friends were not necessary, or return to the beach, sun burning the house chill out of him as he walked. There he would lie once more, mindlessly lazy in the blazing bed, sifting sand into cratered cones around him or setting up palisades of jointed sea straws, idle (he never took a book with him) until supper.

Pat, at thirteen, was growing both tall and moody. He fed his rabbits and now and then took them from their cages; but they were old distractions, and his interest was tinged with nostalgia. He no longer read funnies at night when Bob, who commuted each day to the city, appeared with the paper but went straight past them from the front page to the editorials. He was teaching himself to type as part of a plan to become a novelist. The druggist's son, who was a year older, was Pat's best friend: a clever blond boy who studied magic tricks and was good enough, with a line of jokes and banter and his father's dress suit, which fit him, to entertain for money at birthday parties and once even at an American Legion dance. They were frequently together, sometimes grinning about something, but as often solemn. In the latter mood they followed girls on the beach, and Pat once invited Tony to look at a certain girl who wore a thin yellow bathing suit of a jersey material that fit her golden body so closely that it was possible to imagine she had nothing on.

"Squint!" the older boys cried.

Tony made comments he hoped sounded knowing and at the same time was fearful of the responsibility descending upon his brother. She looked naked, all right, her nakedness amazing on that beach where people could see. The boy screwed his eyes nearly closed, making a haze in which the girl strolled by the surf with nothing on.

During their second winter at the shore Alex had his success with *Pilgrims, Revolt!* and became a celebrity. He was not—Pat and Tony already understood the distinction—a celebrity as movie actors or even some writers were. He was both less well known and more important. He had succeeded in a serious endeavor in the theater, writing with forthrightness about unpopular issues, shaking his fist, really thumbing his nose at the other side; yet he had spoken of these matters as an artist. It was a perfect success because nothing had been sacrificed (Alex and Fran spoke often of the act of "selling out"), but it seemed everything was gained.

"They're paying their money," Pat declared, "to come into a Broadway theater and see just where they're missing the point."

"There was an inevitability about it—a vacuum needing to be filled," Fran said.

Alex's name was in the papers, and their mother and grandmother Rose, when she came to stay, clipped the items that Alex did not send. It was clear, when he came to the house again, that their uncle had changed.

Tony's father, Bob Gamble, was a large man, heavy-seeming in every way, so that to look at him was to feel safe. People listened when he spoke. He was calm, slow, and large. Alex had been quick and light by contrast. Now, though he was still that, he seemed heavy too. Success, Tony felt, had thickened him, though he did not weigh a pound more; and whereas people had listened because he was quick or funny or angry, now they listened as they did to Bob. At the same time, Alex had a special knack of attending. He would come to a stop to listen, even to Tony, who was ten, tug hard at his mustache, gnaw a thumbnail, glaring, it seemed, at each word as it was uttered. Simultaneously, he heard nothing at all, was not even there. Alex's presence burned: absent-mindedness, a new weight of manner and appearance (his shoulders had broadened; his brow seemed broader), that gnawing attention. The boys were thrilled by him; his visits, more than ever, made a crisis of excitement in the house.

His clothes were different too. He was making money and could afford them, but it was more than that.

"He doesn't care about clothes," Pat said.

It was true. The more expensive they were, the more roughly he wore them: thick linen shirts with overlarge cuffs and collars; thick ties, the knots big and square; a good rain-coat; soft shoes, usually black; hairy socks that he wore now with garters. Pat and Tony would lounge on the bed in his

302

room while their uncle spoke of New York and the theater and answered their questions about famous people. Signs of dinner rose, and he said, "Smells good. I could eat a horse. How about you guys?"—casually. He stood knotting the dark tie before a mirror, trouserless. His shirt and shorts were snowy, the garters black with gold bits; his calves bulged; his shoes gleamed. On the dresser top was a pair of silver-backed brushes, a gift from the famous director of *Pilgrims, Revolt!* (He himself always brought gifts on his visits, just the right thing—some remembered requirement or something flatteringly useless and exact: paints for Tony; a handbag for Fran; and for Pat, who was interested in money, Monopoly, inscribed "Yours for the Revolution, Uncle Alexis," which he explained was the way Jack London, whom Pat admired, had signed his letters.) When he brushed his hair, he looked at himself without particular affection. He mentioned Orson Welles. Would they like to come in to see a Mercury Theater production? ("My gosh, would we!") He would talk to Fran: why not? He had an air of ruling that was irresistible, all the more because it was absent-minded.

There were signs of Eve Schiff (always that name, though they had been married)—photographs, a traveling clock. They were carried in his bag and put on the bedside table without ceremony, part of the man. He did not talk about her. Eve's manuscripts would be seen to—edited, published —later. Not now. Now Alex was in the midst of his purpose. He glowed with it. He did not smile as much or make himself as useful. He was not as restlessly amusing, nor as precise in presenting his thoughts. It was as if he did not need to be, as if all that were in his work, which now spoke for him. The boys, unknowing, felt that Alex had prevailed against odds, and they were intoxicated, observing a triumphant man.

What was more, having written his opera's libretto and lyrics, Alex had become a playwright and a poet. With a shrug, Ruth Blum said, "He's now recognized as a major force in the American theater"—deprecatingly because it was true: "Sure!"

There stood the piano, accordioned sheets of music on it crawling with notes and slashed by strings of red grease pencil; the neat worktable with its jar of sharpened pencils and Leonard Lyons' column cut out of the *Post*, the long paragraph about Alex checked in a businesslike way. There stood Alex himself, knotting a tie with swift gestures (Tony still had to murmur, "Over, under, over, under, *up*"—chewing his lip), talking with that air of effortlessness (and division) that was like the tide. He would return to New York the next day or the next week: a business date with someone (a name of importance). He might go to California soon, *maybe* something to do with a film about Spain. A *Pilgrims, Revolt!* company was to travel to a coal town in Pennsylvania to do the show and raise money for strikers. But now Alex stood putting on his trousers, rapidly tucking in the snowy shirttails, ducking into the mirror with the flashing brushes, all the time addressing the boys concerning the exact heart of things just as if they were adults.

They had seen *Pilgrims, Revolt!*, standing at the rear of the theater with Alex, Fran, and Sylvie Tudela, whom everyone called Mme Tudela and who was Alex's mother-in-law. (She was an assistant to the producer of the show and its casting director.) Alex paced and smoked, but Sylvie watched calmly, glancing from time to time at a gold watch pinned to her lapel, or looked in at the lobby door of the ticket office for a word with the men there. The fact that the seats were filled was good, Pat pointed out. They went backstage and observed the leading actor-singer massage his face with tissues while he talked urgently to Alex and Sylvie in a voice different from his stage voice. Alex said at length, "Try it." And Sylvie: "Try it, darling, but tell us before you do."

Tony remembered how gravely the actor had looked into his own eyes in the makeup mirror. He remembered the New York streets at dusk, which seemed as closed as passages in a house, and the electric beads of green and red light rolling across the cars. They had sat under caricatures of celebrities in Sardi's restaurant; waiters brought things to

Sylvie without being asked. There had been an excitement of permanent dusk about the world in New York—of grown-ups' evenings beginning—which the boys would now always associate with their uncle, so that his appearance in their house (their house!) was somehow bitter: he brought that world, then took it away with him.

Having dressed with care, then, bearing out Pat's conclusion, he did not care at all. He loaded his pockets with cigarettes, matches, money, papers, keys, booklets; he thrust his hands hard into the pockets of the expensive jacket (he carried on most conversations that way—the hands jammed into the pockets, tearing nervously at their lining); he smoked, scattering ashes over the good sweaters, burning holes in the flannels.

It was bitter for the boys when he had to go away, but his presence burned. Tony thought of him as burning. He had a nightmare in which Alex burned, flames for eyes, and awakened remembering his uncle at dinner, having risen and shoved back his chair, Rose in a state of alarm as he beat with his hands at the bright coal on his clothes.

•

The boys were to succeed at whatever they tried as adults because Alex had. Pat went at his job of becoming a writer conscious of what he could do. He outlined large projects— a life of the abolitionist John Brown, a book about Sacco and Vanzetti—and did research, putting notes on three-by-five cards, which he kept in metal boxes as Alex did. The difference between the brothers was that Pat did not forget to do his schoolwork. "You have two jobs," Tony's mother said to him, "and you have to do both at this point in your life," admitting that painting was his job as well as school and not putting one above the other. Alex would look over Tony's sketches and paintings. "I don't know a hell of a lot about it, but I do feel I can trust my instinct up to a point." (He had known Tchelitchew and Pascin in Paris.) Certainly Tony had talent; that much was clear. He could draw like a house afire. The only advice he might give worth the giving, Alex declared, was to work on a regular disciplined basis, not when so-called inspiration struck, and with a plan in mind. As to color and composition—he'd leave that to Bob.

With Pat's projects he was more at home.

"Go after the big ones by all means, but there are good little fish to be caught on the way." At this stage he was to try everything; yes, poetry too. He listened respectfully to Pat's plans, the goals he had set. Certainly: why not? But expect to work. There were years of work in this. One found prodigies sometimes in music, but rarely if ever in the other arts. Alex himself had gone through the whole prodigy thing, and a very difficult and destructive process it had been: "I wonder if I'll tell you all about *that* someday?" As far as he went he was candid, speaking of himself. When he drew a line, he said he was doing so.

"Of course, the one thing he isn't," Pat said, "is happy. It doesn't matter what." He explained: "Well, Eve in the first place. The political situation . . ."

Spain in 1938 was being lost. Alex tried to keep his success at arm's length faced with that failure. He had talked of going there; now he did not. He, Fran, and the dog took walks on the beach, the boys occasionally tagging along and listening. Alex kept away from New York in order to work (he was deep in a new opera) and to avoid what he called the blandishments. When he did go, it was to do research, which meant putting on old clothes and "disappearing" into Harlem or the Lower East Side for a day or two at a time and even, the boys understood, sleeping in flophouses. Fran was frightened, though she did not disapprove in theory. One took risks provided they were not needless ones. The brother and sister had discussions concerning the matter, and Pat said to Tony that as a novelist he would do the same thing one day, though perhaps—showing his father's caution—during the day, commuting to the slum or union war as his father went to work. Alex had been taking what he called street-fighting instruction in New York at the gym at which Joe Louis worked out. "The moral thing," Pat explained, "is to put yourself second —take risks—but be prepared. In an unfair world you don't learn to fight fairly. If you forget the rules, you can knock down Joe Louis."

"Courting disaster" was how Bob Gamble described it, and Alex argued heatedly with him: it was all for a purpose.

Oddly, the prospect of failure in the war was not altogether unpleasant to the boy. Alex's success stood behind everything (and, unobtrusive, Bob's successful practice), so that Tony felt safe with failure, could be excited by it. At breakfast on a dark morning, lights reflected in the paneling, a black winter sea in the windows, hearing the news being discussed with energy—if Saul and Ruth were there, with violence— and simultaneously filling himself with sweet hot food for his school day, the idea of losing made the boy's skin crawl with something like joy.

Pat said excitedly, "It's a bad time, Tony." Freedom may have suffered a near death blow, and who knew what might come? "France and England throw Czechoslovakia to the wolves. So much for freedom and honor."

In March of 1939 Madrid surrendered, and that was that.

"Fran told me Ruth cried," Pat said to Tony. "They were speaking on the phone about it, and Ruth burst into tears."

Czechoslovakia was Hitler's. Germany and Italy joined forces. Then, during the following summer, not long before the Gambles were to return to live in the city, the Soviet Union and Germany signed a nonaggression treaty.

"Wait and see," Pat said anxiously.

He was writing a novel about a union organizer and soldier of fortune at Madison Motors in Detroit. He had got to the point where the hero, Kingman, was a prisoner of the plant police in a shack outside town. The head of the local Black Legion was trying to win him over. Kingman, whose beautiful daughter was in love with a banker's son in a subplot, had formed a brigade of Spanish Loyalist veterans to go to Germany and begin a guerrilla war against the Nazis, which was the true reason he was being held. Pat had stopped work at page twenty-five and thought he might have to alter the plot to take current developments into account. In reply to one of his letters, Alex wrote from New York, "Be honest. How would it go in life? If your people are real, they'll behave as they should without much interference from you. Why not let them show their confusion too at this point? I'm sure, as you say, that Saul and Dr. Blum explain it all, but leave that to them. If you're going to 'explain,' then put in a Dr. Blum explaining and have someone argue with him. . . ." Pat tried, but it did not work. He set the project aside.

In the city once more, Tony and Pat began to publish a weekly newspaper, the *Abraham Lincoln Gazette.*

"We know that World War II started long before September 1st, 1939. It started with Ethiopia, Spain, Austria, etc. Of course, who will acknowledge this?" Pat did most of the writing, Tony the design and cartooning. Ruth Blum was distribution editor. Printing, expenses for which were underwritten by Bob, was done on the mimeograph machine at the Committee for Peoples' Rights in center city. Tony's cartoon for a spring issue showed a rich man (dollar signs on his vest) singing a line from the hymn in Alex's *Pilgrims, Revolt!* in which war is praised as the stock market rises. Another sketch was of a figure labeled "Martin Dies" creeping up behind a Hollywood bathing beauty in a suit labeled "red," a club in his upraised hand.

The paper had advertising, whimsical and serious ("Every good labor paper uses Federated Press for accurate, sympathetic, and up-to-the-minute labor news." . . . "Ace Letter Service" . . . The Committee for Peoples' Rights seeking membership or presenting Vito Marcantonio at Town Hall), and subscribers as far off as California. One of these was Fisher Blumenblatt, a friend of Alex's who had become a successful Hollywood writer. He had visited the shore house and told the boys stories of movie stars. Myrna Loy and William Powell were close friends; he knew Luise Rainer and Paul Muni (a serious actor, Pat agreed, even though he did gangsters). Fisher took out full-page ads in the paper: "Alex Weisshorn Picks Workers' Pockets!" "Odets Handicaps Humanity." Alex replied with an ad of his own: "All Blumenblatt Says Is a Bunch of Lies!"

Fisher wrote to the editor explaining that Workers' Pockets and Humanity were two-year-olds at Santa Anita race track, and he took another ad: "VOTE FOR BLUMENBLATT, THE WORKINGMAN'S FRIEND." Pat added a note: "Folks: We are not responsible for the quibbling between celebrities that may go on in this paper. But we enjoy it, don't you?"

The boys came from their suburb to center city to be checked by Dr. Blum or have their teeth filled by Sydney, Ruth's brother, and generally stayed to dinner. Fran often joined them, coming from the C.P.R. offices, and sometimes Bob.

"The Bri-tish and the Fre-ench," Blum declared in his gentle singsong, "are fighting a smoke-screen war, Pat. . . ."

"*Not* against Mr. Hitler but *against . . .*"

"To smash the Soviet-German nonaggression pact and require the Führer to do what he was supposed to do in the first place, which is engage the Soviets in a death struggle to save the imperialist big shots."

Agreeing with each other, interrupting, they appeared to fight. "No!" Ruth would shout, or Fran, meaning yes, and then restate the issue and conclusion. "Smesh" and "pect," Blum said. And Mrs. Blum, grunting with approval at the plainness of her family's arguments: "Exectly." Ruth's calm, preoccupied shrug: "Sure! Certainly!"

A national election was coming up. There had been searches of the offices of left-wing organizations in New York and Chicago, members brought before the Dies Committee and grand juries. There was an antilynch bill before Congress; but there was also Senator Barkley's conscription bill, part of F.D.R.'s deliberate abandonment of neutrality. Pat took notes for the *Abraham Lincoln Gazette* and occasion-

309

ally, though he agreed, attempted to argue. Bob Gamble, if he was there, might disagree.

"Bob, Bob," Blum would say, sadly shaking his head. He and Ruth were mild, half listening, as if the lawyer were only telling a good story. Mrs. Blum drew down her lips, shook her head. But Saul, if opposed, at once took fire. "Lenin himself turned to the criminal classes if he felt it was expedient!"

"Write down, Patrick, that in my opinion—that is to say *my* opinion—there are, as Lenin affirmed, agreements and then there are agreements. Social revolution, not war, is the issue." Blum pronounced Lenin "Le-neen."

Pat spoke of the courage of the British at Dunkirk.

"Sure!" Courage. It went without saying. The British were courageous, Ruth declared, but that did not alter the fact that the war was one of boundaries and national interests.

●

"He's in fine fettle," Fran declared of him as of an athlete in training. Alex was impatient, brilliantly energetic, clear-eyed. By having the roof lifted and adding a small porch, Bob had a studio built over the garages of the shore house, and it was here that Alex lived and worked when he visited. He would storm down the short path from the studio, first for breakfast, having already had a long swim and put in an hour's work, then again at midmorning; he would pause briefly on the side porch of the house to scan the dunes and sea, a cigarette between his lips, then duck into the house; a few words for the maid in the kitchen (stopping, listening hard to her replies), the toilet under the stairs, and out once more with his rolling gait that was like a sailor's, frowning with concentration at the work that kept on inside him.

His guests, down from New York, were theater people: producers, actors, singers, directors, and now possible backers for the opera-in-progress. (The Broadhurst Theater had

310

been reserved for it for the following spring.) He took the professionals to the studio for sessions of work, but the backers' auditions were held in the main house. They sat on the floor, drinks in their hands, some of them old friends of Alex's or Sylvie's—the Park Avenue rich, who, as Pat said, were drawn to their own destruction as a class. ("The rich can be good too," Pat also said in his sage manner; if they couldn't be good, they might be used for good.) Weisshorns, Blums, and Gambles, Philadelphia and New York guests filled the room. Alex had undertaken to finish his work by January. At the same time he was doing incidental music for a new production of *Macbeth*, to be staged in the fall, and the score of a documentary film about Southern tenant farmers who had come to Northern cities looking for work.

". . . the union as the militant reply to the abridgment of our rights, as the new American pioneer crossing the plains, going like the prairies burning; the labor union putting right the Bill of Rights, insistent, firm: bread and butter is being discussed, old-age pensions mentioned, the notion of the forty-hour week, hospital and retirement benefits. . . ."

Alex plunged his hands into the music, then paused and explained in a scholarly tone, leaning back and looking particularly at each person: they were here talking about how things were at that moment in their country. Ask Bob Gamble—nodding in the direction of his brother-in-law, a lawyer active in the labor movement. People were hungry.

Always, finally, Alex talked about hunger.

Pat nodded his long head. Saul stood in shadow by the wall gazing down at the tip of the cigarette in his hand. When he looked up and caught Tony's eye, he gave him a wink and a grin.

The union fink. Alex, crooning, moving into the scene, explained. Alex became the man, creating him: a good family man, a reader of books, a man with a wry ironic style; but also weak. He very nearly brings down everything in ruins. Alex understood the man, was him. This was a *good* man: bitterly. The character of the traitor came into Tony's mind, spilled

311

into it by Alex's art, an intelligent hopeful worker who also wanted a better life for his family. Tony could be like that: frightened and doing what he was told by bullies. (Something of the sort had once happened in class, he thought guiltily.) Then with music, powerfully, Alex made Tony powerful and resistant, so that at the end it was all right. Immediately afterward, Alex did a funny scene that had them all laughing gratefully.

Tony fought through that and other nights before he could sleep, winning one battle after another:

"Oh, so you would lynch a Negro, insult my mother (brother, father), drag Alex or Fran or Ruth before the Dies Committee, call me Jew!"—triumphing each time but not before he had first allowed for his own cowardice, giving the scenes development.

Hunger was the point: people were hungry.

From downstairs until late came the sounds of the party that followed the audition—Alex's voice strong, rather high, his well-mannered (English, Tony thought) tones riding over the others' or, if opposed, abruptly, politely subsiding to attend. A pause for a story (it would be about a celebrity, and it would be what Pat called off color): shouts of laughter; his mother's hoarse pleased laugh; his father's helpless one. There were at least two very famous people downstairs in the house right now, and they laughed as well. Hotly, Tony defended Saul or Fran before a congressional committee. What exactly did they imagine these people would do, the boy wondered, raging, when children were hungry: simply stand by—when nations quarreled and children were bombed in cities. Imperialist nations quarreling! *I* say so! Under oath. *Yes,* typically Jewish! We understand persecution! You don't seem interested in an antilynching bill, or in antihunger bills, or in antibombing-of-children bills. Only in persecuting the ones who help. (Not failing to admit being Jewish, which surprised them all; he did not look it.)

"Are you whispering?" Pat would call from his room across the hall. "I can hear you, for gosh sake! Even with all that

312

going on downstairs. My gosh, you're almost twelve years old!" (Pat, allowed to stay up later, would finally have gone to bed.) "I haven't heard you whispering like that in years."

Tony acted out dramas. When asked what he would be when he grew up, now he said he might become an actor instead of an artist, thinking of these auditions and Alex's powerful effect.

"How would you like it," he raged before the committee, "if you had to register because you're a foreigner? You couldn't live where you wanted. They could throw you out of the country if they felt like it if you spoke up—right now, for example—against getting into the war. . . ."

One of the potential backers brought a friend with him, a tough-looking young man named George (they never learned his other name), who was as small as a jockey and had thick curling yellow hair and angry eyes. The pair came on three successive weekends because the rich man was captivated by Alex and his work and insisted upon attending all the auditions. George, in little bathing trunks with an incongruous (Ruth said) Racquet Club badge sewed onto them, sat on the beach and glared at the surf. "A hell of a lot of that's bull," he said to the boys, speaking of a political discussion that had been going on.

"We don't happen to agree," Pat said politely.

The other had been on the road—a hobo—and in the army. He told the boys stories of top sergeants and mules, of cooks who tried to poison whole companies, of fever in Panama, and even, frankly, of his days in a prison stockade. "The army ruins men, turns them into dogs. That's why I'm against that Conscription Bill, but they don't understand"—jerking his thumb insultingly at the Gambles' house behind them. "Pardon my French," he said when he used a four-letter word. He made bitterly cruel references to women and left an impression (the boys discussed it; Pat said it was obvious) of having joined the army to escape a bigamy charge.

"Well, I think Alex and everyone understand what's wrong with the Conscription Bill," Pat said.

"Yeah?"—indifferently.

The man rolled cigarettes and scratched kitchen matches on a gnarled thumbnail. When he came a second time he brought each boy a hunting knife. "I didn't pay for them. Don't worry."

"He's really shy," Pat said and began to keep index cards on him. Bob said he did not like the idea of the gifts, both because knives were dangerous and because gifts were not called for.

"I wish he'd meet your eyes when he talks," Fran said. And Alex told Fran, mysteriously, that the man was often "on tea." The boys were not to walk down the beach with George separately to where the houses ended. Tony, understanding without understanding, cried, "Don't *worry.* I won't. Of course not!"

The *Gazette*, not normally published in the summer, came out with an extra when Trotsky was assassinated in Mexico City.

"We are against violence of any kind," Pat wrote, "and this may not be the time to point it out. Still, there are those who maintain Mr. Leon Trotsky was not a real political leader at all but an ordinary hack who used the struggle for the liberation of the working class for personal ambition and later for desires for revenge. . . ."

Dr. Blum, canvassed for his opinion in a hammock in the shade at the side of the house, a copy of *New Masses* across his chest, said gently, "He thought he was the only Bolshevik, Patrick, and the best of them. He never understood among other things that you can't run a country the size of the U.S.S.R. with kid gloves."

There was to be a final backers' audition. Alex was not in the mood, but it was too late to postpone it. George came down again with the potential investor in the latter's Packard convertible, heard some of the discussion about the assassination, gave everyone sardonic looks, and sat on the beach, hugging his knees and staring at the horizon. The family kept what amounted to an encampment of mats, umbrellas,

314

chairs, and so on at the beach, carrying food and drinks back and forth. Alex would descend from his studio, swim, join the group briefly, and return to work. Discussions were always in progress. George, who had spoken to no one, finally singled out Saul. "Well, you're full of shit," he said with his embarrassed sardonic laugh. "Pardon my French."

Saul took him on. Alex and Ruth, nearby, joined in. Saul was loud and ready with quoted facts. Alex said that he saw George's viewpoint, listened intently. Ruth shrugged, then declared firmly that she did not agree.

"The Soviet Union is creating for itself time to prepare!" Saul shouted. "Period."

They had gone from the assassination to the pact. The young man wore a ceramic medal on a heavy chain around his neck, a design of twining bodies. (He had told the boys that it was a gift from his rich friend.) As he argued, he clutched and released this object, which Tony thought was fine-looking, swinging it across his narrow chest. "You ain't had the experience to know!" he kept crying.

Ruth fell silent (what was the use?), but Tony saw that she was angry. She jerked her rubber bathing cap down, at the same time shoving her short hair into it. He saw her glance at Fran and shake her head. It was no use. Real anger, as always, frightened the boy. He looked at George. Ruth flung her cigarettes and compact around, slapping them down hard, then yanked at her bathing cap. Only when Alex spoke did the young man appear to listen. He kept his head lowered and scuffed at the sand with a foot. "Well, shit," he said quietly, while Alex, white-faced, glittering, arranged arguments. . . . "You don't know."

The discussion did not stop when they returned to the house. Tony stayed in his room and heard Pat in his. After a time, the house also grew silent. Tony, looking from his window, saw the Packard driven off.

"Apparently an anti-Semitic remark was passed," Pat reported, having investigated.

And Saul at dinner: "Your *Lumpen* and your dirty rich: the

whole business in a nutshell."

Nearly a year later, with Russia in the war, Pat talked coolly about the incident. George had been an interesting type. He might become a subsidiary character in the novel Pat was planning; the ceramic medal (he was going through his cards on George, and there it was described) was an interesting symbol to use. He could make it into a cross, thinking (he did not have to go along with Saul and Dr. Blum, which was the beauty of this family, he pointed out) of the pity of a human life lost, thinking now of Leon Trotsky. Good was in everyone, and death, though necessary, terrible. Tony, no longer a pacifist, wore his hunting knife on his belt whenever there was an opportunity. When America came into the war, Pat said, "Well, it's correct, after all. Let's face it."

Alex shelved the new opera—in fact, withdrew it in the midst of tryouts in Boston. It was critical of the system. As Fran said, the time was inappropriate.

1944

•

Tony had been reading Stephen Vincent Benét and thinking about it, but he could tell it did not go over. He used Housman and Poe, which were easy to remember. They were children in a kingdom by a sea; and here before them was the sea itself. He gave crowns and pounds and guineas but not his heart away. "It was many and many a year ago . . ."

The girl—the season's ingénue—appeared to listen, and he recited well enough. As an apprentice, he had no role in the first production, and his mind was uncluttered. Sounding like the movie actor Cary Grant, he recited: " 'You may talk o' gin and beer while you're quartered safe out here . . .' "

"I love that one."

She had turned her fresh round face to the sea, and the wind blew into it. Her mouth was hidden in her plump cheeks, but he could tell she was smiling. It was a gray day, just right for his mood. He ran a finger under the cast-iron rail and drew off a rain of condensation. (Tony's hands at fifteen were still a misfortune, with dimples where the knuckles should have been. If this girl took his hand, smiling, and turned it over, he knew she was feeling motherly.) He remembered all of "Recessional" and "If" and "O Captain! My Captain!" but knew better than to try them, that they were a little ridiculous. (His father had heard his Kipling poems, learned for school, and for weeks after, when he met the boy, would raise a declamatory finger and cry "If!" knowing that he ought to control himself.) "By brooks too broad for leaping the lightfoot lads are laid. . . ."

The girl's name was Kitty Grand, and that, not Katherine, was the name she was to use in the play programs. She looked something like Fran, Tony told her, with her olive skin tinged pink and dark hair, which she wore short and parted low on one side. She was nearly four years older than Tony, and she had smiled a little at the comparison. "I'll assume that's a compliment." They had known each other since the gathering of the theater staff the week before, and he had already kissed her.

"Oh, very nice indeed," she said in her older way. "Why don't we just leave all the calisthenics at that, my friend?" She was cheerful, energetic, always laughing (he often felt at him), and, it was understood, serious about acting. Candidly, she said, "My father's a third-owner of this place, which is why I'm the ingénue, I guess. But I'm really darned good, you'll see." They became companions. She went through a strict form of discouraging kisses, managing both not to discourage him and to keep him in his place. "You *are* very nice," she would say in a tone of astonishment. They sat on rockers on the porch of the professionals' boardinghouse, where she lived, and Tony would produce the dank tarns of Auber for her, or Alph the sacred river running through caverns measureless to man down to a sunless sea ("For I have drunk the milk of paradise" dropped into the dark summer street in his now deep voice), and Kitty Grand would say in the reproving astonished tone, "Really. Good. You're very nice, Tony"—maintaining the distance.

Now she flapped her booklet of lines—"sides" these were called, with the character's speeches, cue phrases, and directions—against the rail, passed it to him, and dialed a phone in the air. Tony gave the cue, and she cried out in a rather English voice, " 'Maude and I stayed with them in Somali.' Sa*molo*, Samolo. 'I told you about it that time when we had to make a landing . . . *forced* landing . . .' I don't know it. What?"—in a rapid monotone, eyes shut, her narrow suntanned hands at her temples.

Tony said, "Well, the person you're on the phone with answers."

"Don't I say they practically saved our lives? Well, for God's sake, give me what's there. I can forget lines without your help, my friend. '*Hullo*, Maude darling.' No. 'Maude. Darling, the Rawlinsons are upon us. . . .' " He prompted her. Then, "Oh, my *God,*" she cried. Having turned, she turned back, rigid, to face the sea. What was it? Her hair blew all over her forehead in spite of a broad yellow ribbon.

"Coming toward us on the other side. Don't look!"

The season would not open until Saturday night, and this was Tuesday. Tony had not sorted out the others.

"Okay," she said. "Take a peek. Are they doing it?"

Only then did he identify one of the other apprentices—a black-haired boy, tall and thin—and the juvenile lead, who claimed three professional roles and was receiving in excess of Actors' Equity minimum salary (already a great subject between Kitty and Tony). The two were standing by the railing on the shore side of the walk fifty yards down, heads together, discussing something with apparent earnestness. Beyond, looming above dunes of sea grass and bayberry, was the theater, a rambling barn with shingled turrets, and beyond that a water tower stood gray against the gray sky in nets of electric and phone wires.

"So what?"

Tony's gift was concentration. He could not refocus quickly. Birds, theater, figures were all in one tone, nothing singular. "Isn't that what's-his-name?" he asked.

"They were holding hands!" And, hearing him: "I'll say it's what's-his-name! He has such a *nerve*—right in the open." Hadn't Tony seen them?

People talking: "So what?"

"Stop looking, my friend!"

She spoke to the sea, pushing the hair back from her forehead with both hands. Now he faced the same way, shrugging. It was all right. He drove his concentration into the sea.

"Oh, I don't mind," the girl said. "My father hates it. I think as long as the summer people aren't here yet. I suppose they didn't see us. I tell my father it's the theater and that he has to like it or lump it, but he says it's because summer stock has to take the 4-Fs now. It wasn't this way before."

It was odd, Tony admitted to himself, but perfectly okay. When he glanced again, the two were once more walking, now away from them. He looked at their hands. They had made fists, and as they strode along each banged the other's fist.

●

Tony's friend Doc Dougherty, who lived near him in Philadelphia, wrote: "What ho! Gloucester. Tell me when and I'll hop down and throw orange peels. *Good* summer up here. I'm getting in some tennis and sunning, also tutoring a young millionaire in Latin and Algebra at a dollar an hour, so I'm not altogether idle. Nineteen years old!"—underlined heavily, referring to Kitty Grand. "Well, have a joyous time, old bean. I wish I could come down, truthfully, but it looks unlikely. . . .I'm well into *Forty Days* and learning a lot about Bagradian. 'To the ineluctable in us and above us!' . . ."

". . . pretty well, all in all," Tony replied. "We're going to do *Craig's Wife* and I'll get the detective, which means gray hair and mustache. Barrett says my voice is good but tends to be monotonous, so I'm practicing getting it upper and downer—with expression. Barrett plays parts, though he hates to (directing is the big thing) and is a pro. My roommate is from Chicago and he's good. A 'technician' who builds a part by studying a hundred details, then puts everything together. . . ."

The roommate's name was Leo. He was a small fiery young man who wore glasses that he kept ripping off, then thrusting on again to peer at his sides. He walked up and down the theater aisles or in the little lobby during rehearsal, or paced the boardwalk, eyes closed, murmuring lines. "He thinks it through," said Kitty Grand admiringly. "All I can do is feel my way through." When others lay sunning on the beach in the morning, Leo worked in their room; and at night Tony saw him lying in the moonlight, one arm under his head, smoking, reciting mutely to the ceiling; then a nod (a problem solved), and he jabbed out his cigarette, pulled off his glasses, hurled himself onto his side, and fell asleep at once.

"He solves problems," he wrote to Doc and wondered how to do it. "I can't even see where the problems are yet." He worked on variety in his tone and—he supposed he was doing this—on his breathing. " 'The *time* you won your town the race' "—starting high and descending the scale rapidly— " 'We chaired you through the *market* place' "—going more or less up again.

"The trouble with Leo is he's, frankly, ugly," said Kitty. It was a side of the girl that impressed Tony: to make decisions about people, especially negative ones.

The apprentices, who worked without salary to learn the craft, all boarded in the same house—a yellow Victorian mansion in back of town. They would rise late, breakfast, then gather on the broad front porch in the sun with scripts, or novels, or newspapers, light after-breakfast cigarettes, and squint blinded and as if put upon into the bright shore light. There was talk about the difficulty of rising at all and getting into the new day's work. ("Hell, you just pick yourself up and throw yourself into it.") They groaned; there was frank reference to having to line up for the bathroom. The girls wore Levi's, except when they went into town, and smoked even walking on the street the half-dozen blocks to the seafront theater.

Tony wrote home, doing character sketches. ". . . to top it all off he's a Christian Scientist and says he wouldn't call a doctor even if he broke his arm! I feel a bit sorry for him, though, and Kitty Grand and I go around with him. . . ."

The boy he spoke of was the group humorist. He had invented a kind of French, adding *ment*, pronounced "mawn," to English words that were already adverbs. "Truly-*ment*, I'm *sérieux!*"—with a popeyed leer. Now everyone did it.

"Absolutely-*ment, mon ami. . . .* What the hell is my cue —quick-*ment!*" And finally: "Oh, go to hell-*ment!*"

Fran wrote from sixty miles north on the same coast: did Tony know—she pointed it out only to keep him on top of things—that the anecdotes his friend told were all vintage Dorothy Parker? Tony had quoted a few. "I'm sure he didn't mean to pass them off as his own. It's a way of telling a story. . . ."

"Well, I didn't know and neither did Kitty Grand. He wants us to believe they're his. It's all part of the picture of his insecurity. Really a sweet guy . . ."

The young apprentice who had been seen by Kitty holding hands with the juvenile lead left after a week. Barrett, the first director, stayed until midseason—he could be seen running on the beach every morning—then left with his wife, an actress who had come down apparently hoping for work.

"He kept off the drinking until she came," Kitty said angrily. "He's competent, but he'll never straighten out until he gets rid of her."

The replacement, a young man named Gordon Chevron, did not work out as director but stayed on as a salaried player; and the final director was an older man, competent and quiet.

Chevron was unassumingly friendly. He said he knew Tony's uncle. "Oh, my God! Alex Weisshorn? Your name's *Gamble?* You don't look like him! My God, he's just the greatest. I was *in* Alex's *Pilgrims, Revolt!*—the labor road company. Oh, Christ, I was involved with all that—Lady Garment Workers Stage—everything. . . ."

Sooner or later Tony managed to let drop to all of the apprentices that his uncle was Alexis Weisshorn. A lot of them knew the name: *"Pilgrims, Revolt!"* And when they discovered that he was in England, a sergeant attached to the Eighth Air Force's Special Services Unit, they nodded so-

322

berly: "Christ, he's doing something useful, which is more than you can say for us."

"There's a lot of guilty feeling," Tony wrote, "about just amusing summer visitors with a world at war. But if you suggest to them getting into USO work, they say, 'That's all influence. We'd get the dirty details.' Gordon Chevron is an example. He says he was active organizing the Croppers Union in the South, but now he does nothing. He's nervous, I note, and his hands shake. Also, I'm suspicious because though he says he knows Alex *very* well he didn't even know he was in the service until I told him. Most of the others, even two apprentices from the Midwest, know Alex by reputation and think of him as a great theater guy, yet seem unaware really, or just don't 'get' his music side. Which is amazing, considering he's first a musician. Anyhow, fame rubs off and I get credit I don't deserve. . . ."

There was correspondence to decide which play with Tony in it the family should come to see. When it was settled, he wrote Sylvie Tudela in New York inviting her too (she had auditioned him and acted as a reference in his application to the summer theater).

"Sylvie Tu*dela*," he said to Kitty Grand over hamburgers in a place called Pete's near the theater. He spelled it. "She was the toast of Vienna. You hear that kind of thing, but it was true in her case. The students unhitched her horses and pulled her down the street. She was in *The Merry Widow* and so on. Her daughter married my uncle."

"I didn't know he was ever married."

"Oh, sure." And firmly: "She died."

The girl said at once that she was sorry. Smiling, she watched Tony. And then—it was terrible—death made the boy grin too. All of it—the joy of who he was and who his family were—made him grin. It was disconcerting. His jaw ached, keeping it straight. "She was an unusual person herself: a writer. She ate almost nothing," which of course forced them to glance at their hamburgers and, achingly, not smile. "No, really, she was incredible. Her father, Sylvie's husband, died—he was once an officer in the Prussian Army and a member of the nobility—*von* Schiff—of cancer. And Eve in effect stopped eating, got thinner and thinner. . . ."

"It's awful! *Why?* No, I mean, I could understand it."

They suddenly roared with laughter, and Tony felt both ill and fine laughing.

"It isn't that! I started when you said they pulled Mme Tudela down the street. My gosh! It's terrible"—laughing. "It's my mood—after-performance craziness: pay no mind." They heaved sighs, shaking their heads. "It's awful. Really. Come on now," she said, grown up, giving the table sharp slaps. "None of this one-look-and-we-start-again stuff."

On the boardwalk they grew sober. They stood under a lamp, and he observed that the white light was like a moon in her hair.

"If you could just see how you look," he said. "And that's the least of what I want to say."

"Easy, my friend," she said, which was somehow flattering.

Normally, he did not look at her figure or try to imagine it under her dress. Now, rather guiltily, he did. He thought she looked like the actress Dorothy McGuire, who was the heroine of a popular series of movies. Politely, he transferred the image of Kitty under her dress to Dorothy McGuire under hers.

"Claudia?"—the name of the heroine. "I remind you of Claudia?"

"You even dress Claudia-style."

"I thought your mother."

He understood but refused to be teased. "No, I never said you always did. No, my God. I think you could play that role. . . ."

And when he moved in on her: "Are you thinking of Claudia or me, my friend?"

The private lives of celebrated actors and actresses, particularly their sex lives and the possibility of their homosexuality, was a popular subject. The stars were analyzed on this basis as well as on the basis of their acting achievements, and someone always seemed to possess inside information about whoever it was. "Oh, she's known," they said. The girls judged without heat, objectively, but the boys knitted their brows and shook their heads. "Well, I wouldn't have thought so."

"Oh, my God, didn't you know about her? You're kidding! Everybody knows!"

Tony heard his favorite movie stars talked over in this way, always with an air of authority. There was a cowboy with a handsome sad face like a hunting dog's. "Oh, God, everyone's known about that business for years! He's got a little friend he lives with in a house in the Canyon." And Kitty Grand was astonished when Tony pointed out that both this man and someone else mentioned were, or had been, married. "What earthly difference does that make, Tony? It's merely a convenience."

Even Leo, the technician, contributed to such discussions with his matter-of-fact weight: "It's in certain studio contracts that you have to get married. A publicity department requirement."

They went in groups to movies.

"He's known," they would say, leaning forward to announce it down the row.

Tony also began to look for what he was learning to recognize as signs. "Well, what about Lansing, for God's sake?" he demanded, referring to the friend who told Dorothy Parker stories as his own.

"Well, what do you think? I don't care one way or the other. I love Lansing dearly."

And Gordon Chevron?

"Well, that's iffy. He's neurotic, all right. No, offhand. No.

But one thing you invariably notice: these guys are *not* in the service at a time when just about everyone else in the world is. . . . Leo? No"—firmly, her sureness making him jealous. Maybe the technician had kissed her.

"No, thank you. I'm married to my art."

He approved of her honesty and dedication and, accepting this as common ground, talked about his family at length. Her own father and mother, with whom she lived in an apartment in New York, were, she said with a kind of pride, rather ordinary. "I mean, as a businessman he has flair, but all in all . . ." She was impressed by Tony's stories.

"My family *is* a little unusual. I don't include myself in that."

He described the activities of the Blums and Weisshorns, careful not to rank Alex first: his mother's work, the fact that his father was a lawyer for labor unions. "He doesn't seem the type, but he . . . for example, he knows some pretty tough guys—*nice* guys," he said hastily, "but for example, there was a man he used to bring home for dinner when we lived at the shore year-round—a murderer. Not really. He was up on a murder-manslaughter charge. A little tough guy, but really"—what?—"*soft*. I mean, he had tremendous physical strength. During a strike he lost his temper—he was Irish—and hit a scab or strikebreaker, and the guy—poor guy—fell back"—striking the back of his own head—"and hit his head on the bumper of a truck."

"And died?"

"And died! My father got him off eventually, because it was really an accident. And there are the conventions where the men get drunk and throw mattresses and so on out of the hotel windows. And that goes on: right now, this summer. My God, and he walks through all that—unfazed, just plain. He really loves these guys and they love him. He's just the same with them as he is with me or would be with you, and they love him!" Bob liked books about mysticism, Tony revealed. "He's a mystic, really, like a man who has visions, and a darned good—competent—painter too. . . ."

326

There was an evening devoted to discussing Bob Gamble, another to Fran. Kitty listened, nodding. He could tell when she was impressed. "Sometimes," she said soberly, "I'm on the edge, the precipice of liking you very much. And you never talk about yourself, which is something I also like."

"Well"—with a laugh. "There's nothing to talk about there." He described his friendship with Doc Dougherty, whom he had met a couple of years before in a Saturday afternoon art class. "He's a Roman Catholic, of course, so there are certain areas . . . Of course, we have wild discussions. I tell him he's a slave of ancient superstitions and inform him for his own good how reactionary the Church is. . . ." She listened, nodding, smiling, but there was an obscure constraint upon him. When he had said, using Fran's and Alex's style, that his father loved the tough union delegates and they him, the girl's smile flickered. He found himself choosing words. He soft-pedaled the friendship with Doc and made sure he described the games of touch football as well as the intellectual talks. The point was to follow lines that impressed her.

She was interested in Alex but, he felt gnawingly, insufficiently so. "I admire his work. You're lucky having people like him and Mme Tudela in your family."

When Tony got a V-letter from Alex in England, he showed it to Kitty Grand.

". . . glad to hear the summer theater deal is working out. Fran told me about your friend Chevron, but it has not rung a bell yet. I hear also that you're a tall skinny guy now and that Barrett, whom I do remember as a busy interested type around Broadway, compliments your voice. He knows, and you may believe him. Why not a word from you? Pat writes that his novel is going ahead big guns. . . . I've finished a short film (scenario *and* music) about the exploit of a Flying Fortress named Belinda, which Mrs. Roosevelt mentioned in her column not long ago. It's a re-enactment of the exploit with the actual men telling it. Sound like the old *Pilgrims* technique? . . . Were you able to get the July 4 BBC thing on shortwave? I'm curious about the States-side audience on that. I go everywhere now with captains and colonels, if you please. To drop some names: Jock Whitney is my direct boss. Bob Capa took me last night to a boozy party at a pub called Bath House where the giant figure of John Steinbeck loomed large among the bottles. Enough names? News that's good enough for once: the southern landings are going apace, and we seem to be marching somewhere along the road to Paris. It seems really to be The Push. Everywhere: great guys, great allies. *Now* I feel we're really doing our stuff. . . . I get waves of homesickness, thinking of that beach and ocean of yours. . . ."

Kitty stared at the microfilmed rectangle. "He writes as if he were a friend," she said.

They sat on a low step in the theater lobby. He saw with pleasure that she felt, as he did, the electricity, the quiet importance of the letter.

"I feel so useless and dull. What he's doing—*all* those people."

"While we sit here"—Tony making the point—"going in for theater gossip and backbiting."

They had seen a movie with Ingrid Bergman and Charles Boyer, in which the stars honeymooned in a house like a castle on an Italian lake. Inspired by it and by Alex's letter, Tony made a speech about the war. It was to liberate dishonored nations from Fascist slavery of *all* kinds (it existed also in America) and bring about the sort of just peace in which it would be *possible* to live, two people—thinking of himself and Kitty Grand and intending Kitty to think of it—alone on a lake in Italy: the sun, windows thrown open to the late morning, Boyer and Bergman, with the important bed behind them, looking out, she leaning back into his arms.

He did not miss the look in her eyes as, affected, she nodded.

His parents with Ruth and Saul, having reserved a ration of gas for it, drove down the coast to see Tony in *Our Town*. (Sylvie could not come, but Tony promised to arrange for

328

Kitty to meet her in the fall.) He refused to see his family beforehand, but afterward they had supper, including Kitty.

"You were good," Fran Gamble said firmly. "I liked *very* much what I felt was understatement from you both in those roles."

"Well, that was deliberate," said Tony. "It's exactly what we were after, Fran. What did you think of Leo, the Stage Manager? *His* name's going to be in lights."

"Good. I liked Chevron too. We turn out to have friends in common."

"I thought you did very well," Tony's father said. "It's a good play."

"Why wouldn't it be?" cried Ruth. "It lifts from *Pilgrims* at every turn!"

Saul kept looking at him, Tony thought, with surprise. He leaned back in his chair in the restaurant, one leg swung over the other. "Look at this mug," he said gently. "What a good-looking guy he's become in a couple of months. And this gal!" He had a remote gray look that Tony thought was attractive. He could see Kitty liked him. "Of course, you can tell she's a professional," Saul said. He held his cigarette away from her and glanced at her from time to time with stars of moisture behind his glasses, ignoring his sandwich. They all flattered Kitty. Fran said, "We'll have to get her together with Sylvie." Saul engaged her in a long discussion of musical theater, deferring to her.

Alone with her son, Fran said, "She's lovely," in her definite tone, "and talented."

"I *know* she's talented."

"And you're slightly crazy about her."

"Slightly"—grinning.

They had to return that night, but there was time for a boardwalk stroll.

"Well, go to it, old man, and good luck. Your brother's seeing a gal in Atlantic City now—rather hot and heavy."

How *was* Pat?—really.

"Okay, all in all." They discussed members of the family in

that way, with seriousness, like gardeners looking over plants. "He's struggling with this novel. The subject's remote from his experience and there's a good deal of the midnight oil about it as a result. Alex has written to him with his gut reaction to some of it—no punches pulled. . . ." Bob and Kitty walked some yards behind them. They paused now and then to wait for Saul, who made stops to rest; he would put a hand on the rail and look up at the moon each time, as if it had caught his attention.

"He shouldn't smoke," Fran said, "so of course he does, typically, twice as much. He is and always was an immoderate personality. Morris says it's circulation and he thinks fairly serious in the long run. We'll get other opinions, of course. Don't you worry about it. You're smoking, aren't you?"

She hoped not too much. His father, she had been commissioned to say, would be glad if he put it off for at least a year.

"Well, Fran, we just smoke apparently here. We get extremely keyed up in rehearsals. Everybody does. I freely admit I've been drinking a little beer after the shows too. There's a spot called Pete's where we go."

The smoking interested her more, she said. Wryly, almost angrily, Fran flung her own cigarette over the railing onto the dark beach, and Tony, enamored of this night, watched its light fade. Fran understood about being keyed up and needing releases. "Alex is the same, and you're too much part of the family, I'm afraid, not to have similar responses to these stimuli."

It was a good problem. He looked it over soberly. "I'll try. I can wait a bit, I guess." Then he said, "I was a *little* amused when Bob offered to send that book on acting he bought when I asked how he thought I did. *No:* he said I was good first, not that I'm admitting for a minute I was."

"You can tell him you're amused, you know."

"Oh, well."

What did Kitty think of everyone? Tony asked the next day.

"I liked your mother very much. She's so young and pretty and *bright*—my God!"

They were sitting on the beach. Ruth, she said, was friendly and plain; Bob imposing; Saul was a darling.

He had told Kitty that his grandparents were divorced. Obscurely, with everything else, it was a source of pride. It was odd to have divorced grandparents and a stepgrandmother the same age as one's mother. "My real grandmother —Rose—lives near Atlantic City now in an apartment. She's had three husbands, which is pretty something for her"— both deprecating and proud. "The latest—they were living in Pittsburgh—got too old, and his sons just came and took him away. Oh, you can laugh. It's funny enough." And in another tone: "Saul's not well. It presents a bit of a problem right now."

"I'm sorry. You said that just like your mother."

"That's okay."

"You think a lot of all of them, don't you?" She had said this before, he thought with a kind of sadness, which irritated him.

"Not too much! And not in a wrong way psychologically at all. I may be wrong, of course." He understood her. "For example, I'm finished with smoking for the moment simply because they asked me to and I respect the request."

There were a number of differences between his family and others, which were hard to describe. "Everyone has a sense of work to do—of important work that has to get done." But that was inadequate. "I wish you could meet Alex."

"I wish I could. I feel I know him already. He must be great."

"Oh, he's great."

Later, he pointed out that his mother had said nothing at all about the difference in age between them, and the girl grew cool. "Why should she?" And with a distance that struck him hard: "You assume too darned much, my friend. There is no reason on earth why your mother or anyone else has to worry about my age." At a movie on Sunday afternoon

331

with Tony, the juvenile lead, and a few of the apprentices, leaning down the row to address them all, she cried, "That's my idea of a gorgeous man"—of the tall, fair British actor on the screen, addressing Tony too by her inclusive glance, as if he must be interested.

"Oh, God, Kitty," cried a girl. "You'd be making a mistake. He's one."

"Never mind. I don't care if he is. I'll take him!"

●

Tony and Lansing ducked out between scenes and crossed the field to Pete's, which was at the base of the boardwalk ramp. Tony had a cue, but the other boy was off until the next act. It was against backstage rules to leave until the last customer had lit his cigarette in front of the theater at the end of the evening. But Pete's had a new bartender, and because the boys were in uniforms for their roles Tony had been unable to resist the temptation. "Boy, I needed that one," Tony said, drinking half his beer.

They looked at themselves angrily, hollow-cheeked, in the blue bar mirror, tapped the battle ribbons above their breast pockets. Tony looked just right: trim, pressed, shoes gleaming, overseas cap pulled through the webbing belt, fresh crew cut. He turned his head so that the eyes did not move; when his gaze fell on his own image, he looked disgusted, as if he did not like what he saw. He addressed the other out of the corner of his mouth but loud enough to be heard. "People can still live like this with everything that's going on."

Unconvincingly, Tony felt, the other boy said, "My God." He kept glancing at the sign that said, "YOU MUST BE 21 AND PROVE IT."

"Positive-*ment, mon vieux*," he replied to whatever Tony said.

Tony was not due for his entrance until near the end of the

act. He would come into a wealthy living room, find his fiancée's father on the phone, say, "Sorry, sir, I'll wait on the porch," and start out. A gesture from the father: wait. "I'll get back to you, Senator," he was to say into the phone and hang up. Then he and Tony would play the curtain scene.

Tony, on this night, missed his cue by seven minutes.

"My *God! Je*-sus!"

He and Lansing ran out of Pete's, across the broad roadway and brush-filled empty lot, leaping shrubs. They went skidding up the sea-wet ramp that led to the rear of the theater, wrenched open the little door that was set into the big one, looking everywhere, as if there might be more than one way to go.

"Oh, *boy*, Tony!" the other kept crying. "You *are* late! Oh, boy!"

From onstage (brilliant light leaking back, thick-speckled scenery flats swaying) came the croak of Gordon Chevron's voice. An apprentice stood with the curtain ropes in his hands, and Tony caught glimpses of the other apprentices and actors, an unusual number of them crowded backstage, faces both familiar and entirely new in this paralyzing crisis. They stared at him. He heard his name uttered with urgency and sadness. Leo, his roommate, was struggling into a pair of G.I. trousers, preparing to run onto the stage to get Chevron off, while a girl read Tony's lines into his ear, and he nodded, glasses flashing. The director was nodding too, purple-cheeked. He glanced at Tony. "Gamble, you crud," he said.

Tony hurled himself on.

"Oh, sorry, sir! I'm sorry!"

Chevron was thirty-five, a dark-haired, red-faced, fragile-looking man, whose hands trembled even when he was not on the stage. He had told the apprentices—it was with them rather than the professionals, of whom he was one, that he socialized—that once, organizing "croppers" in a Carolina town, he had been jailed on a trumped-up vagrancy charge, taken from the little jail house at dawn, told by the sheriff that he might go, and then been met at his old car by a dozen local men carrying buckets of tar and oil. It was to explain the shaking hands. "Christ, being *handled* by those bastards"— with a gulping, smiling shudder that had nothing false in it. Yet the apprentices were agreed that his stories were fishy. ("Christ, why should he hang around with us?")

He told Tony that he had auditioned for the original production company of *Pilgrims* and thoroughly approved having been turned down. "What did I expect? The guys who came out were the cream in New York at that time, guys who've gone on to greatness since. I couldn't hold a candle to them. Anyhow, I have a lousy voice, and that stuff's close to grand opera, some of it." A company had toured mining and steel towns in Pennsylvania and Ohio in 1939, donating profits to union locals that had been out so long the strike funds were exhausted, and Chevron had been with it, he said. "The problem was to get the guys to come to the show. If they had their union cards, they got in free. Alex didn't care. 'It's proper, their suspicion of us. They have been cheated and betrayed by our class so damned often, Gordy, they quite correctly don't trust us—liberals, outsiders.' We played in union halls, sometimes from the back of the truck outdoors, Alex in his shirtsleeves with a cigarette in his mouth, the way he does? . . . the piano stripped to a skeleton—front off, back off—for volume: the cream of the Group, the Theater Wing, New York City's very best; and we played to two dozen kids and a couple of pregnant women. *And Alex approved.* You have to have known him to understand it." And on another occasion: "Weisshorn's like a saint in the left-wing movement and in the theater, Tony. He has more in his little fingernail than I have in my entire being"—looking down over his narrow body.

"That eagerness to crouch at people's feet is worrying," Fran had said, having first said she liked him. "There's something a bit too easy about it."

Now he sat onstage, telephone held stiffly to his ear, uttering words into it that were half groans. His body would be seized by trembling that started with what looked like a

334

shrug, then seemed to pick him up and shake him. Sweat dripped from his nose and chin; there were dark splashes of it on the canvas-covered stage. Even with a cue, he could do nothing for a time but stare at the boy. The audience seemed stunned. Unaware of doing so, Tony offered it an explanatory grin. (The apprentice clocking laughs from the lobby would tell the director.) They got through the remaining lines. The curtain was pulled across the stage, sweeping debris with it —a paper match, petals from the prop vase of roses—while Tony gazed at its motion with interest. The actor rose, tearing at his wet shirt, taking deep shaking breaths, and walked off. No one spoke to Tony. He sat with Kitty until dawn on a boardwalk bench.

"Better forget it, my friend, now and forever," she said. And with a weary humor: "Draw a merciful veil over the incident."

He learned that Chevron, waiting for him, had hung up the phone, gone to the wings, and said, "Where *is* that fellow?" loudly, waited, staring at the helpless stagehands, then returned, and—it was crazy, Kitty said—picked up the phone once more without its having rung, and continued the conversation.

At rehearsal the next afternoon Kitty whispered with despairing urgency, "You shouldn't have smiled at the audience. That's the worst thing!"

"Did I? Who saw?"

"You mean outside of three hundred people? . . ."

"My God, clocking laughs! I guess she wasn't clocking many just then."

Only the owner-manager, a normally laconic man named Deegnan, referred to the incident, and he delivered a short lecture.

"In the theater, son, whatever our other faults, we are a loyal band. Disloyalty is the unforgivable transgression, the only one that is not forgiven. Your fellow players have the right to feel they can rely upon you, upon your being there. . . ."

He stood over Tony in the dusty daylight lobby. Beyond them through the open theater doors lay the boardwalk, beach, and sea; and the boy, as he listened to the sentimental speech, watched gulls drop to the service poles and stand lifting their wings before taking off again. The white light was irritating. Loyal, of course, was what he was. Anyway, why hadn't someone gone over to look for him in Pete's? "If I have one thing," he would say in the fall after telling Doc Dougherty as much of the story as he felt he could, "—not that it's such a great achievement—it's a sense of loyalty. And here's this Deegnan, an employer exploiting everyone in sight, telling *me* about it. Someone figured out he was getting a total of five thousand dollars' worth of coolie labor out of the apprentices that summer." He was not trying to make excuses. "I was wrong, completely. It was a terrible thing I did. The one thing you don't do."

It was not hard to accuse himself, because at the moment it happened—that glaring onstage failure—and he realized the implication of his fault (it could not have happened to a real actor), his interest in the theater ceased, and he did not care. "I wasn't that good at it, I'll tell you the truth," he would say to Doc, "except for my voice. Oh, I won't necessarily quit. . . ." He was not a quitter, but—he could not help it—he no longer cared. If anything, he supposed, his real interest was probably still painting. He had begun to write poems too that summer.

As if brought to it by what had occurred, Tony and the professional actor became companions. Chevron made it clear that it was all right, that he had taken the incident in his stride. He had often told tales of scene-moving machinery breaking down, of lines blown, and torn costumes, of leading men and women drunk and staggering onstage; and he told them once more and tossed in references to his own moment of terror. "I *know* now!" It was both the game of the theater and history, and neither, he seemed to be saying, needed excuses.

He offered the boy acting tips, which Tony, hating advice,

sought; and on his side he asked the older man's opinion of plays and movies and performances, hanging on the other's judgment, eagerly accepting it: "Yes, I see that now. I never realized. My God." He searched his memory for stories about Alex, seeing that Chevron was interested. His uncle, of course, had composed *Pilgrims, Revolt!* at the Gambles' shore house. "He came down right after his wife died and plunged into it. It was really a rebound. . . ."

"Oh, boy, Tony. What a shame. How did she happen to pass away?"

Disliking the man (it did not occur to him that the other disliked him as well), he told him everything he knew. They would sit in one of the booths at Pete's while the man held forth, using his battered *An Actor Prepares*, hands trembling as they created a sunrise—the birth of reason or love. Tony gazed with dislike at the supplicating paws and red face; yet, guiltily, he gave the other everything he could. (There was the allowable possibility that Chevron might use Tony's connections and thus square the debt.) He gave him, sensing the particular attention, Eve whom he scarcely remembered; she was leaning against a table in the kitchen of their Philadelphia house, addressing him as if he had been a grownup or an interesting foreigner.

"She starved herself to death, really. It was bad of her, in a sense. Well, of course, it was tragic. But strictly speaking, it was a kind of suicide." You did not quit. Alex kept mementos beside his bed: photographs, tiny German animals with jointed limbs, a brass-and-leather nail set, midget notebooks no more than two inches square with poems inside in microscopic script. In fact, most of these were put away now in a bureau drawer in the Philadelphia house, but Tony reproduced them. What he was offering were his uncle's grief and loneliness.

"He's great. Tremendous, tremendous talent, Tony—tremendous heart. What a lucky guy you are to have such a talent in the family."

Practiced, there was now no nervous hilarity in the tale.

". . . promise to eat a meal"—the intimate family stories: "And Alex ordered the whole fancy meal in advance, calling up. Fancy place. They'd get there and after all that, the only thing she could eat was—this happened—an oyster cracker with horseradish on it, if that. And with her favorite food dishes around her." He named some, improvising: roast duck, caviar, filet mignon. He cast about for complex motives, perceiving with a kind of excitement that he was probably right: her father's death; but she had been a writer: "She was disappointed with not making a success at writing and just gave up. . . ."

"God, how rough. Well, I must say I'm surprised to hear old Alex had a wife at all, Tony."

Chevron, on this occasion, sat at his backstage table working cleanser into his cheeks with shaking hands. He was bare-chested, and Tony saw that the man shaved under his arms. Kitty Grand sat reading a magazine on a folding chair that was tilted against a wall of the dressing room. She was in what she called her unfeminine mood—tough, bland, looking things over, not listening to men. Chevron was in a state of irritation, angry because of the performances and because the director would do nothing about them. "He sets us for opening, then zero. I'm not wholly in the dark where directing's concerned. *He* has to keep us up, competing with our own performances. It's his job, not ours alone." His tone, responding to the boy's story about Eve Schiff, was acid with irritation. Tony asked him what he meant.

"Well, Alex is a great person: I mean I assumed he was one of the known ones. I mean I happen to know that from reliable sources."

Tony thought he meant that Alex was a Communist and said, "Well, no." Then he understood and said, "I don't happen to think so."

"Oh, okay. Fine. Me and my big mouth, if you didn't know." And in a moment, having glanced at the boy: "Forget I said it. I'm probably wrong."

Tony would discover the story of the Sharecroppers Union,

338

the jail, and the tar in a novel a year later. It would turn out that Alex could not remember having met the man, nor as far as anyone recalled had he been in a *Pilgrims, Revolt!* company. The actor disappeared from the world with the theater.

Kitty said later, "You should have seen your face, Tony."

It was all right, which was the point: it was perfectly all right. He did not again say it was not true. Formally: it was all right.

"You'll get over it," she said. "Take it from me."

Kitty Grand also disappeared. She had been standing, elbows on the boardwalk rail, looking blandly and with faint accusation at the sea. It was as if she were not there.

●

There were two weeks left of the summer. Tony, the theater season behind him, accompanied his grandfather to the beach each morning. Saul had commuted with the others for a time to do a volunteer stint at Russian War Relief in the city, but he tired easily, and since things were slack anyhow Dr. Blum put a stop to it. He walked slowly. If he took more than a dozen steps without pausing, the pains in his legs made him wince. He was gentle with Tony and the boy's friends who came to the beach. And Tony on his side, moved, was unembarrassed when his grandfather put a hand on the back of his neck and caressed him. Saul, not yet sixty-five, seemed older. Slim, brown, bald, his cropped mustache white, he sat and studied the dancing horizon. "There could be a sub out there a couple of hundred yards"—severely, while Tony and his friend smiled. He forgot what he had said and, presently, repeated himself. The grandson was continually running to the house for forgotten dark glasses or cigarettes. A dozen times in an hour Saul took one of his dips in the surf to ease the pain. Once, emerging, he stood bandy-legged, staring with an expression of dismay at his wrist-watch. "Did I wear it in, for Christ's sake? I did!" He kept shaking it and listening, the plain steel case at his ear. "What's so amusing, wise guy?" he said to Tony's smiling classmate. He smiled too. Once home, he put the watch to dry on the mantel, arranging the wings of the unbuckled straps. "We'll give it a chance. It might start by itself when it dries out."

"I wish I had a grandfather like that."

The boy did not use the word "cute," though Tony saw objectively that there was something like it about Saul—a sweetness that seemed, these days, to increase.

"Hold your horses till I get my breath back, Tony dear."

They would have stopped on the blazing sidewalk halfway to the beach. Saul, looking around at the day as if fondly, passing a hand across his sunburned head, would finally light a forbidden cigarette and, having shaken out the match, look dreamily into the gas of burnt air it made. He would hold a flaming match against the sun, then shake it out with two neat whips of his wrist, inhale the milky smoke. Or Tony would light Saul's cigarette, the grandfather taking the grandson's hand in his narrow dry one and drawing it to his cigarette as if, with its flame, it were a gas jet or torch, then letting it go and watching Tony while the boy lit his own. When he had rested, they would go on.

On the beach he took his dips, stared at the water, and read newspapers.

"Look. . . ."

"Sure, but Alex says the doodlebugs are finished. You're reading what the Nazis say, for gosh sake! They're talking about lifting the blackout in London." Saul took the V-letter from Tony's hand and reread it. Alex had been loaned to SHAEF to make "*the* invasion movie" and would be going to France to collect Partisan songs.

"Why go to France? They could be recorded and sent back." He read aloud the names of the celebrated writers and movie director with whom Alex was working. "I suppose he has to go."

"Sure!"

There was in the letter a fond paragraph addressed to Saul. "Stay well," it ended. "I may be seeing you sooner than we had all thought possible. . . .

". . . the kind of Prussian muck I hope gets wiped off the face of the earth forever," Alex had written, mentioning the destruction of Saint-Malo. "The question is, will it? Only if we are all vigilant and pressing and insistent. The wonderful spirit of the Maquis these last weeks, the Russians all through, taking it and giving it, and the English with the doodlebug —all examples of what people can do if they want to. . . ."

If the bombs were nothing, then why the hell were they examples of what people could do? "I've become a worrier, it looks like." He read "Stay well" as if he had been given an order he could carry out, and nodded.

He and Tony lit the fateful cigarettes. With smoke in his lungs, Saul's eyes sharpened. He grew sober, getting down to the business of national news in the morning papers, of course enraged at once: the poll tax and Southern Democrats, the soldiers' vote. He snapped the papers open, cracked them, Tony thought, as if they were eggs, then folded them into long bankers' tubes, which he neatly flattened. Republicans, barring the handful of win-the-war ones, were exactly the same as Fascists. "Exactly! No iota of difference! They should be shot!"

Pat came down to the beach in Alex's remembered style for a prelunch swim, having put in a morning on his writing. He was preparing to enter his second year at the university —prelaw as a practical consideration: a tall, fair, long-faced young man. He now smoked a pipe. The surgery of his childhood had disqualified him for military service, and he had been both bitterly disappointed and determined to do well at school (he had won a four-year scholarship) as well as at his own work.

"The real war, as Alex says, will be fought right here after that one"—Pat nodded at the horizon—"has been won."

The boys and their grandfather took the slow walk back and showered at the rear of the house. Saul's body seemed as gray as the sand. He propped an arm against the shower room wall, a fist on his hip, and smiled at the floor. His trunks were a wet ring at his feet. He was narrow, gray-brown, the hair on his body white. He said shyly, "I trust in Alex's ultimate safety."

Tony wandered without aim on the island, occasionally took a bus across the causeway to Atlantic City. He found the houses of friends he had not seen in years but then hung back, unwilling actually to find out how they had altered. He stood across the street from his old school and, feeling as if fifty years had passed instead of five, observed the windows of a room in which he had studied, paper tulips left over from the previous spring still pasted to them. That teacher had once caught him in a lie, and he had had to phone Fran from the principal's office. Coldly, she descended at once upon the woman. Would they tell her why the school wished to terrorize the children put in its charge? If Tony lied, he was frightened. *Why* was he frightened? What of? And more, as the principal, turning scarlet, sought replies. ("I almost felt a little sorry for her, Fran," Tony said later.) "Presumably," she had said to him, "the idea is to teach children to become better liars faster." He did the scene now in his mind with satisfaction, he being a father defending, enraged, a son. He could not remember his own lie. A failing test paper to be signed, perhaps.

He visited his grandmother, who lived in a small apartment in Ventnor, and, feeling dutiful, walked with her on the boardwalk while she gazed at the water and sighed. Almost in Saul's words, she said, "I only hope he's all right."

"Oh, he's all right, Nana. They're ready to lift the blackout!"

He watched people on holiday, faces crowding toward them from the long perspective of the walk: why weren't the

342

men in the service? They thrust toward and around them like water, dressed in robes and bathing suits or light summer clothes, menacingly, he thought, so that, towering over her, he took Rose's arm.

Later, he found himself in front of the bayside house of an old schoolmate and suddenly was looking into the girl's eyes across a hedge of pink roses. "My God," she said. "Tony? I can't believe it."

.They sat in canvas chairs under a tree. A movie magazine lay face down, on its cover the actor Clark Gable in an officer's uniform. "The King," said Tony.

"Well, you got pretty good-looking yourself."

They talked about grammar school teachers and friends. The girl, whose name was Marilyn, appeared to be preoccupied and chewed angrily on her lips. Did he remember Adele O'Neill? She had missed a year of school because of a bad heart.

At first he could not. Then, vividly, he recalled a tough-talking older girl and pictured her shrugging at something a teacher had said and rolling her eyes at the houses beyond the schoolyard, as if to ask, "What can you do with this woman?"

Marilyn watched him. "Well, she's dead. I heard."

Tony said, "What?"

The other looked him up and down in a sleepy way, as if she had been awakened from a nap. She said that she had just heard and that here was Tony Gamble after all this time, as if these were prophetically related facts. She kept looking him over rapidly, then letting her eyes slide sideways. "She left the year after you did and went to Washington, D.C. She wrote Christmas cards, and I would send her back a letter. Her father answered last time and said she was too sick to write. Then I got a letter yesterday that she died." It was yesterday. He had no sooner produced the image of the shrugging girl in his mind than she was dead. Marilyn said, "I have the letter inside." She sat hunched over her knees, picking delicately at a scab, then abruptly rose and led the

343

way into the house. She said, "You come down every summer, don't you? And you never bothered to drop in or let anyone know you were around." She had grown heavy-bosomed and wore makeup. Tony recognized her perfume as one Kitty Grand called "common, though expensive." They went into the kitchen for soft drinks. "My mother's at the grosher's. Can you get by me?"

It seemed natural to put an arm around her waist and kiss her.

"We only have a couple of minutes, so make the most of it. . . . Tony Gamble. You were stout, weren't you?" She talked while he was kissing her. She put her large head on his chest. "You would have to show up at the end of the summer!"

He moved his hands without purpose.

"Easy."

When her mother returned, she went to find the letter and came back with it after a time, her expression gloomy. "Dear Marilyn," he read, "Adele passed away last week quietly in her sleep. She came home from a movie matinee and said she would lie down for a while. That was the last her mother and I saw her alive. As you know, it was not unexpected. She often mentioned you as one of the friends at the old school she liked best. . . ."

"Anyway, that's not true. O'Neill hardly spoke to me. I don't know why she sent me the Christmas cards even."

Wasn't there also a boy with a bad heart? He had a little motor scooter to get around.

"That must have been before my time."

They sat on a glider in a room filled with plants. There was a photograph of her brother in uniform on a table filled with framed photos. She indicated this and one of a sailor. "I write him, and we date when he's home. Look how his ears stick out. Did you know him? He was just going into high school when you were here. He's Italian extraction—dark, which I go for"—her eyes sliding to him.

They listened to Benny Goodman and the Andrews Sisters,

344

and Marilyn became increasingly morose. At length, whenever he addressed her she looked sharply away. "You'll be going home in a week," she said.

Tony told Fran about the death of his old classmate.

"Did you know her well?"

"No, but it was a shock anyway. This girl didn't really seem to care too much."

"I think perhaps she did and wasn't able to show it. Some people can't easily."

Making a party of meeting Bob at the station, Fran and her sons often drove over the causeway early, found a table on the Brighton Hotel's ocean deck, and ordered punches. Pat had his pipe. Tony lit Fran's cigarettes. If he felt up to it, Saul came along and engaged the waiters in talk about union problems. When she did not go into the city, Ruth joined them. The drinks were in layers of different colors topped by pieces of fruit, a tiny soldier stuck like a clove into an orange slice. Tony wrote his name in the frosted condensation on his glass. Their smoke flew away into the street and beach below. Pat grinned around his pipe, leaning back at ease after a day of work. "Comes the revolution, everyone gets to live like this."

At their ease, they talked about the boys' future, the war, Saul's health, and Alex. When their grandmother came, she brought her latest V-letter. If its contents seemed unlikely to upset her mother, Fran brought hers. Tony gazed at the horizon and thought of the convoys in danger and of drowning sailors. Everyone was a vivid rose color under the umbrella. He remembered Marilyn's sad glances and decided that she had been frightened and clung to him for that reason.

"Only I'm a little worried about you being upset," Fran said, watching him.

"Oh, I'm okay."

He was conscious of a power within his reach to perform an action without himself being present, to say something without having to hear it. Discussing death in this way, feeling the deceptive drink (their waiter, a friend, had asked the boys' ages and winked), made Tony very cheerful. He would think later that that might have been the moment to mention Chevron and what the actor had said about Alex, only to say at once that of course it was all right, never mind whether it was true or not.

He wandered in the rambling shore house during the final hot week of the summer. There was the tap of Pat's typewriter, Saul's dry cough. On the weekend the crowded house smelled as always of wet wool, sunburn lotion, and powder. He sent objective letters to Kitty Grand. In the course of two days he wrote a dozen poems. He composed them in his mind lying on the beach and wrote them down later. Once, he opened his eyes, which had fallen under a shadow, and there was Marilyn. She introduced the friend with whom she had come from Atlantic City. "We just can't stand the idea of going back to school," she declared. "Can you?" The girls stood above him, haloed in the furnace of heat. Marilyn looked him over. Tony wrote a poem about it. He wrote one about Saul, who, while he was packing and Tony was in his room, went over his possessions for the boy.

"There it is," he had said. "The point is to get rid of things." There were three white shirts, a few sets of underwear and socks, a gray suit, a pair of slacks and an old jacket, a pair of shoes, some other items. Since he had worn it into the water he had no watch; he owned no hat, no wallet, and had no money except the dollar or two he took from Ruth's bag in the morning; no keys. "There's nothing to unlock."

If you let them, things wear you out. It should be the other way around.

He smiled in the sweet way. He seemed to Tony to exist inside the family without touching it, like a man who refuses to sit down in a room because he is waiting for someone.

"Oh, and my glasses, of course." And bridgework: "Courtesy Sydney, which he can have back if he wants."

Tony wrote about it.

He started to read *War and Peace,* Pat's copy. (Pat had

read it at fifteen and written on the final page: "This is the greatest novel ever written in any language. . . . Patrick Robert Gamble.") At the same time he was going through an anthology of war stories, one of which would endure in his recollection. An army surgeon afflicted with boils and carbuncles had a patient the dressing of whose wound was painful. As if to pay, he first allowed the other to lance one of his boils, the worst, with all the other patients looking on, a nurse assisting the wounded soldier in his work.

He wrote Alex. ". . . thinking of trying poetry in a serious way, but I know the correct thing is to try to publish, if possible. . . ."

Alex's letters came with frequency. A concert performance of his War Cantata for solos and choruses—all GI; one chorus Negro enlisted men, the other white; Alex meant to mix them, which would cause trouble—was scheduled for Albert Hall in October. "Also, Col. Jock Whitney, my only immediate boss at the moment, assures me of the opportunity to complete the Big Project without being taken off it." He was living at bomber stations to do research and had made a friend of a flier on a Marauder. ". . . a sense of the relative triviality of my job and consequent guilt coming on me just now," he wrote. "It doesn't often happen, and I try not to go off the deep end about it. A ground crew sergeant wears the tunic of a gunner missing in action, hates himself for doing it, and can't talk to the others. . . ."

An uncle on Bob's side of the family died. . . . "In the sweat of thy face shalt thou eat bread, till thou return unto the ground . . ." (Tony was reading the Bible. "It's poetry, really.")

The family drove into the city. ("The boys ought to be taking part in this kind of thing by now.") Tony and Pat met cousins who were new to them or whom they had not seen since they were small.

"Well, Anthony, I hear you're going to be the thespian in the family," declared a black-suited, dark-skinned boy.

"I may go to art school after all."

He caught a glimpse of himself in a mirror wearing the satin skullcap and was startled. Good, he thought strictly.

In the car on the way back to the shore there was a discussion, Bob claiming he was not sure what the original family name had been. It made Fran scornful. "You must know! It's impossible not to!"

Gamaliel? Ginsberg more likely.

Death was comfortable in the car at night. The moon rode down with them. Fran's wanting the name was only curiosity: if something was being hidden, that was all right; but why? Tony composed lines in his mind: death's power. In his corner of the back of the car, oncoming headlights hypnotizing him, being younger than he was, he thought: Ladies and gentlemen . . . great pleasure at this time: Anthony Ginsberg!" He grinned, aware of himself: *he did not like the name.* Introduced so to an audience, he considered. He would change his name in that case. Why be uncomfortable in small things? (A bit of an anti-Semite?) But he acknowledged the introduction, held up a hand for quiet. . . .

Alex's old friend Fisher Blumenblatt came down on the final weekend in the uniform of an Air Force captain. He had been assigned to assist in the administration of an island in the Pacific. "Call me benevolent leader."

He read a few of Alex's letters, shaking his head. "Staff sergeant! My God, what a guy! All he has to do for a commission is drop one word in the right place."

Fisher announced the death by suicide of a mutual friend, a painter, who had thrown himself from the window of a hotel room in Harlem. "Well," he said, "in a way it was time. But my God . . ."

They took Fisher with them to the Brighton.

"He couldn't . . . they're so tough, these things"—referring passionately to the suicide. "He couldn't *love*, Franny, that's all. Remember Johnny Gregson years ago? . . ."

They discussed Eve's death. Blumenblatt had been a friend. She had weighed at the end seventy-five pounds. Eve had closed so many doors, he declared sadly, that finally there was only one left.

The hotel deck with its scarlet and yellow umbrellas; Fisher with the brass and braid on his summer uniform aflame, his brown, cynically foreign-looking face turned to the sun; the talk; the drinks: everything had power.

On the Sunday Tony took a bus to Atlantic City to meet boys from his school who were vacationing there. They stood on the boardwalk in front of the hotels at twilight, backs to the sea, a heel hooked onto the low rail, elbows on the top one. Their shoes were white in the dusk, or gleamingly polished. There was one whose mother had recently died. He wore a zoot suit, brand-new, trousers tight at the ankles, jacket below the knees, the material a hard bright blue linen. His collar and tie were oversize. He had combed his hair into a pompadour in front and duck's tail behind. Tony understood that it was not the kind of outfit the boy's mother would have let him buy. In the midst of his costume, his pale face was sad and eager. It was as if death had been a license for him.

"What about the can on that one?" he demanded anxiously, indicating a girl with his chin. "No, look!"

"My God," Tony said.

The painter of whom Blumenblatt had brought news had been unhappy, unfulfilled in his work. (He had been 4-F as well, of course.) Tony counted up to ten stories and threw himself—*himself*—from a window. But then he thought that that falling in Harlem (it was the other way out of Harlem, Blumenblatt had said bitterly) might have been as good or useful as falling in love should have been for the man. Briefly containing that death, looking at girls, Tony was conscious of such potency of life in him that he felt dizzy. He was himself, he felt, the heat of life.

The bereaved schoolmate told stories of his brothers' conquests. He snapped his smoked-down cigarettes hard against the lamp standard, where they burst into flowers of orange sparks. The ducal hotels had glaring domes of gold; their faces were lavender; the cooling beach was as pink as bone, the sea the color of Mercurochrome. His own moment past, feeling the other's authority, chilled and sleepily waiting, Tony allowed himself or another self to wish that Alex was dead, though years later he would be certain that he had not wished it.

1945

●

Tony went to New York for a weekend early in the year and met Sylvie Tudela at Sardi's. Kitty Grand would join them at five at the Russian Tea Room, but Sylvie wanted lunch tête-à-tête.

"I don't know. Maybe I lack a certain something for the stage, Sylvie." Feeling this was letting her down, he had been talking about movies. Well, why not? Mme Tudela knew people and could arrange a test. But seated in the famous restaurant, surrounded by celebrities whom she indicated with candid pride—Lucille Ball at a banquette table, Charles Laughton under a pillar with an agent Sylvie knew (she would stop at the table on their way out)—Tony felt oddly upright. "I don't know about the test at this point. I mean, unless you started the wheels."

Nothing had been done as yet. "If you're having honorable second thoughts . . . Heaven knows there's no hurry, darling." Particular dishes were brought to her: sauces, charged water, Nescafé on a plated salver. She sat straight, plump and tiny-waisted, looking at Alex's nephew with smiling eyes. Now and then she covered the boy's hand with hers and gave it a firm pat. A soldierly actor wearing a mustache with waxed ends stopped, nibbled Sylvie's dessert, and talked about himself deprecatingly in a deep voice.

"Idiot," she said absently when he had gone. And to someone else: "Alex writes that the air raids are so much piffle." (Tony had said this to her.)

"Oh, God! How *is* Alex?"

She asked the other, who was connected with movies,

351

"What do you think of this young man? Has he the facial bones for a screen career?"

"It's your decision, darling," she said later, holding his arm and steering him through Shubert Alley for a matinee on Forty-fifth Street. She went to her office—she was on the directorial staff of a well-known production company—but met him backstage at the end of the performance. The star, casting off his costume, cried, "Alex's nephew! My Lord! He looks like him! The sweetest, best, most talented man—the *gentlest* man . . ." He would simply stay at the theater, he said, for the evening performance: "I'll have a salami sandwich sent in, for God's sake, Sylvie!" To Tony: "Were you in front? Wasn't it lousy?" Sylvie worried about the performers, consulted her lapel watch and a list of new cues, frowned at the dancers, and patted them. "Children, don't catch cold, for heaven's sake. Wrap up!" Tony stood in the dark, rope-hung cluttered backstage, feeling as remote and concentrated as if he had been out of doors in a forest.

"I'm not social or something," he said to Kitty Grand in the evening after she and Sylvie had met and talked. "You have to be able to deal with people in a way that I apparently can't. All the kissing, and darlings, and flattery, and Sardi's stuff . . ."

After six months, he had found the girl, in her smart black overcoat and pillbox hat, disconcerting and challenging: grown up. She was both beautiful and strange-looking.

"Kissing bothers you, does it, old friend?" She teased him about his letters. "And I remind you of Jennifer Jones now. I count on you to tell me when I become Kitty Grand."

But she was not that either.

They walked into the park at Sherman's statue, her legs sexy in heels. "I love New York! I guess a native's entitled to as well as anyone else." Her family had a large apartment, but Kitty was staying with roommates in a Village walk-up. She was going to quit college and devote full time to auditioning. "I'll go the rounds, try out for everything—anything. The auditions themselves provide fantastic experience. I'll

352

just do it! I'm going to exploit your darling Mme Tudela. She expects to be used. The whole point now is for me to be good!" She was excited and seemed almost alarmed. He took his cue from her earlier remark and, sitting on a bench, servicemen with girls on nearby benches, kissed her.

"Growing up a bit, aren't we? You needn't feel you have to. It isn't some sort of contest."

After an insistent hour, nevertheless, he had her saying, "I can feel love for you tonight. I can use that word." She held him off, peering solemnly through the dark.

In her apartment entranceway, she said, "If you come in again, my friend, do let me know. I'm trying to figure this out. Was it your recitations of original Gamble work that did it to me? No, you're great, Tony. Those poems you sent. I *mean* that. And I agree on your decision in re the theater for very flattering reasons."

He was staying, as the family usually did in New York, at Edna Loux's apartment on the East River. He spoke of her to extend the moment. "She was Alex's first really important music teacher, and she studied with Siloti, who was Liszt's pupil. . . ."

It reminded her:

"How *is* your uncle, for God's sake?"

On the street in front of his house on Sunday afternoon, he and Doc Dougherty tossed a football back and forth, Tony conscious of the contrast between this and New York and of the ease with which he managed both.

He said, "Oh, we're through, all right."

He had told his friend of the afternoon and evening. He was through with the theater, and he was finally through with Kitty Grand. He said, conscious of the cruelty, "Sylvie feels there's a little something lacking—a professional dimension. . . .

"I might as well say that she finally uttered the actual words. You understand me? And when we said good-by her hand was shaking, Doc. That's the pressure she was under."

Tony had an after-school job in a one-act play that toured

local war plants to encourage bond sales. "When that's over, I'm finished."

He and Doc used the Gambles' season seats at an Academy concert. They bundled their overcoats under the chairs and gazed into the brilliantly lit, bread-colored shell at Ormandy's back. "Tremendous?" Tony whispered of Brahms's Second, and the other boy shook his head in wonder. The music made anything possible and everything worth attempting. His attention wandered quickly into fantasies, his own breathing, joined with the breath of the audience, autohypnotic. Each boy had rolled his program into a tube. Doc wore scholarly glasses with flesh-tinted frames that looked ill at ease on his tense, tough, small face. Tony had black-rimmed glasses, which he wore to concerts and movies. Both were neat with well-creased trousers and polished shoes.

In the interval they ran into Sasha and Pauline Volin, whom Tony had trouble identifying at first. Relationships eluded him. Later, he would work out for Doc that Pauline was one of Saul's sisters. ("Sasha always wears a white vest," he would explain, remembering stories. "It's a cleanliness fetish. The whole family's eccentric one way or another.")

Volin was fatter than he remembered and had pale quaking cheeks and gray lips. "Anthony, don't smoke. Put it out. Take it from me." The man gazed around the ornate lobby at the smokers. "Madness. This fellow"—Doc; Volin's lips shook— "does not smoke, I see. Keep it that way. You know, I like this young man. I like the look in his eye." He cheered up and, while his wife stood silent, reminisced. "Avoid bad liquor and tobacco and you'll be happy men. You couldn't have known your grandfather's father, of course. He died in —what? 1905! Forty years, Pauline, since your father died. Think of the time! Since the Armistice it's already a quarter of a century! *He* was a smoker, as were all of those socialist intellectuals." Doc listened attentively and would say later, meaning it, "That's an interesting man."

Volin's thoughts focused.

"Have Saul give you the story of his father's funeral. Base-

354

ment whiskey was purchased for the mourners, and one suffered as a result from temporary blindness. You had professional mourners. This man was, I believe, the sexton of the temple. I'll recall his name. . . . His name was Solomon Zeide. How's that for a memory? Everybody did it in those days. It wasn't just Saul, you understand. If you needed whiskey, you went to your neighborhood moonshiner. Some of those men are today your multimillionaire distillers. Saul was, in fact, gypped, sold the raw stuff—raw alcohol. You didn't know this?" He described an Orthodox Jewish funeral as if he were talking of rites of which he had read. "Saul had the duty of providing refreshments, and of course the whole thing was highly distasteful to him, and he wouldn't spend a nickel more than he had to. A policeman came to the door of the old Lombard Street house and said that three of these men were in the hospital, Zeide being in the worst shape. Your great-grandmother, who died about the time you were born, put him on a pension, which was typical. She was both charitable and cautious. You get your mother to tell you about Babushka. . . ."

"Oh, she does. I hear a fair amount about all that period."

The lobby was almost clear.

"Saul fainted when the policeman came to the door, or so the story goes."

"I don't believe that's true," said Pauline.

Some days later, having spoken to his mother, Tony said to Doc, "You have to take all that with a grain of salt. Saul and Sasha never really got along, though Fran said it did ring a vague bell."

Tony wandered in the city that winter as he had at the shore but now he went at night, alone, and farther afield each time. He and Doc did not talk about such adventures. It was as if, Tony thought, due to the fact that Doc was a good Catholic, there existed an area between them where, though they could, they should not meet. It made them gentlemen with each other, and this gentlemanliness, an unstated recognition, became their style. But at school (Doc went to parochial schools) with other friends Tony held his cigarette in a different way, walked with his knees bent, and used the four-letter words that he and Doc together never used.

"I might be really late," he would tell his mother frighteningly. "Oh, I'll be all right." He went to observe life in the city, he said. He promised to be extremely careful. Pat as well, during long weekends in New York, would, he said, overhear, study, but deliberately take no part in the world of the streets. He had written to Alex in reply to a letter of warning, "If you get too close, you no longer see."

Tony often came home near dawn, pale with exhaustion and failure, though he was not specific even with himself about what he sought. "Please be careful," Fran said helplessly. "Bob worries so." But they did not prevent either boy from going.

When he was finally in bed with a girl—she was Puerto Rican, very thin, teeth missing so that she had to smile with her lips closed (Tony noted it)—he observed himself attentively. They were in a house in a row of tiny houses in a poor neighborhood: three rooms, it seemed, one on top of the other. An old man and woman waited downstairs for their bed (her grandparents, she said, which he noted politely, not questioning even his own astonishment). The toilet was in a shed in a brick-strewn yard, and Tony had stood there twice, smiling drunkenly into the pungent blackness, surrendered to whatever it was that promised to manage everything. The girl fell asleep ("I don't care to do that anyhow") and the boy worked it out that it had happened to someone else. Yet he recalled everything as vividly as if he had seen it in a movie: the murmur of radio voices through the floor, the bed chiming and sagging, womanly smells that were both strange and familiar, the girl's skin as rough with the cold as a cat's tongue, her dim sleeping smile, even the fact that only his presence had been wanting. . . .

Alex's letters that winter were quietly excited.

". . . a new weekly job on top of all the others, with Forces Network hosting a GI–British Tommy quiz show, making it

356

really a seminar in which the war and its politics are discussed round-table." His War Cantata was now famous. A drama with music dedicated to the Eighth Air Force was about to be produced ("Covent Garden and the London Symphony combined, no less . . ."). He had become a major celebrity.

". . . happy Papa gets on well to the extent of handling another of the monster RWR affairs"—a letter to Ruth, which she was meant to read on the phone to Fran— "and I know you and Fran are doing bang-up jobs at your assignments.

". . . firsthand knowledge once more of what our boys are going through. A good friend, Dewey Pryne, whom I may have mentioned and who has become a close buddy, was due here days ago on flak-leave from France, where he's on a Marauder. I haven't heard, and an uneasiness commences, which may mean nothing. . . ."

In January: "You may have heard I was sweating out a young guy, Dewey Pryne. He's a gunner on a plane, had gotten 62 of his 65 missions, but I hadn't heard in weeks. Okay: now a long letter: he's completed his tour and is on his way to the States—probably to rest, maybe begin again in the Pacific: these kids! I gave him your address"—to Fran— "in case. He's as close to me as anyone and his world views are like ours. I hope he'll open up for you. . . . On the surface: just another guy, but full of charm and tricks.

"My birthday in one week, and I'm trying to decide what if anything there is to say about being 40. I just don't give a damn. But on the other hand I find myself indulging in a good bit of temperament. . . . Pressure on from the Big Chief for our film's completion . . ."

Fran met Pat and Tony for lunch at one of the center-city hotels on a Saturday. She wore her Russian War Relief uniform, which, with its Sam Browne belt and overseas cap, was only now, near the end of the war, familiar enough not to be embarrassing. "I hope to heaven this guy can be a friend," she said vehemently, talking of Dewey Pryne. With his need to be on his own, Alex also required and never came near getting a close friend. "Someone with some kind of—what? Brains, I suppose, for want of a better word, so that there's give and take. . . ."

Early in March Tony and Doc, putting it in so many words, decided to go a little crazy.

"What the hell," said Tony. "The war looks good. Everything looks good."

There had been, in addition, an encouraging letter from the woman, editor in chief of an important poetry anthology, to whom Alex had recommended Tony.

They would have a final fling and put aside boyish behavior: "Which we never indulged in much anyway." They played hooky—Doc with a real pang from his sober school, Tony readily, not letting Fran in on it ("She'd just give me a note getting me excused from classes")—and went downtown for the latest Bogart, for which they had been waiting, catching the first show at ten in the morning, then sitting through it once more.

"Say, Hairy, c'mon, lemme have a little drink."

They played the roles on Market Street and in a trolley car, dealing with the letdown, then in McHale's, a favorite place of Doc's where beer was served to them and where the lunch was set out in bowls and platters on the bar before a rooster-cheeked bartender with a brogue.

"Aw, Hairy, one more?"

"What name? That's not my name."

"Not Haddy?" cried Tony, astonished.

The man had served Doc's parents and asked after his mother (Doc's father was dead).

"She's well," said Doc, being Irish, "and will be the better for knowing you inquired."

Later, they wandered through the polished mahogany corridors of City Hall, which was next door, pushed ajar heavy brassbound entries in hope of a trial or hearing in progress.

"Maybe we'll see Pop browbeating a witness."

They did find two lawyers standing beneath the judge's bench addressing him earnestly. There was no jury, no one

358

seated behind the court barrier. There were a young man, and an older man, and two women before it, the women wearing feathered hats; they were sitting around a table looking ill at ease. There was a man with a notebook. A uniformed guard asked them to go in or move along. Tony said later, unsure, "The tipstaff. . . .

"No," he said then, shaking his head, serious. "I mean, some poor guy's in trouble in there. He was *there*. We might as well have been at school. But we created a conjunction."

Doc understood. "Our paths happen to cross in his time of trouble. Are we therefore, knowing about it, part of it: responsible? Were we anyway?"

They looked on as a police van rolled to a stop in the courtyard below, faces, mostly black, visible, fingers hooked into the mesh screens. "Talk about trouble!"

The boys stood hatless but warm in their long winter overcoats and lined gloves. Doc had his glasses on. Tony's were in his pocket.

"You have these events all going on at the same time," said Tony both vaguely and precisely. "Here's this going on, but you turn away and all that's really going on—except that this is really going on—is the war, for example, or your personal problems. Yet there's a line between you and someone else: only a line, which if you cross it you become perhaps that person."

"Or could that be a definition of madness?" said Doc.

The rear door of the van was opened by a policeman. Another stepped out of the van and stood beside the first. Then a prisoner, a black man, blinking, shivering in the cold, still bent from the cramped seat. Then another.

"They're just about all Negroes."

Tony remembered Leadbelly and told Doc about him. "He came down to the shore once for a sort of benefit with Alex and Asher Moak." He was not specific about the purpose of the pay parties, and Doc was politely incurious. "Really, Ledbetter was his name. A great composer, Asher Moak said. He wrote 'Goodnight, Irene' in jail."

359

"He wrote that?"

Thinking of that (they would call down the row of cells for the song, then listen silently, mouths ajar, eyes dreaming—white men and black) and of the black fingers on the guitar and clutching the screen (the gleaming, brown-pink nails), he said, "You have to do something." He mentioned Tom Joad, as if he were speaking of a friend of the family in trouble. He said briefly, "Like Fran or Alex or even Saul—even now." You had to do something.

"I should have been like Saint Martin and divided my coat in half for that guy." (In fact, Doc was going to look at coats at Wanamaker's; his own, which had been his father's, was threadbare.)

"What good is half a coat, for gosh sake?"

They argued about faith and free will on lower Market Street, in and out of penny arcades, Tony with longing glances at the dirty Movieolas.

"Life is something like a pinball machine."

"Wait a minute, Hairy, just a little one, please? We're avoiding . . . we are *avoiding* the subject. . . . How could He let that guy in City Hall courtyard shiver without a coat, broke, pulled in no doubt on some trumped-up vagrancy charge or the like? . . ." Tony used his capitalized "He" suavely, lending himself to belief at the same moment that he was declaring that God was impossible: some beneficial force heavier than air or lighter—which?—talking Tony over in a blue sky above our sky to assistants *in English?* Yiddish? Come on! (All the time he was trying the possibility. "Dear God," he recalled guiltily, "stop my ears hurting.") Did he mean He did it to get Doc to offer his coat? . . .

"He let John Keats die at age twenty-five, allows Nazism to exist: the camps. . . ."

"Ah!"

He had Tony where he wanted him.

"If one of two contraries be infinite, the other would, ultimately anyhow, be destroyed. Granted? If God means good, then evil impossible. Granted? *However*"—counting out on

360

his long fingers—"Nazism, old Keats cashes in at age twenty-five, et cetera. Therefore *no* God, right? . . . Hold it. Hold it. . . ."

They went up and down in the elevator in Leary's bookstore.

"I don't grant the premise. . . . It's nature. What about the crying girl?" They had sat once in the main branch of the library plugged into a record player, one on either side of it in padded earphones, and Doc had indicated a girl alone at another table. "In utter silence," he had said later, "the earphones on, tears streaming down. *What was she listening to?*"

"What was she listening to: find out, and maybe there's the answer."

"It's only an answer if you don't find out."

They stood in the poetry section. Doc pulled books from the shelves. "Pass the crying girl. Check Tennyson. Check Browning. Pass Keats, Shelley. Check Byron. Pass Walt." They failed Poe, checked Housman. "Fail Kipling."

"Check Kipling."

"Publius Vergilius Maro," said Doc, educated: "Pass."

They thrust their glasses onto their noses. They grinned shyly at each other, classifying poets, discussing God.

Certain people (Tony) did good by instinct, not out of superstitious fear of punishment or hope of reward. They observed the hungry˙of the earth and rushed to do what could be done.

"Superstitious!" Struck, Doc reeled against the books.

"Because God doesn't exist I don't run around hurting people. Why not? Call it selfish: it makes me feel good not to. Or it makes me feel bad to! Conscience ˙ . ."

"Or you're scared to."

It almost made Tony angry. "I admitted the selfishness of it." Good, he saw suddenly, came out of bad. But Doc said, "Pretend you're completely anonymous and all-powerful. The death button is in your hand. . . ."

They were hushed by a salesman. After a time, they started

again. "Pass T. S. Eliot. Check Auden. No, wait: pass him."

They failed Stephen Vincent Benét.

In Wanamaker's Doc tried on overcoats. He made himself yield to the salesman, consulting him. "What do you think?" —a heavy sleeve tugged tight, sighting down his lanky ballplayer's arm. He had an aristocratic manner of inclusiveness that Tony admired, interesting himself in another man's job, yielding to the superior experience and training, but then digging in his heels at that point where he felt he knew something. He went ahead now with an air, working out the formula for overcoats, examining stitching and styling, questioning the man on durability. The salesman knew Doc from other sessions and respected him. It was Mr. Grayson and Mr. Dougherty. A coat was needed and eventually—how money was spent in his family was no light matter—Doc would buy one; but now he was learning. A mountain of coats rose on the table, silky linings making them slide and spill. He chose six to be sent to his house to live with for a week, and then imperiously he would call to have them all picked up.

What about Saint Martin?

Doc would give the old one to a Catholic charity, he declared, slightly flushed. They went questing through the department store. Here, as lights took on brilliance at dusk, and the war went well, and it was remembered that his poems might be printed, Tony felt strong. Goods rose in secure walls. He was enamored of electricity, the colors of lights: a blue that was like ice crystals, cold bright cherry red. They went through shirts on the ground floor and at length, having taken pains, Doc bought a white one with buttons on the collar points for school. They swept the place powerfully, seeking an appropriate exit. Tony's Great-aunt Annette (Saul's sister as well as Pauline?) had once walked all through Wanamaker's, right past the eagle, and out again with her umbrella in full sail. She had been seen by three acquaintances and two relatives, Tony embroidered, and what was more, it had not been raining. "I'm like that, I'm afraid."

"Let's go and give your coat to someone now," he said.

They went into the twilit street.

"Christianity is in the act as moved by the good man's heart," said Doc magnanimously when Tony had protested that he was not qualified. They stood at Thirteenth and Locust, overcoats in their arms. "How much time do we have?"

"You're not going to give your coat away," said Tony.

"Will you? Probably some guy would be insulted."

"I think it's nice of you to let us stay in limbo for our good acts while you get to heaven."

"Historical Society across street," Doc observed, shivering. "Lincoln life mask in there. I've seen it. Also Lincoln horsehair sofa."

Neither boy was a born joker. They were slow in taking fire. Tony watched himself, never quite lost. He actually said to a man apparently headed toward the National Maritime Union's club, "You look cold, sir." The man wore a sweater and jacket but no overcoat or hat. For a moment, clearly, Tony could see in his mind's eye a merchant ship plunging through black water, lightless, propellers in the air. "We happen to have an extra coat. . . ."

"Oh, my *gosh*," he cried later. "Of course, he figured we were spies looking for shipping information. I didn't notice we were in front of the Maritime Union place till that second, smack under the Loose Lips poster!"

They walked toward the Blums' town house, where they were expected for dinner, coats on again.

"Jolly good show, Haddy . . . This city is the color of a rat, but the sky is good." It still shone behind the tall buildings, pale and cold as milk, as if dying, which Tony pointed out. He produced his letter from Maggie Donovan of *Poetry America* and rattled it, read it aloud to the street. (Alex had written to her, then to Tony: "Give Maggie an immaculate MS, also my love. Don't worry, if you meet, about her tough manner; and please tell her that her Charlie is usually— better say always—out of the way of the damned doodles. In fact, they disturb sleep and little more. . . .")

Dr. Blum, meeting Doc Dougherty for the first time, said

in his direct way after brief polite talk, "Father Coughlin says we must forgive the trespasses of Mr. Hitler and Mr. Hirohito. What do you think of that?" The Blums knew about Doc, and Doc knew something about the Blums. He did not defend a priest simply because he was one.

"I have the feeling he tends pretty much toward the paranoiac by now, sir."

"You do, do you?"—wagging his gray head and smiling genially. "Well, well." (Tony could see that Doc liked the old man, accent and all: "Vell, vell.")

His friend read magazines while Blum gave Tony an ultraviolet treatment for acne, then they went upstairs. Saul was dressed, looking more lively than the boy had seen him in months. It made him happy. Saul laid the back of his dry hand against Tony's cheek. When he greeted Doc, he grinned and punched his chest as if they were old friends. Hungrily, he looked from one to the other, so that Tony was aware of his grandfather's feeling as a kind of heat. Later, as if to prove how well he was, Saul got into a fight about a play he and Ruth had just seen, haranguing her as if she, who agreed with him, was his enemy, then turning on Sydney, her brother. "What you don't understand," he kept saying, eyes flashing behind rimless bifocals, cigarette aloft; or: "Let me tell you something, my friends! We are here discussing nothing less than what this world might become in the immediate future. . . ."

Sydney's wife sat with lids lowered. She entered discussions rarely, as if, though their politics were in accord, she and her husband represented an inner confederacy. Sydney's style was frowningly matter-of-fact; he shrugged his agreement like Ruth: "Sure. Exactly. Yelp!"—for yes. He supplied data, made factual corrections: things were not to be apprehended in ideal terms, despite Saul's angry idealism. . . . Tony saw that Doc was impressed all around, though he worried about the effect on his friend of the general assertiveness, the ferocious attacking.

"Anyhow," Mrs. Blum said with finality to cap each disagreement, her cigarette holder between her teeth, "the Red Army, thank God, stands at Vienna's gates."

Tony said later, "The problem here is to get a word in edgewise. You did all right. . . . On the whole, I'd say Saul seemed okay. He shouldn't smoke."

"He seems fine." Enthusiastically, Doc passed them all. "Swell people, Tony! Remarkable."

They went over the house, and in Saul and Ruth's room Tony told the story of Saul's few possessions, how his grandfather had counted them for him.

"Remarkable," said Doc, moved. "Good man."

Tony turned to the entry under Alex's name in a recent *Who's Who in America*, which stood on the windowsill with other references. Doc read it with attention, then leafed through the book.

"F.D.R. There's a long one." He looked up Coughlin, grunting. "The point is to acquire an objective overall view."

Once they were on the street again, both worked to restore their earlier humor.

"Anyhow, the Red Army, thank God . . . "

They stopped strangers.

"We are seeking a man who wears a gray worsted overcoat"—in dry movie-European accents. "He carried a suitcase."

The game, which soon became hide-and-seek, tended to lag. Doc left clues: a glove (he watched from his hiding place because he could not afford to lose a glove) or his morning paper folded to the editorial page, the word "Sarajevo" circled. Later, he pretended to use the phone in a drugstore, saw Tony through the window, and ran, leaving the receiver swinging. He hid in a dripping tunnel under the railroad approaches, where the heels of pedestrians echoed, back against the curved brick wall, features livid in the golden spray of cars' lights. He would say that he sensed then that he was not going to make it. Tony, light as down despite his greater weight, silent, remorseless, sleepy-eyed, was right there. This was work for which he had been trained, which he understood, yet did not like. The dramatic humor became permanent. He stood (he felt drugged) looking into the dark yellow Western Union office half an hour later, while Doc crouched miserably over a pad of forms at the counter inside, writing messages, crumpling them in despair. At length he wrote, *"Dulce et decorum est pro patria mori"* on the pad in large letters and showed it to the window. Neither boy smiled, which was their triumph.

"What time is it now?"

Tony could not dispel games easily. There was no good ending for him. He yawned with depression. Each had told his mother not to expect him before dawn. When Doc suggested the all-night movies at Tenth and Market, Tony said irritably, "It's where the bums sleep. I don't like it."

They could not go home.

In a White Tower restaurant at two in the morning, hamburgers and coffee before them, Tony brought out once more the letter from Mrs. Donovan.

". . . particularly enjoyed your references to nature, for which, it is clear, you have a genuine feeling. Poetry being such a personal medium, especially for the young, it is hard, isn't it, to criticize objectively without seeming rather cold. . . . Anyhow, the point is that in my own estimation you are possessed of talent. . . . I tell you what I'll do: I'll keep two of these and see about one of them for this next book, and you in the meantime are to keep working and send me something else soon. . . ."

It had been beyond his highest expectation—that "I tell you what"—and it seemed as good now, as potential (Alex) and intoxicating, as the morning he had received it. There was little doubt that at least one of Tony's poems was going to appear in print. He decided to be drunk. He began to read the letter to the white-tiled room in what Doc would describe as a very loud voice. The counterman looked at Tony. "You wait a long time for something like that," Tony declared drunkenly.

A few sailors and soldiers with their girls smiled. They had

366

drink-clouded eyes and waited in a friendly way for the boy, who had interrupted their conversation, to finish. But a tall man who had been sitting alone in a corner said without looking at Tony, "Shut up."

Tony did not.

The man turned. He had the congested look of someone who does not feel the effect of his drinking. He rose. Doc, readier than his friend, stood as well. Tony, of course, would blame himself ("It was a dumb thing to do. I was showing off"), but to Doc the man was only dangerous. "Let's go," Doc said.

Tony, believing neither in danger nor in action, was confused. He explained, displaying the letter. ". . . A celebration of sorts," hearing his own elegant tones as if from another place, as if he were not there. Doc knocked Tony aside as the big man swung, so that the fist just missed Tony's ear. The counterman yelled, "Hey!" By then the others in the place had risen.

They tried to walk with dignity, then they ran. When they paused, Tony began to shake. He could not help it. He saw clearly then what he had seen only dimly before—that he was sad, that he was going to be sad all his life. He saw that people were the death of people. He feared them and, fearing them, hated them. When he spoke, his voice shook. He would have to go somewhere at once to relieve himself. "Jesus," he said, defeated.

•

Tony was reluctant to go into the Blums' house. He went instead across the street to examine the little Soutine in the window of Rem Levy's art gallery, and after a moment Rem opened the front door and stood squinting in the sun. He hardly glanced at Tony. He said, "My God, Tony," huskily. He was portly and seemed always to need a shave. He looked exhausted now. "You like the Soutine? It's a little treasure, in my estimation." He hooked a toe under the bootscraper on the top step. "First Roosevelt, now Saul. Some business . . ."

Tony nodded. It was all right. He kept the fact in a separate place. He glanced along the tree-lined street with its tall doctors' town houses and saw his brother turn the farthest corner. Pat had come down after his first morning class at the university (Tony had been called from his class at high school), and he carried a bulging briefcase and walked with a stride that seemed to the brother to be purposeful.

"It's Pat."

"Look, it's Pat, isn't it?" said Rem. "He's coming too. My God." And then: "Did he know?"

"Who—Pat?"

Was Saul finally told that F.D.R. had died?

"I think he was," Tony replied. "Wait: yes. I remember I was down a few nights afterward, and I seem to recall—definitely—that Ruth told him that night. He took it all right. He wasn't that crazy about Roosevelt, Rem. But Alex wrote from London that people—strangers—were stopping him on the streets and paying tributes to F.D.R. because he was, simply, an American in England. A *corporal* taught him: all you say is thank you. There's nothing else to say."

Rem whispered, "Does Alex know?"

"They sent a cable."

Dewey Pryne was in the Blums' house. He had, by coincidence, arrived hours before Saul's death. Tony asked if Rem Levy had met him.

"No. I heard he's there."

Pat's gaze was on the north side of the street, where the house was, and he did not see his brother. The door opposite opened. It stood in a recess above the short flight of marble steps. Dr. Blum appeared, wearing an Oriental dressing gown over trousers and an open shirt. Even from where he stood, Tony recognized the cordovan bedroom slippers thick with talcum. The old man blinked at Tony but did not recognize him.

"What's this?" asked Rem. "He doesn't see you! Morris!"—
in a loud whisper.

The doctor had escorted a man to the door, and the man,
someone unknown to Tony, shook Blum's hand and walked
off down the street toward Pat at a brisk pace. Tony saw with
vivid consciousness the man grow smaller and his brother
larger under the powder of new leaves.

"Who was that, I wonder: funeral man?"

Visible behind Blum in the open doorway were corners of
the curling dragons of furniture in his waiting room, a panel
of silk-embroidered screen. Smoky morning light lit the doctor's tangled white hair and spilled into the room; he
shrugged, thinking himself alone, turned into his house, and
closed the door just as Pat appeared.

"Blum's upset," murmured Levy.

Pat put his briefcase between his feet, hesitated, then drew
a pipe from his pocket. In a moment Tony would cross. He
supposed that Saul lay dead in that house at that moment.
Rem said, "My breakfast's waiting." When he picked up his
morning paper from the step, both he and Tony looked au-
tomatically at the headlines.

●

Saul's body had been taken away earlier. Ruth looked
down from the landing between the second-floor living room
and the bedroom above where Saul had died. Until Ruth told
him, Tony had been thinking, preparing himself by setting
the picture of doing it aside: "I'll go straight up and see him"
—see the body, Saul, dead. It would be correct behavior.

"Pat, Tony, you're here."

Ruth stared down at them. "I wondered who that was.
People have been in and out constantly." She leaned on the
railing and seemed prepared to be conversational. "I was just
sending wires, but word must have gotten out immediately,

369

God knows how, because the phone hasn't stopped for five minutes. Clifford called at six o'clock this morning. Lillian wired." She said, "They took him without his clothes. I was amazed, Tony. The wire from Alex is on the table in there. He's still trying desperately to arrange passage on a transport plane, but the mere fact that it's too late gives it a different priority. Is Fran coming down?"

"She'll be down in a little while, Ruth," said Pat.

"My first response was astonishment. 'What do you do?'—thinking someone would be sent to the place where you rent tuxedos. I'd give them a check. I didn't know. I wasn't functioning at that point. 'Do you rent from Small's?'—in all innocence." She shrugged at their uncertain smiles. "Sure! But I'm supposed, it turns out, to bring something over in an hour or so. They prepare . . ." Ruth at last dug a knuckle hard under each eye, and, sinkingly, Tony saw the tears.

The phone rang.

Dr. Blum, who had been in his office below, came toiling up the stairs, screwing a cigarette into his holder. "Is someone getting it? Clifford called from New York."

"Well, I know I'm through getting it," Ruth said.

They listened. It rang all over the house, then stopped, and they heard Sydney's wife saying in a room above, "Yes, yes. I'm afraid last night. *Oui, grand dommage.*"

Ruth rolled her eyes for her father and the boys. "A little French at this point. Just what's called for . . . Mama has some breakfast ready. Dewey Pryne's here. He got in late yesterday."

They found Mrs. Blum seated beside the dining table. She said, "So. And the next affair is only one week off"—referring to a Russian War Relief benefit. Her features were impassive. She was smoking a cigarette in a smaller version of her husband's holder, her long skirts pushed down between her legs.

"Where's Dewey Pryne?" Pat asked.

She seemed not to hear. Each boy made a modest sandwich from the cold cuts on the table and poured glasses of orange juice. Their hands full, they went and studied a

Braque Rem Levy had sold Dr. Blum as a wartime invest-
ment. Pat said quietly, "Ruth was crying, wasn't she? That
story about the clothes . . ." Finally, he put the sandwich and
glass down, packed his pipe, and held a match to it, talking
out of the corner of his mouth between puffs. "It's terribly
touching. One reason is that it's unexpected in Ruth. You're
surprised."

"I was talking to Rem, and he almost cried."

"That's a real tribute."

A young soldier came from the kitchen with a drink in his
hand. He was bent over it, sipping as he pushed through the
swing door with his shoulder. "Mama?" he said to Mrs. Blum.
"I helped myself to the doctor's Scotch." He saw the boys and
made straight for them.

He was short, no taller than Alex, Tony saw, trim and
tough-looking in a summer uniform with the Eighth Air
Force patch on its shoulder and battle ribbons with stars. He
was in the process of getting a medical discharge ("Fatigue
from the missions is the polite name for it," he had written
to Fran), and it was already settled that he would spend the
summer with Alex and the Gambles at the shore house.

"Jesus," he said, "am I glad to meet you two! But the circumstances . . ." He had a Southern voice. Though he had
been prepared for it, it surprised Tony. Pryne knew at once
which boy was which and addressed them by name. He reminded Tony of someone else. "Alex is trying like hell to get
here. Knowing him, I know what he must feel. There's his
cable over there. It's to everybody. Listen, my God . . ." He
shook his head. Tony knew from the redness in his eyes that
the other had been crying. "Saul took my face like this between his hands"—putting his drink down to show them—
"and smiled so sweetly because I said I was bringing a message from Alex, which was a hug and Alex's love: to take care
of himself. Jesus!" Pryne turned away and shook his head
hard. "He gave me a kiss! I was Alex for him then." He put
a thick hand on the back of each boy's neck and spoke seriously, glaring at each in turn: "*You* two. Do you know how

371

much Alex loves you? He's proud as hell of you both. You and Fran were all he ever talked about. You better deserve it, you bums." Tony examined his response to the man, to his hand on him. Pat, embarrassed, went on puffing at his pipe. Pryne gave them a shake. "Hear?"—glaring. Then he went to stand at a window and look down broodingly, swirling the drink in his glass.

Ruth came into the room wearing a gray suit, her face freshly made up. "Have you all introduced yourselves?" she asked. And, matter-of-factly: "Well, I still can't believe it, can you?"

By afternoon the house was filled, and there was a great deal of shouting and even laughter. Ruth said to the boys, "Three of Saul's old flames are here. Can you beat that?" Tony could not straighten out which was which. A heavy white-haired woman said to him, "I'm Janet McLeod. My mother brought your grandfather into the Movement in 1924. She's dead too."

Pat remembered her. "Your brother fought in Spain."

"That's right!"

Pat was addressing Sydney Blum's laboratory technician. ". . . knew all kinds of people, which I take as a primary positive human characteristic. He would say he knew underworld types but really seemed to know them. Unless I have it wrong, Saul had met one of the victims in the Saint Valentine's Day massacre. Previously, of course. He knew Rothstein, the gambler who was murdered, rumrunners; and at the same time he was a speaking acquaintance of people like Stokowski and Chaliapin. . . ."

"Fanny Brice," added Tony.

"He knew the Barrymores. He used to talk about the old vaudevillians, and he knew a lot of them: Joe Frisco and Pat Rooney, who is not Mickey Rooney's father, incidentally. . . . He was never interested in banking. He just fell into that because it was the family business. His father was the same. A long line of old-fashioned pre-Bolshevik socialists—left socialists. They might as well have sold shoes or apples as gone

372

into banking. That was really Babushka. And what a subject for a book she'd make! . . ."

Each boy had a drink—Tony a beer and Pat a pale whiskey and soda. Their grandmother Rose, who had been staying with them, had come down with Fran. She sat by herself on the edge of a sofa, wearing a round hat of gray satin with a gray veil. Now and then she would tuck the veil up and bring a flared glassful of sherry to her lips. She looked at Tony and patted the cushion beside her. He pretended not to see.

A stocky silver-haired man, eyes swimming, took him aside. ". . . face would light up at the sight of lovers. He loved young people. He never learned to think of himself as old. He'd be with a group of young people—politically active kids —and say concerning some fellow: count him out, he's an old has-been, a reactionary—of a man his own age or younger. He once informed me that he kept score of his conquests, years back, by cutting marks on the bedpost in the old Lombard Street house; at the same time he was a thoroughgoing gentleman who never showed a discourtesy to a lady. . . ."

Dewey Pryne, scuffing the rug with his shoe, was in conversation with Dr. Blum. "That's right, Papa," he said now and then, nodding. "You're right." Tony joined them. He remembered the young man named George who came to the shore house before the war. Dewey Pryne was not like him, yet it was he of whom the Air Force sergeant reminded him. Pryne at once took Tony firmly by the arm. *"This* character, Papa . . ."

Later, Pryne said earnestly to Fran and Ruth, "No, I was going to say he couldn't do it. He did not begin to do you guys justice. I'm not getting it said. I'm tight, which should enable me to say what I could not say normally. . . ." He had touched Ruth's forehead with his own in a salute, grinning. "Listen," he declared, "you asked me to see Alex's father, your father, *your* husband. *I* am in your debt. I thank you."

"Of course," Fran said.

"You're embarrassed, which is part of it—that you should be. Alex hates displays. Not me. Look at old Pat—embarrassed, I think." There were other uniforms in the room. Pryne indicated them. "The war's over. Saul's gone. Okay. But we've come home. And I'll make a prophecy: your brother, your uncle, my friend is going to be the biggest, most important talent in the postwar period. Mark my words. . . ."

"I keep feeling," someone said, "I'll turn around and there will be Saul."

"You hear people say that," Pat said to Tony. "It's true. You get that sensation."

After a time, unobserved, Tony went upstairs to Saul and Ruth's bedroom.

He had no feeling that he could detect concerning Pryne. He made up an emotion. A great guy, he thought. He looked into the mirror above Ruth's dressing table. It was correct to like himself, and he did that as well. The effect of the beer was pleasant. His grandfather had died less than twenty-four hours before in this room. He looked for back issues of *Esquire* on their shelf, chose one, and turned to the calendar girl. When she grew stale right side up, he turned her around. She was in a swing, her body, seen in profile, entirely naked. She had large round pink-gold breasts, a tiny muscular waist, and little-girl curls. Desire flickered—he held her to the mirror—and faded, which was proper.

"Aside from the grief, now he is gone, there is a most intolerable sense of guilt: I neglected him. I saw him too little. I wrote too seldom. I repent an age-long routine. We all do. . . . I tried to get back 'on emergency' after the first cable. No soap. So now, here at this place, I'm awaiting the ordinary type of transportation and will be with you all soon. . . ." Alex's letter came a week after Saul's death. It ended: "Well, the war is closing in a bang of nightmare glory and chaos. I only hope he knew about the join-up with the Russians before he died."

Tony got permission to show the letter to Doc.

"So you'll meet Alex at last," Tony said in a tone of confident pride. "I think you'll like him."

374

They were standing at dusk under a light in the street before Tony's house. Doc had been introduced to Dewey Pryne and passed him. "Good man," he said.

"He's a great guy. His girl friend's an ex-WAC. They're always talking apparently about getting married, but they're in no rush. In effect, when they see each other they live with each other. Dewey's going to spend the summer at the shore with us and get through the first draft of a novel he started in France." Pryne and Alex were to share the composer's studio, which had been made into a small apartment. Matter-of-factly, Tony said so. "I'll be painting. Pat's going to write. An artists' colony."

Doc smoothed a football in his hands, waiting. If a missed catch brought them within speaking range, Tony usually had something to say. He told the other about Saul's funeral. "Nondenominational. Cremation. Fran had to go in back behind a curtain and make the guy stop playing the organ. . . ."

1947

●

The meetings of the local PAC had been held in Tony's two small rooms for the past month, and his landlady complained about it, usually catching him on his way down through the house after breakfast when he was already late for his first class. Finally she pushed a note under his door: "Appreciate it if you put a stop to those activities in my home."

They put the matter on the agenda, but it was dismissed.

"I move we simply forget this—her so-called objections—and proceed with the important business on hand," the chairman said. He had a rapid, irritable style. What, in fact, was Tony talking about? "You pay your rent?" Tony, nervous, could neither let it drop nor say what it was his landlady objected to at the meeting itself. When the others had gone and only he and his girl friend and the chairman, whose name was Lundigan, remained, he said, "She's anti-Negro. She said she didn't want Negroes in her house."

"Or Indians or Mexicans?"

"Now she's concerned about Negroes."

Lundigan, a tall, loose-limbed, easily irritated young art student, was a veteran of the Pacific war. He had singlehandedly created the local American Veterans Committee in this small New Mexican town and out of that a Political Action Committee branch, which functioned on a broader base. His plan was that as soon as he felt it was going smoothly, he would resign the chairmanship of the PAC branch and resume his work with Amvets. He urged Tony to try for his post: "Why go home now? You just got here, for God's sake! Why not spend the summer and really dig into this work?"

After the meetings he would peer around in the gabled top-floor room at Tony's work. "Braque! Come on!" Or: "Why early Picasso? You've got a teacher over there in the school to show you the road! What the hell are you mixing sand with your paint for, for God's sake?"

He said, "The point of any activity in this town is to break down racial barriers. What more sensible place to start than in your rooms here? What are we going to do, bar those guys, good guys—vets—because of some old Kluxer's widow?"

Tony was fond of his top floor rooms. In the farthest one a corner of the unmade bed was visible. A tower of dishes stood in the sink in his kitchenette. He had acquired a puppy, and newspapers with yellow stains on them were everywhere (the meeting had had to be held with a window open). His girl, wrapped in a GI greatcoat, sat as she had throughout the meeting, bent over a sketch pad. Lundigan seemed to have closed the subject. He addressed the girl: "You live here now, cutie, or do I get to escort you home? That's all the landlady needs on him."

Tony put the puppy on a leash. He, Lundigan, and the girl walked to her boardinghouse, where the chairman waited while they kissed. Later, he said, "Don't let the old lady get your goat, Tony."

The woman was waiting on the second-floor landing when he got back. She was short and had tightly waved brass-colored hair. She looked frightened. "I put in a call just now, and in a while he's going to call back."

"Who?"

"You'll soon know. You go on up, young man, and when I holler for you to come to the phone you come down."

He went up the final flight to his rooms, the dog under his arm, put away the pretzels and empty beer bottles, and found places for the glasses in the sink.

"All right, come on," she called when the phone rang, though she had not yet answered it. He went down again. "Another thing," she said, offering him the receiver. "I never said you were to have the dog there. I mention it because I said it to him"—with a shake of the phone. (The dog was Very II. Tony had thought of Eve and Alex when he bought it.) "The dog is just one more thing."

The voice said, "Gamble, this is Chief Brodbeck. Mrs. Bruce says you're giving her uneasiness."

"I'm not giving anything like that."

"Don't feel you can rent a room in that area to have political meetings in. There are other places for such activities."

The man's voice was authoritative, but he spoke with the cheerful reasonableness of the region and kept pausing as if to remind himself of the subject of the conversation. Once Tony heard him say off the phone to someone in the same room, "Put it down there, and I'll get to it in a minute. I got this here to see to now." He sighed at the beginning of each sentence. "We intend you to respect Mrs. Bruce's feelings in this and suspend those meetings or vacate the room."

"I have a right to have guests." His voice was low.

"Now, never mind that. Bear in mind to respect Mrs. Bruce's wishes in this matter. It is her house. She's an old friend, and that's enough for you to know. If you prefer, you can come down here and we'll talk it over, but it seems to me it's a matter we can settle on the telephone. Mrs. Bruce, to be plain now, is a lady of the old school." She stood on the stairs to the first floor, waiting. Tony saw her nod as if she could hear the man's words. "She doesn't wish Negroes in her house. That's her privilege. I'm being plain with you— Anthony, isn't it? I don't have time now to go into it, Anthony."

"Well, you shouldn't say that."

He found that if he tried to raise his voice above a whisper it shook violently. Hearing this, the woman on the stairs glanced up, astonished. He remembered the man in the White Tower restaurant. He remembered what Lundigan had said. He was not going to back down.

"You can come see me if you want. You want to come down here to talk?"

"Of course not."

"Because I can arrange it. I'll have a car sent out right now; you can come. We'll talk it over. I can't spend the night on the telephone with you, Anthony. I understand you have a young lady comes there to visit you—an artist like yourself. That won't do. Mrs. Bruce is of the old school. How do you want this now?"

"What do you mean?"

"I want you to promise me there'll be no more political meetings such as I had described to me, and just quit generally in offensive behavior to Mrs. Bruce. I hear you keep a dog, which is offensive to her, but she says: accept that. Now, I want your promise and that will be the end of it."

"Well, how can I do that?"

The man could not hear Tony.

"I said they're my guests."

"Now, you just tell me that's the end of it, and we'll say no more on it. Put Mrs. Bruce back on."

Tony said, "Well, if that's what . . . if that's the law . . ."

"That's it."

He would work it out with Lundigan. They would solve it. What about Lundigan's room or one of the others? It was April, in any case. There were only two more meetings scheduled.

"Well, if that's it, the law regarding it . . ."

"Put Mrs. Bruce on."

As he went upstairs, he heard her say, "All right," in a tone of self-justification. "It's my house, isn't it? Just so, Chief Brodbeck. That's all right, then."

He made a gift of the puppy to the graphics teacher and his wife, went home a week before the end of term, and then to the shore with his family. He took over the studio until Alex would arrive in August and hung his paintings around both there and in the house. Fran took a color photograph of him standing on the studio porch in a bright red sweat shirt displaying a canvas as tall as he was. He worked hard and in a few weeks made a start on a dozen canvases.

Fran knew about Tony's political activity—there were let-

379

ters concerning it back and forth—but nothing yet of the incident with the police chief. Little was said about his coming home earlier than expected. He began one angry, Gropper-like painting—a cartoon in color—of a fat man, naked except for a loincloth made of an American flag and a policeman's hat, clubbing down Negro and Mexican pickets.

"You can't, Jake," his father said, referring to the use of the flag. "No matter how sore you are about something. To begin with, it's a matter of taste"—which, believing solely now in the power of art, Tony discounted.

Over cocktails in the glassed porch that faced the sea, Tony at length told his mother the story, exaggerating his cowardice. He lit their cigarettes. "Some tough guy." And, thinking of Alex, whose precepts he remembered and whose courage he assumed: "I sure didn't risk a hell of a lot that time, did I?"

They talked it over, action and reaction, in the sunny room. A day's work was behind Tony. His second sherry, bright brown, stood on the table beside him. Who he was, what he was, what he would do in the life that was opening remained still to be discussed.

Alex came down from New York.

He had put on a few pounds, which he would soon take off. He was affectionate and attentive. There were gifts. His energy appeared to be limitless and seemed to include everything. Pryne had gone to Chicago to try for a job, and Alex said to the family, "He's drinking too much and doesn't see any real reason not to. We're not around each other, and he's been alienating anyone else who might be of help or use." Pryne had married the ex-WAC (Alex was best man). "It's what he needs." Alex too had been drinking. Now he did not. "I hadn't been working well. That's over. I'm deep into things again."

He played scenes from the new opera for the family, sitting very straight at the upright in the studio. He worked with his cigarette in the center of his lips, head back to avoid the smoke, squinting, abruptly bending to make out his own notes and scrawled blue or red changes. He jammed the cigarette out, spread the multileaved sheets across the face of the piano, slapped them into place as they slipped. Fran listened with her head bent. Bob nodded. Pat looked out the window at the sea, his glance sad. Tony observed himself sitting and listening. He saw that he was moved, that art was a force for good if it was good in itself; in that case, he saw that it had to be tragic, whatever else it seemed to be.

Once,.during an evening walk, he and Alex talked about art and duty.

"Of course, you risk everything every time out. You have to do that. The trouble is that inevitably either you force others, people close to you, to share the dangers or you give in and surrender some weapons. I don't mean that an artist ought to be alone, though it must sound that way."

Tony saw only that art, not life, could be the sole arena. He would not be a coward in art! But Alex said presently, "We are responsible for what we do and for what we are," which cast a veil over everything again.

"So, then what you do is risk everything?"

"Well, you try," the older artist said in a kindly way. He had heard about the police chief. "Not uselessly. In your own line."

Good.

At length Anthony dared to ask of Alex's work if it was going well, something one did not do lightly.

"I *think* so. Yes," with an air of triumph.

This was a major project. Alex would declare it was the best summer of work he had ever had. He burned with work.

1964

•

Alex sat in the prow of the boat, trim in jeans, a striped shirt and a pair of rope-soled shoes. He was concentrated upon the line that ran over his finger and into the dark water, drawing it up now and then to pick off the persistent rags of green weed. Just on their right, channel markers stood on twisting poles, and across the sun-blinded bay they could see their boat-rental dock with its red fuel tank and repair yard. A sulfurous marsh bank lay near at hand, colonies of polished blue-black mussels hanging stranded as the tide dropped. Alex's arm supporting his weight on the gunwale had a foreign, powerful look. When the boat swung from its anchor and tautened their lines, Alex glanced sharply at Tony, as if for guidance in the strange place, gnawed his mustache, then looked down once more. It would be a good serious joke to come home with some fish.

"Bite?"

His uncle's carved sunbather's face hung over the water, scant hair cropped close, white around the ears now, the flaring Jewish nose and unshaved boxer's jaw (he would shave before cocktails) advancing solemnly upon his image: a deep frown. He performed the work seriously; it was the business now of catching fish, a serious joke.

"I don't *think* so."

Heat released the dried-fish-scales smell of the boat and the marsh's rank odor.

Later, Alex talked about Eve, which he had never done (he had never before gone fishing). As anyone else might, he had a photograph in his wallet. Though he had seen others, Tony had never seen this. She stood in a bathing suit on a stony beach in, he said, Capri. She shaded her eyes with a bony hand bent almost to a right angle, looking out to sea. Alex stood by her, legs apart, fists on his hips, returning the observer's glance with a youthful belligerent courtesy: "As you see. Here we are." She is pale. He is brown, slim, and trim: a gymnast, neatly muscled. Both wore the frank cotton bathing suits of the time, and Eve smiled her broad smile of total knowledge, which pressed her eyes happily closed. (Anthony began to create her.) She was pale, her complexion a problem, thin as a reed. The rocks around them had bleached white in thirty years; a string bag filled with beach gear hung from her wrist: cigarettes, notebooks, Tauchnitz novel. Though she loved it, she seemed to be watching for her death in the sea.

"I'm a morning person. She was a night person."

But mornings were for work, and she could not wake. She saw sleep as death and loved sleep too. When she lived alone in New York and Paris she used three alarm clocks set at fifteen and five-minute intervals. Living first with Randall Schiff, then Alex, she required them to pummel and shout her awake at seven to get her to her desk: an hour's work on the novel before breakfast, because she fervently believed in the morning hours. It was terrible. She fought waking. "Bastard, let me sleep! Let me go!"—sinking back into the sea caverns of her dream, which was just what Alex feared. "Wake me"—fast asleep: "Wake me up right now, darling! I have to work."

Having lived it, Alex sounded as if he had no idea that it was family piety and talked about Eve's actual death as if it were no more than an important story. He had taken the waxed cardboard box with its greasy ashes onto a Boston–New York coastal freighter and, punctiliously ("I was out of my mind," he would say to Tony) having secured the captain's permission and advice concerning wind direction, shaken them over the rail of the ship into her sea. (Tony would create the fragment of bone and the fainting. Fran had long before supplied the story of the fight with the cab driver.)

•

Was that all there had been to that? It was like taking an altar into the sun, turning it over, and having a look at how it was made. Alex lit a cigarette, using the Zippo he had owned since he had been in the Air Force, while Tony drew up the anchor. They were pleased: a success. How about trying another spot? And Alex: what was the name of the thing they were supposed to catch—*flounder?*—only half kidding, though of course he knew. Neither understood anything about fish, which was all right. The afternoon—such a thing had not happened in this way before and would not again—was a hit. Now his uncle appeared to reconsider the whole subject of fishing. They were, after all, here. He looked at his watch, at the bait of squid drying on the deck. He was deep into a new work; Tony was writing a new novel. Obsessively, every moment, each either fled in his mind to his current impasse or specifically avoided doing so. They might row around the bay for a bit. Would Tony like Alex to row? No, no. "It shouldn't be a total loss," they had taken off their shirts to deepen their tans. The man who rented boats had warned them that a storm was imminent, but the sun still shone. Tony rowed into the blind late-afternoon water, and for a time there was only the mild sound of their wash and oarlocks. He headed toward a flat crust of clouds and marsh grass half a mile distant. Heat, with a few mosquitoes, came from the mainland.

Alex said that Eve called making love moonlight. In spite of the other disclosures, this one was unexpected, because the uncle and nephew were not, really, on frank terms. Fran related family history as she recalled it or as it had been told to her, but not this. "Making love," Alex said again, as if he were fearful that it might need to be explained.

Tony understood but did not yet know what to do with the information; it hung, authentic from 1930 and that old drama; then it made a silence between them, which as it grew became dense. It was as if a plea had been made, and for an only time, briefly, the nephew saw an aspect of the uncle's reality. Alex talked about moonlight some more, elegantly and in a clinical way, and both were relieved by this approach.

They did not bother fishing again.

Alex discussed politics, his mood altered.

He did not sleep well at night. He dieted compulsively and could not now gain back what he lost; old ailments cropped up. He had been given an important and desirable commission of work and a considerable amount of money, but the work did not develop. The sky darkening, enraged by an injustice to sense, he shouted across the water his opinion of an editorial in the morning paper. And then it seemed that with the sun gone, their shirts back on, he had come to feel either frightened, or impatient, or ashamed of the suddenly assaulting irritation, and he said nothing more.

●

But ashore, in front of the island drugstore, Alex looked around cheerfully at this place that seemed foreign with him in it. A storming wedge of sea lay at one end of the short street, the flat bay at the other. His hands were filled with things he had just bought in the drugstore, including a new Zippo. It was exciting—as if he had been to the open-air market. He stood tough-looking, bald, the pugnacious chin thrust up, and took a breath. "Well, that was fun. I enjoyed it," he said.

He thanked Tony for suggesting the expedition: a good break for them both ("both" was flattering; they were artists).

The composer now seemed to see a way around his problem and was already in his new day, intent upon it. If they were not avoided, problems provided solutions, except death, with which one had nothing to do. ("A thread," Alex would say and take one from Tony's shoulder; nothing except death was unimportant.)

As they had been awkwardly tying up the boat, Alex energetic, self-obliterating ("I won't be *much* use at this"), yet dancing from stern to prow, cigarette in the corner of his mouth, shoving things up on the dock, getting in the way, the Zippo had gone overboard, the accident of a wide gesture—*look* at the clouds piling up—and he said at once, almost instantly, "Fine!"—the self-hatred blazing, then disappearing. It was as if such sure bad luck had to restore his good humor. He had been precise with the boatman, addressing him respectfully, as he did headwaiters. And in the car he said, "Dewey Pryne gave me that," calmly.

Did he ever see Dewey Pryne?

"No"—startled, almost, it seemed, shocked. "Not in years."

At the uncle's injunction they drove straight to the drugstore. Alex bought an identical lighter and put it in his pocket.

•

Later, Bob Gamble and his son Tony watched the weather report on television. When Alex came in from the studio he seemed preoccupied, alert, his gaze going all over the room. Why wasn't Fran back yet? His sister had gone to fetch their mother from her apartment for the evening, but she had only just left. He nodded. He had shaved after his swim, changed into faded blue slacks and an oversized shirt open halfway down his chest. The gifts he had bought for Tony's children had been arranged on the coffee table earlier. Now he carried cigarettes, the new lighter, a tube of tablets, glasses in a case with a clip, and the *Saturday Review* folded to the Double-Crostic. He settled into an easy chair under a window, pushed on the glasses, and began to work the puzzle, chewing the inside of his cheek. Now and then he would call for help or read aloud the quotation as it had been worked to that point. When he was addressed, he would look up at once, brilliantly irritable, to understand exactly what was being said.

He would wait—looking at his watch—fifteen minutes for a drink.

Tony made a martini and drank most of it. (Each brother had half of the summer. Pat and his family used the house in August.) Tony's wife, Elizabeth, came downstairs with the girls in dresses, and Alex rose to his feet, kissed her and the girls, and complimented their outfits. The gifts were presented. Gertrude came from the kitchen with the canapés, and Alex, first checking it over with her, took the platter from the maid. When he lived with the Gambles he paid his share of food and bought all the liquor. Tonight there was caviar, which had come with him from New York a month before. He had grown tired of the Gambles' insistence that it be saved for an occasion and before his swim settled the matter with Gertrude. Here it was: a surprise. No one would touch the platter, waiting for Fran. A smell of roasting meat and onions filled the house. When cars pulled down their street they glanced through the windows. Alex now demanded answers for the puzzle from Elizabeth Gamble. Bob Gamble opened the case beside his chair and dipped into it for blue-covered briefs, tissue carbons, through which he glanced confidently. At length he signified to Tony that he was ready for his Manhattan, and, once it was prepared and in his hand, Alex presented his canapés.

"Why not wait for Fran?"

No, no . . .

Well, they were fine. Briefs set aside willingly, he captured a child and rode her on his foot: *"Hup*-diddy-up!" though it was tiring. Alex insisted that Tony's wife eat a canapé and listened with attention to her opinion. Tony was sent for the serious-looking contáiner in Russian. Then Tony, who no longer smoked, made a second martini, which he placed on the mantel, as if to put it beyond his reach there, and Alex allowed him to mix him a bourbon and water. The children drank Cokes. Bob improvised stories for them, but they wriggled on his lap or dragged his glasses down his long nose, and he was reduced to pretending he had forgotten their names or saying, "That's a nice red dress," when it was yellow. Alex thought of something, stood with the *Saturday Review* under his arm, and told a funny story about someone famous with whom he had been staying before coming to the Gambles— an incident during a game of charades.

Rose and Fran arrived—traffic had been bad, the bridge up for the most magnificent yacht ever—and Tony was ready with his grandmother's Old Fashioned, his mother's gin and tonic. Alex once more presented the canapés—he had taken only one himself—and began the story of the afternoon. (Also, he lit his first cocktail cigarette with the new lighter; he would not say—it was as if he had forgotten—that it had been lost in the bay and found in a store.) Tony, listening, tucked his drink, which was now his third, onto the mantel after each fiery sip, and there it waited for him. He was tight. The sun found a break in the clouds, filled the room, and, as he saw, lit his drink magnificently. He was hungry. You took a swim, a drink; the sun came blooming out; dinner was nearly on; neither child had spilled her Coke. . . .

Until late in the evening, Rose and her son played Scrabble. He drummed his fingers on the table as she tried out words, and she in turn ticked her hard nails on the dictionary's cover. She stopped in thought, ticked them. Would it be all right (again!) if she were to look something up? And when, to earn permission by the rules to do it, she said aloud the word she had in mind, it sounded so odd in the silent room, everyone reading, that they glanced up at her. There was no such word, Alex declared irritably. She gave a wriggle and ducked her head: if she might look it up . . . He thrust on his heavy glasses, snatched the book, went through it, then handed it over, a square finger at exactly the place where her word would have been if it had existed, and watched her courteously through the smoke of his cigarette.

"Here it comes," said Bob Gamble when the sky rumbled. They listened.

"We'd better keep clearly in mind that we have to get Mama back," said Fran. It was ten.

●

The storm broke over the beach house at midnight. Bob Gamble was asleep. Fran had been reading in bed—Henry James that summer. Tony and Elizabeth had been asleep, but they were awakened by the noise. Their children were to sleep through it. "Cars in the windows?"—were the windows in the various cars up? Alarmingly close, the thunder broke upon them in repeated discharges. Lightning made a nearly continuous illumination.

"Cat out?"

The street and beach kept opening whitely to view. Wreckage, visible from the window beside the bed, rocked two hundred yards offshore. Anthony had been dreaming horribly, so that Elizabeth had had to wake him twice before the thunder did it. " . . . cat."

Their street had filled with water. The dune grass was crushed flat, but the sea well out was calm, as if quelled by the storm's weight. From the rooms over the garage where Alex worked and slept light gleamed.

"Alex is up. Woke up or was up."

When he woke once more, finally, thrown out of the brief sleep by a dream of burning, Tony replied to his wife's question concerning the cat. "I think she is." The studio was dark, but as he watched a light went on again and stayed on.

"We'd better get her in."

"Dreamed I was burning."

But he meant Alex. He said of the electric fire crackling around them, "It's damned close." It made a white room out-of-doors; shadows leaped from hedges and poles. Tony saw Alex's head appear in the studio door at the top of the flight of outside stairs. He looked around and drew it back. What was he looking for? Anyone could see it was raining!

They got up at last, Elizabeth to check the children, while Tony, first writing descriptive notes on an end page of a mystery, descended. His mother, with a raincoat over her night clothes, gray hair loose, was coming into the kitchen with an armful of Alex's manuscripts that had been wrapped in a *Times.* "It might flood!" Tony did not think so—not as high as Alex's rooms certainly; yet a neighboring garage had been taken out to sea in a hurricane some years before.

"Look at her!"

Fran had got the younger Gambles' cat in. It sat soaked beside the water heater in the utility room. "That's a wet cat! Alex saw lightning in his studio! We think it struck the studio. No visible damage." She looked exhilarated and scared. One cigarette had smoldered to its filter tip in an ashtray on the sink counter; another, which had been lit and put out by the rain, was between her fingers. "I checked the cars!"

Tony took her bundle and put it in a chair in the living room.

"My God!" Alex ran in from the kitchen with a brown canvas work bag in one hand, an army duffel bag in the other. He wore a rubber poncho, legs and feet bare under it, an old beret, and a thick sweater. His eyes were brilliant. "One more trip."

"I'll get it!" Tony cried.

"Nope! I know what I need and just where to put my hands on it. Lightning right there," he said. "Went right through the room and out again!" He returned to the storm, ducking into it, calves bulging under the poncho; in places water swirled to his ankles. Fran called, "I'm coming!"

"No!"—in the wind. But she went.

A moment later they splashed back, Alex carrying a letter file and his calendar diary, Fran a metal card box. Let the rest go: a few clothes; he tugged at his mustache ends, grinning fiercely. "I saw lightning, Tony. Understand, I saw it *in* the room."

Elizabeth had come down. They sat in the living room, lights dimming with each explosion, the sister and brother breathing quickly, fresh cigarettes lit. Fran poured brandy. "Let's see if we can't stop colds right here"—sipping from her own with shudders.

"A bright blue spark in the center of the room! My initial reaction, not thinking what it was, was *great!* Gorgeous. And in the same moment that the notion of its beauty was forming, of course it was all over. Why didn't it go through me? I was in the center too! Yet you keep away from walls. . . ."

"Well, you're a poor conductor."

Alex roared. "I should have thought of that! Perfect!"

Gertrude had come in from her room. "I heard you. I got worried about Mr. Weisshorn."

"I'm okay, Gertrude." He had jumped up, alert as a boy. "I thought I'd try the house for the night under the circumstances."

"*I* can't sleep," she said. She was an anxious woman, older than she appeared to be. Alex took her hand. She ought to drink something. A liqueur. Anthony poured it and a Scotch for himself. It was a good thing Ormandy or Bernstein had not been there: excellent conductors. Bob Gamble blinked from the head of the stairs, and Alex went to the foot at once, reassuring: "Everything's okay, Bob. I thought I'd try the house since the elements were doing their stuff. You go on back."

Later, Alex described once more the blue spark that had swollen and exploded in his room. "It was round—a flaring, blue-white, *round* . . . really a *bomb* of light in the dead center of the room. It hung there. . . ."

Then?

"Then I beat a damn quick retreat!"

Gertrude looked frightened. Fran asked, "Why is there no lightning rod on that place?"

"Is there not?"—quiet, turning to this clear fault. Then he looked at the ceiling. "Is there one here?" No one knew for certain, *but they ought to know:* it was ridiculous not to! He stood frowning in the Gambles' living room. A man had been killed by lightning on a beach at Water Island two years before. " . . . spare you the details."

"You do not stay on a beach in an electric storm. Wasn't someone killed years ago by lightning next to the pond at Yaddo?" Alex had told her so, Fran thought.

There had been a suicide; she was mixing up the events. Eve had been terrified of lightning, yet always braved it, plunging directly into storms. The dog, Very: they had walked him in thunderstorms to help him lose his fear, and he had.

It was all said with an eye on the ceiling. They would see to lightning rods next day after lunch. He and Tony would go to a hardware store. Alex would have them installed; it would be his contribution. "On the other hand, shouldn't a television antenna act as a lightning rod?" he suddenly asked, staring at the set, and at once began turning its dials. "Vertical hold," he said carefully. "You could hook onto this. Then there mightn't be so much involved." He and Fran discussed technicalities, improvising mechanical principles, the composer squinting, turning to rub his jaw in thought, but also grinning at himself, as if to say, "What the hell do I know?" His and his sister's looks were bright. He used his new lighter, and his thumb on its rough wheel was a communion with working parts; pins of bright fire jumped up in his eyes. He snapped it shut, grinning. He clowned for Elizabeth and Tony. "What do you think of our flood epic? A little theatrical?" In the midst of this they noticed the bruise on his forehead.

Fran moved to look; Alex held still, submitting. "Why not?" Speaking of theater, wasn't this par for the course? A small cut and slight swelling. Fran said, "Okay." Hadn't he

392

noticed? What a guy! Now he went objectively to a mirror, bent the carved, cropped head, and lifted the chin in every direction; he looked fine and suddenly old and glanced around, self-mocking and grim, as if to see if the others saw. He supposed he had hit his head in the dark in the midst of the excitement and not noticed. He turned from himself.

Fran left and came back with alcohol and cotton. Altered, Alex approached one of the bundles of notes and manuscripts and searched it. Something missing. Never mind what: a black loose-leaf notebook, then, with the entire thing—only the plan for the opera; that was all—the rage beginning.

"Put on the rain gadget—poncho!"

"I'll dry off with a towel."

They watched him thrust into the storm, up the studio stairs. When he returned, streaming water, empty-handed, he said nothing, and searched again.

"You had it all the time in there"—as he held it up grimly for everyone. How was his head now? It had never been anything at all.

Gertrude had gone back to bed, Elizabeth had gone upstairs as the storm began to weaken, but Anthony's uncle seemed ready to demonstrate life without recess; he was the survivor of his own bad dream, as if to say this was how it was done.

In the morning Tony went onto the beach. It was wet and chilled, covered with brittle craters. What he supposed was the wreckage he had seen offshore the night before had been washed up—crates tied onto a raft, all of it crusted with barnacles, oil, and sand, one of the boxes lettered with a manufacturer's name. Alex stood in the surf wearing a pair of tiny striped trunks he had picked up during a working visit to Israel and what he said they called a dumbbell cap, also striped. He faced, nearly, the rising sun, too thin, somewhat bowlegged, with good calves, which the Gambles did not possess. He had shoved his grizzled jaw toward the sun and stood captured, like a dozing horse, eyes lidded.

When Tony looked along the beach he saw two sheds that appeared to have turned slightly, as if to ward off the weather of the previous night. A lifeguards' station three blocks below was collapsed at one corner where a piling had given way; a gull stood on its flagpole. The roofs of houses up and down this stretch of coast—rambling old brown-shingle structures like the Gambles'—were wet still, and the sun was making them steam.

"Not going in?" Alex called, having seen him. "You're out of your mind!" He created a comic grimace, plunged in himself, ignoring the damaged shore, the seaweed and shattered shells, and swam out. His cap lay where he had stood. Tony heard him call, saw him grin and wave from the raw sea.

Gertrude gave them early breakfast, and Alex sat briefly over his mail, which included a thick letter from the William Morris Agency and air mail from Europe. He had written a note and put it under the flap of his cigarette box: "Lightning rods." He turned his powerful forearms with gray hair on them, dealing with mail, frowned bitterly at William Morris, shook out clippings, royalty statements, and a check. He would not complete the current opera. The manuscript had been lost once in Rome airport, and he had had to redo it. The project (it was about Sacco and Vanzetti) had been commissioned by the country's foremost opera company; the Federation of American Music had adopted a resolution concerning it; there had been letters to the *New York Times* claiming that the composer had been a Communist and therefore ought not to have been given the job. Some of the clippings concerned this. The bruise on Alex's forehead had faded. Tony offered to help carry the manuscripts and books back to the studio, but that had been done. His uncle glared at the view beyond the dining room windows, biting the edge of his thumb. Then: "Work. I'm off," and left.

Later, himself working in his and Elizabeth's bedroom, which had been his as a boy, Tony heard Alex faintly from the studio: the piano, a phrase repeated, then sung in the hoarse voice. Uncle and nephew had lost one day by going fishing.

EPILOGUE | **1968**

1970

1968

•

A consul arranged shipment of the body in its sealed coffin, as well as manuscripts, books, and clothing. An initial cable had arrived from Alex himself—they would suppose later that it had been, at least in part, dictated by the consul and put over Alex's name—saying there had been an automobile accident. Could Fran arrange to come? With a military flavor: "... soonest." Then the consul wired in his own name. Alex had died in a hospital as a result of the accident. Ultimately it was learned that there had been no automobile accident. He had been beaten and robbed, left shouting for help at dawn in the waterfront district of the Mexican port town near which he had been living and working for four months.

Of those arrested, tried, convicted of manslaughter and robbery, and sentenced to a few years in prison, one was a Jamaican black, a sailor without a ship at the moment. There was another, older man, illegally in the country, who had a record of previous arrests, one on a charge of homicide. The third was a kitchen worker in a local hotel. Alex had given an efficient description of them, and they were picked up.

Anthony Gamble, his brother, and his father stood by the coffin. The younger of the brothers would insist to himself that he had rested his hand upon the lid, remembering the feel of it, but he did not. The director of the mortuary, asking for authority, looked from one to the other.

They would open the coffin, reveal the bruised face, or they would not. For a moment they did nothing, said nothing.

Not surprisingly, once dead, the tide that had been the man would not drop punctually. The nephew looked into window glass and vases, an obsessive modest glancing so schooled by now that the image only reminded him of the fact that if he was looking he was not working. Beyond the cool passage in which they stood was the establishment's cinerarium—it had been described as such by Mr. Brall—a tall room in the Gothic shape of a cannon shell. It was pierced by narrow windows and through these could be seen the park where Alex would remain, as green in February as in May.

Pat had come from New York the morning following the news of Alex's death and a week before the arrival of the coffin. The brothers walked around the corner from the apartment in overcoats and rubbers. Though Pat was doing better, they were both going bald, one dark, one fair, in a nearly identical way. The younger had begun a mustache, but in a week, as if frightened by the self-advertisement of it at this point, he would shave. Insistently nondramatic on the surface (they did not conquer as Alex did; if they had led in their careers, they had effaced all style in doing so), they went to buy bourbon, gin, and dry vermouth.

"I was the one who told Rose," Tony said with the twist such bragging gives of shame and pleasure. At eighty-eight, she was living with her daughter and son-in-law. They would allow her to believe for several days that Alex had died in an accident in the white Fiat. It was credible since he would have felt he had to drive in Mexico at least as recklessly as he had years before in Rome. Then Elizabeth and Tony had been captive in the front seat of that same car while Alex, ragingly rude, more Roman than Romans, used the machine to comment upon the always obdurate work-in-progress (the particular manuscript of which was to be lost in any event).

"Was it bad?" Pat, a lawyer, asked and answered himself: "It had to be."

They talked cautiously on the surface of shock, shiftily around the man, unprepared to think of how to settle his ghost. Then, wordless, they turned homeward with the bottles. Tony wondered if he might not say that he had once wished this, but he was almost certain he had not. Alex himself always allowed the possibility, and Pat would have said it was all right. ("They may dislike me one day," Alex declared of his "nevviews" in their presence on a gratifying summer day on the beach just after the war and the London years. The boys worshiped his saying it. "My God," they replied, delighted to find that he would be wrong about something. "Okay, we'll just see!" Why not? The point was, much more important, they loved him.)

There was to be an informal tribute in a New York theater at noon a week after the Philadelphia funeral, which had been itself without ceremony. The curtain would be up, work light on, props in place for the opening scene of the matinee: friends on stage addressing their affection for Alex to friends in the audience. Patrick and Anthony attended, representing the rest. There would be a memorial concert of Alex's work in the spring.

Tony had found no way of thinking about Alex's mother and sister (cast so in his mind now rather than as his own mother and grandmother), and he would not "do" them. Sylvie had been dead for years. What the nephew pictured was his uncle, frail, furious, thin, though not as Eve had been for her getaway, glaring at his relatives, challenged: it was not incorrect, this behavior, the man in the picture said. He clutched at the air with a vivid Mediterranean gesture of drawing down the one moral idea to be recommended, if not for their activity then for study. "What you don't yet appear able to understand . . ." In a nightmare Alex wore a full brown wig, cruelly false-looking, and seemed to be seeking approval for it.

These things happened. There might have been a mistake in identification. Brall, the director of the crematorium, waited for their reply. "Let him go," Bob Gamble's look declared to his sons, meaning Alex. The sense of having been liberated by death came with its attendant grease of guilt.

399

Tony would not be able to work at his writing for a long time. A famous singer had put ashore in the little harbor, almost a lagoon, of the banana plantation where Alex had rented his cottage, having set off from a movie producer's yacht in its longboat. The sea was already bleached by heat at seven in the morning. Alex had lived here. She glanced northward toward the Mexican seaport town to which he had driven for his celebration: died there. She met the aged caretaker of the group of empty cottages on the lonely peninsula. She spoke in French. A dog followed them. The caretaker showed her the cottage where the composer had kept house alone; he conveyed his sorrow. (Alex, she knew, looked closely at any man or woman who might conceivably need him—a friend or a stranger in the street: "Are you all right? Perfectly? Can you manage?") As if to settle with the composer, he gave to the singer a half coconut shell containing pre-Columbian fragments and her hat filled with turtle's eggs; he watched her climb down to the beach and set off, waved to her. . . . Reading of the adventure in a letter from the woman, Fran would snort with what had the appearance of anger.

Tony recorded Alex's last thoughts. What will Mama do? What would Papa have thought? What would Eve, she being less certainly dead, have said?

Driving at dusk toward the murderers whom he had not yet met, he shouted in the Fiat that it was not good enough after all, referring to the good day of work he was celebrating. At the same time, as always, the news was in his mind. There was fighting on the Citadel walls in Hué. The Marines had tied a flag to a bamboo pole, thrust the pole through the cane seat of a chair, and placed the chair on the wall. The citizens of Hué looked on with deep interest, stepped through no man's land during lulls. " 'They're crazy,' " declared a Marine in the *New York Times*. " 'Bullets zing up and down these streets all the time and these people think it's a side show.' " Alex used this week-old *Times* folded into a club to strike the tabletop in the dockside bar, launching the attack that would lead to his death.

400

Tony himself avoided violence, though he accepted gin (it's perfectly all right; I can manage) and had become habituated (kiss me) to work, relying on the notion that artists are made from such waste. His hand coming down short of the sealed, lead-lined coffin, emotionally sixteen years old, the nephew desired ceremony—a funeral, in fact—to persuade the other, persistent vitality to relent; yet he said concerning the opening of the coffin that there was no point to it. ". . . no point, is there?"

There had never been a thought in his mind, in that particular line of thoughts, except to be an artist—it hardly mattered what kind—as Alex was, so that he had been damned almost from the outset as well, and gin had already led him to suspect that an acceptable reward for a good day of creative work was oblivion.

1970

•

With the head of the creative writing subdepartment, the citizen-soldier or life-soldier (Gamble thought of his student as both), the visiting poet, and some others, Gamble dropped out of the candlelight march and went into a bar. Each one blew out his candle and placed it in its paper cup on the table before him. The poet had taken one of the pens from a rank of them in the bib of her overalls and was writing on a beer pad. "I don't believe in the soul in the ordinary way," she said, using a kind of cockney accent. It was nearly midnight. They watched the silent student body file past outside, from six to a dozen abreast, eyes alert in the moonlike candlelit faces. Now and then a few dropped out, came in for a beer, and returned to the street. The poet showed her work around the table.

"Good," said the subdepartment head, and then earnestly: "Good, Minerva!"

"Shark from hell's not bad."

She addressed them persistently, recalling her life in New York. "I didn't get arrested for political reasons," she said. "I used to steal."

Graduate students in the next booth listened, beards hanging over the partition. "Minerva!" one cried. She offered what she called a typical evening at home. ". . . sexual tension building. At the same moment I'm talking to a friend about McAlister's *Viet-Nam: The Origins of Revolution.* I feel hungry as hell from the all-protein diet, which must be what caused the horniness in the first place, and I'm very conscious of *dying* for something sweet, also wondering if the friend

402

feels it—either the sexual tension or my hunger or both, if they can be told apart. Simultaneously, my daughter in her room, lovely, is *singing* in this lovely voice, deep already at fourteen—really talented—about love, accompanying a record." (The graduate students purse their lips.) "The temperature in the room keeps dropping, water runs in its pipes, jets go overhead, motorcycles start up on the street below. The fantasies switch from one sex to the other; instead of loving flesh I'm dreaming of scenes in which people merely suggest doing so. All this going on at once."

"Far fuckin' out," the graduate student, Gamble's ally, said mildly.

"All the time, simultaneously depressed as hell: the knowledge that all I get as reward for this *long exhausting evening* is my little husband. . . ."

She was searching her clothing as she spoke, exploring even the hammer loop on her thigh, and she produced at last a mirror. "It's what the poets don't *get* but are trying for: simultaneity of experience. . . ." She searched the grimed crannies around her cheeks. A lock of gray hair, that part Gamble's daughters called bangs as distinct from the rest, even when it was as long as the rest, fell across her face as often as she tucked it aside. "Well, baby, they'll kill us all at last"—referring to the dead and wounded students. "Baby, they'll kill us each and every one unless we stand up to them."

The graduate student who had led the rebellion in Gamble's initial night seminar came past.

"How are you?"

"How in hell should I be?"

"You never bring *me* any of your work, Paul," the poet said, putting a hand on his hip. "My God, feel that."

He was running the New University, he said, and too busy.

They were now breathing deep smiling breaths, looking around at each other, out at the procession.

"We're still occupying the payroll office in the Administration Tower," the young man declared with an air of bringing

403

news. "We left a skeleton force for tonight, but we'll beef it up to thirty or more tomorrow. You fuckers are getting too much money. You too, Minerva."

"Between you and I," the poet said, "I agree. Lorca: *Que esfuerzo del caballo por ser perro. . . .* I got arrested once for stealing the waiters' tips in Lüchow's. I've been in jail in Paris and London."

The citizen-soldier told them suddenly about nursing at the young mother's breast, taking his turn after the baby. "To more or less see what it tasted like."

"And? More or less?"

"It wasn't so sweet as I expected, but it was good."

The students in the next booth had missed the beginning of the exchange. They kept saying, "What?" The poet said, "Fine." But she looked uneasy and in a moment declared with a laugh, "My God, you kids!" Finally she was silent while the others talked. When she spoke at length it was in a heavy voice, new to them. "Jesus, I'm rah-ther depressed." Color had appeared in her cheeks, lattices of pink capillaries; her eyes, which had been made clear as porcelain by the Scotch she drank, had clouded again.

"We ought to rejoin the procession," someone said.

They did not.

At her motel-apartment door, to which she had been escorted by Gamble and his boss, who was also her boss, the poet said, "If I spend the rest of this night alone, I'll take an overdose." And immediately: "Of course I won't. I use that one from time to time."

"We're drunkish."

"I miss my little husband"—swaying in her doorway.

"Should we have stayed with her?" Gamble asked later.

"I think it's just as she indicated."

They walked through the deserted town. A line of freight cars blocked the street, and they had to make a detour, which brought them near the tomato ketchup factory. "You should get a whiff of this when they're in production. It's sickening. You're lucky you won't be here. This is the time to be here."

The night, the emptiness of the streets, now that the procession was ended, had released a smell of lilac more powerful than any the warm days could raise, and both men sniffed the air. They were powerfully earnest. Tony kept saying, "The point is . . ." The other, with his gray beard, was youthful and energetic.

The first enemy is the man who would do you an injury, and never mind for the moment the finer points, Gamble said. He saw at once the flaws in what he was saying, calling them fine points. He looked around in the deserted streets. There were crushed paper cups, candles in the gutter. He was not interested, Gamble told himself accusingly, in politics. His glance was ferocious. Kill children, would you?—the terrible sexual fantasy of revenge coming now.

Having prevailed over the evening seminar, he would set to work for the first time since Alex's death. He collected the last of his checks from the comptroller's office, which had been freed of its sit-in students (it marked the end of the palmy days for teachers of creative writing, as well as the end of student political resistance), and went home to resume firsthand dealings.

He gave up drinking.

Before he began a new book in this house that had been his father's, a gift to him and his wife, he called for his family. (He remembered the moment in this way; it meant this.) When they had gathered around him in the dusk of a Friday in late May, they sat silent for some time looking out of the well-furnished room through its windows and doors at the flower-filled suburban street, comfortably waiting, as if before the beginning of an entertainment.